HUSTLE

TROUBLEMAKERS & HEARTBREAKERS
Book One

Mary Cain

ISBN-13: 978-1-934518-01-4
ISBN-10: 1-934518-01-8

First Edition: April 2024

This book is dedicated to Isaac,
the best card I was ever dealt.

1

THE MEET-CRAZY

Drew

COORDINATION AND CAFFEINE were like Chris Hemsworth and wet panties. Drew Miller couldn't have one without the other.

She descended the staircase outside her apartment slowly, unable to grasp the railing for support thanks to the heavy stack of sketchbooks and drawing materials piled in her arms. Even with sunglasses on, the early morning sun sent pricks of pain through her eyes, which resulted in a dull ache in the center of her forehead.

Her favorite coffee shop was a mere two hundred feet from her apartment, but it felt like three times that far as she endured the sweltering Savannah humidity. Just before she reached the door of the shop, she stopped to adjust her things so she could open it without dropping them.

A man in a black leather jacket sidestepped her, opening the door for her.

Or at least that's what she'd thought he intended to do. But no.

He slipped inside the door as if he hadn't noticed her standing there and the door swung closed.

Drew reached for the handle before it closed all the way. As she attempted to step forward, the heel of her Betsey Johnson peep-toe stiletto caught in the sidewalk crack. *Snap.*

The sketchbooks slipped from her arm, clattering to the ground.

She fumbled for the tin of colored pencils and nearly saved them from the same fate, but instinctively reached for the railing that separated the outdoor patio area from the entranceway to keep from falling on her ass.

When she'd righted herself, she bent down and retrieved her broken shoe. These shoes were the only high-end item she'd bought her entire time living in New York City, and only because her father had sent her money for her birthday with the message that if she spent it on anything sensible, he'd let her brother—who'd given her a book called *Unfuck Your Brain* and signed her up for a twelve-week Pilates class—pick out her gift next year. Lee believed self-help books and a consistent exercise routine were the keys to emotional wellbeing.

Her mind was still fucked, but her ass and abs were impressive.

She held her breath as she inspected her Prisma color pencils for damage. The force of the fall had popped the case open. Two had broken in half. It'd be a miracle if the cores of the others weren't fractured. Nothing was more aggravating than having the pigment fall right out of her pencil every time she attempted to sharpen it. There went thirty bucks.

The universe literally did not want her to become a successful fashion designer. Waitressing through one more tourist season in Savannah would break her. She tried to take a deep, calming breath but ended up wheezing.

You have your master's degree. Your former classmates would kill to be hired for the jobs you've turned down. Even if things don't work out exactly as planned, you will *land on your feet—wearing perfectly intact designer pumps.*

Chin up, she gathered her things, adding her mutilated shoe to the top of the pile, and awkwardly opened the door enough to hobble inside. At her usual booth, she set her sketchbooks and useless colored pencils on the table, then took her place in line, trying not to make it obvious she wore only one shoe.

There was only one person in front of her—the guy who'd let

the door slam in her face. Maybe he hadn't seen her outside. Although for someone to have missed her and her forklift-worthy heap of drawing materials, they'd have to blind.

Since he was staring at the menu suspended from the ceiling, she ruled that excuse out.

Thirty seconds ticked by while he stood there, reading the menu like it held all the answers to life.

No coffee shop etiquette. She doubted he had any type of etiquette.

Hoping to burn a hole through his thick skull, she glared at the back of his head.

Did he not know people had schedules? Jobs to be on time for?

She cleared her throat and peered around him. "Excuse me, if you aren't ready to order, do you mind if I—"

"I do mind," he said without sparing her a glance.

For real?

The bouncy-ponytailed barista behind the register looked beyond Drew and bit her lip.

Following the barista's gaze, she noted two more customers had gotten in line behind her.

"What's your most popular drink?" Mr. Inconsiderate asked her, leaning into the poor woman's personal space.

The barista looked at him like he was Ryan Gosling, a slice of cheesecake, and a cure for cellulite all rolled into one. "I make the best iced caramel macchiato around."

"Do you, now?" His accent was indiscernible, but definitely not southern. He had one of those rough, throaty voices that could send a shiver down a woman's spine. That didn't happen to Drew, of course.

The barista nodded and reached for a clear cup and a marker. "Want to try it?"

He righted his posture. "Nah, I don't do sweet."

Her head hammered with the force of a gazillion tap dancers

on amphetamines. A short fuse and an unsatisfied craving for caffeine nullified the small bit of southern hospitality she possessed.

"What's in a Java Avalanche?"

She clamped her jaw to keep from screaming. Had this guy never been to a coffee shop before?

With a deep, meditative breath, she closed her eyes, and transported herself to her happy place—a place where waves crashed against the shore, where she could wiggle her toes in warm sand, where a bottomless cup of coffee was never out of reach. She imagined herself hip-deep in crystal clear water, a school of colorful fish swimming around her ankles.

An irksome voice crept into her imaginary vacation. "Is the house blend any good?"

Her reverie transformed into a scene where she held the inconsiderate jack-off's head under the tranquil waters. Drew leaned to the side, catching the barista's attention. "I'll have an Ameri—"

"Excuse me." His voice splintered the air as he turned to face her. So chilling. So forceful. So unaware of who he was dealing with. So oblivious he stood in the way of her and her anti-venom.

His deep blue irises flared as he stepped toward her. He had a perfect five o'clock shadow, despite it being eight in the morning. His dark-brown hair was cropped short on the sides, but longer on top, and styled so that it stood up, rather than laid on his forehead. The dark-and-dangerous vibe he had going on dimmed her annoyance with the barista. Gorgeous was the only adjective she could think of to describe him, but then again, thanks to a lack of caffeine and her unexpected attraction to him, her brain wasn't fully functioning.

"Would you order already? I have stuff to do," Drew said.

"And that's my problem because…?"

She glanced at the barista, hoping she'd remember Drew came in every day and always tipped well.

"He was in line first." Her wimpy tone paired well with her I'm-just-doing-my-job shrug.

It was a toss-up on who she wanted to yell at more. But only one of them ground the espresso beans. She choked back the words welling in her throat and bargained with the universe to grant her a few ounces of patience.

His fingertips drummed the thick oak counter.

Screw this. If no one else here had enough balls to let him know what a parasitic dickface he was, she'd gladly step up to the plate.

"Just fucking order!" Her voice reverberated throughout the room.

He whirled on her, sending a wave of bamboo and spearmint her way. Total nose-gasm. "I'll order when I'm good and ready."

"I swear some men are conceived by anal sex," she muttered. "No way being this much of an asshole is a learned skill."

His smile spread into a full-on, five-hundred-watt smirk. A kind of lopsided one that would have made her thighs clench if he hadn't already made it to the top of her list of people she'd like to set on fire. "Who lit the fuse on your tampon?"

Her anger rushed forward like a landslide. She moved closer, her nose an inch from his. "Acting like a dick won't make yours any bigger."

"You don't like me? That's a shame. Let me pour you a tall glass of *get over it.*"

2

MAKING MEMORIES

LOGAN

JUMPING IN LINE in front of Drew Miller was like pulling an alligator's tail.

That mouth. It was as sexy as it was vicious. Logan had stared at those red and glossy, pouty lips way too much over the past week. His inability to resist becoming distracted by her frustrated him.

Drew was a stunner, but he was a natural hustler. He could do this. He hadn't gotten as far as he had in his career without knowing a thing or two about bluffing.

With a little recon, he'd learned she always left her apartment at eight on the dot, walked across the square to the coffee shop, ordered an Americano, and paid with exact change.

Another useful tidbit he'd gleaned—she had no patience and a doozy of a temper. Information that proved useful in developing a plan to deceive her into believing he didn't want anything from her. She'd initiated their encounter—or so it appeared—just as he'd expected.

While he had anticipated her reaction to *him*, Logan's reaction to her knocked him off his motherfucking axis. Her fire gave him a thrill almost as good as winning the World Series of Poker on a straight bluff. Maybe even better.

His attraction to her was a complication, but he was no amateur. He wouldn't let it get in the way.

Compassion was a burden that would bring a confidence trick to a screeching halt. Every time. That was the first thing Uncle John taught him right after he'd agreed to teach him the family business.

Now, Logan had to prove to himself he could stare into those brilliant green eyes and show no mercy. His sister's life depended on it.

Drew crossed her arms, and God love her, pressed her exquisitely round breasts upward. Her scowl could have fueled a nuclear holocaust. "You can't stand there all fucking day."

She didn't intimidate Logan—much.

"Do you really think *you* could stop me?" To emphasize his challenge, he took another step closer, the tips of his boots touching the toes of her pumps—pump, *singular*. She'd abandoned the broken one.

"Are you suggesting I kick your ass right here? Because that can be arranged."

Pssh… She was bluffing.

Her finely arched eyebrow lifted.

He gulped, swallowing a colossal wad of his masculinity. What would he do if she physically attacked him? A vision of him grabbing her wrists and pinning her against the wall popped into his head.

Get your shit together, man. Just a hot chick with a hotter temper. Nothing you can't handle.

Anyway, he had accomplished his goal: piss her off.

He was done. For now. She wouldn't be suspicious of their next interaction. She'd remember him, and he'd have a solid reason for approaching her. In no time, she'd be telling him everything he wanted to know.

Logan turned back to the barista. "I'll take a coffee, black. Put her frou-frou drink on my bill."

"You…you…" Drew sputtered.

He tried not to laugh, fearing she might hyperventilate if he pushed her any further. He accepted his coffee, then looked over his shoulder on the way out the door.

Her eyes looked like they were going to purge themselves from their sockets.

Nope, no way he could resist. "Go find an anger management class, crazypants."

She started toward him, but her missing shoe caused her to stumble. Nearly went down too but steadied herself by grabbing onto a table.

And on that note, he let the door swing closed and got the hell out of there.

She was going to be such an easy mark.

3

THE DIRTY DECOY

LOGAN

A SALTY BREEZE KICKED UP, sweeping through the moss dripping from the oaks lining the banks of the Intracoastal Waterway. The instant Logan planted his foot on the dock where he kept the *Gypsy*, the unshakable sensation of being watched poured over him. An icy vine of trepidation slithered down his neck.

So, this was how it felt to be on the other side of the scope.

Preferring not to be a stationary target, he strode on, closing the distance to his yacht. A rush of wind lifted a wisp of blond hair above the rail of the fly bridge.

He sprung from the dock, his boot thudding on the gunwale, and dropped into a spongy vinyl-covered chair on the aft deck. "Nice try, Morgan."

A stomp resonated through the level above. His sister slid down the ladder with the grace of a spider descending its web. She wore gray scrubs but had abandoned her practical nurse's shoes for beaded flip-flops. The flimsy, translucent skin engulfing her eyes had become the signature of her burnout. At one time, Morgan was sequins and Sambuca and skydiving and pure spunk.

Then she met Eric.

She'd left her whole life behind to follow that scum to Savannah, and he'd not only broken her heart, but he had also gotten her mixed up in some ill shit Logan was still trying to clean up.

His cell vibrated in his pocket. He glanced at the text message.

Limo needs wash and wax. One hour.

He scowled at the phone. Now, he had to drive out to the cesspool that was Pooler. What a lovely day it was turning out to be.

He'd rather wash and wax six limos than do what the cryptic message indicated. Being Bob's underling irked Logan in the worst way. They both might be grifters, but Bob was of an inferior breed. There were no limits to the shady things he would do for a buck.

Morgan snatched his phone from the table and read the message. She plopped into the chair facing his and reached for the pack of cigarettes on the small teak table.

He dug the lighter from the cup holder in his chair and tossed it to her. Once they had both lit up, she gave him her *I'm waiting* stare.

"I don't want to talk about it." He took a long drag, then exhaled. The hit of nicotine curbed the acrid burn climbing its way from his stomach to his throat. Another drag smothered it. For now.

"You don't have to do this, Logan."

Yeah, okay. He was tired of having this same conversation. Mostly because he got sick to his stomach whenever he was reminded that Eric had talked his sister into stealing prescription drugs from the hospital she worked for, so that his boss, Bob, could sell them on the street.

Their uncle had raised them since Morgan was an infant. Her moving two thousand miles away had been rough on him but learning she had done something so despicable had sent him off the deep end.

Uncle John didn't deserve that level of anxiety now that Logan and Morgan were adults. Not only had he adopted them when their mom died, he'd given them an amazing life. It'd taken hours to convince him Logan should be the one to intervene.

Getting busted would have ruined Morgan's life. Luckily, she'd never gotten caught. When things went south between her and Eric, that cheating bastard, she could have walked away or taken revenge by slashing his tires or throwing his shit on the lawn and setting it on fire. Like a normal person. But no.

She'd been so furious that while she'd been taking all the risks, Eric had been off screwing someone else, she broke into Bob's safe and swiped fifty large. But before Logan could talk her into giving it back, she'd donated half of it to the hospital and the other half to a charity that raised awareness on prescription drug abuse.

His original plan—to use the *dinero* he'd planned to take to the poker table that weekend to payoff Bob, so he wouldn't go through with his threats to rat out Morgan to the hospital—hadn't panned out.

Bob wanted more than that. Drug dealing was a side hustle. His main gig was extortion. Insisting they meet on neutral ground turned out to be a mistake. Logan had brought his camera with him, thinking he'd snap a few shots by the river while he waited for Bob to show. His interest in photography excited Bob. It was a skill he could exploit.

For months, Logan had taken blackmail photos for him. He hadn't liked that job any more than he liked conning Drew Miller, but if he wanted his sister to continue to wear scrubs instead of an orange jumpsuit, he didn't have a choice.

"How about you let me clean up my own mess? Let me repay my own debts?" Morgan asked for the thousandth time.

He sank farther into his chair. "It's not your debt anymore."

"You hate what you're doing." She stubbed out her smoke, then chewed on her nail.

"It is what it is, Morgan. Besides, it's not like I'm robbing her. I laid the groundwork today. Soon she'll be telling me everything I want to know and never be the wiser."

She scoffed and tossed her long hair over her shoulder. "Don't be too confident. Not everyone is susceptible to being manipulated."

Oh, yes, they were. Lesson number two in the John Cash Con Artist Curriculum: *If I know what you want, I can take everything you have.*

"I don't know what your hang up is," he said. "After what you did for Bob, you have a lot of nerve judging me for *this*."

Her face fell. "I had a lapse in judgment, but I didn't betray anyone other than myself."

"You're right. If I do this, I'll be taking myself out of the running for that humanitarian-of-the-year award."

"It's not right to manipulate her. This girl is someone's sister too."

"But not *mine*." Morgan was his blood. If it meant protecting his sister, he'd hock all his vital organs.

"I think you're wasting your time with her anyway. She doesn't know anything."

He aimed his finger in her direction. "She doesn't know she knows anything. There's a difference."

LOGAN ROLLED HIS AUDI INTO THE PARKING LOT of a limo rental company in the rundown shopping district outside Savannah city limits. He parked alongside a ten-year-old, rusted Escalade limo, then sat for a while, dreading going into the musty office.

Bob used the limousine rental company to launder money from his array of illegal business ventures. When he spotted the fat bastard staring at him through the plate glass window, he groaned, then got out of the car. Walking across the lot, he tried to hold his breath. This part of town smelled worse than the typical sulfur stench of downtown Savannah. It had the lovely addition of rotting garbage and burnt rubber.

The building had one office in the front and another in the back. The back was a dump. Papers everywhere. Balled up fast food bags overflowing from the waste bin. And a hefty stack of 80's nudie mags in the bathroom—a place Logan would never set foot in a second time.

The front office's furniture was dated, but the carpet was clean. Thanks to Bob's *secretary*.

Logan nodded to her on his way to the back. She smiled and fluttered her fingers at him, the rhinestones on her neon yellow acrylic nails glimmering in the light.

He stood, rather than sit on the grimy, ripped club chair across from Bob's desk.

Bob stubbed out his cigarillo in an overflowing ashtray. "Got anything for me?"

He wanted to choke Bob for making him drive all the way out to this dump to give him updates they could've handled with a quick phone call.

"Not yet. This shit takes time." And finesse. Something Bob knew jack about.

"So will finding a new job once the hospital board finds out what your sweet little sister has been up to."

He stopped himself from making a fist. Bob wanted to push his buttons, back him into a corner, make him sweat. Well, too bad.

"We had a deal," Logan reminded him. "This is between you and me now."

He had refused the job at first because it called for far more orchestration and intervention than taking blackmail photos, which was all Logan had agreed to do for him when they'd struck their deal.

Then Bob dangled the carrot. His debt would be considered paid once he'd completed the assignment. Then he'd never have to see Bob's ugly mug again.

Logan didn't mind a little recon. Spending a night casing a joint with Benny Teodori was always a good time. On the rare occasion Benny asked for his assistance in a heist, Logan would play whatever role was needed. He got satisfaction out of running a short con on any pretentious asshole who got in his way. But sitting at a card table, winning a high stakes game—on his own merit—was more Logan's style than choreographing and executing long cons. Didn't matter now though.

It would be worth it in the end. He couldn't wait to be back on the poker circuit, soaking up VIP treatment, working his way from the fifth highest-ranked player in poker earning's history to the top highest. He missed the game, but his ego could wait. Morgan came first.

Finding out who filched one of Sam Miller's paintings from his house wasn't going to be easy. Drew's father had painted it well over a decade ago, but the painter's recent rise in popularity in the art industry made it valuable.

"Why are you so hard up to know who stole the painting anyway?" Logan asked. Art theft was far too nuanced for a thug like Bob. He liked quick and easy money.

Bob reached into his desk drawer and pulled out a flask. "None of your business. Do what I tell you to and stop asking questions."

"The more I know, the better chance I'll have at getting to the bottom of this. Unless…you don't know anything. This ain't your type of gig, Bob. Feels to me like you're doing someone else's dirty work."

"I'm not available for contract," Bob grated out and took a swig from his flask. He saw himself as top dog. The type of guy who didn't work for others. Regardless of what Bob claimed, this reeked of outsourcing. If there was anything Logan understood, it was outsourcing through blackmail. That's how he'd ended up as Bob's grunt.

"Extortion feels pretty shitty when it's the other way around, don't it?"

"I wouldn't know."

"It happens to the best of us." He shrugged. For this to work, Logan needed Bob to believe he didn't think any less of him for falling susceptible to a shakedown. Shouldn't be hard to convince him. He couldn't think any less of Bob than he already did. "You don't have to tell me what he's got on you. I don't fucking care. But the more I know about him and his motives, the quicker this job will go, and the sooner you'll have him off your back."

Bob pulled a cigarillo from his pack and held the tip between his teeth as he lit the end. The nauseating aroma of cherry-flavored tobacco smoke wafted across the desk. He stared at Logan, clearly mulling over his decision, like he had anything to lose.

"My *associate* wants to pull a dirty decoy." He crossed his arms, cigarillo dangling from his lips.

"He wants to lift the painting from the thief, keeping his hands clean by never having stepped foot on the original crime scene?" That didn't help Logan. "How'd he know it was stolen in the first place?"

"Didn't say."

The crime hadn't been reported to the police, which made it an even more brilliant scam. Nearly zero chance of taking the fall for an unreported crime *and* the painting would be easier to unload if the buyer didn't realize it was stolen.

The theft wasn't public knowledge, so either someone in the Miller family had leaked it, or the thief had bragged about his score. The latter was highly unlikely. It'd be easy enough to trace it back to him or her, and if that were the case, Bob's extortionist wouldn't need him.

Confirming someone in the family had loose lips wouldn't help Logan because it didn't answer the question that plagued him: Why wasn't the theft reported to the police?

Fuck. Back to square one.

That caliber of theft took careful recon. Lots of it. Which meant getting inside the house. Which meant getting by Drew.

She no longer lived at home, but she, and she alone, had scheduled and paid all the servicemen who'd visited the home in the past six months. Logan would bet his Audi the culprit was posing as a cable repairman or a cleaning lady.

To narrow down the list, he'd have to squeeze her for details on each suspect. And he'd have to do that without revealing that he knew the crime had taken place. Difficult and time consuming, but not impossible.

Drew's hotheaded nature made her predictable. It also meant twice as many steps to reach his goal. His plan wasn't linear. It was more like one of those crazy cloverleaf exit ramps. She couldn't be sweet talked. He'd seen men approach her. Every single one had been shut down hard. So, Logan hadn't wasted time trying to get on her good side. He'd gone straight for her bad side.

"What else do you know?"

Bob blew a plume of smoke in his direction. "That's it. He wants to know who took it and where they have it stashed so he can steal it out from under them."

Liar. There was more. Like why the hell the guy chose *this* idiot for such a challenging job.

There was nothing left to gain here, and he was past ready to leave. "When I find out something, I'll let you know."

He turned to leave, but of course Bob wasn't going to let him have the last word.

"It's been two weeks, Cash, and you haven't got shit. Maybe your sister is the one with all the talent, and you're just a punk with a camera."

Logan whipped around and without skipping a beat, called Bob's bluff. "Put Eric on this job then."

He scoffed and the ash from his cigarillo fell on the desk. He didn't make a move to clean it up. Fucking slob. "Don't get your panties in a wad. I said *maybe*. I'm giving you the opportunity to prove yourself."

Prove himself? Logan almost laughed. "Look, I know what I'm doing. Like I said, these things take time."

Bob leaned across the desk and narrowed his bloodshot eyes. "Yeah, well, this deal has an expiration date of one week or your sister pays the price."

"Then stop wasting my time with these meetings." He wasn't going to bother arguing with a crook like Bob about honoring his word. Until Logan found out who stole Sam Miller's painting, Morgan would be under threat. Tired of looking at the worthless jackass, he turned and left.

Through the glass door of the lobby, he spotted someone he hated even more than Bob about to enter the building. Eager to blow off some frustration, he shoved the door open with enough force to knock Eric off balance and propel him backward.

"What the fuck!"

He choked back his laughter. "Sorry, I didn't see you there."

Morgan's ex—the person who got her mixed up in all this in the first place—gaped at his pristine white sneakers. "You scuffed my shoes, man."

He stepped toward him, so close their noses all but touched. "So, do something about it."

Eric took two steps back.

Logan excelled at intimidation. The only time he'd ever failed was when he'd gone up against Drew Miller. His tactics had bounced off her like Nerf darts off Kevlar. He'd poked at the rattlesnake, and she'd struck, fangs, venom and all.

And he'd liked it a little too much.

Meeting her feistiness with his own brand of smart-assery had been entertaining as hell. Under different circumstances, he would love to find out if sex between them was as electrifying as he imagined it would be. His hands tangled up in that long auburn hair. The sweet arch of her back as he thrust into her from behind. Damn.

Logan preferred to keep his hookups casual and quiet, but he'd make an exception for the chance to walk into a poker tournament with her on his arm. He bet she had just the dress for the occasion.

But that wasn't the reality Logan lived in. Nope, he resided in a real-life nightmare where a douchebag like Eric could get an intelligent woman like his sister so wrapped around his finger, she'd abandon a promise she'd kept since she was a little girl.

Eric tried to skirt around him to go inside, but Logan mirrored his movements, blocking him. "I don't wanna fight you, Logan. You know how upset Morgan got the last time."

"Can't upset her if she doesn't know about it. I'm not gonna tell her, and she's not hearing it from you because I already told you that if you contact her, I will tack your balls to my fucking dock using a screw gun, tie your ankles to the stern and—"

"She showed up at my place last night." Eric's left eye twitched. "I told her she needed to leave. But if you don't back off, next time, I'm inviting her in."

He didn't believe him. Morgan had learned her lesson the hard way, but she had learned it. Eric would say anything to avoid an ass whooping like the one Logan had dished out when he'd arrived in Savannah. "It blows my fucking mind that my sister ever saw anything in a little bitch like you."

Logan brushed by, bumping Eric with his shoulder.

The little shit stumbled backward so hard he landed on his ass.

4

SWEET LIKE SRIRACHA

Drew

THE JERK-OFF who'd verbally assaulted Drew the day before slid into her booth across from her. *The nerve.*

"Let's start over," he said, pushing a paper cup across the table in her direction.

She gave him a quick once-over. His sleek, dark brown hair and Ramones T-shirt cemented his bad boy image, not to mention the leather motocross jacket. She knew his type.

Except, there was *something* about him that made her a little breathless. An intensity in his eyes that sent tingles all the way to her toes.

Ugh. Was her coffee dosed? She didn't do the bad boy thing. She didn't do the boy thing period. Not that she did the girl thing, either. Dating required more of a bullshit tolerance than she possessed. Not to mention free time. Which did not exist in her world.

Every day her alarm went off at 6:45, allowing her to hit the snooze twice before she crawled out of bed. By 7:50 she had showered and chosen an outfit. Hair. Make-up. Leaving her ten minutes to get her things together and make it across the square to the coffee shop.

No later than 8:15, she planted her ass in the only window booth and spent an hour sketching designs to enter in the Emerging American Designer competition. Tomorrow was the deadline for applications. If she didn't have her collection illustrated, matted, packaged, and postmarked, she could kiss her dream goodbye.

"I'm kind of busy right now," she said, turning back to a sketch of an evening dress inspired by the moss that dripped from the oaks in the square.

"That's kind of your thing, isn't it?" he asked. "Busy. In a hurry. Running people over in your stilettos. Pushing your way to the front of the line."

She glared at him. She did not run over people or push to the front of the line. Some might see her as a little strung out. But those people didn't know her. "You don't know anything about me and my…things."

He chuckled. "But I am curious. About your *things*." His lips parted to reveal flawless teeth, a flicker of a smile in the depths of his eyes.

Her stomach lost equilibrium and she got woozy for a minute— like she'd stood up too fast. Her body was a frickin' traitor. It would be nice if it got on the same page as her brain, which understood this guy was a worm.

"Look, I don't come here to get hit on," Drew said, slathering on the iciness thicker than buttercream. She turned her attention back to her sketchbook and made a fluid motion with her graphite pencil, creating long, flowing hair on the croquis.

"Oh, good. Then you won't be disappointed when I don't ask you out."

Her eyes widened so much she almost burst a blood vessel. He was quick, she'd give him that. She bit the inside of her lip. *Do not smile. He's the enemy.*

She picked up another pencil. As soon as the point touched the paper, the pigment came loose. When she'd inspected her colored pencils for damage after this jerk had caused her to drop them, the damage hadn't seemed as bad as she'd initially feared. Clearly, that assessment had been inaccurate. The red, semi-crushed piece of pigment on her paper made her think of murder. And she had the perfect victim.

He spread his leather-clad arms across the top of the bench, then grinned at her. Again.

"Can you leave me alone?"

"Why?" he asked.

"*Why?*" He couldn't be that oblivious. "Because I don't like you, that's why. Not to mention, I'm trying to work."

"What are you working on?" He leaned in, forearms braced on the tabletop.

She snapped her sketchbook closed. "I'm sketching."

"No shit. Do you think I'm blind?" A laugh crossed with a huff left his throat. "*What* are you sketching?"

"You may not be blind, but you sure as hell don't know how to take a hint."

"I do realize you don't want me sitting here with you. I just don't care."

"Awesome," she muttered under her breath.

He took a swig of his coffee, then drummed his fingers against the side of the paper cup. "So…what're you drawing?"

"Fashion illustrations." She placed the red pencil into the case with the others, even though it belonged in the garbage.

"Are you a designer?"

"I'm going to be. If you ever leave me alone so I can work."

He tilted his head. "How do you do that?"

"Do what?" She slid her sketchbook off the table to put it into her bag, then stopped and pushed it back where it had been. As much as she wanted to get away from him, she refused to be the one to leave. She pressed her shoulders into the hard wood of the bench and crossed her arms.

"Become a fashion designer. I don't know anything about it."

Just her luck he was interested.

He made a motion with his hand, prodding her to go on.

She scrunched her eyebrows together. Did he really care? "Most people start out as design assistants or interns and work their way up."

"But not you?"

Drew shook her head. "I'm entering a contest, which I might stand a chance of winning if you leave me alone so I can work on my entry. The top three finalists get to show their collection on the runway. First place prize is $400,000 to start your own label and a mentorship with an established designer."

The two runners-up got $125,000, but if Drew didn't get first place, she was fucked. Talent, she had, experience…not so much. The name of the mentor had yet to be announced, but it was guaranteed to be a reputable American designer with connections Drew would kill for.

When she was enrolled at Parson's, she'd sold a series of designs to a well-known fashion house. She'd been thrilled. Until she saw her designs in Macy's. With someone else's name on them. She'd known when she sold them the label's name would be on them. But actually seeing her designs and not being able to take credit for them? Oh, no. She did not like that.

"So, winning would be like a shortcut to becoming a famous designer?"

Drew stared at him for a beat, then flipped open her sketchbook and grabbed a light gray pencil and began rendering the sequined fabric on the dress she'd drawn earlier. Stupid questions didn't deserve answers. Not ones asked by this guy, anyway. Her focus stayed trained on the page for as long as she could manage before the silence got to her. She glanced back at him.

He flashed his pearly whites.

She ran her tongue over her top row of teeth. Five years in braces and her smile couldn't begin to compare. "What?" The word came out sharper than the pencil in her hand.

"Shouldn't you be in New York? Aside from Paris, isn't that like *the* place for fashion?"

"I did my undergrad there."

"Ah, so you graduated in the spring, then came back home so you could save on rent while you work on this contest."

This guy apparently thought he was some type of detective.

"Wrong. I finished my undergrad two years ago. I have my master's now." The plan for her fast-track to a design career developed shortly after she'd started high school. But after living in NYC for a month, her end goal changed. Not the being a famous designer part. The part where she lived hundreds of miles from her family. Fame over family didn't appeal to her. No need to choose, though. That's why she had to win this contest. With that money and mentorship, her vision could be achieved—right here in Savannah. "Why do you assume I'm from here?"

"Your accent. It's painfully obvious you're Southern."

Ouch. She'd had guys say her accent was cute, some even said sexy. It had been a lot less pronounced when she first got back from New York. Since then, it had thickened, but it still wasn't the slow, twangy drawl most Savannahians shared.

"Besides," he said, "why the fuck would anyone choose to live here?"

She shifted forward, staring him right in the eye. "Why the fuck did you? Would leaving violate your parole?"

Amusement danced in his eyes as he took a sip of his coffee. "Believe me, it's temporary. My sister moved here first. I'm helping her sort things out and then packing her up to move back home."

"Why'd she move here if it's such an awful place to live?"

"To be with some dickhead who doesn't deserve to breathe the same air as her."

Anguish thickened his voice when he said it, and she accessed him for a moment. She hated him a little less knowing he was protective over his sister. Her own brothers nearly lost their shit when they found out she'd be attending college in New York. They'd calmed down considerably when they'd visited and saw she'd sacrificed a social life to get ahead and graduate a year early. She empathized with him a *little*, but she still didn't like him, nor did she have the time to chitchat.

She turned her attention back to her sketchbook. "Well, safe travels home. Wherever that may be."

"Las Vegas. Ever been?"

"No." Was anyone really *from* Vegas? If she hadn't already made up her mind that she couldn't stand him, she might be intrigued. To keep herself from asking questions about his upbringing, she selected a blue pencil and worked to render sparkling sequins around the hem in a disappearing gradient on the way to the waist of the dress.

"Maybe you'll go sometime."

"If I ever go to Vegas, it isn't going to be with you, 'kay?"

He laughed *at* her this time, making her feel like she was on the outside of an inside joke. "Oh, I bet you're a delight to fly with. Do you try to cut in the security checkpoint line?"

She rolled her eyes. "Can you leave now?"

"I could, but I won't." His slow wink stirred a flutter in her stomach that crept downward.

What did she have to do to get rid of him? She studied the corrugated sleeve around her coffee cup. If she didn't look directly into his dark, challenging eyes maybe she could form a coherent thought. "What did you say your name was?"

"Logan." He ran his hand through his hair—which had that whole James Dean vibe going on—and his lip curled on one side.

"Logan," she said, as nicely as she could, avoiding direct eye contact, "I'm Drew. I like my privacy and my little booth where I normally get a lot of work done. I would really appreciate it if you gave me some space."

She forced a smile and raised her gaze to judge his reaction. He wasn't smiling. Or frowning. He was just…there. Staring at her with the vaguest expression.

Then suddenly, he slid from the booth.

A wake of minty bamboo washed over her.

Before walking away, his gaze tracked over her face, assessing. "I like you better when you're salty."

5

AARAIDAN

Drew

DREW HOOKED the chain from one side of the stairway to the other to discourage tourists from sitting in the upper outdoor seating area after hours, then dropped her apron onto the bar and dragged her body onto a stool.

She pulled her tips from her apron and fanned the thick stack. Thanks to a pharmaceutical convention in town, she'd made more money in one day than she had in the past two weeks. After rent and groceries, she'd put the rest, plus the seven hundred dollars she would get for subletting her apartment for the weekend, toward materials for her collection.

The new bartender moved toward her, wiping the bar with a rag and missing several spots as he fixated on her chest. "Looks like you made out pretty good tonight."

His skin was golden, his brown hair slightly bleached from the sun. A hemp choker with a shark tooth on it circled his neck. No disfigurements. No unappealing features. No obvious body odor. But there was a dullness to his eyes that made Drew wonder if someone had found a way to clone life-sized Ken dolls.

She pushed a wad of bills toward him. "Here's your cut."

He picked up the stack, folded it in half, and tucked it into the tip jar next to the register without blinking. "Bartending is bloody awful, but it pays the bills, aye? I cannot wait until I can support myself with my art."

She felt the same about waitressing. "You're an artist?"

Not to judge a Ken doll by his bourgeois appearance, but this guy didn't seem the creative type.

"Photographer. Trying to build my client-base." He shook his shaggy hair out of his eyes. "Can I give you a ride home?"

His Irish accent might have swayed her into saying yes, if the other waitresses hadn't warned her that he had hit on every one of them. And scored with a few in the week he'd worked there.

"I don't think so," she said.

"Aw, c'mon. Go change while I wrap up and I'll give you a lift."

The underwire in her bra chafed as her chest filled with air. Tension clutched the back of her neck like claw. "How do you know I'm going to change?"

Her uniform—a T-shirt with the restaurant's logo and khaki shorts—didn't fit her vibe. Most days, she came to work straight from her studio, and rather than walk through downtown Savannah looking like a camp counselor, she brought the shirt and shorts in her bag and changed in the bathroom.

He raised his hands in front of him in a defensive gesture. "Don't get the wrong idea. I've seen you coming and going a few times. You always look nice when you aren't waiting tables."

"You don't think I look nice now?" she asked, wondering if he was smart enough to realize he had backed himself into a corner.

"Cut me some slack here, will ya? I think you look great in those shorts. So, do I pass? Can I give you a ride?"

"Thanks, Aaron, but I live close by. I'll walk." Total lie. She'd have to hoof it fifteen blocks, which was fine in the daytime, but she wasn't brave enough to cover that much territory after dark. Once she escaped Aaron, she'd snag a ride from one of the other waitresses.

"My name's Aidan." He wrung out the towel as if it were his worst enemy's neck.

She squinted and faux-flirty smiled. "Are you sure?" In any other setting, she wouldn't have cared if she insulted him. Not after he'd taken the upstairs tour without buying a ticket. But she had to work with him, and she depended on him to make her drinks quickly and correctly, or else her tips would be kaput.

"Let's have a beer at my place and I'll make sure you never forget my name."

Seriously?

Even if she had time to date, a guy who found his jewelry in the oral cavity of giant fish and made promises about his performance in the bedroom was not the way she'd go.

She opened her mouth to simultaneously boost his ego and reject him, but a voice at the outdoor entrance distracted her.

"What's kickin', little chicken?"

Her heart fluttered at the same time logic zapped her brain and slammed her back down to reality. It couldn't be.

She slid from the stool and sprinted to the entrance.

A tattered denim-covered leg swung over the chain. A familiar set of eyes met hers. Her brother winked at her.

Drew threw herself at him, not sure if she was laughing from joy, or because she'd gone mad. This had to be a hallucination. "Aubrey, what are you doing here?"

"Coming to see you."

She wiggled out of his bear hug. "You're supposed to be in Egypt."

He nudged a nail in the floorboard with the toe of his shoe. "We lost our grant."

Shit. "Want a drink?"

"It's about time you asked."

At the bar, Drew ordered them each a vodka tonic with a twist.

Aidan slung his bar rag over his shoulder and grabbed two glasses from underneath the bar.

While he made their drinks, she whispered to Aubrey, "The bartender is on a mission to violate my 'no dating guys I find pretentious' policy."

Aubrey kept his voice low. "I'll get him to back off, but it'll cost you."

Aidan set their drinks in front of them with the enthusiasm of a sloth on Valium. Aubrey's was missing the lime twist, but a perfect spiral rind artfully wrapped around a mini plastic anchor swam in hers.

She took a sip and savored the smooth taste of top-shelf vodka. "When did you get in?"

He checked his watch. "Thirty minutes ago." He hissed after tasting his drink. "Can I get a splash of cranberry in this?"

As if he hadn't served her brother rubbing alcohol, Aidan rolled his eyes and grabbed a juice pourer from the cooler and dribbled red liquid into his glass.

"I'm Aubrey." His shaggy brown hair fell in his eyes as he extended his hand in Aidan's direction. "Drew's brother."

Lifesize-Ken's face lit up. "Aidan. You live in Savannah?"

If he thought he was going to get in good with her brother and increase his chances with her, he was an imbecile.

Aubrey cleared his throat and locked eyes on his glass. "Well... usually. When I'm on *this* side."

Blond manscaped eyebrows shot up. "You did time?"

Drew bit her lip to keep her laughter contained. Her brother had never gotten more than a parking ticket.

"Just a few months." He shrugged. "It's cool, though. I've been working on resolving my latent aggression issues and the blackouts only happen when I forget to take my meds. Or mix my meds with alcohol."

Aidan's gaze connected with the glass in Aubrey's hand. "Blackouts?"

"Yeah. I wake up and surprise, I smell like kerosene and Tyler is in the ICU burn unit."

"Who's Tyler?"

"Drew's ex-boyfriend." Aubrey rubbed the side of his nose with his finger. "Decent guy. Hope the next round of plastic surgery does the trick. At least he doesn't have to worry about getting his hair cut ever again."

Aidan's Adam's apple bobbed beneath his shark tooth. Mumbling something about having a lot to do, he went to the other end of the bar to wash glasses.

Drew turned to her brother. "So, what happened with Egypt?"

He took a long sip of his drink then stared into the glass. "The university didn't want to pay our expenses for another year."

"What are you going to do now?" Despite Aubrey's passion for anthropological archaeology, the digs he'd been on had been unfruitful. But so far, he'd kept finding ways to get funding. Stubbornness wasn't a just character trait in the Miller family, it was a way of life. Hopefully, it would help them both find success.

"I heard you're recruiting models." He wiggled his eyebrows.

She nodded. "How are you in stilettos?"

One shoulder lifted. "Some would say I'm the next Gemma Ward."

She twirled the ice in her glass with the swivel stick. "Seriously, do you have a plan?"

"Yep. Come home, spend some time with my family, hit Congress Street every night, eat a lot of fried chicken, and then reevaluate the situation."

Not Drew's idea of a plan. But anal retentiveness wasn't for everyone. When they were kids, Drew arranged her crayons in rainbow order. Aubrey melted his and molded them into zombies.

"Does Dad know?" she asked. The instability of Aubrey's career worried their dad, even though Aubrey didn't seem bothered by it.

He shook his head. "Dad has enough to worry about. Which reminds me. You owe me a favor."

"Cashing in already?" She cut him a look. "You set me up."

"No, the timing was convenient. That's all."

"Just spit it out. What kind of idiotic scheme are you going to get me tangled up in this time?"

As soon as she could walk, Aubrey had started suckering her into all kinds of outrageous plans. Normally, she found his antics amusing and went along without too much arm-twisting, but, at the moment, her plate was full.

"I'm going to catch the thief who stole the painting," he whispered.

She choked on her vodka tonic. "Oh, please, no. Aubrey, you're not Sherlock Holmes."

He had spent a lot of his life pretending to be, though. It was cute when he was eight. At twenty-three, not so much.

"That painting is all we had left of Mom. I can't sit by and do nothing."

Her insides clenched. Their mom was gone. The painting was gone. Nothing they could do about either. Drew and her brother had very different methods of coping. She preferred to move on, full steam ahead. Aubrey liked to poke. And prod. And make a gigantic mess out of things.

"Well, Aubs," she said, more than ready to get this crazy notion out of his even crazier head, "I don't know what you think I can do. You might fancy yourself Sherlock Holmes, but I'm not Watson. Besides, I've got Claire's wedding coming up and a contest to win."

Puppy dog eyes bore into hers. "I wasn't around when it happened. You were. All I wanna do is ask a couple of questions."

By a couple, he meant a gazillion.

She shook her head.

"Come on, Drew. I *did* just scare the bejesus out of that bartender for you. You owe me."

He wasn't going to let up. It would probably be easier to give in now rather than listen to his constant nagging.

She slumped her shoulders. "Fine."

6

MILLION-DOLLAR MISFIRE

LOGAN

LOGAN PAID for two coffees and prepared to launch into the next phase of his plan. It was going to hurt—literally—but it would be worth it.

Drew sipped a latte, drawing materials methodically laid out on the table. Soon, she'd get up to fetch her second dose of caffeine, but before she stood from the booth, Logan would place himself in the perfect position for her to bump into him. If she was in her usual rush, and he was counting on it, he'd be wearing his black coffee all over his Queen of Hearts tee. She'd feel terrible, thinking she'd caused the spill.

That was all there was to this phase of his con, but it was a vital part. And fucking brilliant.

He crept behind the wall separating the coffee bar from the sitting area and approached her from behind. She set her paper cup on the table. When it connected with the surface, it made a hollow sound.

She grabbed her wallet and slid from the booth with her head lowered.

He snuck to her side, putting himself in line with her elbow, ready to douse himself in scalding liquid.

Instead of her elbow, her heel landed on his foot. The point of her stiletto stabbed through his canvas sneaker. The unexpected pain was so sharp a black haze dotted his vision. He hissed and twisted, both coffee cups flying in the direction of the table.

Both cups hit the surface, their plastic tops popping off, and spilling all over…professionally matted fashion illustrations. *Mother Fucker.*

That didn't go as planned. At all.

"What the hell," Drew yelled, lunging for the napkin holder. With frantic movements, she attempted to salvage her papers. "Don't you look where you're going?"

She turned with a wad of wet, brown napkins in her hand, her lips pressed together.

Logan cringed. His game was way off. "I'm sorry. I was bringing you a latte. As an olive branch." Minus the I'm sorry, that was the line he'd rehearsed to give to her after he'd doused himself in steaming liquid.

Drew blotted at the espresso mixed with frothed milk soaking the illustrations. Ink ran over the pages until they resembled Rorschach inkblots.

"That," she said, punctuating the word, "was over sixty hours of work. It has to go in the mail today."

Well, damn.

He ground his teeth against the pain and worked to clear his mind. To find a way to salvage this. To prevent his murder.

"I'm so sorry. Let me help you clean that up." Logan snatched a napkin holder off a nearby table, yanked a few free, and wiped at the mess. "I'm really sorry."

He dared to look at her. Her face was purple again. And her shoulders were vibrating.

Holy shit.

Logan's jaw fell slack. He couldn't keep saying he was sorry. It wasn't fucking working.

In all his days of grifting, he'd never been this sloppy. Was it bad luck or—no. It couldn't be his attraction to Drew. That was ridiculous. She was sex in a pair of stilettos, sure. But that was nothing he hadn't seen before.

Vegas was flush with women like her. Most of them a lot less mouthy.

So much was riding on this. His sister's career and freedom. Severing his relationship with Bob. Returning to his poker career.

Drew gave up attempting to dry her work and gathered her things. Her face was doing that getting-ready-to-explode thing again.

He swallowed hard. "How can I make this up to you?"

She was supposed to be asking him that question, not the other way around.

She didn't even look at him as she said, "By getting the hell away from me."

Mission: fail.

7

THE QUEEN OF COPING MECHANISMS

DREW SET HER portfolio on her dad's kitchen table and released a deep breath. She'd spent a solid five hours redoing her illustrations. If she got them to the post office by four o'clock, they'd be postmarked today. First, though, she had to mat them on presentation board.

She was still mad as hell at that guy, and if she ever saw him again, she'd take pleasure in dumping scalding coffee over his head, but her new illustrations had turned out undoubtedly better. Color pencils were her go-to. They were a safe option. But they also took more time. Using markers to color the new illustrations had saved time, but it'd been a risk.

That risk had paid off. Her pulse raced as she pulled them from her portfolio. There was no question these were better than the others. The vibrant colors. The details. These illustrations *would* get her accepted into the contest.

But first, she needed to borrow her dad's mat cutter.

She jogged down the stairs to the walkout basement, but froze on the last step, gawking at the large corkboard positioned on an easel.

"What kind of fucked *Beautiful Mind* shit is this?" she whispered and walked over to it. She ran her fingers over the red yarn stretched taut across the board. Her eyes settled on a picture of her mother.

"This is how crimes get solved."

She turned and rolled her eyes at Aubrey. "Oh, right. I forgot you worked for the CIA."

Losing his funding and having his dreams dashed yet again must have pushed him over the edge. This cork board with sticky notes and photos and handwritten math equations screamed mental illness.

"You don't really think you're going to find the person who took it and get it back, do you?"

He shrugged. "Something feels off about it. Dad has a studio full of his work. Why would they break into the house and take that one?"

Why did it have to be that one? She'd had that thought a million times since the theft. The painting was the one thing in the entire house she would have grabbed during a fire.

Years and years ago, her father had painted a large-scale painting of Drew and her mother. For several sunny spring days, they had sat on a blanket together, surrounded by pansies and lilac bushes in her mother's garden. While she listened to her mother read books, her father painted.

"Maybe they didn't know about the studio."

Aubrey shook his head. "Doesn't make sense. If someone wanted to steal his paintings, they would have done their research. They'd have known about the studio."

The rest of the family had already gone through this two weeks ago. There were several different theories, but the outcome remained the same: the painting was gone. Of course, Aubrey hadn't been here for any of that. He probably needed to vent a little about the unjustness of it, as they all had.

"It was just luck. They couldn't have known what paintings he had here versus the studio. Maybe they figured he stored the most valuable ones here for safekeeping."

"That's the thing, though," he said, pausing in front of a folding table scattered with paperwork. "They stole the painting most valuable to Dad. And he doesn't even seem that upset about it."

"I can't do this with you right now. I'm on a deadline."

"You don't think it's weird he didn't call the cops?"

Drew raised an eyebrow. "What are you getting at? You think Dad staged the whole thing?"

"No." Aubrey shook his head, then winced. "Maybe."

"What!"

He ruffled a hand through his hair. "Maybe he needed the money or something."

"Dad doesn't need money. He just sold an entire collection of paintings. But if he was going to sell a painting for some quick cash, do you really think it would be that one?"

"I don't know. It's not like he can collect the insurance on it since he didn't file a police report." He sighed and his shoulders fell. "Things don't add up."

"Aubrey, I don't have time for this. My illustrations got ruined, and I redid them, but if I don't get them matted and postmarked in time, I can kiss winning the contest goodbye. I need you to help me."

His expression changed from determined to puzzled. "Ruined?"

Normally, she was very careful. The illustrations had been wrapped in plastic and stored safely inside her portfolio, ready to be transported to the post office, but she couldn't help looking them over one last time. "It's a long story."

"Okay, I'll help, but I still have a lot of questions I want to ask you."

Aubrey walked to the easel and tapped a technical drawing of the living room window, the one that had been broken during the burglary. "I measured. The painting wouldn't have fit through this window. Close, but no cigar."

Drew blinked. But no, her brother—who had made *technical drawings* and measured windows and suspected their father stole his own painting—still didn't appear to be joking. "We didn't have a security system then. They could have come in through the window, grabbed the painting, and waltzed out the front door."

"I fingerprinted all the doors."

She plopped onto an oversized wicker rocker with worn, dusty-blue velvet cushions. "You fingerprinted the doors," she repeated, her voice deadpan.

"And then I got everyone in the family's fingerprints off something only they would have touched. A bottle of your perfume. Dad's coffee mug after he left for work. Some Playboys Lee left in the top of his closet when he moved out. Grant and Marjorie willingly let me fingerprint them."

To keep from screaming at Aubrey for dragging them through this all over again, she stroked the soft fabric covering the chair. "Ever heard of gloves?"

"Drew, there are too many holes. You might be able to ignore it," he shoved his thumb into his sternum, "but I can't."

It felt like her brain was filled with a swarm of buzzing bees. He'd said he would help her. Did he not hear the part about only having an hour to get her illustrations matted and mailed off?

"I want to make a spreadsheet with every person who has visited the house over the past six months or so. Even people we trust." Aubrey paused for a moment, tapping his chin with his finger. "I'm thinking we should have a column for dates, times, et cetera, but also it would be helpful to record what rooms they entered. And if their visit was expected or unexpected. Oh, and—"

Whoa. "Aubrey, this is getting out of hand. Your time would be better spent talking dad into hiring a private investigator."

He plucked a tack out of the jar on the mantel and pointed it at her. "Sometimes, you have to take matters into your own hands."

"And sometimes you have to let things go."

"Typical."

"Excuse me?"

"Whenever anything bad happens, you shut down. You don't deal with it. You go into avoidance mode. How many years did you spend in therapy, and you still won't let anyone mention Mom around you?"

Her chest burned as though it contained embers and Aubrey had picked up the poker and stirred them to flame. "You weren't there! I was right there with her. So don't tell me how to deal with losing her because you. Don't. Know. What. It. Was. Like."

"Yeah, well, she was my mom too, and losing her didn't hurt me any less than it did you. I wanna keep her memory alive, but you're determined to bury it with her."

She shot out of her chair. "I don't want to fight with you, Aubrey."

"That's exactly the problem. You'd love to walk away right now and never talk about this again. It's why you've never had a boyfriend. You won't let anyone close. All you ever do is work, work, work, so you can avoid, avoid, avoid."

Pinching her nose and closing her eyes, she said, "Maybe if you had a job, you wouldn't be so concerned."

He stayed quiet for so long that she opened her eyes to make sure he was still there. His jaw had a stubborn but wounded set to it.

She sighed and rubbed her forehead. "I didn't mean to dig at you for being unemployed."

"Yes, you did."

"We both know you could go out today and find a job, no problem. If you need time off, I'm not judging you for it. I just wish you'd find something to do besides play Sherlock Holmes."

He sniffed and stuck the tack into a small free space on the board.

Drew would personally string up the low-life responsible for taking it if they found him, but Aubrey's little investigation bordered on obsessive. The painting was gone. She'd made her peace with that.

"So, you're in league with dad?" he asked. "You think I should get my teaching certificate and some sweater vests?"

"You're so off, it's not even funny. I want you to be having fun, not *this*."

A loud snort jarred her. "What do you know about fun?"

8

SIZZLING SHRIMP CAKES

Drew

"TOSS ME YOUR CAR KEYS," a deep but twangy Southern voice called to Drew on her way up the outdoor staircase leading to her best friend's beach house. She'd gotten her illustrations to the post office in time, thankfully. Aubrey had helped her, but he'd been tight-lipped the entire time.

She turned, making sure she didn't squish the garment bag draped across her arm and wrinkle Claire's wedding gown.

Matt, Claire's fiancé, stood at the bottom of the stairs with his hands cupped together, ready to catch.

"Did I block you in?" She'd parked next to Claire's SUV, but she'd been in such a rush she hadn't paid any attention to where his vintage Mustang was parked.

He shook his head and took the stairs two at a time. "According to the sticker on your windshield, you're two-thousand miles overdue for an oil change."

Sometimes, it was nice having a mechanic as her best friend's fiancé. Other times, like now, when he was giving her the stink-eye for her lousy car maintenance, not so much.

Taking her car to get serviced meant time away from working on her collection. "I know you think being overdue for an oil-change is a grave sin, but—"

"*Two-thousand miles* overdue."

Okay, so yeah, maybe that was pretty bad. She hadn't realized it'd been *that* long.

"Just give me your keys," he said. "I'll change it for you while you're doing wedding crap with Claire."

Matt was a nice guy, so it didn't surprise her he was offering to help her, but part of her knew doing a good deed was only half of his motivation. "You're not going to be able to sleep tonight unless I let you change the oil, are you?"

His mouth turned up on one side, revealing the dimple in his cheek. "Nope."

"The keys are in the cup holder."

Matt trotted back down the stairs, calling over his shoulder, "Claire's down by the beach with the photographer."

Inside the house, she bustled up to the second floor and hung the dresses in the spare bedroom. The wedding was in two days, and she had promised to help Claire with last-minute preparations. Hopefully, she would get back to her studio before dark and squeeze in a few hours of sewing.

On her way through the living room, the bathroom door swung open, nailing her in the face. "Ow!"

Drew clutched her nose and let her entire vocabulary of cuss words fly.

"Oh, damn. I'm so sorry."

She managed to see who was apologizing through her stinging, watering eyes. Her focus landed on a sprig of brown chest hair, exposed by a collared shirt open one too many buttons, and a shark tooth dangling from a thick neck.

"Aaron?" Blood dripped through her fingers.

"*Aidan.* Shit. Hold on." He rushed into the bathroom and came out with a wad of tissue. "Here."

She grabbed the tissues from him and pressed them to her nose. There was blood in her mouth, on her chin, on the floor, and her white linen shirt. Fuck. She wouldn't be able to get the shirt off to soak without getting more blood on it, so she plopped down on the couch and dipped her head forward.

"I've never been so sorry," he said in his knee-weakening accent. His only attractive trait was losing its allure. Hard to be wooed by anything after having your face bashed in.

She drew in a breath, then released it, tasting the blood dripping down her throat. Her nose felt like she'd been rammed in the face by a rhinoceros. "What are you doing here?"

"I'm the wedding photographer. You?"

Of course, he was. "Maid of honor."

He moved closer and pried the blood-saturated tissues away from her nose, then scrutinized her face. "It probably hurts worse than it is." A slow grin formed on his lips as he ran the backs of his fingers down her cheek. "Would never forgive myself if I messed up such a perfect face."

"I'm fine," she said, swatting his hand away, then snatching back the tissues. "You can go."

Aidan sat next to her, stretching his arm behind her. "Have you ever thought about modeling?"

He'd totaled her face a minute ago and now he was hitting on her?

She tried to reason with herself that this was Claire's wedding photographer, someone she shouldn't punch in the nuts.

He moved closer, cornering her between the arm of the couch and his body. "Modeling isn't always about clothes. You could come to my flat. I'll show you what I mean."

"I *know* what you mean." He was about as subtle as the door that had smacked her in the face. "Back the fuck up before I break *your* nose."

He leaned closer. His lips hovered near her ear as he said, "You don't have to pose for me. We could just get to know each other."

Drew dropped the blood-soaked tissues and brought up her palm up, aiming for his nose, the way her brothers had taught her.

He grabbed her wrist. "I like feisty women."

She yanked her arm, but he didn't lose his grip. Panic bloomed in her chest. She raised her knee and tried to turn her hips, going right for his junk.

He blocked her. Again. "Why do you American girls always play hard to get?"

"Did you ever think it's your tactics and not our nationality? I find it hard to believe the girls in your country drop their pants when you treat them like this."

He let her go, putting a hand to his chest as though she'd stabbed him in the chest. Honestly, she'd do it if she had a sharp object. "Are you implying I have trouble getting laid?"

Drew moved to stand, but he tugged her back down.

His hand landed on her bare knee, then moved upward.

"*Dude*, move your hand or you're going to lose it."

He snickered, and moved even closer, looming over her.

"Get *off* her," Claire echoed, rushing into the room. Her eyes zeroed in on the blood saturated tissue under Drew's nose before her mouth twisted into a snarl.

Aidan immediately snatched his hand away and stood.

Claire had her arms crossed, barefoot tapping on the floor. "You're fired."

"I think you got the wrong idea," he said, hands held up as though she was pointing a gun at him.

"I don't." Claire pointed in the direction of the back door. "Get out."

He lowered his chin to his chest and made his way past Claire, grabbing his camera bag off the kitchen table.

"Sizzling shrimp cakes," Claire said, coming closer and inspecting

Drew's face. "What did he do to you? I'm gonna kill him."

Drew grabbed Claire's arm to keep her from going after him. "He hit me in the face with the bathroom door." She held up the bloody tissues for her to see. "It was an accident. Nosebleed, but I'll recover."

Claire took Drew's chin in her hand and turned her head from side to side. "There was more going on there than him performing first aid. Are you okay?"

She shook her head, not because she wasn't okay, but because she didn't think Claire realized what she had just done. "Your wedding is in two days."

"Oh, sugar. Drew," she said, pressing her hands to her cheeks. "What am I going to do?"

"I'll fix it." She pushed herself off the couch and walked through the kitchen, making it to the screen door only to watch Aidan's car skid out of the driveway. She bustled down the steps of the elevated house and into the garage.

Matt stood by a workbench, wiping his hands on a rag. "What's up?"

"I need my car."

"I thought you were staying for dinner."

Her fingers sifted through her hair, pressing into her head, which had started to pound. "I need to go after the photographer."

"Why?" His tone was all what-did-you-do-this-time, but she could hear the smile in it. He loved teasing her about her temper.

"Claire fired him. He was…doing some…not nice things."

Matt straightened his posture. "Not nice things?" His eyes locked on her nose.

The blood wasn't running into her mouth anymore, but probably only because it had gelatinized under her nose, acting as a dam.

"He did this to you?"

"On accident. He opened the bathroom door when I was heading for it. But then he started hitting on me. I told him it wasn't happening. He must have selective hearing. Claire came in and saw what was happening and freaked out and fired him. I need to go talk to him or you won't have a photographer at your wedding."

His face sobered. "No."

"No?"

"There's no way I'm letting that dick back on my property. And even less chance I'm letting you go bargain with him to take pictures of the wedding."

Drew huffed. She didn't *want* to go after that asshole, but she didn't have a choice. The wedding was in two fucking days. "We work together. He's a bartender. I can reason with him."

"Let's circle back to the part where I will bloody *his* nose, as well as many other body parts, if he steps foot on my property again." Matt leaned against the hood of her car, arms crossed.

"You understand how far in advance you have to book a photographer, right?"

"Is Claire upset?"

"Not as much as she should be."

He walked to his workbench and grabbed some kind of big wrench doohickey, like the discussion was closed and he was getting back to tinkering with her car. "You mean more to her than a bunch of pictures."

"Pictures of your wedding," she said, stressing the W-word. "I need to fix this."

"I'm not letting you go after some jerk-off who deserved to be fired without a new set of tires for Leona."

"New tires?" She didn't have the funds for that. "Wait, Leona? You named my car?"

He shrugged. "I can get new ones and have them on by tomorrow. Seriously, you have no business driving her until you've got new rubber."

Drew closed her eyes. A bloody nose? No big deal. Having to

rush to redo her illustrations and get it postmarked in only a few hours? It'd proved to her how capable she was. But ruining her best friend's wedding? Unacceptable.

She *would* fix this.

9

CASHING IN

Drew

DREW CLOSED HER EYES and took a deep breath, opening herself up to be lulled by the buzz of the cappuccino machine and smoothie blender. For some reason, those noises coupled with the light chatter of the other customers, created the perfect soundtrack to inspire her designs.

Usually.

Today, it was like someone had switched the recording to American Idol's worst auditions. If that guy in the next booth blew his nose one more time…

What was he doing? Trying to dislodge his brain?

Maybe she was a little irritable, but she had reason to be.

The wedding was tomorrow. Claire and Matt had forbidden Drew to talk Aidan into still being their photographer. Her godfather was a photography professor at SCAD, and he would have done it despite lifestyle photography not being his specialty, but Uncle Rich was already on a plane to Dallas to speak at a conference. He'd contacted his students to see if anyone could do it, but the college was on break, and most had gone home to visit their families, or headed to Florida to wild out.

She and Claire had called every photographer in the city and all of them were booked. It was just Drew's luck she needed a photographer on a Saturday during peak wedding season.

The universe had a sick sense of humor. She was sure of this because when she'd passed the jerk-off who'd ruined her illustrations sitting outside, his expensive camera practically jumped off the table and smacked her in the face. He was the last person on earth she'd ask a favor.

He hadn't shown any sign he'd seen her. Slouched in a metal café chair, he'd kept his mirrored aviators locked on the folded newspaper in his hand.

"Just get it over with," she muttered. With her drawing materials collected and a second latte in hand, she headed out the door and stopped in front of his table.

He didn't look up.

Drew cleared her throat. "Mind if I sit?"

Although his eyes were hidden, his eyebrows rose over the rim of his aviators. He lowered the newspaper to the table and gestured to the chair across from his.

She set her things on a nearby table and took a seat across from him. "Logan, right?"

He nodded.

"I thought of a way you can make it up to me for ruining my sketches."

Using one finger, he pulled his shades down the slope of his nose and peered at her with those dark, daring eyes.

"I need a photographer."

He pushed the sunglasses back in place, then lifted the newspaper. "I'm not a professional. It's just a hobby."

She spun the cardboard sleeve around her cup. People didn't buy cameras of that quality unless they were serious about photography. And at this point, if he was a mediocre photographer, that would be better than what Claire had. Which was no one.

"I'm in a real jam. My best friend is getting married tomorrow and her photographer quit last minute."

"Why?"

"Why what?"

"Why did the photographer quit?" He took another sip of his coffee.

With the lenses concealing his eyes, it was like being on the wrong side of a one-way mirror. And like a guilty suspect, she squirmed. She didn't want to get into what had gone down with Aidan. That was none of his business.

"That's not important." Before he pressed further, she went on. "I know I've been…"

"Mean," he supplied, gesturing outwardly with his hand.

"Are you kidding me? You fucking ruined my illustrations the day I was supposed to send them off."

"Oh, you were nice to me before that?"

Her eyes widened. She pressed her lips together to keep from saying anything that would prove his point. He'd gotten in her way *and* said his share of mean things, but calling attention to that wasn't going to help her.

He snorted. "Say it."

"Say what?"

"Whatever salty remark you're just barely suppressing."

She gripped the edge of her chair. "I wasn't going to say anything."

His lip curled into a hint of a smile. "You must be really desperate."

"Claire's my best friend, and if anyone deserves to have a perfect wedding day, she does."

He tilted his head and raised his eyebrows. "You have friends?"

"Just the one," she snapped back, unable to keep her mouth in check any longer. "Maybe you'll have one too, after you agree to do me this favor."

His deep, rumbling laughter sent her stomach tumbling. Her smart mouth repelled most men, as intended. Every now and then, some dickface like Aidan believed his persistence could cut through her icy exterior, as if they tried hard enough, they'd penetrate it and find a sweet, gooey center.

Logan didn't so much as flinch at her blatant hostility. It was as if he intentionally provoked her for fun. Clearly, he had mental issues.

The sensation coursing through her resembled exhilaration, but that couldn't be right. More like some weird adrenaline rush from her fight instinct being triggered.

"You owe me," she said, wishing he would go ahead and agree so she could get away from him and rid herself of this bizarre reaction.

Slowly, he removed his sunglasses and set them atop the newspaper. "I don't take those type of photos. Just landscapes."

"Well, it's a beach wedding. You would be taking shots of the landscape, only there would be people in front of it."

He ran a hand through his hair. "Fine. I'll do it."

Did he just say—Really? "You will?"

He slid his phone across the table, then picked up his paper and resumed reading. "Text me the details."

She sent herself a message with his phone, then saved his number in her contacts. "Tomorrow at nine. That's when we're going to start getting ready. Claire wants some shots of the bridal party getting their hair and makeup done."

"Uh-huh," he muttered, not looking up.

Apparently, they were done. She chewed her upper lip. Things didn't feel conclusive. What if he was just telling her he'd do it and then left her hanging?

Although, she did have his number, so worst case she'd badger the shit out of him until he showed.

10

VERBAL ASSAULT KINK

LOGAN

UNCLE JOHN WAS RIGHT. Logan really was one lucky son of bitch.

He had botched his plan to make Drew feel guilty. But somehow, he'd gotten a second shot. She'd come to him. All on her own, without any devious plotting on his part.

Taking pictures of her wasn't going to be a hardship, either.

Hers was the first face he saw when he arrived. His heart skipped three beats. She sat in a wicker chair on the screened porch of her friend's beach house. Her head was covered in curlers the size of soda cans and a soft white robe enveloped her body. She pouted her lips as a woman in a smock applied lipstick.

He stood paralyzed at the top of the stairs leading up to the stilted beach house, watching her laugh while trying to keep a straight face for the makeup artist. It was the first time he had ever seen her like this—unguarded and playful. Happy. Her green eyes sparkled as she threw her head back and let out a deep laugh. He wanted to be in on her joke.

An earsplitting whistle snapped his attention in the opposite direction. He turned and spotted a man in board shorts and a T-shirt. He motioned for Logan to join him in the backyard.

"Logan, right?" the man called, holding his hand up to block the searing sunlight.

He nodded and joined him in front of another set of stairs leading to the back deck.

"I'm Matt, the groom."

He shook his hand. "Nice to meet you."

Matt shoved his hands into his pockets and rocked back on his heels.

"You seem too relaxed for a guy about to get married."

"I know what I'm doing." He glanced up at the house. "Claire is another story. She's a wreck."

Claire wasn't the only one. Seeing Drew had messed with his cool. He needed a couple minutes to get his shit together before he faced her.

"You don't think she'll back out, do you?" he asked, unable to hold back from teasing this bastard about to sign his life away.

Matt shook his head. "I'd drag her down the aisle if I had to, but I know she'll get there on her own."

Logan couldn't relate. At all. He had no desire to be in a relationship, let alone get married. And if he ever did lose his mind and ask a woman to marry him, the fuck if he'd be this chill knowing she had cold feet.

"I wanted to give this to you before I forget." Matt handed him a plain white envelope, then beckoned him toward the steps to the back deck. "After you get set up, Claire wants you to take some pictures of the girls getting ready. I'm not allowed in the house. Just go in through this door, and someone will give you orders. You can count on that."

He peeked inside the envelope, saw it was a check, and tucked it into the interior pocket of his jacket before heading up the stairs.

The kitchen buzzed with wedding preparation, but an older woman in an apron pointed the way out to the front porch. He passed through the living room and opened the swinging screen door.

The makeup artist dusted Drew's face with a huge round powder brush as she stayed perfectly still.

A blonde wearing a pair of frayed jean shorts and a white tank top paced the length of the front porch while another woman followed her, trying to pin some locks away from her face. When the screen door hinges creaked, she stopped and smiled at him.

"Logan?"

After he nodded, she clasped his extended hand, covering it with both of hers. "I'm Claire. I want you to know how grateful I am. You're a lifesaver."

The woman with the hairpins seized the moment to whisk some of Claire's hair back and secure it. But she only got two pins in before the pacing resumed.

Claire reminded him of his sister. Or at least of how Morgan was before she'd gotten mixed up with Eric—all sunshine and determination, even when under the gun. An unexplainable urge to help her shake her anxiety tugged at Logan. "What are you so nervous for? I just met Matt, and shit, if you don't marry him, I might."

She laughed.

His gaze flicked to Drew.

Her lips twitched, but she didn't laugh.

"Did he seem nervous?" Claire spun her engagement ring round and round her finger while she waited for his answer.

He shook his head. "I got the feeling he made up his mind a long time ago that he was never letting you go."

"He says this is just a celebration with our friends and family. That nothing is going to change—except my last name."

Logan shoved his hands into his pockets and shrugged. "That doesn't have to change either, unless you want it to."

His attention once again bounced to Drew.

She quirked a brow.

"I want to marry him. I'm *going to* marry him. I just…" Claire hugged herself.

"It's a major turning point in your life. You can't see what's around the corner, and that's scary as hell."

"Yes," Claire said in a *someone finally gets it* tone. "I've been so focused on getting here, and now I am here, and I don't know what comes next and it's freaking me out."

"The honeymoon comes next," he said with a wink. "Going anywhere good?"

"Antigua."

He whistled appreciatively. "So, here's what you do. Whenever you start to freak out about the future, remind yourself that the future is sandy beaches and rum punch, steel drums and pink sunsets, and lots of getting tangled up in the sheets with your *husband*."

The smile that emerged on Claire's face made him feel a little less like scum for using this opportunity to con her best friend.

Logan got to work, snapping shots of everyone on the porch. The entire bridal party consisted of the bride, Drew, and the flower girl.

"You could only choose one bridesmaid and you picked her?" he asked Claire, keeping his back to Drew so she couldn't see his smile.

"It's not going to work," Drew said in a sing-song voice.

He turned and watched her dig through the cosmetic bag perched on her lap. "What's not going to work?"

"I'm in too good of a mood to let you ruin it. If your kink is verbal assault, I'm more than happy to accommodate you, but it's going to have to be another day."

Yeah, that was his kink alright. Before he'd met her, he'd never have thought he'd get so hot for someone with such a salty mouth. It was so bad he'd caught himself replaying their conversations in his head while he laid in bed.

11

HOW DARE HE BE LIKABLE

Drew

"I'LL BE NICE, IF YOU WILL." Logan extended his hand.

"Deal." Drew placed her hand in his. As his long fingers curled around her hand, her stomach flipped—not the nauseating kind of flip, but the kind she got right before she did something gutsy. The warmth that flooded her body wasn't all that unpleasant, either. She snatched her hand back.

Logan's hand fell to his side, but his soul-stroking gaze refused to release hers.

Whatever he was looking for, she didn't want exposed. It was bad enough she had gotten glimpses of him she wished she hadn't.

She didn't want to know he was secure enough in his masculinity to crack jokes about marrying another man. She didn't want to see the hint of a guy who's supportive of feminist actions, like a woman keeping her last name after marriage. Drew especially didn't want to watch him empathize with her wedding-jittery friend and help her relax without missing a beat. Evidently, his talent for rapid responses wasn't limited to flippancy.

She wanted him to be the antagonistic jerk who'd gotten under her skin. He could at least be ugly. Or a sloppy dresser.

The charcoal jacket, matching flat-front trousers, and white dress shirt he'd selected for today not only showed that Logan could go from leather-jacket rebel to Hugo Boss model seamlessly, but he was also damn good at buying clothes that fit him *really* well.

Drew tore her gaze away and focused on her makeup bag, digging through the contents as if it contained a route to escape. If only her eyeshadow palette doubled as a portal. "Go take pictures."

He grunted like her hasty dismissal was typical, then sauntered away.

Fighting a battle she couldn't win, she watched him walk toward her goddaughter, who sat on the swing at the end of the porch, hair braided into a halo and entwined with baby's breath.

She gritted her teeth as the camera shutter *chitch*-ed over and over again.

His concentration was spot on, snapping shot after shot of Claire and Autumn, his vibe charming and chill.

Chill was not a mood accessible to Drew on her best day. She didn't want him to see her ruffled, though. Maybe she could pull off blasé.

He paused to shrug out of his form-fitting jacket and roll up his sleeves. His shoulder muscles rippled under his shirt.

Her thighs tingled and a dull ache blossomed from a place she refused to try to pinpoint. She almost sighed out loud. Had his body always been so…thirst-inducing?

She was noticing too much. Like the way the seat of his trousers filled out when he crouched. And the deft movements he made as he switched lenses and adjusted his focus.

"Can I take some shots of your dress before you change into it?" he asked Claire.

Claire held up the brush from the pink polish she'd been applying to Autumn's fingernails. "It's in the bedroom. First door on the right."

"Whoa," Drew shouted. "I'm the only one who is going to handle that baby until it's on her body."

That gown was her blood, sweat, and tears. Literally. When Claire had told Drew Matt proposed, she'd started designing her wedding dress immediately. She'd finished it months ago and cried when Claire had tried it on for the first time. Logan had already ruined her work once before. She'd managed to fix that catastrophe, but there would be no replacing Claire's gown the day of her wedding.

Logan headed inside, as if he hadn't heard her.

She flew out of her chair and darted after him, her heart beating rapidly, partly because she didn't trust him alone with the dress, and partly because she didn't trust herself alone with him after her uncontrollable bout of lust.

Blood pulsed loudly in her head when the snap of the camera traveled from the bedroom into the hallway. She rushed in and found Logan taking photographs of the gown hanging on the armoire. Lucky for him, he hadn't touched it.

She pushed by and gingerly removed the gown.

He whistled. "That's some dress."

Ivory lace, fitted to the knee, flowing out like a trumpet. The silhouette was perfect for Claire. A pink sash wrapped around the waistline, concluding in an exaggerated bow that would trail behind the bride in place of a train.

"Thank you." She laid it on the blue and white circle quilt and fussed with the drape of the fabric. The camera flashed repeatedly as she arranged the tulle under the skirt.

"You made it?"

"Surprised?"

After a few moments of silence, she turned to find him staring at her.

His camera hung limply at his side, the lens directed at the floor. He opened his mouth, but before a word came out, his stare dropped to her chest.

Drew had never seen Logan at a loss for words. He was too sharp-tongued, too quick-witted. But right now, mouth agape, eyes glazed, he appeared to have faltered.

She glanced down, then gasped and pulled the lapels of her robe together. If her left breast had been any more exposed, he'd have seen nipple.

Heat spiraled through her body, rushing toward her face. "Are you finished?" she snapped.

"Calm down. I didn't see any—much." He took a deep breath. "Sorry."

"Yeah, I bet you are."

"You're the one who flashed me!"

She tugged at her robe again, adjusting the belt to make sure it stayed in place, then crossed her arms for additional insurance. "Just do what you're here to do."

With her back to him, she kept her gaze on the dress while he resumed photographing. Okay, so, she couldn't really be mad at him for looking. Her boob had been right there in his face. Still, he needed to get the hell out so she could be mortified in private.

"Can you hang it by the window?" he asked.

She transferred it to the window overlooking the beach, placing the hanger on the curtain rod. The sunlight poured in and illuminated the lace. "I thought you only did landscapes," she said. "You seem to know what you're doing."

"I wasn't going to come into this unprepared. I did my research, found out what the standard wedding shots are."

He didn't have to do that. Asking him to be the photographer was an act of desperation. In this situation, he could have gotten away with doing the bare minimum. Why did it make her feel some kind of way that he wanted to do a good job?

He rose from his crouch and rolled his shoulders. "Shoes?"

She shook her head. "Barefoot wedding."

"Okay, then, that's all for now."

Drew closed the bedroom door behind them and pointed to where the back door was located. "The guys are in the garage."

"Can't wait to get rid of me, can you?"

"Nope."

Logan shook his head with a smirk stretching his lips as he put his camera into his bag. "No reason to get all bashful. I've seen tits before. Although, maybe none as nice as yours."

Her mouth fell open.

He winked at her, then strode off before she could form a coherent comeback.

Drew shook off her stupor, grabbed the champagne bottle she'd stored in the fridge, and snuck two glasses from the caterer's crate on the kitchen table. The mother of the groom *shoo*-ed her out of the busy kitchen, smacking at her rear with a dishtowel.

She stood in front of Claire on the porch swing and dangled the bottle in front of her.

"Yes, *please*."

Drew handed her the glasses and uncorked the champagne. "I have presents too."

"You always have presents," Autumn said, clapping.

"Can't keep my title as best godmother ever if I didn't." Drew winked at the girl and poured the champagne. She handed one glass to Claire, and then they clinked them together. "To the bride."

After a sip, she retrieved the canvas tote bag by the door. Drew pulled a pink paper and twine wrapped shirt box from the bag and handed it to Autumn.

She shredded the wrapping in a nanosecond. "Mom," she shrieked and held up a doll-sized dress while grinning from ear to ear. "It looks just like my dress."

"Well, we couldn't have Phoebe feeling left out," Drew said, amazed at how receiving the little girl's approval always made her heart swell.

"Thank you so much, Aunt Drew." Autumn jumped off the swing and hurled herself into Drew's arms. "I'm going to go try it on her." She scampered into the house, clutching the dress to her chest.

Claire took the thin white package Drew held out to her. She pushed the tissue in the box aside revealing a pair of lace gloves with buttons at the wrists. "These are gorgeous. Are they vintage?"

"They were my mom's," Drew said, forcing herself to recite what she had gone over in her head all morning. Talking about her mom always made her ache, but Claire was the closest thing to a sister Drew had. "She bought them on her honeymoon in Paris and kept them on her vanity. I always wanted to play dress up with them, but she told me I couldn't wear them until my wedding day."

Claire shoved the box at Drew. "I can't wear these."

"Yes, you can. You helped fill the void she left, and I know she'd want you to wear them." Her voice cracked on the last word. Drew took a deep breath and blinked back the tears. She didn't pay a small fortune to have her makeup done only to ruin it before the ceremony.

Claire released a strangled sound and wiped at her watering eyes. "Are you trying to make me cry?"

Fanning herself to try to cool the rush of emotional heat radiating through her, she shook her head. "Just say you'll wear them. They're your something borrowed."

"Okay, I'll wear them, and you're going to wear them at your wedding."

"Yeah," Drew said through a choked laugh, "because I'm on the marriage fast-track."

"You never know when that's going to change. Tomorrow, you could meet the man you're going to spend the rest of your life with. Maybe you've already met him, and you don't know it."

Drew rolled her eyes. "Please don't use your wedding as an excuse to play matchmaker."

"No, I would never do that," Claire said, and in the next breath, "So, do you still think Logan is totally awful?"

After he'd agreed to photograph the wedding, she had told Claire the entire story of how she met Logan.

"I don't think he's totally awful *looking*."

"That whole laid-back rascal vibe he puts out is hard not to like."

"He was nice to you, Claire. Of course, you like him. Are you going to overlook his smart-ass remark about choosing me as your maid of honor?"

A slow smile stretched Claire's mouth. "Would you have paid any attention to him if he'd been nice to you?"

"Yes," she drawled out.

Claire raised an eyebrow.

She opened her mouth to make Claire promise not to try to set her up with Logan. Before she had one syllable out of her mouth, Avery, Autumn's twin brother, exploded from the house like a bat out of hell. He tripped over the rug and fell to his knees, a small velvet box flying out of his hands.

Both women stood to help him, but he grabbed the box and bounced right up.

As he approached, panting, his blue eyes sparkled. "This is from Dad." He thrust the box at Claire.

"Thank you." She pulled him in for a hug.

That box held delicate blue earrings made from beach glass. Drew had asked the most important people in Claire's life to participate in the tradition. The twins had collected shell fragments off the beach and Drew had them strung into a beautiful anklet. Something new. Before he walked her down the aisle, her dad would give her something old.

"I'm going to go check on Autumn," Drew said, leaving them to their important mother-son moment.

12

A FULL DANCE CARD

Drew

"Your dance card sure has been full tonight."

Drew stared into her father's eyes, deadpan. "That's because I'm a phenomenal dancer."

He shook his head, but a small smile crossed his lips, then he twirled her, bringing her under his arm and back to his front. There was no one she would rather dance with.

The backyard—always its own little slice of paradise—was magical with a capital M. She'd been too busy getting ready and being a part of the ceremony to really appreciate the transformation, but wow.

A dance floor had been erected in the yard and several small clusters of round tables with white linen tablecloths and folding teak chairs surrounded it. Sand and seashells had been sprinkled in the center of every table. Large and small cylindrical vases nestled in the center of the sand, a white candle inside casting a warm glow over each setting. More candles glowed inside glass hurricane lanterns hanging from the trees.

"Matt's brother seems to appreciate your *dancing skills*."

She threw her head back and groaned. "Can we not talk about this right now?"

"I'm only pointing out the obvious."

She snuck a glance at Matt's younger brother. As best man and maid of honor, they'd made their entrance to the reception together. The goofball had the genius idea to enter the reception dancing to a Michael Jackson song, complete with fedoras and moonwalking. It'd been fun, and everyone seemed to love it.

All decked out in his Army dress uniform, Colin looked handsome. He had sandy blond hair, like his brother, and being a soldier, his body was in top form. Despite being a relentless flirt, he wasn't pushy, and she'd never felt anything other than safe and comfortable in his presence. But…that's all she felt.

A little chill ran down her spine, intuition telling her someone was watching her. Her gaze cast around the edges of the dance floor, until her eyes locked onto Logan's.

She forced her attention to her dad's tie and kept it there.

"I'm not interested in Colin, Dad, don't worry," she said.

"It's you not being interested that worries me."

It worried her too. Because while Colin did nothing for her in the attraction department, the fill-in photographer evoked desire so intense it made her entire body flush. Ugh, why him?

"Dad…"

"Life is about balance."

"I'm not balanced?"

He opened his mouth, then shut it.

"This wedding is making everyone delusional. I don't need a man to be happy."

"I didn't say you did." He looked her dead in the eyes. "You work too hard. I don't want you to miss out on the good things life has to offer."

She could point out that she'd learned her work ethic from him. He always made time for her and her brothers. Family was number one. It was for her too. But her dad didn't have much of a social life. He hadn't been on a date in the fifteen years since her mom died, at least that she knew of.

But she didn't want to have that conversation. If he didn't have such passion and commitment to his work, she might feel differently. Her dad didn't show any signs of being lonely. Which was great because it would be hard to see her dad with a woman. But if she thought it would make him happy, she'd suck it up and pretend to be happy for him.

Her dad had come to the wedding stag. That said it all. He still wasn't ready for any romantic entanglements.

As for her...

"Dad, I'm twenty-two. I'm supposed to be working hard. I'll have plenty of time for the other stuff later."

"I know, but—"

"You're ruining what could be a lovely father-daughter moment."

His expression turned soft. "I worry you're going to miss out on having what I had with your mother."

Talk about straight to the heart. She rested her cheek against his shoulder. He wasn't the only one who worried she'd never have that.

13

STOP TRIPPIN'

LOGAN

"WHAT'S STOPPING YOU?"

Out of the corner of his eye, Logan took note of Claire, who'd moved to stand next to him on the edge of the dance floor.

Her gown swished as she swayed to the music. He'd never paid attention to women's formal attire, but he found himself floored by this dress. Drew's talent was impressive, but he had failed to find the words to tell her that. Probably due to her unintentionally showing him her tits.

Her hair fell in soft curls over her bare shoulders and spilled down her back. Her dress was the same shade of pink as the bow on Claire's gown. It was simple, clean, elegant.

He needed to unglue his gaze from Drew, and he would, in another minute.

The woman he had never seen in anything other than designer pumps was barefoot. It was a different, softer side of her. A side he wanted to experience.

"Stopping me from what?" he asked, knowing full well what Claire was suggesting.

"You haven't taken your eyes off her for the past fifteen minutes. Ask her to dance."

He could have denied wanting to, but Claire seemed like the kind of person to call bullshit without hesitation. "I'm working."

"I'm the one paying you." She sounded every bit as bossy as her best friend, no small feat. "And I say it's okay."

He was always professional when the circumstances called for it, but he had another reason for keeping his distance. As she danced with one man after the other, he'd gotten progressively agitated. That shit had to stop. He couldn't have her.

Her current partner was an older man, somewhere around his mid-fifties, with a manicured beard and neat ponytail. He twirled Drew around the floor with more grace than any of her other partners. And he made her smile and laugh more too.

"Who's she dancing with?"

"Sam Miller. Her *father*." Claire looped her arm through his and tugged.

His gaze shot to her, and he shook his head.

"If you aren't going to ask her to dance, you're going to have to dance with me. This is my wedding. You can't say no to me."

He searched the backyard for her husband and spotted him standing by the bar, talking to his father-in-law and drinking a longneck bottle of beer.

Even though his father-in-law appeared to be deep in conversation, Matt's gaze never wavered from the woman dragging Logan onto the dance floor. He grinned and held up his beer as if to say, "Good luck, buddy."

"Set your camera down," she ordered, stopping by the special table reserved for her and Matt.

He could tell Claire was not going to relent, so he put his camera on the table. One dance wouldn't kill him.

Until they ended up right alongside Drew and her father, he'd believed he was leading. He glared at the woman in his arms, though only half-heartedly. Uncle John could turn her into a fine con woman in no time.

She smiled back, then turned to the couple next to them. "It's bad luck to leave a wedding before dancing with the bride, Mr. Miller."

He turned his attention from his daughter to Claire. "I've never heard that before."

"That's because I just made it up." She said it in such a cheery tone that Logan laughed. Man, he liked her spunk.

As the song ended, Drew's father let go of her and extended his hand to Claire.

She thanked Logan for the dance and accepted the hand of her new partner.

The band began to play a slower tune.

Drew started to walk away. The best man, dressed in Army Class A's, was heading in her direction. He had already danced with her twice and had flirted with her nonstop from the minute he walked her back up the aisle at the end of the ceremony.

Before G.I. Joe made his move, Logan reached out and grabbed her hand, tugging her back and spinning her into his arms.

The momentum forced her to flatten her free hand against his chest to keep from plowing into him.

He slipped his hand behind her and pressed it against the small of her back and waited for her to protest.

Drew moved her hand farther up, so her fingertips pressed against the starched collar of his shirt. That small, innocent action made his pulse ratchet up. He needed to get away from her. Leaving her stranded on the dance floor in the middle of a song didn't seem like such a hot idea, though.

Especially since he'd gotten lucky after his original plan had gone off the rails. He'd skipped several steps ahead of where he'd be if things had stayed on course.

She smelled like oranges, or maybe lemons.

He bet the skin on her bare shoulder tasted like citrus too.

He took a step, and she followed his movements fluidly. *Unexpected.*

Unlike Claire, she let him lead. The feel of her body brushing against his flayed the restraint he had on his body's reaction to her. If he didn't put space between them, and a lot of it, he was going to lose the last little bit of that restraint from his chokehold.

She was uncharacteristically quiet. But her body language didn't convey any displeasure. If her silence wasn't due to animosity, could it be that she enjoyed dancing with him?

Stop trippin'. His head was so fucked. And he needed it unfucked because he still needed to find out who stole her father's painting and that required a lot of calculation and forethought.

Logan put space between them. Preventing her body from grazing his as they swayed together wouldn't help much. Not as long as he had her hand in his, and proximity to her warm body and sweet scent.

She directed her gaze up at him. "What's wrong?"

"You, being this quiet. Didn't know it was possible."

"I didn't know it was possible for you *not* to be annoying."

He snickered. "No one has ever called me annoying."

"How about obnoxious?"

He cracked a smile. "That's my girl. I was wondering how long it would be before the biting remarks started flying."

"I'm not your girl," she whispered, staring at his chest.

"And what a shame that is," he whispered back before he could stop himself.

Her gaze flashed to his, her eyes big and bright as the song ended.

He cleared his throat and let his arms drop.

The singer of the band announced it was time to cut the cake.

"You're a good dancer, Logan. Who would've guessed?"

"I do have a few redeeming qualities, believe it or not."

"I should probably…" She tilted her head in the direction of the cake and the people swarming it.

"Uh, yeah." Fuck. He was supposed to be photographing this shit.

Logan walked in the opposite direction as Drew, hurrying to grab his camera before they cut the cake.

He snapped several shots of it and the newlyweds. After feeding Claire a small bite, Matt kissed the icing from her lips. Classy.

After the newlyweds made their exit, the reception died down. With the bride and groom gone, there wasn't much else worth capturing on film.

He couldn't pass up the opportunity to make progress siphoning info from Drew. Getting her comfortable with him was a vital part of his plan, but he suspected they'd made a wrong turn and were cruising toward a type of thirst he absolutely could not quench. It wasn't only the feel of her curvy little body against his—although that had felt wickedly good. Holding her, having her in his arms on the dance floor under the stars, he wanted to keep her.

14

COULD HAVE FOOLED ME

LOGAN

HE COULDN'T FIND DREW ANYWHERE. Damn it. How hadn't he seen her leave?

As he was about to head for his car, he caught a glimpse of pink on the beach.

Drew's silhouetted body moved in the moonlight, walking alone in the sand with a champagne flute.

Grabbing a bottle of champagne off one of the tables, he headed in her direction, wishing he could do what he was about to without it being part of a con.

But it was a con. One that was going to keep his sister safe and earn his freedom. It was going to feel so fucking good to be out from under Bob's thumb.

By the time he reached her, she was wading in the water ankle-deep. Prickles slid across his palms. He'd never wanted to touch anything so bad in his life. He had to keep reminding himself why he was there. Once he got the information he needed, he would never see her again.

His stomach twisted. He wouldn't have even known she existed if he hadn't taken the damn assignment.

"More champagne?" he asked, walking closer.

She glanced over her shoulder. Her gaze stayed on him, her

expression unreadable. Maybe she had been waiting for someone. Someone that wasn't him.

Too damn bad.

He lifted the bottle so she could see he hadn't uncorked it yet. "I swear it's one hundred percent arsenic-free."

Her lips twitched. She walked toward him with her glass held out.

He removed the cage and foil from the bottle and used his fist to twist the cork up and out of the neck. He filled her glass, then took a swig from the bottle. "Have a good time tonight?"

"I'm glad it's over, to be honest."

"Why?"

She faced the water again. "I love Claire and Matt. Being part of their wedding was an honor, but it was also time consuming. You have no idea how many dress fittings we did, or how much time I spent with her on the guest list and stuffing the envelopes with save the dates and invitations."

She didn't sugarcoat things. Ever. But he would bet a small fortune she hadn't once uttered a word of complaint while helping prepare for the wedding.

"Were you able to make your deadline?"

She cut her eyes at him. "That's what you're going to bring up right now? Do you always shoot yourself in the foot, or is it something special you reserve for me?"

He gazed at the moonlight reflecting in flickers across the water. "It's only with you."

As someone with a reputation for being smooth and charismatic, it was fucking ridiculous, not to mention embarrassing, how often those qualities vanished when in her company.

The sound of waves crashing filled the space for several seconds, then she said, "I made the deadline."

The weight crushing his chest eased the smallest bit. "Were you happy with what you sent in?"

She fidgeted, drawing in the sand with her toes. "I don't know why I'm telling you this because you deserve to feel awful, but...my illustrations turned out even better when I redid them."

His chest resumed a slight pressure he could live with. It'd settled there when Morgan left Vegas, and it'd only gotten worse since. Until he got this mess with Bob cleaned up, it would stay there. "How long until you hear if you're a finalist?"

"Three or four weeks."

"And in the meantime?" Logan shifted his gaze to the ocean. Maybe if he didn't look at her too much, he'd have a better shot at maintaining a level head.

"I keep working under the assumption that I'm going to be a finalist, so that if I do get chosen, I'll be ahead of the game." Her voice held a note of conviction that made him smile, and foiled his plan to keep his eyes off her.

"What does that entail?"

"Buying fabric, drafting patterns, sewing." She ticked the tasks off on her fingers as she spoke.

"Sounds like a lot of work." And it sounded like she wasn't the least bit daunted.

"It's an insane amount of work, but I know I'll never be happy working for someone else. As an intern, I never had much say in what I designed. Now, I make *all* the decisions. Having my own studio is just butter on the biscuit."

The corner of his mouth lifted, but he left the butter on the biscuit comment alone. "Your own studio? That's pretty sweet."

"Well, it's not *all* mine. My dad and I share a space. I have the second floor. He has the first."

"What does your dad use his studio for?"

"Painting."

Logan's shoulder blades grew closer, his neck stiffening. He'd successfully steered the conversation exactly where it needed to go. So, why'd he feel like such a failure?

He wanted to guide the conversation back toward her designing. It was fascinating, and not because he had an interest in fashion, but because of how genuine she was when talking about it.

But he couldn't.

"Is he able to make a living at it?" There were more than a few articles written on Sam Miller lately, lots of hubbub about his rising success. Logan knew what his paintings sold for. Her dad could quit his teaching job at the college.

"Yes." She eased down to the sand, sitting with her knees pulled to her chest. "Thanks for doing this. Photographing the wedding. You saved my ass."

She didn't want to brag on her father?

He sat beside her, digging the heels of his shoes into the powder-soft sand and took a swig from the bottle before wedging it into the sand so it wouldn't tip over. "An ass like yours is worth saving."

She turned to rest her chin on her shoulder, eyes bright, lips pressed together, trying to rein in her smile.

The air left his lungs like he'd been hit hard enough to knock the wind out him. If there was ever a moment—no, a look—he wanted to capture, this was it. He'd seen her give the same look to Claire as she handed off her bouquet before taking her vows, to her godson when he asked her to dance, and later to her dad as he'd twirled her around, to Matt during her Maid of Honor speech when she thanked him for being the man her friend deserved.

His tie was way too tight. He reached for the knot, but his fingers hit the skin under his open collar. Shit. He wasn't even wearing one.

Drew wet her lips. During the ceremony, they had matched the pink of her dress, but now, they were naked. Her lashes lowered and she shifted closer.

His stomach dropped out like he was about to go down the mother of all rollercoasters.

For fuck's sake. He had as much of a chance resisting her as he did getting hired by the NSA.

He covered her mouth with his, their kiss sweet from champagne and salty from the ocean air. Logan ran his tongue across her bottom lip while his hand traveled up her back and neck to tangle his fingers into her hair.

Her lips parted and he couldn't resist sliding his tongue into her mouth. Her arms circled his neck and her tongue brushed back against his. He grunted, bemused by how cooperative she was considering her normal combative nature.

Hungry for more, he cupped the back of her head to keep her mouth on his. The throaty moan she made when he sucked her bottom lip gave him an instantaneous hard-on. He pulled her even closer and relished the way her body curved into his as her fingers dug into his shoulders. He twisted his fingers in her curls, gripping her hair in fistfuls. The purring noise she made killed him.

She didn't mind a little roughness.

He could work with that.

She angled her head, allowing his tongue better access to hers and slid her hands from his shoulders to his chest.

He throbbed for her touch, and he doubted that feeling would subside until he was deep inside her.

And that couldn't happen.

He had to stop. She was a job, and he knew better than to get more involved than necessary. He was going to stop kissing her as soon—

Before he had a chance to finish his thought, she ripped her mouth from his and pushed away from him. Her chest rose and fell in quick drags. "What the hell?" she muttered. "I don't even like you."

"Could have fooled me."

"You can't just go around kissing people!"

Logan smiled. "Sure, I can. That doesn't mean they have to like it as much as you did."

Her mouth fell open wide enough to hold a hockey puck. She sputtered. "I've had too much to drink. I'm not thinking clearly."

Bullshit. She might be working toward a buzz, but he'd been watching her all night and she hadn't had more than two glasses since the reception started.

Grabbing the champagne bottle from the sand, he held it in her direction. "Want to add some actual truth to that statement?" He didn't want to get her drunk, but maybe another drink would help loosen her tongue, since clearly his own tongue hadn't done the trick.

She stared at the bottle for a few seconds, then reached for the glass next to her side. Held up in the moonlight, sand glittered in the bottom. She turned it upend, trying to unstick the powder-fine granules.

"I don't think that's going to work." He waggled the bottle at her.

Her nose wrinkled and she held her hand up. "That's okay."

"You'll let me put my tongue in your mouth, but you won't drink after me?"

Her glare blistered him. She snatched the bottle from his hands and held it to her lips.

He focused on the waves crashing because watching her lips on that bottle was torture. "You and your dad looked pretty tight when you were dancing. Guess you get your artistic talent from him."

She gave him a look like he'd asked if the champagne had bubbles in it. "He just had his first widely recognized exhibition. Sold every piece." Her words carried a bite.

"You aren't happy about that, huh?"

"It made his work a target." She dropped her gaze to where she'd been digging a small hole in the sand with her toe. Her teeth pressed into her lower lip.

Now, they were getting somewhere. Logan rested back on his elbows, trying to communicate that he wasn't all that interested. "What do you mean?"

"One of his paintings was stolen from our house."

Really now. "Are the police investigating?"

"No. He refuses to report the crime."

The lack of police involvement had aroused Logan's curiosity when he'd first taken the assignment. Why wouldn't her dad report the crime? Logan had a theory. "Maybe he thinks it was someone he knows and that's why he hasn't gone to the police."

"No, it's not that. He doesn't want people to know it was stolen, period."

Oh. "He thinks it'll disappear forever if word gets out." But word *had* gotten out. Bob's associate knew the painting had been taken or Logan wouldn't be here right now.

He had seen some photographs of Miller's work. The guy had skills. But who would go to this much trouble to steal one of his paintings? Let alone two people? He wasn't Picasso *yet.*

"Yeah. If it's made public that it's stolen, that narrows the market it can be sold to." Drew shot him a glance. "I shouldn't have told you."

"I won't tell anyone." At least no one that didn't already know. But he wouldn't tell them shit about her dad's reason for keeping things hush-hush. All Bob cared about was the score, not the details. "So, has he hired a private investigator?"

She scooped up a seashell and tossed it toward the water. "Nope, he's opposed to that too. Honestly, I don't know what is going on in his head right now. It's like he's expecting the thief to knock on the door and give it back."

No cops. No investigator. What *was* going on in Sam Miller's head? If there was going to be any hope of getting his painting back, someone needed to be asking questions. And they needed to be doing it now.

15

MR. COOL AND MS. FORTUNE

Drew

DREW SHOULD GO HOME. She needed to get up early to play catch-up.

But she wanted to stay.

Being around Logan made her head spin. Her feelings toward him were conflicting. The first time they'd met, he'd rubbed her like sandpaper on an open wound. But tonight, his nearness was like silk sliding across bare skin.

Sitting on a moonlit beach with him was the most relaxing thing she had done in longer than she cared to admit. Even though she had no intentions of this going anywhere, it was nice to spend an evening drinking champagne and wiggling her toes in the sand with a hot guy. She didn't know how badly she'd needed to put her stress about her collection and her family obligations on the back burner and let herself be a woman.

Other than he was hella good looking, a photographer, and bantered like a boss, she didn't know anything about Logan. "So, Las Vegas, huh? Did you work at a casino?"

"Professional poker player."

Her eyebrows plunged, but she forced herself to relax. If she wasn't careful, she was going to get premature wrinkles. Lately, there'd been too many reasons to scowl. "A professional poker player?"

His lips twitched into a grin. "Google me if you don't believe it."

"You don't play anymore?"

"A little. No high stakes games in Savannah, though."

"What do you do all day then?"

"I've taken a few photography classes at SCAD, but this summer I've been bored as fuck. I mostly read and take walks when I'm not hanging out with my sister."

"You said she moved here to be with a guy?"

He nodded. "On a fucking whim. Nothing went as planned. Probably because there wasn't a plan, which is classic Morgan, but she's my little sister and I missed her and I want everything to work out for her, so, here I am."

"Oh, that's so sweet, Logan."

"Oh, that's so sweet, Logan?" He shook his head. "What the fuck is that? Did you get a personality transplant?"

She frowned, and the frown turned into a pout. He was calling her out on being fake, and the super annoying thing was, he wasn't wrong. His confession about his sister was unexpected, but it *was* sweet. Drew wasn't used to thinking nice thoughts about Logan—except for when those thoughts were about his body—so, she'd said what she figured any other person would say.

"Fine. You want me with no filter? Done."

"It's sexy when you say exactly what's on your mind."

She snorted. "Even when I'm thinking how much I can't stand you?"

"Especially then."

"Oh, my God, you need mental help," she said, her voice tumbling out in teasing lilt.

His eyes connected with hers again, dancing with laughter, but not giving into it. "Probably."

Behind them the sand swished underneath feet. Drew turned to see three figures heading their way, carrying armloads of firewood and one of them hefting a cooler.

"There you are," Colin said to Drew as he walked past them with the cooler. He'd traded in his dress uniform for board shorts and a T-shirt. "I was worried you'd gone home."

"Not yet, but I'm about to," Drew said. *Thanks for crashing my party.*

Logan pushed to his feet and held his hand out to her.

She grabbed hold and he pulled her up.

Colin set down the cooler and his buddies dropped the wood, then dug beer cans out of the cooler. "C'mon, stay."

"Yeah, stay," one of the other guys said.

She shook her head. "It's been a long day."

"You're gonna make me sleep in that big house all by myself tonight?" Colin asked.

"You'll survive," she said. "Goodnight, boys." After taking a few steps backward in the sand, she locked her gaze to Logan's and nodded in the direction of the house.

Logan walked alongside her to the house, not saying a word.

When they reached the outdoor stairs, she turned to him. "I've gotta go inside and get my bags. So, I guess, um, goodnight?" Oof. The uncertainty in her voice was cringey. Hopefully, he didn't think she was hinting at them spending the night together.

He flashed her a lopsided grin. "I have to come up and get my camera. You'll have to wait a few more minutes before you celebrate my departure."

Drew took the stairs ahead of him. As she made her way up, she wondered if he was looking at her ass. And if he was, did she mind?

Ugh. Being around him scrambled her brain.

At the top, he walked across the deck and grabbed his camera bag off a lounge chair.

She stood by the back door and waited for him to make his way over by her, her heart pounding. Whatever the hell these visceral responses to him were about, it needed to stop.

"Thank you for coming today," she said.

He lifted one shoulder. "I always pay my debts."

As much as she'd initially wanted him to take a hike when he'd gotten on her nerves at the coffee shop, she hoped this wouldn't be the last time she saw him.

She reached for the screen door, but stopped with it half open, leaning into the frame. "You know, I think it's a good thing the other photographer didn't work out. You did a way better job than he could have."

Logan raised an eyebrow. "You haven't seen any of the shots yet."

She shrugged, then smiled. "I could tell you knew what you were doing. Plus, I really didn't like the other photographer, so you get a huge ratings boost simply for not being him."

"Nice to know I'm the lesser of two evils." He moved forward and nudged her inside, pulling the screen shut between them. Then he put his hands on the frame and leaned forward. "Bye, Drew."

Their faces were so close. Close enough he could have kissed her if the stupid screen door hadn't been between them. She lifted her hand and fluttered her fingers. "Night."

She'd packed her things up before the ceremony, knowing it would be a drag to have to do it at the end of the night. After slipping on her sandals, she hoisted her giant canvas duffle and purse over one shoulder, a garment bag over the other, and grabbed the bag with the robe Claire had given her as a bridesmaid gift. With her free hands, she lifted the sewing kit she'd brought in case of last-minute alterations or repairs. Making two trips might be the most sensible thing, but she wanted to get home and get to bed.

Halfway down the stairs, Logan intercepted her and reached for her duffle and sewing kit.

"I had it under control," she said as she adjusted the strap to her purse.

"Oh, I don't doubt it," he muttered. "Is that blue Honda yours?"

"Why?" she asked, knowing she wouldn't like the answer, because whatever it was had caused him to come back.

"Your tire is flat."

"Perfect." She stomped down the stairs ahead of him, muttering every four-letter word she could think of. "I guess I should have listened to Matt."

She tossed her things on the backseat of her car. None of it was stuff she'd need tonight.

When she turned, Logan was using his phone light to inspect her tire. "Let me guess. He told you that you needed new tires."

She twisted a curl of her hair around her finger. "He might've said something along those lines."

He stood and got in her face. "That's dangerous. Do you have a death wish?"

"Do you know how much four new tires cost?"

"Less than a funeral," he nearly shouted at her.

"I don't need a lecture on safety. I just need a ride." She grabbed her sewing kit and duffle bag and added them to the backseat.

He still hadn't offered to give her a ride when she turned back to him.

"Can you give me one?" she asked.

Logan's brows were drawn together, and his lips formed a tight line. Maybe one favor was all he was willing to give her.

"Okay. Whatever. I can just stay—"

"No." He swept his arm in the direction of the shiny, black Audi parked several feet away. "I'll give you a ride."

She locked her car and strode to his.

Logan passed by her and opened the passenger door but avoided eye contact.

Whatever his problem was, she couldn't understand it. They'd been getting along. He'd kissed her, for crying out loud. A lot. He'd kissed her a lot. On the beach, and even when he'd said goodnight to her, he'd been smiling and joking around with her. Where was *that* Logan?

He stayed silent as he closed her door and got in on the driver's side.

Once he'd driven out of Claire and Matt's quiet little neighborhood, and onto the highway, he turned on his stereo.

The White Stripes blasted through the speakers, making her heart thump. At least she wanted to believe it was his fancy sound system causing the vibrations.

His mood—whatever that was about—seemed to shift as they headed toward Savannah. He had one arm draped over the wheel, his opposite elbow propped on the open window frame. He appeared pensive, but no longer scowled.

Was he thinking about that kiss?

She sure as hell couldn't stop.

Drew caught herself scraping away her nail polish and froze. Great, now not only was her peace of mind ruined, so was her manicure.

She pulled her hair over one shoulder and leaned toward the window to catch more of the salty breeze rushing by. Sweating wasn't something she was prone to, but at this moment, every pore seemed to be dripping.

She looked to his side of the car and frowned at his profile. He looked so...unaffected.

He hadn't been Mr. Cool when they kissed. Oh no, he hadn't been anything close to collected then. His hands tugging on her hair. And his tongue. His tongue should be cut out and studied by scientists. It didn't seem natural for such a small muscle to be so diligent and yet so very erotic.

She licked her lips, cussing herself for being so turned on by a stupid memory.

Studying his trimmed five o'clock shadow in the dark as streetlights illuminated the car in brief flashes, her stomach quivered.

Did he even realize she was in the car with him? His eyes never wavered from the road.

He had probably forgotten the kiss even happened. Asshole.

She wanted to know one way or another how he felt. He didn't mind being rude to her or standing up to her. Whenever they spent more than two minutes together something between them sparked. But he also had this way of looking at her...like he understood what she was about. Like a girl wants a guy to look at her at least once in her life.

She couldn't shake the hot press of his lips or the way it made her feel when he roughed her up. *Stop thinking about it.*

Frustrated in more ways than one, she shifted on her seat and tried not to let on how bothered she felt. He was already cocky enough.

"Downtown?" he asked as they neared the exit for Victory.

"Yeah," she squeaked out, then cleared her throat and sat straighter. "Take the Islands Expressway until it turns into East President, then turn on Broad and head up Liberty."

As he navigated back into the heart of the city, they sped past car after car.

"The speed limit is twenty-five," she said.

"The cops don't use radar down here. They're more worried about drunk drivers swerving all over the place and military beating the shit out of college kids."

"If the laws aren't enforced, it's okay to break them?" She looked over just in time to catch his grin, then was thrown back against her seat as he punched the gas. The motor revved, sending a rush of adrenaline through her body. As they neared Drayton Street, she gripped the hand-rest. "Turn left here."

With the deftness of a stunt car driver, he whipped the car left and fishtailed down Savannah's main drag.

Her heart jumped into her throat.

The car slowed and he resumed driving like a normal person.

Drew backhanded him across his biceps. "Are you unhinged?"

16

IT'S NOT A BOAT

LOGAN

"IT'S THIS STREET." Drew pointed at a street that branched off Forsyth Park.

Logan didn't understand why she didn't have him take her to her apartment. Maybe she didn't want him to know where she lived. He didn't want her to know that he knew, either. Then he'd have to explain how he'd surveilled her for days before they'd first met.

Her dad's neighborhood didn't exactly promote privacy with each house mere feet from the next. Even at this late hour, a man walked his dog and a group of college-age kids passed through. It'd be tricky to break into one of these houses and leave with a painting unseen.

He pulled into a small driveway behind a white Beetle convertible and switched on the interior light. She'd probably insist she could carry everything herself again, but he wasn't going to sit there and watch her juggle it all.

As he reached for his door handle, she put her hand on his shoulder. "Hold on."

He turned toward her, hoping she was going to suggest they make out, while simultaneously hoping it was anything else.

"I don't know whose car that is. I think my dad has...company."

He rubbed his jaw. "Is that unusual?"

"Yes." She leaned her head into the headrest, staring up at the ceiling. "Actually, I don't know. I haven't lived at home in a while."

"Did you just move back in?" Maybe her directing him here didn't have anything to do with not wanting him to know where she lived. From what he knew of her, she didn't seem like the type to get evicted. Could be her lease was up and she'd moved in with her dad to save money while she worked on her collection.

She chewed her lip and shook her head. "I rented out my apartment for the weekend."

"Rented it out?"

She released a huff and tucked her hair behind her ear. "Yeah, like a vacation rental. I make a couple hundred dollars and all I have to do is stay at my dad's. But I was so busy with the wedding, I forgot to tell him I'd be staying with him."

That was a pretty smart scam. No, not a scam. Just a way to make extra cash. A legit way.

"I don't want to walk in on him—" She squeezed her eyes shut, then shook her head rapidly. "This is awkward. I can't—I'm going to have to stay somewhere else."

Logan ran a hand through his hair. Nothing ever went right when he was with her. Everything was always a clusterfuck. "Do you have any other family you can stay with?"

She released a dramatic sigh. "My oldest brother lives on the south side, but his wife is pregnant, and they go to bed at like seven o'clock. I don't want to wake them up. My other brother is at some extreme obstacle race thing in Atlanta. Aubrey is living at home, but he's probably still out drinking. I'll call him, maybe it will be less awkward if we go in together."

He drummed his fingers on the steering wheel while she held the phone to her ear, listening to it ring and ring and ring.

She tapped the touch screen, then shoved the phone back into her purse. "No answer."

"Maybe it's not what you think."

Her head whipped in his direction. "It's one in the morning. I'd rather not meet my dad's girlfriend at this hour—if she is his girlfriend. Considering he went stag to a wedding and didn't leave until after ten o'clock…I'm guessing this is more of a…"

"Booty call." He couldn't hold in his laugh.

"Shut up," she muttered. "Just take me to a motel."

Yes, ma'am.

As soon as he pulled into the parking lot of the motel she'd directed him to, he spotted a drug deal going on right out front. Across the street, a group of women were clearly working. A few sketchy-looking individuals loitered around the premises.

Logan kept driving, right back out the other end of the parking lot.

"What are you doing?" she asked, twisting her head to look out the window at the motel he sped away from.

"You can't stay there." He took a right and veered into the valet lane of the waterfront Hyatt.

One block over and everything was upscale, bright lights, a doorman. That was Savannah for you.

"Look," he said, parking the car and turning toward her. "I'm not going to let you stay in some seedy motel room."

"*Let* me?" Her eyes turned fiery.

"I'm looking out for you."

"That's not your responsibility."

He got out and walked around to her side.

When he opened her door, she didn't move, just kept her ass parked, arms crossed, staring out the windshield. "I'm not staying here. I can't afford it."

He didn't expect her to pay for it. He knew from following her around over the last few weeks that she worked double shifts waitressing. Not something he could see her doing for enjoyment.

"I'll pay for it."

She snorted. "No, thank you. I'm not owing you."

"You won't. It's a gift."

Drew shook her head. "No."

Logan gritted his teeth and clutched the edge of the door until pain flashed through his palm. "I'm not taking you back to that motel."

"I'm not staying here."

Un-fucking-believable. He swung her door shut and stomped around to his side.

"I know it's out of the way and everything, but could you take me back to Claire's?"

Deliver her to Colin?

Hell no.

He threw the car into gear, took a hard left onto Bay Street and kicked it into high gear.

She stayed quiet until he turned onto a dead-end street. She jolted up, one hand on the dash. "Where are you taking me?"

"My place." He drove through the gate to the marina and rolled into his usual parking spot.

"I don't want to stay with you." Her voice came out uneven and edged with panic.

"I'm trying to do you a favor."

"I didn't ask you to do me any favors, Logan."

"Too bad." He sighed and changed his tone to a less agitated one. "Relax. It's going to be fine." *Who was he trying to convince?* They were going to have a slumber party. There wasn't a damn thing *fine* about that.

"Just because I'm spending the night with you does not mean that I'm going to—"

His throat rumbled with laughter, cutting her off. He could be charming, but not *that* charming. "I know. You don't even like me."

"I don't dislike you one hundred percent of the time, either. When you're not intentionally antagonizing me, you seem like a pretty good guy."

He was the antithesis of a good guy. Whether he liked it or not, in this situation, he was the bad guy. Logan was never going to be a candidate for sainthood, yet the more time he spent with her, the more he wished meeting her had been unpremeditated.

He had to get through the night without things getting messier. First step, get out of the damn car and put some space between them. Thinking straight with her this close was like trying to swim in a tar pit.

Neither of them said a word as he led her up the dock. The only sounds disturbing the quiet were the water sloshing against the hulls and the soft pad of Drew's sandals on the planks.

Once he'd stepped on board, he turned to help her.

"This is where you live?"

"Is that a problem?"

She shook her head and accepted his hand.

Once she'd stepped down onto the deck, he unlocked the cabin, then motioned for her to go in.

She stood in the center of the living room, her head swiveling. "This doesn't really seem like your style."

"Too beige?" He walked past her and dropped his keys on the oak coffee table.

"Exactly." She ran her fingers along the back of the white leather captain's chair, then stroked the tortoise shell wheel. "I've never been on a boat like this."

"It's not a boat. It's a *yacht*."

She released a soft snort. "Whatever. Most people don't have houses this nice."

Logan walked past her, down to the kitchen. Over his shoulder, he said, "C'mon, I'll show you where you're sleeping."

After she took the narrow steps down to the galley, he pointed to the booth that served as the dining table. "That's it."

"You want me to sleep on a table?"

He'd like to do a lot of things with her on the table, but sleeping wasn't one of them. He unlatched the table from the wall and lowered it onto the platform supporting the benches of the booth. Once he'd popped the cushions out of their positions, he revealed how they formed into a makeshift mattress.

He pulled a set of sheets out of the trundle drawer and set them on the table-turned-bed. "I'll get you a blanket and a shirt to sleep in." Right after he smoked a much-needed cigarette. Being so busy at the wedding, he hadn't had the chance to light up all day.

"Where are you going?"

To get the hell away from you. "I'll be back in a couple minutes."

Logan went onto the back deck and slid the door shut behind him. He pulled a cigarette from his pack and held it between his lips as he patted his pockets to find his lighter. After he'd lit up and taken a drag, he expected the agitation to subside. At least a little. But fuck. That shit had a death grip.

He pinched the bridge of his nose and shook his head. His focus needed to be on how he was going to play this with Drew going forward, but instead, his mind kept wandering to her inside, mere feet from his bed.

Going down to that beach turned out to be the worst idea of his life. He'd wanted to talk to her unguarded, and he had. He'd learned plenty, but he still didn't have enough intel to get him shot of Bob. If spending more time with Drew got him answers, was it worth his sanity?

A few minutes passed and the heavy cabin door slid open a crack. One of her bronzed legs emerged, then the rest of her too-fuckable body. Damn that tight dress and whatever push-up device she had on underneath.

It figured a woman in Drew's line of work would know how much cleavage to show without being trashy. His gaze followed the curve from her breasts to the flare of her hips. His hands would look so good on her body.

"You smoke?"

"No." He tossed the cigarette overboard by pure reflex before turning to face her.

"I've never seen you smoke before."

He placed his hands behind him on the rail. "I wasn't smoking."

Things were getting too personal. He should have gotten her a nice hotel room and insisted on paying. No matter what she'd said.

"Really?" Drew leaned against the gunwale and settled those shimmering emerald eyes on him. The way they glowed was almost feline.

"I'm a closet smoker." Where had that come from? If it wouldn't make him look crazy, he'd slap himself.

Her mouth twisted to one side. "Why?"

He wiped his face. "My uncle would have killed us if he caught me or Morgan smoking. He always says, 'If you're going to have a vice, make sure it's a good one.' Morgan and I have hidden our smoking since we were teenagers. He's a freak about dental work. Gives us whitening treatments every year for Christmas."

Could he be any more of a girl? Giving her that information had come way too natural. *She's the mark.*

The mark.

The mark.

The fucking mark.

He needed to put an end to the conversation and go to bed. Being friends, or anything more for that matter, was out of the question. Besides, having a platonic relationship with Miss Sex-On-Legs wasn't feasible.

"Did your uncle raise you?"

"Yep."

The curiosity in her gaze tugged at his good sense.

"My mom had postpartum depression after she gave birth to Morgan. She unalived herself. My dad went to prison while she was pregnant. I don't remember either of them."

The sympathetic pout of her lips made him uncomfortable. He tied no emotion to the facts. His first memory was playing cops and robbers with Uncle John, and it was a damn good one.

Not open to getting dragged into a full-blown conversation about his unorthodox upbringing, Logan yawned and stretched. "I'm tired. I'm going to bed."

She opened her mouth to say something, but he breezed by her and headed straight for the safety of his bedroom.

17

A GOOD HOST LIKE THAT

LOGAN

LOGAN WOKE FROM A DREAM about fucking Drew on top of her favorite table at the coffee shop. He closed his eyes and tried to reenter the dream, desperately wanting to finish it.

No dice.

Damn that woman. She tormented him even in his sleep.

He groaned and turned his head to the side. The clock on his nightstand read four in the morning.

A rustling sound came from the kitchen. He crawled out of bed, threw on jeans, and went to investigate.

Drew was on tiptoe, looking through his cupboards. She looked sexier in his Ramones shirt than any of her designer labels. The view of her toned thighs stupefied him.

He hadn't meant to sneak up on her, but as long as she didn't know he was there, what was the harm in appreciating what was right under his nose? Her hair, slightly mussed from sleep, but still curled from the wedding, swayed across her back as she moved to the next cupboard.

His erection jerked. He rubbed his lips and tried to stop fantasizing about how good her thighs would feel wrapped around him. They were thick enough that they'd hug him tightly and not feel boney.

"What are you doing?" he asked, hoping to distract himself from being a pervert.

"Looking for a glass," she whispered, not even flinching. "I wanted a drink of water. I didn't wake you, did I?"

"No, I just woke out of a dead sleep to see if you were thirsty. I'm a good host like that." He grabbed a bottle of water from the fridge and handed it to her. "I'm already awake, you don't have to whisper."

No going back to sleep now. Maybe a stiff drink would help.

He poured himself bourbon and leaned against the counter, avoiding looking at her, but her stare was like a heat ray.

"Want some?" He offered the glass to her.

She hesitated and then reached for it. She winced after taking a sip, then took another, more careful, drink.

Having her on his boat, in his shirt, drinking his favorite liquor gave him a high that made it all too easy to ignore reality.

He grabbed a glass and poured himself another. *Think of something else.*

Like putting a closed door between them. A locked door. Hell, maybe he should consider putting an ocean between them. The way Drew stole his train of thought was lethal.

"Logan?" The huskiness in her voice stroked him like silky fingers sliding from his ears to his neck.

He slowly raised his gaze. "Yeah?"

"You live on a boat."

"No shit?"

She shoved his shoulder. "There's got to be some kind of story."

"And you want to hear it."

Her head bobbed as she drank the rest of her bourbon.

"Listening to me and pretending to act interested is so painful you need to catch a buzz first?"

She threw him a witchy smile. "Maybe before a few hours ago. Now, I know too much to not be genuinely interested."

He took a sip of his liquor, then rubbed his finger across the rim of the glass as he debated how much to tell her. "I told you what I do for a living. I play poker, which is how I won this." He twirled his finger in the air.

She eyed him. "You won this?"

"You think this is what I would pick out?"

She laughed and moved closer in the tiny galley, one shoulder pressing against the fridge, her nearness testing Logan's willpower. "You said there weren't any high stakes games in Savannah."

"I took a trip to Miami to visit a friend from the circuit. He lined up a game for us at a real estate mogul's beach house. After I took all his cash, he used his yacht to double down and try to get back what he'd lost."

"Why didn't you sell it or trade it in for something more your style?"

"Initially, I didn't plan on staying in Savannah long. Thought it'd make a decent place to crash until I found a buyer. Now I'm kind of attached to her."

"Her? Your boat has a gender?"

Logan's lip curled as he poured a splash into each of their glasses. "She's sexy as hell, takes me for a ride, and is likely to kill me. Sounds like a woman to me."

Or more specifically, the woman standing right in front of him.

Her gaze dropped to her toes. "Are we going to talk about it?"

"About what?"

She peeked at him from under her lashes. "The kiss."

His spine snapped straight. He set his glass in the sink. "No. No, we are *not* talking about that."

"Wonderful. I'll never bring it up again." Her chin jutted up and she swiped her auburn hair from her face, then darted up the steps leading into the living room.

Oh, hell. Now he'd done it. He hadn't meant to hurt her feelings.

That kiss would haunt him for the rest of his days. Talking about it with her…he couldn't imagine worse torture.

What was there to say? She liked it. He liked it. And it could never happen again. But if he told her that, she'd want to know why.

He should give her time. Let her cool off. Not like she was going to walk home wearing only his shirt. She didn't have shoes or her purse. Once she'd settled down, she would come back in, and in the morning, he'd take her home.

Logan glanced toward his bedroom, then in the direction Drew had gone. With a deep sigh, he trudged up the steps and through the living room.

She stood on the aft deck, finishing off her drink, then raised the empty glass to eye-level and examined it. Her arm pulled back, like she was going to chuck it.

He closed his hand over the top of the glass before she had the chance to release it. "Take it easy." He pried it from her grasp and set it on the patio table. "You got me all wrong."

She spun. "That's just it. I don't *get you* at all. You flirt with me and kiss me, and then act like you don't want me around."

He *didn't* want her around. But not because she repulsed him. It was best for them both if he stayed away. Probably best if he let her think he didn't like her one bit.

But damn it, seeing her all dejected, he was ready to make one of the worst decisions of his life.

"I didn't want to talk about the kiss because the last thing I need is to remember that shit. It's hard enough trying to resist you standing here in my shirt, all legs and perky tits."

Drew blushed so hard he could see it in the dark. The glow from the overhead dock lights might as well have been specifically designed to accentuate all that silky smooth skin.

"I want you, but it can't happen."

"Why not?" she asked, her voice barely above a whisper.

Oh, only a hundred reasons. Or one really good one. She was his mark.

"Because I can't give you what you deserve."

She pressed her lips together, like she was trying not to laugh in his face. "An orgasm?"

He groaned. "You know that's not what I'm talking about."

Drew moved toward him, gazing at him with those vibrant green eyes. "Then, you could? Give me an orgasm, that is."

"Several," he said hoarsely.

"Just one night, Logan." She was too close. He could smell her shampoo. "That's all I want. I'm too busy for anything more."

The minute her stomach brushed against his, his brain clocked out. She pressed up on her toes, hands on his bare chest. Every part of his brain screamed for him to get far, far away from her. His body had other ideas.

He slid his hand around to the small of her back and held her there, dipped his head as hers tilted. Their lips met.

The spicy taste of bourbon on her lips hit him deep within, her own intoxicating ammunition. Prompted by his fingers pressing into her neck, she angled her head backward. Her compliance sent a jolt to his cock.

He deepened the kiss, greedy for more, taking the initiative when she opened her mouth, pushing his tongue past her teeth. Those slender fingers of hers traveled up the back of his neck, creeping into his hair. Latching onto her bottom lip with both of his, he sucked.

A throaty whimper escaped her throat.

Logan tore his mouth from hers, pulling her hands from his hair, and dropping them to her sides. "Inside," was all he could get out.

He let her slip by before taking a deep, staggering breath and following her.

She stopped in the kitchen, turning around, looking lost.

He pinned her against the fridge with his body. He held his face an inch from hers, bewitched by the harmony of their ragged breathing.

Curling his hands around each of her wrists, he stretched them above her head. "You're going to look so good underneath me," he muttered before lowering his lips to hers.

She gasped into his open mouth.

Using one hand to keep both of hers locked together, he smoothed his palm down the center of her chest, then up to cup her breast.

She answered with a moan that traveled from her throat to his, which made his insides burn as though doused with firewater. He couldn't get enough of her. From head to toe, she was soft and warm. His hand rushed over her exposed skin, eager to touch every inch of her perfect body.

He'd meant to grab a handful of her ass, but she steered his hand back to her breast. Logan angled her head farther back and brushed his lips against her neck.

He nuzzled her neck, getting lost in the scents of orange blossoms and ocean. The thought of having access to all the places that scent clung to drove him nuts...and tasting her?

That was a whole other realm of enjoyment.

No reason to wait. He dipped his head and sucked the skin between her neck and shoulder. She tasted like salted caramel—sweet, but with an edge.

"Fuck," she hissed.

"That's the plan," he whispered against her ear as he thumbed her nipple through the soft T-shirt, arrogantly pleased to find it already drawn into a tight bud. Using his teeth, he nipped her earlobe and tugged.

"Taking. Too. Long."

He lifted her and guided her legs around his hips, almost dropping her when his hands cupped her bare ass.

Drew slammed her mouth to his, pulling, sucking, and nipping.

He struggled to find the bedroom. It was less than six feet away, yet with her kissing him like that, he could barely remember how to take one step.

She used just enough tongue to lure him, drawing it back into her mouth, beseeching him to chase it. When he'd make contact, she'd rub her tongue against his and moan.

He leaned her against the wall and adjusted his hold on her.

She took the opportunity to tear at the button on his jeans.

Fueled with pure need, he tried for the bedroom again. Logan miscalculated the distance to the threshold, bumping Drew's head against the wall. "Shit. Are you okay?"

Her laugh dissolved his worry. "Are we there yet?"

He wanted to laugh with her but nipped her earlobe instead.

Pulling her from the support of the wall, he turned toward the bed. He tossed her in the middle, opened the bedside drawer, and dug around for a condom. Slanting his mouth hungrily over hers, he pushed his jeans off.

Drew's hands slid down his back, sending shivers up his spine. A nice little buzz clouded his thoughts, helping him ignore any qualms he had about letting this happen.

He worked the shirt up over her head. His hands moved up the inside of her thighs. Damn, she was so wet, and he hadn't even gotten started.

To give her a taste of what was to come, he swirled his finger against her damp flesh. She arched against him and whimpered. It drove him on. He stroked a path with his tongue from her ear to her chest and sucked the taut skin between her breasts.

"Logan—" She gasped, her body rising and falling beneath him.

Why'd she have to say his name all needy like that? Ignoring his body's demands for warm and wet, he slid a finger inside her and muffled any sound that dared to come out of her mouth with his own.

The way she greedily pulled at his hips broke his patience.

He tore the condom wrapper open and positioned himself between her thighs.

She thrashed and arched her lithe body to beg for more.

He interlaced their fingers and stretched her arms above her head. Underneath him, she looked fucking magical. Her face painted with soft light from the moon. Lips rosy, hair tousled, and nipples begging for attention.

Remembering how she'd responded to his roughness on the beach, he buried himself inside her in one forceful thrust.

Drew cried out. Not with pleasure.

She was still, no longer rubbing her beautiful body against his.

Logan brushed her hair away from her face. "That hurt?"

He hadn't been *that* rough. She was so wet, but so fucking tight. Her thighs quivered.

She took a deep, shuddering breath. "I'm okay."

His gut clenched. That was the tone she used when she was faking being nice.

Why would she—

She wasn't a—

Was she?

He released her hands, but kept his eyes locked on hers. "You've done this before, right?"

She kept her gaze trained on his collarbone.

"Drew."

No eye contact.

Logan put his finger under her chin and tipped it up. But there was something he'd never seen in her before—vulnerability—and he couldn't bring himself to keep pressing her for an answer.

How old was she? What the fuck?

He had never taken a virgin to bed before. Never.

What a fucking nightmare. He'd felt bad about this playing out when he thought it was going to be a one-night stand. Now, he felt like the scum of the earth.

She'd waited this long, and then picked him. *Shit.*

"Does it still hurt?"

"No," she whispered. "It sort of...stings."

Sweet mercy, what should he do? Pull out? If he moved, he might make it worse.

"Breathe, Drew," he said as soothingly as he could manage. "Try to relax."

She inhaled and let out a shaky breath.

"If I knew, I wouldn't have...so fast...so rough... I didn't mean to hurt you. I'll make it up to you, I promise."

The first tear streaked down her face, and she dipped her head away from his, burying her face against his shoulder.

Logan let her hide. He didn't think he could handle seeing her cry. With deliberate tenderness, he rubbed up and down her arm. "We don't have to do this."

"I want to," she whispered. "Unless you don't."

He probably shouldn't want to. This whole scene should have killed his erection, but he was still buried inside her, which felt fucking incredible even though he hadn't moved a muscle since she'd cried out in pain. Add in her soft, full breasts. The silky feel of her thighs around his hips. The way her lips had slightly swollen from his kisses. Yeah, he wanted this.

If they kept going, he needed to make this good for her. He was obligated to make her forget the pain and focus on the pleasure. If not, she would be disappointed she had waited so long and then chosen him.

His ego couldn't take that.

Once her breathing had somewhat leveled, he searched for her lips, coaxing her to meet his. He reignited the spark between them with his mouth, tugging at her lips and stroking with his tongue in an undemanding rhythm. Until her mouth made an O around his tongue and sucked. Logan tangled his fingers in the hair on one side of her head and tore his mouth from her, only to dive right back in to taste her addictive sweetness.

Her nipples brushed against his chest. He liked that. He withdrew with painstaking care and waited for her to react. Before a second had passed, she pulled him back inside using her legs.

She whispered his name, her voice syrupy with pleasure.

Somehow, he found the last shred of his control and used it to take things slow. Calculated movements. The sure and sensual glide of his body over hers. His hand, skating from her raised knee to her hip. Wet lips on vulnerable soft spots.

The little gasp that slipped out when he ground his hips into hers drove him to do it again. Another gasp. He dipped and dragged his whole body along hers, letting their sweat-slick skin make the movement fluid.

"Fu-uck," she muttered.

Logan chuckled and pressed his forehead into hers.

Without a drop of hesitation, she leaned her face up and pressed her half-open mouth to his. The kiss broke as he withdrew, only to slide back up her heavenly body.

Her breathing was labored, and her hands shook as she ran them up his arms.

"Put your arms around me."

Her fingernails pressed into his biceps. Apparently, she no longer took orders now that the pain had subsided. She let him know when she wanted him to increase the pace by sliding her hands to his hips and squeezing.

He couldn't hold back for much longer. Not with her moaning into his ear with each thrust. He used his thumb to stroke her clit. When he felt the first tremor, he thrust with more force.

Her moans got louder. A lot louder.

He squeezed his eyes shut and came so hard his ears rang.

The haze ebbed from his mind more quickly than he'd have liked.

Holy mother of hell.

He had slept with his mark.

And he wanted to do it again.

18

YOU STARTED IT

Drew

DREW FLIPPED OVER AND SIGHED. Several minutes had passed since Logan slipped out of bed and her body had cooled, losing the incredible heat he'd stirred in her.

Wrapped in a blanket, she went to find him.

He wasn't in the bathroom or the kitchen. She climbed the steps to the small living room. Not there either. A tiny red dot flicked through the tinted cabin door window.

She slid the heavy wood and glass door open and poked her head out.

He was perched on back edge of the boat. He'd put on jeans, although he'd not buttoned them. His lips turned down and he studied the cigarette between his fingers. Was he feeling guilty for smoking or for…?

His gaze flicked up, then he took a long drag. The heaviness of his stare sent a fever flooding her veins. After exhaling, he crooked his finger at her.

She looked to the left and then the right, like a child about to the cross the street. The sun had started to rise, but there wasn't anyone else on the docks. The sky glimmered in pinks and oranges along the horizon. The rest of the sky was bright blue aside from the clouds.

When she moved within reach, he slung his arm around her

middle and pulled her close. "What the hell, Drew?" he asked, his voice scratchy.

Well, that certainly put a damper on the rising heat engulfing her body. "Are you mad?"

"No, I'm not mad." He took another drag from his cigarette before leaning to the side to stub it out in an ashtray on a small table. "Though it would have been nice to know ahead of time."

"If I'd told you, would you still have had sex with me?"

"Probably not."

"Exactly." He was making a bigger deal out of it than it was. The pain was more than she'd expected it to be. Otherwise, he wouldn't have ever known.

"I don't get it. How the fuck were you still a virgin?"

Her face flushed. Most awkward conversation ever. "I didn't do it on purpose. I wasn't saving myself."

Logan shook his head, his eyebrows drawn down. "If you'd wanted to, you could have had sex before now. *Easily.*"

She didn't want to admit she'd never had a boyfriend. Besides it being embarrassing, he'd just point out that she didn't need to be in a relationship to have sex. They sure as hell weren't in one. "I worked my ass off to graduate high school early. I didn't reserve a lot of time for fun. College was no different. I wasn't concerned with going to parties, and I was younger than everyone, so I couldn't have gotten into the bars if I'd wanted. I did what I do best and knuckled down, finished my degree early, came home to get my masters at SCAD, and now I'm continuing that pattern, so I'll have a shot at winning this competition."

"Why me?"

The way he asked that needled her. As though he'd been chosen for some appalling task.

"Can you stop acting so traumatized? Virginity is a social construct. Having sex with you didn't change my identity. I didn't give you some special part of me that I can never get back."

He laughed, his shoulders shaking.

Drew started to turn away, but he circled her with both arms and pulled her tight against him. Pissed she was being laughed at, she resisted, her hands braced against his chest to keep distance between them. The blanket slipped off one of her shoulders.

Logan leaned in, his mouth hot against her neck as he nipped the sensitive skin there. "I'm laughing because you think I'm acting traumatized."

"You are," she said, but a sigh laced her words. She tilted her head to give him better access to her neck.

"I'm flummoxed because people don't usually have sex with someone they'd like to push off a cliff, especially not their first time."

"My mind has been spinning since you kissed me on the beach," she admitted. "I couldn't sleep and tonight's probably the last chance for me to let my hair down for a long time. I don't want to turn gray without ever having had sex."

"Oh, I get it," he said, his tone slightly amused. "You used me."

She rolled her eyes. "You started it."

"What?" His tone was sharp and filled with laughter.

"You could have gone home after the wedding. I didn't invite you to come out to the beach. I didn't ask you to kiss me."

The playful expression lighting his features dimmed. His gaze dropped. "I shouldn't have brought you here. This was a mistake. There are things you don't know about me that—"

She gasped. "Are you married?"

That would be exactly the kind of thing that would happen to her. At least lately. Aubrey would say it was a message from a higher power to do some soul searching and find meaning in something besides her career.

His eyebrows drew together. "No. Why would you think that?"

"You said it was a mistake. We're on a boat." She waved her hand around in a quick sweep of the deck. "Who lives on a boat?"

"What is your hang up with that?" Logan glared at her. "Never mind. I'm not a cheating creep who brings women here to fuck them without his wife finding out."

His tone sucked any and all lightheartedness from the moment. Up until this moment, she hadn't succeeded in offending him. When she'd intentionally attempted to run him off with her snide remarks, no such luck. Apparently, his Achilles heel was being accused of being a sleazy, cheating manwhore.

"I'm sorry," she whispered. "For insulting you, and I'm sorry you got stuck with me tonight. I'm sorry I woke you up."

Logan sucked in his breath. "What? No. I don't want you to be sorry about—"

"You get to have regrets, but I don't?"

"I only regret that I hurt you. If I'd known, I'd have taken it slow. I could've made it better for you." He snuck his hands inside the blanket. His palms spanned her ribcage, sending goosebumps coursing over every inch of her skin. He rubbed circles with his thumbs, skimming the underside of her breasts. His touch would have been a lot more enjoyable if his face didn't show he was deeply lost in thought.

"Logan," she started, but his thumb brushed her nipple, and a moan stole her voice.

"You're so tempting," he muttered, then dropped his hands to her hips.

She wrapped her arms around his neck, encasing him in the blanket with her and pressing her mouth to his.

He nipped her bottom lip with his teeth.

Loud footsteps on the dock forced her back to reality. She pulled her mouth from his.

Logan jerked his chin in greeting to a white-haired man in green seersucker shorts. The man waved back and chuckled as he strolled by.

He turned back to Drew, hungry eyes melting away her embarrassment. "Wanna use me again?"

Drew nodded.

His hand slid down her belly, his knuckles skimming her pubic hair. Her pulse thumped between her legs. Tingles rushed from her thighs all the way to her toes. Her nipples grew painfully tight, and she wanted badly to press her chest to his, to rub against him.

She sunk her teeth into her lip to keep from making noise.

He gave her one thorough, tongue-teasing kiss, then pulled her inside to his bedroom. Standing behind her as she stared at the bed, he tugged the blanket off her shoulders and down her back. His finger grazed her spine, following the blanket's path.

Drew leaned her back into his chest, turning her head to find his lips.

He slid his hands over her torso in opposite directions as he kissed her, reaching his intended destinations at the same time, her nipple and her clit.

A gasp-turned-moan escaped her.

He barely had to touch her to get her squirming. His fingers skimmed the parting of her skin in featherlike strokes. In excruciatingly wonderful contrast, he pinched and plucked her nipple.

Wetness surged between her legs.

Logan's hand slid from her inner thighs up to her belly, trailing that wetness over her skin. He moved around her. He sat on the edge of the bed and pulled her closer, then placed his mouth above her navel and licked. His wicked tongue trailed up to her cleavage, his hands cupping her breasts as he tasted her flesh.

She opened her eyes and looked at the top of his head. She couldn't resist pushing her fingers into his messy hair.

He stilled his actions and ever so slowly turned his gaze upward. His dark eyebrows and angular forehead cast a seductive shadow over his eyes.

Her stomach fluttered and her thighs clenched. Of course, he was the first man she'd let touch her this way. No one else had ever made her body ache with a single look.

Logan cupped the side of her head and pulled her mouth down on his, the other hand guiding her body to straddle him. His erection bumped against her through his pants.

She lowered her hips and ground against him as his tongue plundered her mouth.

A grumble, muffled by their kiss, came from his throat. His hands gripped her hips and held them away, keeping her from rubbing against his cock, but he didn't stop kissing her. His lips glided against hers, a gentle suck here and there.

Since his hands held her hips hostage, she decided to do some exploring. She ran her fingers down his shoulders, over his chest and stomach. His muscles rippled and rolled as her fingertips brushed over them.

She flattened her palm and stroked him through his jeans.

Logan released her hips and grabbed her hand. "No," he breathed, then effortlessly flipped her onto her back.

"Yes."

"Always arguing."

"Only when I don't get my way," she said.

He stood over her, staring at her naked body.

Her stomach muscles tightened. Her spine stiffened. Even though his eyes were full of electricity, and she could practically feel how much he wanted her, she became bashful. Drew grabbed the sheet and pulled it over her.

A split second later, he pulled the sheet off and tossed it on the floor.

"Logan!"

He rolled his eyes as he dropped his pants and stepped out of them. "I get that you're new to this, but it's something we do naked."

19

LIKE A KITTEN ON TRANQUILIZERS

LOGAN

LOGAN STARTED THE COFFEE POT and headed to the bathhouse. As he lathered his hair and let the water beat against his chest, he had trouble wiping the memory of Drew's body coming alive against his from his mind. He didn't want her to ever forget how good it had been, but he wished he could.

Fuck me. Logan scrubbed his scalp and body extra hard, but no amount of scrubbing erased the dirty shame of what he'd done.

It wasn't bad enough he'd conned an innocent woman. Oh no, he had to take her virginity. He was going straight to hell.

She was right. Virginity was a social construct, but the first time was supposed to be special. Not a one-night stand.

How the hell was he supposed to continue his assignment? Fry her some eggs, drill her for information, and then, fuck her again?

Jesus.

As soon as he could, he needed to get away from her. He couldn't think with her anywhere around. But how was that supposed to go? *Hey, Drew. Thanks for the hot sex last night. I'll call you a cab. You can wait for it by the road.*

It was quiet when he came back on board. He poured two cups of coffee, added milk and sugar to one, then went to check on her.

She slept like a kitten on tranquilizers. All snuggled up, practically purring, but in such a deep sleep, she didn't even stir when a passing boat's foghorn blared. She slept on her stomach, the sheet barely covering her lower half. Her hair was strewn across the pillow in a chaotic auburn mess. One arm rested under her head, the other curled over the edge of the mattress. He moved to the side of the bed and set the mugs on the nightstand. In doing so, he caught sight of the swell of her breasts pressed into the mattress.

His cock throbbed, recalling how soft and full they were.

He glided his fingers along the silky skin of her back and whispered her name. He had to say it twice more, the second time practically shouting, before she responded.

Eyes still closed, she rolled onto her back and stretched her arms.

He turned his body away, sitting like a rock on the edge of the bed, forbidding his mind to commit the image of her in his bed naked and sleepy to memory.

"You smell good." Her voice hovered on a yawn.

"It's probably coffee you smell. I brought you a cup."

"No, it's you," she said. "Soap and shaving cream."

He wouldn't have thought anything could smell better than Drew did last night when he had danced with her, but he was wrong. Right now, her scent mingling with his, was the best shit ever.

He gritted his teeth.

A whole minute passed, then the mattress bounced. Sounds of her rummaging around on the floor came from on the opposite side of the bed.

"Sorry," she said. "Morning-after etiquette is a new concept for me. Give me a second, and I'll be ready to go."

He looked over his shoulder, watching her slip out the bedroom door to retrieve her bridesmaid dress from the galley. "I'm not rushing you."

With the dress held in front of her, she nudged the door closed until he couldn't see her anymore.

"About last night—"

"There's nothing to talk about," she said through the thin door. "I don't want to be your girlfriend, Logan."

He hadn't planned on asking, so he ignored the queasy feeling sinking to the pit of his stomach.

20

POACHING THE PRODIGY

LOGAN

"I QUIT."

Bob glanced up from his desk to the doorway where Logan stood. He scowled until his eyes all but disappeared behind his fat cheeks. "Come again?"

He took a few steps inside and slapped a black legal folder on the desk. "I'm off the job. This is my intel."

He'd do a thousand other jobs for this crook, but he wasn't going a step farther with this one.

Bob flipped open the folder containing the list of outsiders who'd been in Sam Miller's house before the theft. "This is shit."

"There's nothing else." That wasn't true at all, but he'd cut out his own tongue before he gave Bob anything about Drew. "Whoever did this didn't leave a trail."

"Bullshit." He closed the file and shoved it back across the desk. "What am I supposed to tell my associate?"

"Tell him to get over it. Find another painting to steal. Whoever took this one made a clean getaway."

That might not be true. He hadn't asked Drew enough questions to be sure. But he couldn't go anywhere near her again. Didn't trust himself. When he'd dropped her off earlier, he'd caught himself about to lean in and kiss her goodbye.

He should have never touched her. Danced with her. Kissed her. Brought her home with him. He'd been sloppy, causing more damage than a Molotov-cocktail.

So here he was, trashing his one shot at severing the leash Bob had him on and putting Morgan's job and her freedom on the line. If that wasn't punishment enough, he couldn't shake the recurring flashbacks of his night with Drew. Her laughing on the beach, digging through his kitchen cabinets in nothing but his shirt, naked underneath him, watching her fall asleep eclipsed by a post-orgasm glow.

After what he'd taken from her, there wasn't a chance in hell he was going to help screw her family over.

Bob snarled like a rabid dog. "Fine. I'll tell him. Have a nice life, kid."

Whoa. Hold up. That was too easy. Tucking his hands into his pockets, he asked, "That's it? We're done?"

"I'm feeling charitable today."

Nope. Something wasn't right. Last time they spoke, Bob was desperate for Logan to get the information the guy who was blackmailing him was after. "Or you found a way to get this prick off your back."

Bob stayed quiet, eyes trained on his recently emptied ashtray.

Logan stared him down. "I know you didn't tell me everything before. I promise you, though, I'm going to find out. This is your one opportunity to decide whether you want me as an ally or enemy if your half-baked plan doesn't work out like you want it to."

The chair behind the desk swiveled to the side. Bob stared at the wood paneled wall. "He knows about my operation. Everything. Has photos. Recordings."

"Fuck, Bob." He raked a hand through his hair. "Does he know about Morgan?"

"He's been watching—for a long time."

"Is that a yes?"

"That's a *I don't fucking know*." Bob reached into his desk drawer and pulled out a plastic flask of cheap vodka.

"Well, you better fucking find out," he shouted and smacked the desk. "I held up my end of the bargain. Now, it's your turn. If Morgan isn't safe, then neither are you, you slimy bastard."

Bob's eye twitched. "He didn't mention her. Just you."

Logan put his hands on the desk and leaned down to Bob's eye level. "He did what, now?"

He lit a cigarillo and blew out a plume of smoke. He fiddled with the lid on his lighter, clicking it open and shut repeatedly. "You're slick, Cash. You might not like your job, but you're damn good at it. The rest of these guys are about as useless as a screen door on a submarine."

Not much satisfaction in being praised for photographing people at their worst or for conning an innocent woman. "What's your point?"

"This guy, he asked for you. Said he wanted you on it, no one else."

The hair on Logan's neck stood on end. "Who is he?"

Bob shrugged. "Wouldn't give me his name. I've never even seen the guy. Got an envelope with proof of the dirt he has on me. The rest of our communication has been by phone."

The shifty bastard stared back at him, and for the first time since Logan had known him, Bob gave it to him straight. "The deal was that after you did this, your debt would be cleared. His idea, not mine."

"Keep talking, and tell me everything, or I swear—"

"He knew I had something to hold over you," he blurted out. "Said you were smart, and you wouldn't work for me otherwise. My guess is he wants you to come work for him."

"Oh, I get it," Logan said, pushing off the desk. "If you give me up, you think he'll leave you alone."

Bob gave a half-shrug.

"The next time he calls, you tell him from now on I deal with him directly."

He stormed out of the office, bile rising in his throat. This new threat was ten times worse than Bob. He was smarter. Which made him more dangerous.

21

CUCKOO AT THE COFFEE SHOP

FOR THE PAST YEAR, this coffee shop had been her sanctuary.

Then Logan happened and fucked it all to hell.

The bell on the door chimed. Drew's head snapped up, then her heart plummeted. Two girls and a guy filed in. The guy wore a yellow SCAD T-shirt. Like she wouldn't have been able to point him out as an art student from his orange and green hair or the anime costume his girlfriend sported.

Drew pondered that balance her dad had mentioned. A relationship and a budding career. Could she stay on course with her goals if she didn't devote every single ounce of her energy to it?

A solid hole formed inside her chest at the thought of never exploring that connection she got a glimpse of whenever Logan was near. But what if she got sucked in and couldn't find her way out? With so many things in her life, Drew was all or nothing. She threw herself into anything she felt passionately about one hundred percent.

And the passion between her and Logan couldn't be disputed.

Drew tapped her pencil against her sketchpad and rested her chin in her other hand. *Where was he?*

Oh, no.

It had finally happened.

Yep.

She had lost it.

The last time she saw Logan, she'd told him she only wanted to use him as a one-night stand. Now she wanted him to show up, and what for?

To beg her to go on a date?

He'd never do that. Begging wasn't his style, and in one of their first conversations, he told her he had no intentions of asking her out.

She didn't know what she expected, but she did know she missed the way he'd grazed his deep, enigmatic eyes over her body, and made her all weak-kneed.

She groaned out loud. Apparently, a little too loudly. At least ten people turned from their laptops, newspapers, books, and conversations to stare at her. Dipping her head, she searched for some sanity.

When she found none, she gathered up her things and marched out the door.

22

A VERY SEXY RHINOCEROS

LOGAN

LOGAN PULLED INTO CLAIRE AND MATT'S driveway on Sunday evening. He parked behind Drew's dark blue coupe.

His heart quit beating. When it started back up, it beat twice the normal rhythm. Logan didn't want to come face to face with Drew. It was a guaranteed disaster. He didn't know what would happen, but whenever he was around her, everything always went to hell.

Don't be a pussy.

The sound of tires on gravel caught his attention. Matt waved as he drove his gleaming 1969 Mustang Boss around the other cars and pulled into the garage.

Logan grabbed his laptop case and headed for the house.

Matt unfolded from the car wearing mechanic's coveralls and lifted a case of Red Stripe from the floor of the passenger side.

Shouting boomed from the house, catching both men's attention.

"I already slept with him!" Drew's voice.

Shit. Shit. Shit. Shit. Shit.

Matt darted a glance at Logan. His eyebrow rose, then a goofy smile spread across his face.

Logan's jaw twitched.

"You lost your virginity to a one-night stand?" Claire shouted, sounding more like a mother than a friend. "*What* are you doing, Drew?"

"Maybe we shouldn't go in just yet." Matt tore open the case of beer and tossed one to him.

"Claire didn't tell me Drew would be here."

"Something tells me Drew didn't know you were going to be here, either."

"I think I'll just give you the thumb drive with the wedding photos and get out of here."

"Sorry, man. Can't let you do that." He shoved his hands in his pockets and rocked back on his heels. "I'll catch hell if I let you get away."

Logan slumped against a workbench.

"What's going on with you and Drew?"

"Nothing," he said, staring out the open garage door.

"I thought I heard her shouting at my wife that she had sex with you." He shrugged and then said, "Guess she was talking about some other guy."

Even though Logan was positive she'd been talking about him, the slightest possibility that one day she'd be talking to Claire about another guy irked the hell out of him. "She was talking about me," he muttered. *Fuck me.*

"Yelling stopped," Matt said. "Probably safe to head in."

Logan doubted that, but he might as well get it over with. They chugged their beers, tossed the bottles into a recycling bin and headed up the outdoor staircase and into the house.

Drew read a magazine at the kitchen table.

When the screen door swung shut, Claire turned from the sink to look at them, but Drew kept her attention focused on the glossy pages.

Matt walked over to his wife, the case of beer dangling from his hand. "Miss me?"

"Uh-huh." She gave him a kiss, then leaned around him. "It's nice to see you again, Logan. Thanks for coming."

"No problem." He glanced at Drew. She was pretending he didn't exist. "Here's the thumb drive I loaded all the photos onto. I'll get out of here. I don't want to make anyone uncomfortable."

"You aren't making me uncomfortable," Drew said sharply, without looking up from her magazine.

"Please stay," Claire said. "I want you to be the one to show us the shots."

Holding in the frustrated sigh in his throat, he set his laptop on the table and pulled up the slide show of photographs. He had taken over four hundred shots during the ceremony and reception. Only about half of them were worth printing.

Matt stuck the beer in the fridge. "I'll be right back. Gotta change."

Claire turned to Logan and smiled the mother of all polite smiles. "Can I get you something to drink? Sweet tea? Beer?" She opened the fridge. "Chocolate milk?"

He forced himself to return her smile. "Beer, thanks."

The only sound through the whole house was Claire popping the top off his beer bottle until Matt strolled back into the kitchen, dragged a chair from the table, and straddled it.

Drew was doing a hell of a job pretending to be blasé, but her jaw was tight and every other minute she uncrossed and re-crossed her legs. The sundress she had on shifted higher with each moment.

Logan's mouth went dry. He'd been between those thighs once, and given the opportunity, he wouldn't be able to resist burying himself between them again.

Claire was as transparent as plastic wrap. She was doing her best to be a gracious host, smiling and offering him a new beer when his was still half-full.

Matt was the only one of the lot who didn't try to disguise his thoughts. He was grinning like an idiot.

"Drew, look at this picture of you fixing my train before I walk down the aisle. Wow. This is like the best picture I've ever seen of you. It's so *real*."

Drew rolled her eyes, shoved away from the table, and sauntered out of the kitchen.

Logan didn't get it. Wasn't sure he wanted to.

She'd said she didn't want anything more than that one night together. Maybe she'd said that to save face.

As he flipped through the slides, Matt and Claire let him know how talented they thought he was. The candid shots impressed them most.

"I didn't even realize you were taking most of these pictures," Claire said.

The mark of a good photographer is capturing the moment without intruding upon it. He wanted to be creative with his work and give Matt and Claire a variety of images, instead of the standard boring series of poses most wedding photographers offered. Since he wasn't a wedding photographer, he figured that'd give him a leg up, and was glad it'd paid off.

He was closing his laptop when Claire said, "Stay for dinner."

"Just say 'yes'," Matt muttered under his breath. "It might sound like she's asking, but she's not."

"I'd love to." Logan would rather cut his eye out with a rusty spoon, but Matt was right. Claire was the kind of person you didn't say no to. She was so kind that if you did, you'd feel like shit afterward.

Logan and Matt went outside to light the grill while Claire patted out burgers. She came outside a while later and drank a beer with them.

"What's Drew doing?" Matt asked her.

"Pretending to sunbathe on the side porch." She turned to Logan and said, "She's not mad at you. She's upset with me for meddling."

"If you say so."

"I'm not saying Drew is normally a ball of sunshine, but she has been having shit luck lately." Matt wrapped an arm around Claire and pulled her in close. "I can't blame her for being in a bad mood."

His stomach knotted. He shouldn't ask... "What's happened?"

"A few nights ago, someone broke into her apartment," Matt said.

Logan's body went cold. "Was she there?"

Claire shook her head. "Thankfully she was working late at the studio."

"What did they take?" The urge to hunt down the bastard who'd done this overwhelmed him. First, her dad's house gets broken into, and then her apartment. Fishy. Fishy as hell.

"It's not like Drew has anything that valuable, but they did find her waitressing tips. She's been saving for months to buy what she needs for her collection."

A growl rumbled in his chest. Someone was going to pay for this. Logan would make sure of that. "I can't believe she didn't tell me."

Claire's forehead wrinkled. "You two haven't seen each other since the night of the wedding, have you?"

"Not since the morning after," he said under his breath. He'd stayed far away, so it's not like she'd had a chance to tell him anything. But that's the way she wanted it and the way it had to be.

Matt choked on his beer. His wife elbowed him in the ribs. He laughed so hard for so long he started wheezing.

Several high-pitched shrieks came from the porch. Two blond munchkins barreled down the porch and ran full throttle toward the beach, one of them holding onto a big, black-and-white floppy hat.

Drew flew down the steps after them. "Come back here with that!"

"I'll be back," Logan said and followed the chaos.

"Tell them it's time for dinner," Claire shouted after him.

When he reached the sand, Drew had Autumn around the waist with one arm and reached for her hat with her other hand.

Avery dangled it in front of her but stayed just out of her reach.

"This isn't funny!" she said even though her voice was filled with laughter.

"Throw it here," Logan shouted to Avery and held his hands out. The kid tossed him the hat like a Frisbee and stuck out his tongue at Drew.

She let go of her captive and spun around.

"Your mom says it's time for dinner."

"Okay, but don't give her the hat back!" Avery shouted as he and his sister raced back to the yard.

"You *will* give me that back," she said.

"What will you give me?"

"You know what?" Her voice had a serious bite to it. "Keep it."

Drew tried to storm past him, but he grabbed her hand. "Matt told me your apartment got broken into."

She tugged her hand free. "And that's your business because…?"

It wasn't. It was absolutely none of his fucking business. But it bothered him on a level he wasn't ready to analyze. It didn't help that he suspected the robbery might not be entirely random. Until he knew for sure it had nothing to do with the break-in at her father's house, his mind wasn't going to stop this incessant spinning.

"Did you report it to the cops?"

Her nostrils flared. She looked like a rhinoceros about to charge. A very sexy rhinoceros. She tried to shoulder past him, but Logan took a step to the side, bringing them chest to chest.

"Did you report it?"

Her gaze flicked to his. "Yes. I reported it. Happy?"

"Not even close." Logan tipped her chin up and connected his gaze with hers. "What did they take?"

"Money. Three months' worth of tips."

"Anything else?"

"My laptop."

"You pay your bills on it?"

She swiped his hand away from her face and crossed her arms.

But this wasn't her normal pissed-off ice queen stance. More like she was hugging herself.

"Cancel all your cards and get a new bank account. Probably wouldn't hurt to change all your passwords, either."

And just like that, the white flag fell to the ground, and she was ready to battle. "Fuck off, Logan. Who do you think you are, ordering me around?"

"Someone who cares about you, I guess," he said, releasing a huff. "You don't wanna be my friend? Fine. I don't give a shit. But I'm not going to stand by while bad stuff happens to you."

"It's none of your concern. We're nothing. Not friends. Not fuck buddies. *Nothing.*"

That little rant, meant to wound in the deepest of ways, would have worked on anyone else. Not him. She was a freaking artist when it came to pushing people away. Logan saw right through it, though, and his skin was thick enough to handle it.

So, he pretended as if she hadn't said it. "You need to get your landlord to put in a security system. You shouldn't be staying there alone until it's installed."

"Not that it's any of your business, but I'm moving in with my dad. After tonight, I won't be staying there anymore."

Not good enough. Without the proper defenses, she shouldn't be there at all. Not even for a night. "Spend the night at your dad's tonight."

Her jaw flexed as she gritted her teeth. "I have to finish packing. I need to be out by tomorrow or I won't get my security deposit back."

"Fine. I'm helping you pack then."

"What?" Her mouth dropped open. Then snapped shut. "No, you're not."

He shrugged. "Try and stop me."

Her eyes filled with fire. "I don't like you, Logan. When are you going to get that through your thick skull?"

Damn it, she was sexy as hell when she got all worked up.

He looked up at the sky so he would stop noticing. He'd finally gotten a handle on those haunting images of her the night of the wedding, but now they were back with a vengeance. "I thought we'd gotten past that."

"Why would you think that?"

Logan couldn't help but bring his gaze to hers. She had to be joking. "Because you gave me your—"

Before he got the rest out, she shoved him. Hard. Then flipped him off.

He covered her fist with his, pushing her middle finger down. "Regret it?"

She stared at him for a long time, her jaw clenched. Then her eyes shifted to the sand. "No."

"Then, what's your beef?"

With a swift jerk, she freed her hand from his grip. "You've been avoiding me. I meant it when I said I didn't want a relationship, but I didn't think I'd never see you again."

He had his reasons for staying away, but she'd made it clear on more than one occasion that the coffee shop was her turf, and he was unwelcome there. "Don't act like I'm a jerk for giving you what you asked for."

"I'm not."

He waited, daring her to stand by her lie.

"Okay, maybe it seems that way, but I'm…frustrated."

"Sexually frustrated?" Shit, he shouldn't have said that. He was joking, trying to lighten things up, but considering the circumstances it was probably not the best thing to say.

"No." Drew sharply turned away, froze for a moment, then turned back toward him. "I don't know what you're so cocky about. I mean, I thought it was good, but it's not like I have anything to compare it to."

Splashes of red flew before his eyes. *Compare?* Yeah, that was not happening. She was his. Logan strode toward her and put his hand on the back of her head. He was about to lean in and remind her how off the charts their chemistry was. One kiss was all it would take to kindle that flame between them, rid her of that anger.

But then he saw something in her eyes. Hurt.

Drew hid her vulnerability behind that fire of hers. Whether it was anger or embarrassment, or even pain, she used her tried and true defense mechanism to deal with her unwanted emotions. She lashed out. Said things she knew would distract others from seeing that vulnerability.

If he touched her now, if this went any further, whatever hurt she was feeling right now would multiply when he went back to Vegas.

He let go and took a step back. "I think you're the shit, Drew, but it wouldn't work between us, and we both know that."

She rolled her eyes and scoffed. "As if I'd ever consider dating an asshole like you."

"Oh, good," he said in mock-relief. "Because I'm not into uptight bitches."

Even though she rolled her eyes, she was doing her best to choke down a smile. "I probably sound like I forgot to take my crazy pills. First, I want you to leave the coffee shop, then you stop coming, and I want you to come back."

"Yeah, well, I learned early on that you were crazy. Lucky for you, I'm a sick fuck, so it turns me on."

She laughed, then shook her head. "Claire wigged out on me when I told her I slept with you and got me all worked up. But you're right. Anything between us would be a total disaster."

A total disaster. That chafed. She wasn't wrong, though. He'd decided to keep an eye on her until he knew if the break in was random or related to the painting theft. Now, he had to figure out how the hell to keep his hands off her during that time.

"Claire invited me for dinner. You cool with that?"

"I suppose." She snatched her hat from him, put it on, and headed toward the house.

Logan followed behind, watching the twitch of her hips, all the while grinning his ass off. Under different circumstances, Drew was exactly the kind of woman he would let drive him crazy. And enjoy every second of it.

23

CRAZY PILL REFILL

Drew

DREW MADE AN EXAGGERATED GAGGING sound as she approached her friends. Enough with the PDA. Didn't they grope each other enough on the honeymoon?

"You're killing my appetite." She swung her leg over the picnic table bench. The spread was impressive. Typical Claire. Juicy cheeseburgers, red skinned potato salad, pasta salad, homemade pico de gallo, grilled zucchini, corn on the cob, freshly baked peach pie.

The twins already had their plates fixed and their faces were smeared with ketchup. Drew crossed her eyes and stuck her tongue out at Avery. He mimicked her and she winked at him. She caught Logan watching her and turned her attention to filling her plate.

"Is photography your main line of work, Logan?" Claire asked.

"Nah. Just a hobby."

"He's a poker player," Drew said. "Apparently, a good one."

Logan took a long pull from his beer, his eyes locking on hers, sending a ripple of energy all the way to her toes. His stare said things that couldn't be put into words. Everything else became white noise, and for a moment, Drew feared he might actually be able to read her thoughts.

She would rather eat mud than have him know what she was thinking. Logan was not only uniquely attractive, but his background was intriguing. He was one of a kind, and not in a *I try to be different* kind of way.

"That's badass," Matt said. "You go to Vegas a lot?"

"He's *from* Vegas." She stuffed a forkful of potato salad in her mouth, so she'd stop answering for him.

"How'd you end up in Savannah?" Claire asked.

"My sister moved here, and I moved here to be near her."

"That's so sweet." Claire made eyes at Drew, silently communicating that Logan was a catch in her book.

See? That was the normal response to hearing Logan had done that.

"We're having a 4th of July celebration," Claire said. "It's the twins' birthday, and we're going to have a cook-out and watch fireworks on the beach. You should come, Logan."

She was inviting him to the kids' birthday party? That was not good.

Pretending not to want him was taxing on her mental health. If she had to spend an entire day around him, she might actually need crazy pills.

Drew looked forward to the twins' birthday each year. She had been with Claire the night they were born and was the second person in the world to hold those precious little buggers. Every birthday since, she had helped blow up the balloons and hang the streamers.

"It's gonna be awesome," Avery said. "We're gonna have a water balloon war and a limbo contest."

"Sweet," Logan said.

"There will be adult activities too." Matt raised his beer and smiled.

"I'll be back in Vegas by then."

Drew stopped chewing. She let her burger fall to her plate, landing with a *plop*. Going stag to a party had never bothered her. It meant showing up when she liked, not having to bother making introductions or entertain anyone, and leaving when she felt like it.

I don't want him there.

Holy crap. Yes, she did. She totally wanted him there. Her mind wouldn't stop filling with images of him slinking his arm around her waist as the twins blew out their candles. Or sitting between his legs as they watched the fireworks from the beach. Or him between her legs after the party…

Drew snatched up her plate and stomped to the house. She scraped her plate into the trash, then looked for something to clean in Claire's spotless kitchen. Seriously, how did a mother of two not have a dirty dish in the sink or a crumb on her counter?

"Are you okay?" Claire asked through the screened door, her arms filled with serving plates. There was an underlying tone of amusement in her voice.

She held open the door for her friend and glared at her. "I'm wonderful."

Claire set the plates on the table, then retrieved the rest of the leftovers Matt met her with on the deck.

Drew pulled the foil and plastic wrap from a drawer and held her breath waiting for Claire to say something about Logan.

She didn't let her down. "I like him."

"You like everybody."

"He wouldn't let us pay him."

"What?"

"For photographing the wedding. Matt wrote him a check, but when we got home from the honeymoon, it was tacked to the corkboard next to the phone." Claire pointed to the board next to the ancient wall-mounted house phone. "We thought maybe he'd lost it, and someone found it and stuck it there, but when I talked to him on the phone, he said he'd put it there. He said he owed you a favor and nothing we could say would make him cash our check."

"Well, that's just dumb."

"Is it?" Claire asked.

She grumbled. No, it wasn't dumb. It was freakin' nice as shit.

Must be nice not worrying about money. It had hurt to cough up the near fortune for her new tires. Matt and Claire had tried to loan her the money, but she couldn't let them do that. They had just paid for a wedding and a honeymoon and had two mouths to feed.

She didn't have any idea how she was going to scrounge up money to produce her collection now that all her tips were gone. Getting the security deposit back and living with her dad would help some, but not enough.

Her dad had offered to give her the money. If she hadn't already been accepting free rent at the studio, not to mention the loan he'd given her to buy dress forms, sewing machines, and all the other industrial garment sewing equipment she needed, she might have accepted.

"Logan's going back to Las Vegas. Forget your little matchmaking attempt, okay?" Drew pointed her finger in Claire's face.

She swatted it away. "Plans change. Maybe he needs a reason to stay."

"Seriously, Claire, it's not going to happen. We're not you and Matt."

Claire put the last of the leftovers in the fridge and opened a beer. "No, you're Drew and Logan. But that doesn't make it any less special."

24

THAT SHIT'S NOT FOR ME

LOGAN

WHILE THE KIDS PEDALED their bikes up and down the driveway, Matt and Logan talked under the hood of the car.

"I know it's none of my business, but I gotta ask you something, man." Matt tapped a wrench against his palm. "Did she tell you?"

"Tell me what?" Logan took a swig of beer.

"That it was her first time."

It was none of his business, and if anyone else had asked, Logan would have told them where to get off, but Matt put off an energy that encouraged you to laugh at yourself.

He leaned against a workbench and crossed one ankle over the other. "She didn't tell me. I found out on my own. *During.*"

"Oh, man." Matt hooted with laughter as he lowered the hood over the engine.

He shook his head, unable to hide his smile. It hadn't been funny at the time, but looking back on it, he had a hard time not laughing.

"You're a brave man." Matt slapped him on the back. "Gonna have your hands full with that one."

"It's not like that. We both agreed us being together would be a bad idea."

"It's the bad ideas that are usually the most fun."

Wasn't that the truth?

"Our lives are on different tracks. It'd never work," Logan said.

"I hear ya, man. When I met Claire, I was all about being a bachelor. The more time I spent with her, the more the time without her started to suck. Freaked me out pretty bad when I found out she was a mom. Didn't think I was ready for all that, but I fell in love with Avery and Autumn faster than I did Claire. Never imagined that my life would turn out this way, but anyone tries to take it away from me and it'll be a fight to the death."

He hadn't realized Matt wasn't the twins' biological father. He figured he'd knocked up Claire when they were young, and they were just now getting around to marriage.

He gave Matt mad respect for stepping up and raising those kids like they were his own. He hated thinking about what his life would have turned out like if Uncle John hadn't taken him and Morgan in.

Claire and Matt's situation couldn't be any more different than the situation between him and Drew. That didn't stop him from wondering if he'd miss his bachelor lifestyle if Drew were in his life.

She'd definitely keep things interesting.

"I think what you and Claire have is great. You seem really happy. But that shit's not for me."

25

THE ANTITHESIS OF BEIGE

DREW TURNED THE DEADBOLT, then turned and surveyed her living room and kitchen. Packing would take all night, but there was no way around it. She needed to get everything moved tomorrow. With any luck it would only take a few hours for her brothers to help her get all her boxes and furniture loaded into the U-Haul and unloaded at her dad's.

Best to get the worst job done first. Clothes and shoes.

Knock! Knock!

Drew jumped. Her heart banged against her ribs.

She sucked in a calming breath and pulled the curtain back.

Son of a shit fuck.

She unlocked the deadbolt, jerked open the door, and gave Logan her dirtiest scowl.

He raised his eyebrows and flashed a grin with a wickedness to rival the Antichrist.

"How do you know where I live?"

"I followed you when you left Claire's."

Great. Not at all overbearing or stalkerish. "Go away."

Logan made a *psssh* sound and squeezed past her. "Where do you want me to start?"

Door still wide open, she turned to spit out a snarky comment, but Logan shrugging out of his leather jacket stole her ability to speak. The muscles in his back swelled and rolled with his movement, his white T-shirt tightening across his shoulders.

Her thighs tingled and her breasts ached.

Drew wasn't a toucher. She avoided hugs whenever possible. Shaking hands, also not her favorite. But holy hell, she wanted to run her hands all over his back and arms.

Logan draped his jacket over the stool at her small breakfast bar and faced her.

She wouldn't mind getting a good feel of his front side, either.

In three strides, he was in front of her, close enough that if she wanted, she could lick the sharp line of his jaw. Kissing him was only the worst idea ever. But she wanted to do it anyway.

She turned her face up.

He reached past her and pushed the door shut. He walked back to the kitchen, grabbing one of the many empty boxes stacked in the corner. "Do you have newspaper or bubble wrap for your glasses and plates?"

She shook her head, hoping to clear all the absurd thoughts from it. "I really don't need—or want—your help."

"Too bad." Without looking at her, he opened a cabinet and pulled out the three dinner plates she owned. "I'm not leaving, so get over yourself and give me some direction. Or I'll find things to do on my own. Your choice."

She grabbed a stack of newspapers from the paper bag by the door and slapped them against his chest. Drew kept an eye on him at first to make sure he was doing things to her standards, but it didn't take her long to learn Logan was as anal as she was. It kinda turned her on.

Before placing items inside, he flipped the box over and put extra tape on the seam, and another strip running perpendicular. Each glass got rolled neatly in a sheet of newspaper, with the ends tucked inside to secure it. Inside the box, he placed a balled-up piece of paper between each, for extra protection against breakage.

His closet and drawers probably looked high-end retail display worthy. Perfectly folded shirts. Jeans rolled Marie Kondo-style. He was a boxer briefs guy, and she'd bet his underwear looked exactly like they did when they came out of the package. Speaking of underwear and packages...

Drew swallowed and turned on her heel, demanding her body stop that clenching between her thighs. She tackled the bedroom and bathroom, and with Logan doing the kitchen, it didn't take long to get through the rest of her apartment. After she'd carried the last box from her bedroom and set it next to the others by the breakfast bar, she pulled two bottles of beer from the fridge and offered him one.

Logan sat on the floor with his back against the cabinets, wrapping her cereal bowls in newspaper. His gaze coasted over her body as he reached for the bottle, uncapped it, then took a swig—without ever taking his eyes off her. "I wouldn't have guessed you for a beer drinker."

The cool liquid running down her throat was divine. Not like beer? There wasn't a thing better on a humid night like this. "Why not?"

"Too classy." He shrugged and took another swig.

He thinks I'm classy. The smile tugging at her lips was almost impossible to suppress, but she was nothing if not willful, so she squashed it. "I have three older brothers. Not much opportunity to smuggle Chardonnay from them."

"How did you turn out so"—the weight of his stare as he once again assessed her, sliding his gaze over her body, delivered a pulse to her core that grew into a throb—"*girly* with three brothers?"

"I'm pretty sure I came out of the womb ungovernable." She lowered herself to the floor and leaned against the pantry door. "That and I used to blackmail my brothers whenever they broke something or got into a fight, which was daily, so I never had a shortage of pocket money to buy magazines and makeup."

Logan chuckled. "Your poor brothers."

"What's your family like?"

"Uncle John is a character. Always has a joke or a new card trick. Everyone likes him, even his m—" His mouth stayed open, but no more words came out. His eyebrows lowered, and he continued to sit here, as though some outlandish phenomenon had just taken place.

"What were you going to say?"

He finished wrapping a piece of newspaper around a bowl before meeting her gaze and studying her in silence, as though deciding if he could trust her with the truth, then said, "His marks. He's a grifter."

"A what?"

A half-grin tilted his lips. "A grifter. You know, a con artist."

She blinked a few times, waiting for him to laugh. When his expression didn't change, she tucked her legs under her, and settled in to nag the rest of the details from him. "Like George Clooney in Ocean's Eleven?"

Logan snorted and shook his head. "No, nothing that dramatic. Short cons on tourists mostly."

"What's a short con?" It was like he was speaking a different language.

"It means the trick is done and over quickly. Not a lot of set up involved. He used to be into bigger stuff, but he toned it down when he adopted Morgan and me."

"He's a pickpocket?"

Logan smirked and shook his head. "No. That's more up my sister's alley."

The beer bottle slipped from her grasp as she went to set it on the floor next to her. Foamy, amber liquid spread across the floor, which wasn't even close to level. She jumped up and snagged a roll of paper towels.

Scrambling, together they cleaned it up before it ran under the fridge and down the heat register. Logan stood, tossed all the wet towels into the garbage, then extended his hand to her. He pulled her up and didn't let go.

They stood there for a solid minute, holding each other's stare.

Drew's gaze dropped to his mouth.

"Stop thinking about kissing me," he said, his voice thick.

She pulled her hand from his and whacked his arm, but he didn't even flinch. "I'm not."

"You wet your lips." Accusation thickened his voice, like she'd broken the law. Okay, not the best comparison since Logan clearly didn't judge people for engaging in criminal activities.

"No, I didn't," she blurted out. *Gah.* She had. By reflex.

He ran his fingers through his hair. "You're trouble."

"Me?" The word came out a squeak. "Look at you…with your…"

Logan stuck his hands in his pockets. His expression conveyed he was waiting to hear the rest. And expecting an insult.

She couldn't articulate her perception of him. Rolled up T-shirt sleeves. The hair. Those piercing eyes. The shamelessness in his attitude. One look and anyone could see he wasn't the type of guy that played by the rules. There wasn't one thing vanilla about Logan.

"Well?"

"You're a trouble*maker.*" That was the word. An instigator. What was it he'd said when she'd failed to verbalize why the décor of his boat didn't align with his personality? "And you're the antithesis of beige."

"The antithesis of beige," he said, like he was trying it on. "I'm gonna put that on my tombstone."

"Good idea," she said, grinning. "Because it's very likely that I'm going to strangle you if we spend any more time together."

"Maybe I'm into that."

She pressed her palm to her forehead. "Let's talk about something else. Back to your family." Grifters? Pickpockets? Short cons? "You're not actually serious, are you? About your sister?"

He shrugged, hands still in his pockets. "Our upbringing was unconventional. Morgan started out with picking pockets. It was more of a party trick than anything. Uncle John got a kick out of his four-year-old niece handing his friends' watches and wallets back to them. By the time she was a teenager, she could crack a safe."

Drew's jaw dropped.

"I'm going to shut up now. I don't know why I'm telling you any of this."

"No, no, no," she said, putting on her best I'm-cool-you-can-trust-me face. "What about you?"

Up until now, she'd found him mildly interesting. Someone out of the ordinary. Now, his intrigue factor topped the charts. Logan Cash was easily the most fascinating person she had met.

"Me?"

"I seriously doubt that you're the upstanding citizen in your family."

He gasped and mimed getting stabbed in the heart.

She responded by thrusting her hands on her hips and cocking her head.

"They have real jobs. It's not like they make a living robbing casinos or plotting to steal the Mona Lisa. Morgan is an ER nurse and Uncle John has a legit job too." He hoisted a box from the floor onto the kitchen island. "He teaches rich women how to play table games while their husbands gamble high stakes. When he's done with them, they usually take home more winnings than their husbands."

"You still haven't told me what you do."

26

THE FRIENDS OF DREW MILLER SOCIETY

"I PLAY POKER. At least I used to before I became my sister's full-time babysitter."

"So, what, do you like count cards or something?"

She didn't seem bothered by the possibility that he might be dishonest enough to cheat in a professional poker game. Logan hoped that was a good omen. He didn't want her smacking him silly when she found out she'd been his mark.

Not that he was sold on the idea of coming clean with her. The only thing he was sure about right now was that he was going to stay close to her until he was certain she was safe.

"No. I mean, yes, I can count cards, but that's not—" He rubbed his jaw. "Counting cards isn't considered cheating in poker. It's not the same as when you do it in Blackjack."

"Do you play Blackjack too?"

"Sure, on a night out with friends, just for fun."

"You don't cheat?"

He walked around to the other side of the peninsula that separated her kitchen from her entryway and slid onto one of the two stools. Putting space between them was mandatory if he wanted to keep all their clothes on. "You can't cheat at casino games, Drew. In Blackjack, if you count cards—which, by the way, is easy if you understand basic math—you'll know when your odds of winning are the highest, and that's when you raise your bet. It's not illegal to count cards, but for obvious reasons, casinos don't like it, and as private establishments, they reserve the right to boot your ass if they're so inclined."

"So, you don't cheat in the casino?" Her eyes glimmered the way they had earlier when she'd teased Matt and Claire about their rather overt PDA. That playfulness was a rarity and fucking sublime. Like a double rainbow or a royal flush. "How about outside of the casino? For instance, if you played poker with a bougie cum dribbler at a private game in Miami?"

Cum dribbler. Having three brothers may not have hindered her femininity, but damn if it hadn't contributed to that filthy mouth.

Wait a second.

Logan had done it. Gained acceptance into an exclusive club. The Friends of Drew Miller Society. No idea how he'd accomplished that, but he'd take it.

"*If* I played in a private game and used a strategy to facilitate winning, I'd call it hustling, not cheating."

"What's the difference?"

"Cheating would be manipulating the deck. Hustling is manipulating your opponent, so he believes he's a better player than you, or misleading him throughout the game so he *thinks* he knows when you're bluffing."

"What if it doesn't work?" she asked.

"It's cute that you think that would happen to me."

"Okay, then, Mr. Humble." She rolled her eyes, but her smile stayed in place. Palms flat against the counter, she leaned closer. "I don't think I'd stand a chance at poker."

"With your temper, you'd make an awful poker player. But you could crush it at the Blackjack table with the right training."

"You could teach me to count cards?"

Hell yes, he could. Logan could teach her many illicit but highly enjoyable things. They could get on a plane to Vegas right now and commit all kinds of sins in Sin City. "Why? You wanna go win some money?"

That would be one way Logan could help her recoup her stolen tips. Unlikely she was down for a spontaneous trip, though.

"There's no casinos in Savannah," she said, a little pout on her lips.

Should he tell her they didn't have to limit themselves to Savannah, or even the surrounding states? No, he would keep that to himself. The idea of whisking her off, sharing a hotel suite...it was a bad one, even if it was fun as hell to think about. "How about Biloxi? Atlantic City?"

"Not Vegas?"

"You said if you ever went to Vegas, it wasn't going to be with me. Remember that?" He propped his forearms on the counter and raised his eyebrows.

Pink swept her cheeks. Drew Miller blushing? Unheard of.

"You made a terrible first impression on me, and then tried to hit on me. Of course, I shot you down." Her voice came out melodious and honeyed. She could have given him a scalding insult in the same tone, and he'd have found it charming.

He dropped his head onto his outstretched arms, laughing so hard his shoulders shook. Fuck, he was so screwed if this saucy, impish side of her didn't go back into hiding.

"I wasn't hitting on you," he said, when he got himself together enough to speak. "And I sure as hell didn't invite you to Las Vegas."

With the sexiest smirk, she leaned in even more, her cleavage beautifully showcased. "What about Biloxi or Atlantic City? Was that invitation genuine?"

Trying to gauge whether she'd truly consider going, he studied her face. In this moment, he couldn't read her. Time seemed to pass slower.

The smart thing would be to tell her it was banter, nothing more. But Logan was a fool when it came to this woman. "I'll take you wherever you wanna go, baby."

Her throat emitted the slightest gasp. Her chest rose and fell more vigorously. "I can't travel right now," she said and straightened away from the peninsula. "Too busy and too broke."

He started to tell her she wouldn't have to pay for any of it. That he wouldn't let her even pay for a pack of gum while she was with him. But he checked himself. It was all true, but Drew wasn't the kind of woman who'd jump at the offer to have him drop coin on her.

"So, now you know all the dirt on my family. Your turn. Spill the tea on the Miller dynasty." It was disturbing how true that was. In the times they'd spent together, he'd told her the saga of his biological parents and disclosed that he'd been raised by a con artist. She knew why he'd come to Savannah in the first place. How he'd won the *Gypsy* playing cards. Oh, right, and she knew he was a smoker. Christ. He'd been the one that was supposed to get intel on her family, not the other around. He didn't know anything other than surface details about the Millers. Except for the reasoning behind her father not reporting his painting stolen, information that was basically useless.

Trying to bleed her for clues was over. He'd quit. Asking about her family was partly to change the subject, but he genuinely wanted to know more about her life.

Drew pulled the corner of her lip inward with her teeth, head bobbing side to side. "Like I said, I have three brothers. Grant is the oldest. He's a history teacher, and very popular with his students. His teaching methods are way outside of the box. He's married and his wife is pregnant with their first."

She let her hair free from the twist she'd put in it when they'd started packing, and finger-combed it until it cascaded down her back. "Lee is five years older than me. He's a personal trainer. He's all about nutrition and getting his body into top athletic shape, so most people assume he's not creative or erudite, but he reads over three hundred books a year, and he can decorate a cake like you wouldn't believe. Then there's Aubrey."

Logan waited, but she didn't elaborate on him.

The way she'd said his name, like he was a scab that wouldn't heal, indicated some tension between them.

"You two don't get along?"

"What?" A laugh bubbled out. "I'm closer to him than anyone. He's an archaeological anthropologist and his research grant was revoked, so now he's on this crusade to find my dad's stolen painting. And he's driving me mad." She ran her palms down her cheeks. "Under any other circumstances, I might humor him, but I have so much on my plate right now."

"Any word on the contest?"

"Not yet. Even if I do make it as a finalist, my odds of winning have tanked now that the money I was saving up to fund my collection is gone. Not going to win using cheap-o polyester off the clearance rack at JoAnn's Fabrics." Drew dropped her head back and groaned. "I can't even think about what the four-hour trek to Atlanta is going to cost in gas."

Logan bit back an offer to drive her to Atlanta and buy her whatever she needed. Sure, if it was as easy as handing her his Amex, it would be no sweat. But he didn't have the patience to sweet talk her into accepting what she would see as charity.

It was killing him not to ask what progress Aubrey had made investigating the painting theft. He had far better access to information than Logan had. Now wasn't the time to pry, though. He couldn't do it without raising her suspicions. The backlash he'd receive if she found what he'd done wasn't his only deterrent, or even the biggest one. Drew had suffered enough bad shit happening lately. Getting worked up about his motives for inserting himself into her life wouldn't be good for her stress levels. She didn't need that while trying to focus on winning the contest.

Logan set his beer bottle in the recycling bin next to her trash can, snagged his jacket off the chair and inched backward toward the door. "I can help move everything to your dad's tomorrow."

She maneuvered around the peninsula and came close enough to touch. "You're leaving?"

Leaving her apartment, yes. He wouldn't be going far. Camping out in his car, he'd be able to keep an eye on her apartment all night.

But the disappointment in her voice cut through him like a switchblade.

"It's getting late." It wasn't even ten o'clock. But another five minutes with her might be more than his moral compass could navigate. Time to split before he did something really dumb. Like kiss her.

"Oh…" She moved her hands like she was going to put them on her hips, but dropped them back to her sides, then started to twirl her hair around her finger, only to quit that too, and cross her arms like she was cold.

He'd never seen her awkward. Under any other under circumstances he'd find it hilarious, but she wouldn't have a reason to be awkward if he wasn't holding back with her. Whatever this was between them, he wanted to explore it, but he couldn't.

The only woman he'd wanted to pursue on a deeper level turning out to be the one he'd done wrong might be karma for his ambivalent approach toward morality. Talking to Uncle John about this would make him feel better. If there was a way to fix it, his uncle would know. But his pride wouldn't let him make that call. The only reason John had stayed in Vegas was because he trusted Logan to fix Morgan's mistakes. He was supposed to be cleaning up her mess, not making his own.

"Well, thanks for helping me. My brothers will be here in the morning, so I'll have plenty of help."

That was probably just as well. He'd be exhausted after keeping watch all night. She'd be safe with her brothers while he got caught up on sleep.

She flicked at the door chain. "Are you no longer worried about me staying here alone?"

"Are *you* worried about it?" If she didn't feel safe, he wasn't going anywhere. Spending the night here would make protecting her easier. He might be able to get some sleep. On the couch. Alone.

She gave a little shake of her head. "I want you to stay, but not because I don't feel safe."

His throat constricted. What had he done to merit this level of torture?

Those bright green eyes stared up at him.

Logan stared back. He couldn't have looked away if there was a nuclear raid.

She leaned up on her toes, pressed her thighs against his, and brushed her lips across his.

Fuck. He was a weak son of a bitch.

He pulled her close and slanted his mouth across hers, his hand tangling in her hair. Kissing her was as hot as he remembered. The feel of those plump lips. The way her body melted into his. And the barely audible moans she made in the back of her throat.

He broke his mouth away from hers. "I thought we agreed this would be a disaster."

She tilted her head. "We agreed that a relationship would be a disaster. I was thinking more the lines of…"

"Using me for sex again?"

Her eyes danced with laughter. "Do you have a problem with that?"

No. God, no.

He fucking loved the idea.

He brushed his pelvis against hers. His erection pressed uncomfortably against his fly. "Does it feel like I have a problem with that?"

"Um, no."

He dragged his fingers down her neck, past her collarbone, and over her breast. His hands grazed her thighs and skimmed up under the skirt of her dress. Both hands clutched bare ass.

Holy hell.

Time to catch his breath and stifle the barbaric notion of tossing her over his shoulder and carrying her to bed.

"Do you always go commando?" Last time, she hadn't been wearing any either, but he hadn't dwelt on it.

"Almost always." She held her head high. "I don't want to take a chance on panty lines."

"Isn't that why women wear thongs?"

"They drive me crazy."

You drive me crazy. "I have to get something from the car. Unless you anticipated me staying here?"

She shook her head no.

"Be right back."

As fast as he could move without running, he went out to his car to grab his rucksack.

Drew was in the bedroom when he returned, trying to wiggle the zipper on the side of her dress free without much luck. He dropped his bag on the end of the bed and pushed her hands away.

"It's really stuck," he lied, as he pretended to tug on the zipper. "We might have to cut you out of this dress."

She took three steps away from him. "I'll keep it on then."

He lowered his gaze so she wouldn't see the laughter in his eyes as he pulled her close. Then he promptly unzipped her.

Her glare seared him.

He reciprocated by pushing down the dress until it fell around her ankles, leaving her in nothing but a strapless bra. Damn. All that tanned skin. And those tan lines. Every inch of her was soft and curvy and perfect.

He kissed her hard on the mouth while he unclasped her bra.

Drew pushed his T-shirt up over his abs, and he stopped kissing her to pull it over his head.

He walked her backward to the bed and nudged her down. He covered her body with his, and his eyes shut as he absorbed the ecstasy of being skin to skin with her.

It must have been eighty degrees in the apartment but then again, maybe they were responsible for the heat. Her skin scorched his lips when he kissed the base of her neck.

She bumped her hips against him, squirming, begging with her body for more friction. Moving his hand between her thighs, he brushed his fingers against her heat. She let out a ragged moan. He stroked her until she whimpered his name.

Hastily, he undid his belt and pants, then shoved them down his legs.

She used her feet to help him work them the rest of the way off.

His boxer briefs met the same fate. He took her breast in his mouth, swirling his tongue around the nipple.

She gasped and dredged her fingers into his hair.

Sinking deep inside her tight pussy consumed his mind. He reached for his bag, retrieved a condom, and rolled it on.

As soon as he laid next to her, she pressed her body against his side. Her mouth sought his. They kissed while he ran his hands over her body until he felt as if he would erupt.

He rolled her onto her stomach and when she started to protest and roll back over, he covered her body with his, then brushed his lips against her ear and whispered, "Baby, you're going to like this. Promise."

Palm flat against her pelvis, he guided her ass toward his cock. She moved against him, rubbing her wet sex against his.

Logan held her hips in place and pushed the tip of his cock inside her.

She gasped, then moved her hips backward, trying to take more of him.

"Not yet." He dug his fingers into her hips to from ramming inside her and fucking her like a savage. He bit his lip and moved inside another inch.

"I don't have the patience for this, Logan," she said, her tone husky with need. "I want you. *Now*."

He grunted and withdrew. She was so tight, but so wet, and he easily slid back inside. With his head thrown back, he closed his eyes, and planted himself deep inside her. His groan almost drowned out her moan.

He settled into a rhythm that made her louder, slipping nearly outside her opening, then thrusting back, deep. He ran his palm up the cat-like curve of her body, loving her positioned this way. Her ass high in the air. The looks she threw over her shoulder. Those eyes that were both pleading and threatening.

Despite knowing continuing to watch her would push him over the edge, he couldn't look away. He gritted his teeth as sweat broke out on his forehead.

His hand moved over her hip, dipping between her thighs, stroking her until her head dropped to the mattress. Her orgasm gripping his cock did him in. Logan squeezed her hips with both hands, pouring himself into her with one last, long thrust.

When he felt capable of moving, he eased out of her, ditched the condom, and collapsed against the mattress.

Drew turned and he spread his arm out for her to fold into him. Without hesitation, she curled against his side, and rested her head on his chest. Her mouth slackened and her body relaxed further.

He trailed his fingers down her spine and back up, eliciting a murmur, followed by her leg draping across his thighs.

Logan'd had no-strings sex plenty.

This wasn't it.

27

AWW, BABY, YOU GOOGLED ME

DREW WOKE SO HOT, the sweat-dampened sheets clung to her skin. The building was almost two-hundred-years-old and the central air that had been installed a few years ago performed as though it was just as ancient. It always went on the fritz during the most humid nights.

Her hand slid across the mattress, coming up with nothing but bed linens.

She untangled her legs from the twisted sheet. Searching through the boxes she had packed her clothes in, she found a dress slip. It was either that or a long-sleeved T-shirt. She pulled it on as she headed into the hallway. Down the hall, light flickered against the wall. As she got closer to the living room, the faint sound of applause reached her ears.

Logan sat on her couch with the television on, hunched over her coffee table, playing solitaire.

"I couldn't sleep," he said without turning to look at her. A late-night poker game lit up the TV screen.

She sat on the couch—the opposite end, since cozying up to him seemed too relationship-y—and stared at his profile. Her nipples tingled and tightened. The glow of the screen amplified his sexiness. It seemed impossible she'd ever be as attracted to another man as she was to Logan. Drew refused to let herself go there. Even though she accepted that he didn't have a place in her future, it made her uneasy to envision it.

Finding a less painful place to direct her attention, she glanced at the screen. There were three players left in the game. The one with the least amount of chips was the youngest by decades. He wore a slouchy beanie and a lip ring.

"Want to play cards?"

She whipped her head in his direction. "Poker? Against the fifth-ranked player in career poker earnings history? I'll pass."

"Aw, baby, you Googled me."

She liked the way he called her baby, his voice thick and playful. His hungry gaze ate her up. He leaned closer, one hand pressing into the cushion between them, the other grazing the outside of her knee and sliding upward. "Not poker. Blackjack. You can get your first lesson in counting cards."

An ache pulsed between her thighs. She fought the urge to shift her hips toward his touch.

He continued his route upward, skimming over the thin fabric of her slip, up her waist, and curling around her ribs. "Have anything to use as chips?"

"Hmm?"

His wicked smirk snapped her out of her lust coma. "Do you have something to use as chips so we can play cards?"

Drew leaned around him and pulled a bag of butterscotch candies from the drawer under the coffee table. The only deck of cards she owned was still inside. She glanced at the game of solitaire he had laid out on the table. "Do you always carry a deck of cards ozn you?"

"No." He scooped up the cards from his game and shuffled them in one smooth, fluid motion. "I carry at least four."

"What did you do with all that money?" She tried to sound only mildly curious. He didn't live the life of a multimillionaire. He lived on a boat—a nice one, but still, a millionaire could have afforded better—

and his car, although a high-end model, wasn't the type of car most men would buy if they had that kind of dough.

"I still have most of it," he said. "Paid for my sister's nursing school. I play the stock market a little bit. I'll probably splurge on something one day, but I haven't found anything I couldn't live without yet."

He shuffled a few more times, then instructed her to place a modest bet, which she deemed to be two candies. Using the cushion between them as a playing surface, he dealt them each two cards, with one of his facedown.

"In a casino, they use six or eight decks. I'm going to teach you with one for now. You know there's a basic strategy to whether you hit or stay, right?"

"Uh, sure."

"Christ." He wiped his palm across his jaw, then grabbed his phone off the table. After tapping the screen several times, he handed it to her. "This chart tells you whether to hit or stay based on your cards and the dealer's cards."

"Don't I just try to get twenty-one?"

"No," he said, a huff in his voice, clearly offended she was such an amateur. "Forget counting cards. You need to learn strategy first."

Applause on the television distracted her. The guy with the beanie had lost the hand. "Did he for real just lose ninety-thousand dollars?"

He flicked a glance at the screen. "Yep."

"Holy fuck."

"You gonna hit or stay?"

She checked the chart on his phone. "This says I should stay, but I only have fourteen. Why wouldn't I hit and give myself a better chance at getting twenty-one?"

"Baby, as long as your cards are higher than the dealer's without going over twenty-one, you win. If the dealer busts, you win with whatever you have unless you busted too."

"But my cards suck."

He chuckled and tapped the facedown card. "Let's assume this card is a ten."

"You have a six. So, you'd have sixteen. That's higher than fourteen, Logan."

"But the dealer has to hit unless they have seventeen or higher. What are the chances that the next card is going to be five or under?"

"Not good?"

"Right. Probability says there's more of a chance that the next card is higher than five, and if it is, I bust."

"Fine. I'll stay."

"Good girl." He flipped the card over. A jack. "Dealer has sixteen." He dealt himself another card. A king. "Dealer busts."

He took two candies from his pile and slid them over to her.

She unwrapped one and popped it in her mouth while he dealt the next round. The poker game kept drawing her in. Beanie's stack of chips was dwindling.

Logan cleared his throat, and she returned her focus to Blackjack.

Not sure whether to hit or stay, she turned the candy in her mouth over with her tongue and glanced at him.

He zeroed in on her mouth. His eyes smoldered.

Her entire body quivered.

He shook his head slowly as though she vexed him.

She arched her brow. "Now, who's thinking about kissing who?"

"It's a hard habit to break," he said in a lazy drawl. "I've been trying since the first time you blistered me with that sassy mouth."

"You should really see a therapist about that. Or better yet, a psychiatrist. It's probably best treated with heavy drugs."

"I'll just borrow some of your crazy pills."

They'd played several hands of Blackjack, and she was running low on candies. Would he accept the half-dissolved one in her mouth?

On the TV, Beanie—or Chao, according to his little box—got the two of hearts and the seven of clubs.

"He's not going to win with that." She couldn't keep the dejection out of her voice. He seemed like the underdog, and she had been rooting for him.

"He will."

Yeah, right. She shot him a cynical look.

"Watch." Logan gathered up the cards. He set them on her coffee table, scooped up the remaining candies and put them back in the drawer, then leaned back and stretched his legs out.

"Giving up on me?" she asked.

"I'm giving up on teaching you outside of a casino. Or while there's a poker game on."

Chao raised the pot.

The other players called.

The dealer dealt out three cards face up in the center of the table, an ace, a jack and a ten.

"Those three cards are the flop. There's a possibility for a straight if a player's hole cards are a queen and a king."

"Hole cards?" Drew asked, scrunching her forehead.

"The two cards they were dealt."

"But no one has a queen and a king."

"Right, so Hansen will fold if the next card isn't a ten or a queen."

Each player's cards were represented in a little box next to their name. Hansen had a ten and a six. "But he's got a pair of tens."

He shrugged. The next card was a four.

Hansen folded. Just like Logan said he would.

The other player at the table—Jones—had an eight and a nine. He raised the pot.

Chao went all in.

Jones had a big enough chip count to call the bet, but he folded.

"He just won seven million dollars with the worst hand at the table." Wild. It might be Logan's normal, but it wasn't hers.

"Told ya."

"How did you know?"

"Because that little fucker cut his teeth playing cards in my penthouse."

Penthouse? No, she wouldn't get sidetracked by that. "You taught him to play poker?"

"He grew up in my building. The other kids picked on him, and his parents worked a lot, so I kept an eye on him."

"You babysat?"

He snorted. "No. Charlie was like fifteen. I'd have him over and we'd order pizza, play video games."

"And poker."

"Yeah, well, the kid was persistent once he found out how I made enough dough to afford the penthouse. I taught him the game, but he got to where he is because of *how* he is."

"What do you mean? How is he?"

Logan scooted closer to her and toyed with the hem of her slip, pushing the lace edge farther up her thigh. "Quiet. Introverted. People assume he's soft. No one would ever guess he's as ruthless as he is at the card table."

"Ruthless enough to beat you?"

His grin sent a wave of vertigo through her. Damn this man and his cheeky expressions. Claire was right. He was a rascal. A very sexy one. "Do you really have to ask me that?"

"Such a hot shot." She tucked her hair behind her ears and pretended his fingers didn't feel hot enough to blister her skin as they stroked a lazy track across her thigh. "It says this is the championship round. If he's good enough to make it this far, why couldn't he go up against you and win?"

He leaned back against the couch cushions. "Because he doesn't think he can."

"If he was confident that he could beat you, he could?"

"If Lady Luck was on his side that game, maybe."

She wanted to see him play sometime, to see him in his element. Maybe she'd catch him playing in a televised game. But that wasn't what she really wanted. What she really wanted was to be there with him when he played. She wanted him to find her amongst the spectators and for those deep blue eyes of his to fill with lust. She wanted to celebrate with him when he won.

Get a grip. This was temporary. Just sex.

"Luck might help, but he's winning, and he's had terrible cards." She turned to see his face.

He twisted a hank of her hair around his finger. "Those other guys don't know how to read him. I don't need to see Charlie's cards to know if he's got a good hand."

"But he can't read you?"

Logan shook his head. "No one can. Except maybe Uncle John. He claims he can, anyway."

"So, you have a tell?"

"Everyone has a tell."

"What's mine?" Waiting for the answer made her uneasy.

He stacked his hands behind his head. "You have the same set of tells in real life as when you play cards. You throw your shoulders back when you have a good hand or when you feel in control of a situation. If you have a losing hand or feel vulnerable, your temper gets prickly. When you kept losing at blackjack, you started gritting your teeth and a few times you made a fist."

She tried not to let his observation bruise her pride. Logan had spent a lot of time learning to read people. "Do you wish you were there?"

He lifted her legs and draped them over his lap, then leaned in to nuzzle her neck. "Depends."

"On?"

"The alternative," he rasped against her ear. "If my other option is being with you, then no."

Warmth radiated deep inside her. "You know you don't have to sweet talk me to get in my pants, right?"

He flicked his tongue over her earlobe. "You asked a question. I gave you an answer."

She closed her eyes and tried to focus on the physical pleasure he was doling out and not her emotional response to his flattery. Getting accustomed to it would be a mistake. This—whatever it was—wouldn't last. He was only in Savannah temporarily, and her life was full. It was fine.

His mouth successfully distracted her. The touch of his lips was faint, coasting over her skin, heading toward her chest. He sucked her breast through the fabric of her slip. The barrier should have dulled the sensation but heightened it instead.

Drew sunk her teeth into her bottom lip. The wet fabric clung to her skin when he removed his mouth. Everything he did to her turned her to goo. "Is there anything you're not good at?"

"Staying away from you." His eyes met hers and held.

Her stomach flipped and her heart pounded so hard it made her chest sore. She'd lose her mind if she continued to examine what was happening between them. This was supposed to be her using him for sex, and vice versa, so that's what they were going to do. Shifting, she straddled him and draped her arms over his shoulder.

He tugged her slip up around her hips and gave her a devilish grin.

An ache spread through the lower half of her body. She leaned in and brushed her lips over his.

His breath was minty with a trace of tobacco. Logan cupped the back of her head and pulled her face closer, kissing her harder, stroking his tongue against hers.

She felt him growing between her thighs. This was good. How it should be. No pretty words. No intense looks. No getting caught in emotional quicksand. She didn't have the extra bandwidth to crawl out of a void with the power to consume her.

The texture of his jeans wasn't unpleasant against her sensitive, throbbing flesh, but the barrier frustrated her. She dragged her palm from his shoulder, down his chest, down his warm, hard stomach and the crisp hair that tickled her fingers, stopping at his waistband to tug at the button. It popped open and she lifted herself enough for him to work his pants off.

Her impatience only allowed for him to get them halfway down his thighs before she lowered herself, pressing her sex against his. Her eyelids flickered, the sensation too decadent to allow her to focus on anything else.

"Fucking hell," he muttered, his nose and mouth pressed to the space under her jaw. "How can this feel so fucking good and yet not enough?"

Even if she'd been capable of speech, she didn't have an answer for that. She rolled her hips, her clit skimming the hair above his cock. A pulsation of heat overpowered her senses.

He growled and curled his hands around her thighs, his fingers digging into her ass cheeks as he bumped his hips up, grinding into her.

She whimpered and dropped her forehead to his shoulder. The greedy, gnawing urge to have him inside her grew stronger. Teeth pressing into her bottom lip, she shifted so his tip pressed against her entrance.

His grip on her tightened, immobilizing her. Heavy breathing warmed the skin above her breasts, forcing her nipples to tighten further, straining against the silky fabric. "You're gonna kill me." His voice came out deep and scratchy, sending even stronger pangs of want through her.

Sorry? No sense in saying things she didn't mean. Usually, Logan pulled the strings, and she was the one disoriented and teetering toward madness. And okay, so right now she was in exactly that state, but at least he had joined her.

"I want to sink inside you so bad right now." He nipped her collarbone. "Get off me before I lose my ability to remember why I shouldn't."

She must not have responded as quicky as he'd have liked, because he slapped her ass. Drew sucked in a heap of air, then shifted her weight to one side and swung her leg over, crumpling onto the couch cushion beside him.

Logan stood, shed his jeans, snatched a condom from his bag, and sunk into this previous spot. As soon as he'd rolled the condom over his thick cock, he hooked his hand under her knee and tugged her back over top of him. The path his hands took from her knees to her thighs to the sides of her breasts elicited a gush of wetness from deep in her core. He crept higher, hooking his fingers under the straps of her slip and tugging them down her arms. Her breasts spilled out and he moved his hands back to her sides, clutching her ribs. His thumb swept out and lathered her nipple in sensation.

She brought her mouth to his and kissed him with a complete lack of inhibition. The chemistry between them was too good. Too exquisite for words.

The hand not teasing her nipple slid from her waist and gripped her hip. In a desperate jerk, he tugged her down.

She moaned against his mouth as he surged inside her, then tore her lips away to gulp for air. "Logan…"

His mouth covered her nipple, and he swirled his tongue against it, pinching the other between his fingers.

Drew's head fell back, and she slid her hand up his neck, into his hair, cupping the crown of his head to keep him right there, doing exactly what he was doing. Having him filling her felt incredible, but it wasn't enough. She shifted her hips against him, instinctively exploring, needing to find something to appease the ever-growing ache inside her.

His mouth left her breast, and his lips skimmed a path upward. He covered the space where her shoulder met her neck and sucked. "Baby, you're in the driver's seat right now. Fuck me like you want."

Drew gripped his shoulders and lifted herself up, then lowered herself. Pleasure flooded her body. She repeated the move, this time rocking into him as their pelvises met.

He groaned, the sound vibrating against her chest.

While she moved her body up and down, back and forth, he touched her everywhere. Places she didn't even know would feel so erotic to be touched.

Her thighs trembled and heat flooded her body. She moved faster, desperate for that burst of pleasure that would send her spinning into oblivion.

Logan shifted his hips, creating a new angle between them. That did it. A spiral of hot, white pleasure exploded inside her.

Frenzied moans spilled from her. She felt Logan's stare on her but couldn't bring herself to care or stop. Only when the ripples of pleasure subsided did she manage to open her eyes. She couldn't meet his gaze, though, and buried her face against his shoulder.

His hand wrapped around her hair, gripping it at the base of her neck. He tugged, forcing her to look at him. His eyes washed her in inescapable gravity, pulling her to him in a way that had nothing to do with her body.

Right then, Drew knew things had gone so much deeper than they'd agreed they would go.

28

FRESHLY-CAFFEINATED LITTLE CONTROL FREAK

LOGAN

LOGAN HAD TO SHOUT DREW'S NAME and shake her to get her to wake up.

She opened her eyes for only a second before snuggling against him.

Spending the morning in bed with her, savoring her all sleepy and sweet like this appealed to him more than it should. Leaving, going back to the Gypsy, crashing for the next several hours, should be at the top of his list.

"Baby, you have to get up."

She groaned, a protest so cute he smiled and brushed his lips across her forehead.

"Someone is knocking on the door."

The covers flew off as she shot up. "What time is it?"

He propped himself on an elbow. "Almost eight."

"Shit," she muttered and ran to the bathroom. She came back in a thin cotton robe, hastily tying the belt. "My brothers are here. Get dressed," she hissed.

He pulled his jeans on, not taking time to button them, and decided to fuck with her a little. "Do you want me to let them in?"

"Are you crazy?" She picked his shirt up off the floor and threw it at him. "Put this on and button your pants, for God's sake."

"Drew"—he grabbed her from behind and pulled her against him—"how old are you?"

"Twenty-two."

Hell. Younger than he'd thought. When he'd done intel on her, he'd guessed her approximate age based on her education level. Twenty-two was fucking young to have a master's degree. Still, she was old enough not to be embarrassed a man had spent the night. "Don't you think it's safe to assume your brothers understand you're a grown woman, and it's perfectly acceptable to have a man stay the night?"

"I'm their little sister. It's never going to be okay with my brothers if I have a man stay over." She pushed away from him and checked herself in the mirror. The knock came again, loud and impatient.

"Do you want me to sneak out the back door?" The apartment didn't have a back door.

"Of course not. I'm going to send them to get coffee and then you can sneak out the front," she explained, like it was the most obvious plan.

"I'm not sneaking out."

She shot him a look that said he better not make things difficult and headed to answer the door.

He pulled on his shirt and buttoned his pants before padding down the hallway barefoot.

A man with biceps the size of bowling balls stood in the doorway while Drew tried to convince him to go across the street and fetch her a coffee. Although he was more than twice her size, he had the same green eyes and dark auburn hair.

Bowling balls spotted him as soon as he stepped into the kitchen. His eyes narrowed and his jaw tensed.

Drew glanced behind her, then scowled, sending the message loud and clear she was pissed he'd disregarded her plan. After she'd burned a hole in his eyes with her death glare, she turned to the man in the doorway.

"Lee, this is Logan." She looked around Lee's shoulder. "Where are Aubrey and Grant?"

Logan wasn't intimidated by the brute, even if he did best him by a hundred pounds. He empathized with the guy. Anyone who'd ever showed interest in Morgan landed on his shit list. So far none had made it off.

"Grant is going to meet us here with the U-Haul. Aubrey isn't coming," he said without taking his eyes off Logan.

"Why not?" she asked.

Damn. He'd hoped to ask Aubrey about his investigation of the painting theft. Just casually, feigning mild interest.

Spending the night had taught him he was incapable of staying close enough to keep an eye on her without touching her. His conscience might be able to cope with fucking her a few times if that's all it was. Whatever this was, it wasn't something he could stop. Drew had tapped into a part of him he hadn't been aware existed. He refused to label it, but what she'd cracked open couldn't be sealed back up.

Time to switch teams. Hell, more like switch leagues. Once he uncovered who had broken into her apartment, found out who the fuck Bob's associate was, and got a lead on what had happened to her father's painting, then he'd come clean with Drew.

Lee finally ripped his murderous glare from Logan and flashed Drew a crooked smile. "He told me not to tell you, said you wouldn't understand, but I think maybe he misjudged you."

"What are you talking about?"

"He went to Destin with a girl he met. He called me last night to tell me he wouldn't be making it back in time to help with the move."

"Oh," Drew choked out.

"You going to make me stand out here all day or what?" Lee seemed to be more at ease now.

When she moved out of her brother's way, Logan moved forward and put his hand out.

Lee hesitated before giving him a firm handshake.

"Lee is the middle brother. Grant is the oldest and Aubrey is just eleven months older than me," Drew said.

"I'll get you a coffee while you get dressed. Lee, you want one?" he asked.

He shook his head. "I don't mess with that shit. Grant will probably take one, though."

Logan slipped on his shoes, then headed across the street to the coffee shop. It was a short walk, but he dragged his feet, giving Drew and her brother time to say whatever needed to be said.

He wasn't worried. She was tough enough to hold her own against anyone, even her bruiser older brother.

He returned with her Americano and two regular coffees in a drink carrier.

Lee was on the phone and Drew wasn't in sight. He set the coffees on the counter and went back outside to give him privacy. Two drags into his cigarette, Lee joined him.

"Drew is taking a shower."

"Okay." He knew what was coming.

"She's young."

"I get it. I have a sister."

"Is she Drew's age?"

"Uh, a little older." This wasn't the interrogation he had expected. Why did Lee want to know about Morgan?

"How old are *you*?"

Ah, so that was it. Lee thought he was too old for his baby sister.

"Twenty-nine. That's only seven years." Less than a decade, but not by much.

"I can do math," he snapped. "You might think she's old enough because of her age, but she isn't as…"

"Experienced?"

"Mature. Let's use that word," Lee said. "She isn't as mature as most girls her age."

He wondered if he knew his little sister had been a virgin. He doubted she would have shared that juicy tidbit with her brother, but he obviously had some knowledge of her inexperience.

"Look, I can tell she likes you a lot. That's enough for me to tolerate you, but I swear—"

"You'll kill me if I hurt her," Logan finished for him.

"I'm glad we have an understanding."

"You should give her a little more credit." Implying that Drew was immature, even though he knew Lee didn't mean any harm, rubbed him the wrong way. "She lived in New York all by herself and came home in one piece."

"Damn it," Lee snapped. "She's my little sister. I don't care how sophisticated she dresses or how cultured you think she is. She doesn't know squat about men. If you make her cry, I'll crush every bone in your body."

"Fair enough." He stubbed out his cigarette as a U-Haul truck pulled up in front of them. The man driving was older and leaner than Lee. He didn't share the strong family resemblance Drew and Lee did.

"This is Logan," Lee said to him. "Drew's boyfriend."

"About time," he muttered and shook Logan's hand. "I'm Grant."

He let the boyfriend comment slide. Correcting Lee that they were fucking, not in a relationship seemed like a terrible idea, and at this point, he'd accepted it was more than sex, although labeling it as a relationship… he wasn't sure that fit.

Most of the boxes from the kitchen had been loaded into the truck before Drew emerged. Logan was hefting a box of pots and pans when she came into the kitchen.

Her hair was pulled into a ponytail and her face was freshly scrubbed, not a speck of makeup. This was the first he'd seen her in anything other than a dress or skirt. The navy biker shorts had his mind drifting to last night when he'd been between her incredible thighs. She'd knotted a white David Bowie T-shirt at her hip. The shirt had been cut so it fell off one shoulder, revealing the strap of a sports bra the same color as her shorts.

"Damn," he muttered under his breath.

"Did you say something?" she asked as she reached for her coffee.

He set the box on the counter and crowded her against the cabinets. "You look fucking hot in Spandex."

He nuzzled her neck, glad her brothers were occupied taking apart her bedframe. "Lee gave me the hurt-her-and-you-die speech."

"Good." The stutter in her breathing made his dick jerk. He worked his hand under her shirt, skating his palm up toward her tits. If they were alone, he'd be pulling down those goddamn stretchy shorts and making her come on his face.

"My bed tonight," he muttered against her ear.

"I can't. It's going to take at least two trips to move all my stuff to my dad's, and I'm waitressing the dinner shift. I need to squeeze in a few hours of work on my collection, and the only time I'm going to have to do that is late tonight."

Her workaholic tendencies posed a problem. Keeping tabs on her until he could be sure she was safe would be difficult.

He pressed his hands against the counter edge and straightened his elbows, bringing them eye to eye. "You have to eat and sleep. So, do it with me."

"Is that all we're going to do?"

He winged an eyebrow up. "What else would we do?"

Her eye roll made him grin. "I can't get sidetracked. This unexpected move is already putting me behind schedule."

"How about this? You go to the studio now, while I help your brothers move everything, then I pick you up from work later."

Why did he have such a hard time reading her? The look she gave him could be gratitude *or* hesitancy. He didn't fucking know.

"Wouldn't you rather work on your collection now, while you're freshly caffeinated? Or later when you're exhausted from moving and waiting tables?" If he had to list the pros and cons of the alternative he was offering, so be it. "I'm better at heavy lifting. It'll get done faster with me helping."

"That is so sexist."

"It's facts, baby. You wanna compare biceps?"

Her gaze flitted to his arms.

"Or we can ask your brothers whose help they'd prefer." It'd probably be a relief not having this little control freak supervising.

"I don't—"

He kissed her to shut her up. She could probably come up with fifty-two bullshit reasons why his offer wasn't the most sensible and beneficial option.

A muffled noise of euphoria escaped her mouth and shot straight to his cock.

Logan put a hand on the small of her back and urged her closer. At the full body contact, her posture liquefied.

He pulled his mouth from hers. "Text me later with what time to pick you up."

The reluctance faded from her face. "Okay."

Lee's voice cut through their private moment. "Can you stop defiling my little sister and help us move this mattress?"

"I have to help move a mattress," Logan said, as if she hadn't been present for her brother's demand. "I'll finish defiling you later."

29

OKAY, KILLGRAVE

LOGAN

"TELL ME THAT YOU HAD NOTHING TO DO with Drew Miller's apartment being ransacked," Logan demanded, not amused at being back in Bob's company.

While he'd helped Drew's brothers move all her shit to her dad's house, he'd asked Morgan to discreetly keep watch over her. If she spotted anyone suspicious lurking around the studio, she was to call him. Both crimes had occurred while no one was home, probably deliberately. That was a good sign that whoever it was didn't have any intention of hurting anyone.

"What are you a cop now?" Bob asked.

"Answer me. Did you have anything to do with it?" Actually, he hoped Bob was behind it. Better the devil he knew, and all that.

Bob ran a wad of twenties through his bill counter. Five fat stacks covered his desk blotter. "You left me in the lurch. Eric was more than happy to fill your shoes."

"Eric?" he shouted, his head ready to explode into smithereens. "Why the fuck did he think Drew knew anything?"

He shrugged. "Why did you?"

Logan's head throbbed and his eye twitched. There was nothing in the file he'd given to Bob about Drew. "You had me followed?"

"Don't act so violated."

"Last time we talked, you said this prick blackmailing you would leave you alone if you cut me loose. Why do you have Eric sniffing around?"

Bob cleared his throat once, twice, three times before grabbing the trashcan under his desk and hocking a loogie into it. "I got to cover all my bases, Cash. Maybe he'll lose interest in me once he finds out you're no longer part of my operation. Maybe he won't. I've looked over your intel—or should I say *lack* of intel—it's worthless. I need something to satisfy him when he contacts me."

"It's been over two weeks since I gave you that. You haven't heard from him?"

"Nope."

That made as much sense as everything else in this whole debacle. Logan cracked his knuckles. "I want to talk to him. *Today.*"

"I don't have his number."

He groaned. "Fine. Tell him when he calls you."

Bob glanced up and shook his head. "Didn't anyone ever teach you not to poke a bear?"

"I'm not a pussy like you. This guy doesn't scare me."

"Then you're stupid. He *knows* things, Cash."

"About you. He isn't blackmailing me, Bob. And I'm not going to give him the opportunity. He's a mere mortal, like the rest of us, vulnerable to being manipulated if I get into his mind. And believe me, I will."

"Okay, Killgrave, I'll tell him to call you. Don't mean he will." Bob kept on running cash through the machine, not sparing Logan a glance.

He ran a hand through his hair. Bob was right. He had to force this guy's hand if he wanted to guarantee he'd call him. "Tell him I know who took the painting."

Eventually, he'd find out who stole it, but he wasn't going to get any closer to that information until he talked to this guy. He had a feeling he knew more about the crime than Drew did.

"And call your lackey off," Logan said. "I don't want to hear that Eric has come within a hundred yards of Drew."

He tried to convince himself Eric being behind the break in as a good thing. Eric wasn't dangerous. If he set off that temper of Drew's, he'd end up either crying or pissing himself. Hell, it didn't have to be one or the other. That little bitch could wet his pants while tears ran down his face and he begged for mercy. Better still, now Logan knew who he needed to make suffer for vandalizing her apartment.

Bob's weight shifted in the chair, the vinyl squeaking. "I ain't doin' no such thing until I know this jackoff ain't gonna sell me up the river."

"Rein Eric in, or I'll drown you in the fucking river."

30

DEVIOUS

Drew

THE KITCHEN HAD CLOSED, and Drew was down to two tables. The performer tucked in the corner of the outdoor seating area was a few songs into his last set, and the table of six—a group of couples visiting Savannah for the first time—sang along like tweens at a Taylor Swift concert. She banked on them drinking at least two more rounds.

Her other guests, a couple, looked to be in their late sixties. They'd ordered dessert and were enjoying the entertainment—the drunk tourists, not the paid performer.

Drew placed a slice of key lime pie and a peach cobbler ala mode on her serving tray and carried it through the indoor portion. Her body moved like a rusty bike chain, her joints protesting and her muscles jerking. According to her phone, she'd taken nearly 20,000 steps today. She was thankful Logan had coerced her into working on her collection this morning, saving her from a long night at the studio.

Turns out, he not only had a talent for aggravating the hell out of her, he shined in the altruism department. And when he decided he knew what was best for her, he was relentless in getting his way. Maybe that wasn't such a bad thing. Sometimes, she took her autonomy a little too far.

Damn it. She had to stop thinking about him all the time. Forming an attachment would be the worst thing she could do.

After delivering the older couple their desserts, she checked on her other table, who did indeed want another round. She went to the bar and waited for Aidan to finish serving his bar patrons.

This was her first night working with him since before the wedding. Thankfully, he'd kept their exchanges strictly work-related.

"Another round for the six-top?" he asked while gathering up empty bottles and glasses customers had left behind.

She nodded, then rested her elbows on the bar flap and watched the one-man act strum his guitar and sing.

Aidan set the last of the six drinks on her tray and flicked a glance at her. "I've been wanting to apologize all night for how I behaved at your friend's house. I was a total asshole and I'm sorry. I don't know what I was thinking."

Did Aidan have a twin or something? Aaron, perchance? That was one of the sincerest apologies she'd ever heard.

She didn't believe in second chances. Cross her once, and that was it. Forgiveness took compassion and understanding, and well, those didn't come naturally to her.

Shitty personality aside, Aidan was a topnotch bartender. Customers complimented his cocktails, and his ability to remember her drink orders and make them lightning fast made her job easier and boosted her tips. They'd never be besties, but it'd be nice to work together without contention. So, she'd make an exception this time.

"If I accept your apology, do you promise you'll never pull that shit again? With *any* woman?" She needed to clarify that last bit. Too many men who behaved the way he had walked the earth. If she could influence even one of them to have more respect for women as a whole, she'd take it.

He nodded vigorously.

"Fine. You are forgiven, but that's not an invitation to ask me out. Got it?"

"Yes. Absolutely."

She pulled her tray off the bar and went to serve the drinks.

The tourists decided they must have a round of shots before they closed their tab, so Drew went back to the bar and waited while Aidan put the ingredients for the specialty shots in a shaker.

"I felt terrible leaving your friends without a photographer so close to the wedding. Please tell me you found someone to take the job."

It would be petty to tell him she'd gone home with the guy who'd replaced him, right?

"She did," Logan said over her shoulder, scaring the bejesus out of her.

She spun and grabbed hold of his biceps to balance herself. Christ, how had he gotten this close without her hearing him approach? She started to tell him he was early, but his mouth slanting over hers prevented it.

One hand on her hip and the other cupping her jaw, he kissed her so thoroughly everything south of her belly button clenched. When he finished, she stared at him, stunned. He'd kissed her in public. *Really* kissed her. It felt very relationship-y.

Then again, so did picking her up from work. So did helping her pack and move. So did meeting her brothers. So did spending the night together two nights in a row.

Logan smirked and gave her ponytail a quick tug.

"You're early." When she'd texted him to give him the time she needed to be picked up, she'd told him to park on Bay Street and wait for her in his car. She should have known the rebel in Logan—which undoubtedly made up no less than ninety percent of his personality—would lead him to do the exact opposite.

"I'll sit at the bar and have a drink until you're done."

A drink at the bar. The bar Aidan was manning. She half turned to gauge his reaction to Logan's shameless public display of affection.

Aidan's expression didn't hold any detectable jealousy or bitterness. Maybe it'd be safe to leave them unsupervised for a minute or two.

"This is Logan. He, uh, photographed the wedding."

Aidan's head angled a bit to one side. It was obvious the second he pieced together that his actions had been the catalyst to her and Logan getting together. His jaw drew taut and the veins in his forearm bulged as his hand tightened around the cocktail shaker.

Drew put her back fully to Logan and gave Aidan a look that broadcast a warning not to do anything stupid that would undo the progress he'd made with his apology.

His shoulders slouched a smidge. Gaze climbing and shifting beyond her, he set down the shaker and extended his hand across the bar. "Aidan."

Logan's chest brushed against her shoulder blades as he outstretched his arm and shook hands with Aidan. "How's it going?"

"Not bad." He picked the shaker up and poured the shots into the glasses he'd lined up on a little wooden paddle with a slot for each. He raised his gaze from the shots to Drew. "If you wanna get out of here, tell them they have to close their tab and open a new one at the bar."

"Thanks." She waited a beat until he'd headed toward the other end of the bar and turned to Logan. "Take a seat. I'll be back in a minute."

The group whined, but good naturedly, after she gave them Aidan's message. She checked in with the older couple to see if they needed anything further, and when they declined, she pulled the bill folder from her apron and set it on their table.

One down. One to go.

Logan had taken the empty stool all the way at the end and had already been served what looked like a whiskey neat.

She watched him out of the corner of her eye as she tapped the POS screen and waited for the bill to print. Her heart raced from the weight of his stare.

One member of the six already had his credit card out and handed it to her before she had a chance to set the small leather folder on the table. Her other customers were already on their way toward the exit and had left cash to cover their bill and her tip.

After taking the six back their receipt, she moved close to Logan. "I already cleaned up the rest of the deck, so after I clear these last two tables, we can go."

"Take your time." He nudged his head in Aidan's direction. "So, that's Matt and Claire's original photographer?"

She nodded.

"You never did tell me what you did to the poor guy to make him quit."

Even though she'd told Logan that Aidan had quit, rather than been fired, it chafed that he assumed that *she* was responsible. "I don't want to talk about this."

"He doesn't seem easily rattled. You must have really let that temper of yours fly."

She gritted her teeth. "I didn't make him quit."

"Did you do that thing where your face turns purple, and you look like you're deciding on the best murder weapon? It's honestly terrifying."

Her back tensed and her throat constricted. Logan didn't know what had happened and she didn't think it would be good for him to find out, but his amusement was pushing her to her snapping point.

"Yeah, like that." He pointed at her.

"He didn't quit," she blurted out. "Claire fired him."

His face sobered and he swiveled toward her on his stool. "Why?" The uneasiness in his tone had her wishing she'd kept her big mouth shut.

"Let it go."

"The fuck if I will. Either you tell me, or I'll make *him* tell me."

She took a deep breath, released it, and rubbed her hands over her face. "He tried to make a move on me."

His gaze shot to Aidan, who was busy closing out tabs at the other POS, then back to her. "Tried." The word came out flat. He studied her face, as though he'd be able to learn more details about the incident just by looking at her. "Then what happened?"

"I pushed him away."

"Keep going," he said through his teeth.

This conversation was headed nowhere good. "He persisted."

Now it was Logan's face turning purple. "How *persistent* was he?"

"It's not as bad as you're thinking."

"Did he put his mouth on you?"

She shook her head.

"His hands?"

She took a deep breath and nodded.

"Where?" The chill in his voice nearly made her shiver.

"Logan, I work here. I don't have an overflowing bank account like you do. My tips from the entire past three months were stolen. I need this job. Not to mention, I'm exhausted. If you put your hands on him, someone will call the cops and we'll be stuck here making statements when we could be on your boat, where I'd like to get naked and then sleep for several hours."

"Where did he touch you?"

"Let this go right now, or you can drop me off at my dad's house when I get off."

That seemed to get through to him. He faced forward, his expression stony as he took a drink.

"I'm going to take that table their check and clear the tables. Promise me you're not going to make a scene."

He continued to stare ahead.

"Logan."

"Fine," he muttered, dragging a hand through his hair.

She waited a moment, then decided to trust him to behave, and walked away. After serving the check, she bussed the other table, keeping a watchful eye on Logan.

He'd not made any moves to confront Aidan, but his tense posture showed it was costing him. He flipped a poker chip back and forth across his knuckles, his jaw tight.

She wasn't afraid to set and hold boundaries. Good thing he wasn't testing this one, though, because his protective, possessive vibe was sexy as hell, and going home alone would be pure misery.

As fast as her tired feet would carry her, she took the full bus pan to the kitchen, then ducked into the locker area outside of her manager's office to grab her bag. She'd never changed clothes so fast in her life. No telling what would happen if Logan was left to his own devices.

The seat Logan had been in was empty when she came back onto the deck. Her stomach knotted and her gaze darted around the area. Aidan was in one piece, which kept her from full-blown panic. She turned and spotted him leaning against the wall next to the door to the dining room, phone to his ear.

The predatory look on his face as he explored her body with his eyes pushed that knot in her stomach into her throat. "Gotta go." He tapped his phone and shoved it into his pocket.

He pushed from the wall and stalked toward her. His hand settled on her waist and his mouth brushed her ear. "Wearing panties today?"

Heat pulsated through her core. The black mini skirt hugged her hips and would have shown her ass cheeks if not for the subtle flounce ruffle at the bottom. The blouse she'd paired it with was a loose-fitting, short dolman-sleeve, in a faux-wrap style. The classic look called for statement shoes, so she'd spent forty minutes digging through boxes, looking for her turquoise patent leather wedges.

"I'm not telling," she whispered back.

He took a step back and gave her another once over. "That's

alright. I'd rather you show me."

She'd never blushed so hard.

Drew stopped on the sidewalk along Bay Street while Logan pulled his key fob from his pocket and hit the button.

He looked left, then right. Depending on how he'd walked down to River Street, it would be easy to get disoriented and forget where he'd parked. Up the street, headlights and taillights flashed. He grabbed her hand and pulled her in that direction.

They stopped next to a four-door sedan. Logan walked around the rear of the car and made his way to the driver's side.

"What happened to your car?" Maybe it was in the shop, and this was a rental. A junkie one. A quick glance inside the window changed her mind about that possibility. There were clothes scattered across the backseat and a bunch of other clutter.

"Nothing." He opened the door and stared at her over the roof.

"Okay, so…"

"I agreed not to put my fist through that prick's face, but I didn't promise I wouldn't fuck with him."

"This is Aidan's car?" Her voice came out in squeaks. "How did you get his keys?"

"They were behind the bar."

"How did you get behind the bar without—" She shook her head. "Never mind. What the hell do you plan to do with his car?"

"Relocate it."

"He'll think it was stolen."

He shrugged.

"He'll call the cops."

Logan fished in his pocket, then tossed his keys over the hood. "You don't have to come. My car's back a few spaces. I won't be long." He folded into the car, shut the door, and the engine roared to life.

Drew looked at the keys to his Audi, then back at Aidan's car. Shit. She yanked the door handle and got in. "Great. Now I'm an accomplice to grand theft auto," she said while securing the seatbelt.

His laugh boomed through the vehicle as he pulled onto the main drag. They came up to a red light and his gaze took a slow sweep of her. "That face? That skirt? There's not a cop in this city that would arrest you just for sitting in the passenger side of a stolen car."

"What if he's gay? Or married? Or what if it's a woman? A straight woman."

"Baby..." The light turned green, and he accelerated. "Sexual orientation is irrelevant. One look at you, and anyone would turn fluid."

"You're crazy," she muttered. Her lips wouldn't stop from quirking into a smile, though.

He turned left, drove a block, then hung another left. The parking space he pulled into was one block shy of the cross street of where Aidan had parked his car.

"Um, isn't it going to be kind of obvious when the police find his car a block away from where he parked it that it getting stolen wasn't random?"

"No, they're going to think he's a fuckin' idiot who forgot where he parked his car."

"His stolen keys would indicate otherwise."

Logan dropped the keys in the cupholder. "They didn't get stolen. They're right here. He's got a knack for forgetting where he leaves stuff, huh?"

"You're ridiculous." And devious, which made her want him even more. What was wrong with her?

31

WRECK ME, RUIN YOU

LOGAN

LOGAN HADN'T SEEN DREW IN TWO DAYS. Even though she hadn't outright asked for it, her excuses for not being able to see him indicated she needed space. So, he gave it to her. As much as he could, anyway. He'd limited and timed his calls so that they'd be on the phone while she walked to work, or when she'd be leaving the studio after dark. Logic told him the odds of her being harmed were slim, but not seeing her, not being able to touch her, turned him irrational.

He glanced up the dock, then checked his watch. She should have been here thirty minutes ago. Anxiety tormented him, but it stemmed from a gut feeling that her standing him up was a deliberate choice.

The onrush of their entanglement freaked her out. She hadn't said it. It did, though.

It's not like he wasn't freaked out too. Nothing should have happened between them. He was no good for her. He never should have kissed her. Never should have let her spend the night. Never should have crossed her path, to be fair. It hadn't gotten him anywhere with the assignment Bob had dumped on him. The only thing it had got him was a massive amount of guilt.

Life would be so much simpler if he'd never met Drew. He couldn't get the sassy-salty, secretly playful, gorgeous woman out of his damn head.

Where was she?

His mind went places it shouldn't. Dark places. Places where fucks like that bartender she worked with touched what was *his*. Drew had yet to share another shift with him, but she was a knockout and men who believed they were entitled to touch women without consent weren't a minority.

The dark places weren't the only problem for his psyche. Dopey, absolutely absurd fantasies plagued him. All the shit he wanted to do with her. *With* her, not *to* her. Travel. Spend time with his family. Go to that fucking birthday party for her godchildren.

Logan had gone soft.

So soft that he'd gone above and beyond to tempt her into spending the evening with him. Promised her a sunset dinner cruise. He'd cleaned the Gypsy and fueled her up. Cooked dinner. Spent an hour selecting mood music.

At least it kept him busy while he waited for Bob's puppeteer to contact him. He needed to get to the bottom of this stolen painting bullshit, and he didn't have much to work with. Drew's brother might have information he could use, but he'd yet to meet him.

He pulled his phone from his pocket and found Drew's name in his recent calls. Standing him up was not going to fly. If he believed she wasn't at all interested in spending time with him, that'd be a different story. She needed to get over this idea that he'd get in the way of achieving her goals. He might distract her a little, but she needed someone to pull her out when she became too immersed in her work. Not someone. *Him*. Logan wanted to be that for her. When she needed to recharge her batteries, he wanted to be her power supply.

The second he tapped her name on his phone screen, she appeared on the dock, a white baby doll dress swishing against her thighs as she strode to him. The silhouette suited her curvy body. Navy-blue trim below her neckline emphasized the swell of her breasts. Half of her hair was rolled up and secured on top of her head like a pinup girl, exposing gold anchors dangling from her ears. Cherry-red fuck-me heels held in place by a strap that curved up her heel accentuated her long, silky legs.

The vibe she was rocking turned him on with such intensity he'd already decided exactly how he'd fuck her—with the skirt of her dress shoved up and the top pulled down, her ass on the small built-in desk across from his bed, in those shoes with his arms tucked under her knees, raising them next to her tits.

"Sorry I'm late," she said, stopping on the dock a foot from the Gypsy, not looking a bit sorry. "The police found my computer and I went to pick it up."

"That's good news." But not really news to him. He'd tracked down Eric, and with a little persuasion, convinced him to hand over her computer. Then he'd slipped it onto a detective's desk in the police station without being seen.

Logan had wiped it for prints, since his were on it along with Eric's, but man, he'd love to see Eric in handcuffs. The computer was easy enough to return to Drew, the money was going to be trickier. Eric claimed to have spent it all and after seeing the new rims on his car, Logan believed it. Still, he'd find a way to right things and restore her stolen funds without her getting suspicious.

"Take those off," he said, pointing at her shoes.

"Excuse me?" With the face she made, you'd have thought he asked her to strip naked right there.

Later, on the carpet inside the cabin, she could strut around in them as much as she wanted. "You'll fuck up my teak."

She stared at him blankly.

"The wood," he said, gesturing at the immaculately varnished deck.

With a huff, she held onto the piling and slipped out of her shoes.

She stuck them into the big bag slung over her shoulder. An embroidered red anchor decorated the front, tying it in with her nautical aesthetic.

He took the bag from her, set it on a deck chair, then took her hand to assist her onto the boat. Once both feet had landed firmly on the gunwale, he put his hands on her waist, lifted her and spun, then lowered her to the deck.

After steadying her, he gave her another once-over. "Where's your sailor hat?"

Her jaw dropped. "Are you making fun of me?"

Very slowly, he shook his head. "I like you all tricked out. It's sexy as fuck."

Her gaze slid to the side, like the compliment didn't affect her, but she pressed her lips together to ward off a smile.

If she'd been on time, he'd take her inside and make his fantasy a reality. It wouldn't be much of a sunset cruise if the sun had already set, though. Good thing he'd already warmed up the motor.

Those green eyes he'd never tire of looking into shifted back to him, first meeting his, then dropping to his mouth. For once, he read her without ambiguity. She wanted to know why he hadn't kissed her yet.

Good question. One he couldn't answer. Because why the fuck hadn't he?

Logan cupped her jaw and leaned in. She met him halfway, causing him to smile against her lips, foiling the *not seeing you for two days wrecked me* kiss he'd intended to lay on her. Getting his mouth to cooperate with what he wanted to do failed. Each attempt turned into a quick smooch; his lips insistent on pulling into a smile.

He gave up and moved back, leaving space between their upper bodies, but keeping his hand splayed an inch above her ass, her thighs pinned to his. This view was magic. Face still angled up, eyes hooded, lips parted and waiting, clearly wanting more than he'd given. His smile grew even wider.

The needy daze vanished. Her shoulders squared, her softened posture stiffening. "What? Why are you smiling like that?"

"Because you missed kissing me. *A lot.*"

"Oh, get over yourself."

"How much did you think about it while we were apart?" He leaned in and whispered against her ear, "Did you have trouble sleeping? You know I wouldn't have turned you away if you showed up here in the middle of the night, right?"

Her warm breath trailed across his throat as she angled her head in his direction. "I have enough bad habits."

Logan tucked his knuckle under her chin and tipped it up, locking his eyes to hers. "I'm bad?"

"So bad," she said in a low, breathy voice.

He growled and sealed his mouth to hers. This kiss sure as hell didn't lack intensity. It said I'm-going-to-ruin-you-like-you've-ruined-me.

Drew wound her arms around his neck and melted into him. She tasted so fucking good.

He continued to nip and suck at her lips as his hands drifted lower, finding the edge of her dress and sliding under it. The fabric shifted, riding up on his arms as he explored higher up her thighs.

An unintelligible murmur escaped her throat. She pushed on his forearms.

He tore his mouth from hers and dragged in air like he'd broke the surface after a deep dive. "What's wrong?"

"We're in public."

Right. The marina only had a few slips, but there'd been movement this evening. They could pick this up once they got out into the Sound, where they'd be isolated.

"Want a drink before we head out?" he asked, reluctantly letting go of her.

She nodded.

"Wine? Beer? Liquor?"

"Wine."

He took her hand and pulled her along with him into the cabin and to the galley where he poured them each a glass. "Can you help me cast off?"

"Are you serious? What am I supposed to do?"

"Steer." He went up to the living room where the helm was located and started the motor. She appeared at his side, sipping on her wine. He took her glass and set it on a side table. "You can't drink while you're behind the helm."

"I'm not driving."

"You have to."

"No, I don't." She crossed her arms and shook her head.

"You were late, so yes, you do. It'll take longer if I do everything myself, and I don't want you to fall in trying to jump back on after you release the lines. Come on, don't be a wuss."

He positioned her in front of the wheel and showed her the controls. "You steer just like you would your car. This is the throttle, if you push it forward, the boat will move forward, if you pull back on it, it will reverse. Keep it in neutral until I tell you." He put her hand over the lever and showed her how positioning the throttle lever straight up and down would keep the motor idling.

"I can't do this," she said, shaking her head.

"Yes, you can." He guided her hands to the wheel and wrapped her fingers around it. "Keep it straight, just like this."

He left the cabin and hopped onto the dock to release the stern and spring lines.

"Logan! Please don't make me do this."

He laughed and walked toward the bow. "Put the throttle in forward, but not too much," he shouted from the dock. He waited a minute and then gave the command again. "C'mon, Drew, you got this."

The *Gypsy* pitched forward. He let the bowline loose, waited for the yacht to get far enough out of the slip, then leapt back on.

He hurried into the cabin and stood behind Drew. She tried to move out of his way, but he held her there while he maneuvered the boat out of the marina. When they reached open water, he let the motor idle and pulled up the fenders.

"That was scary," she said, as he returned and took the wheel. "I could have crashed your boat."

He rolled his eyes. "Come back here."

"No way. I'm not getting anywhere near that wheel again."

He pushed on the throttle and headed down the Wilmington River.

Drew stood at the open cabin door, watching the marina disappear behind them. As it turned into a tiny speck, she picked up her glass of wine and took a seat on the deck.

He navigated the boat southeast, where the river spilled into the Wassaw Sound, then moored in a secluded cove where the water was calm, and no other boaters would bother them.

Logan set up a small table on the deck. Then he served her his chicken marsala. He'd made a trip to the gourmet grocery store and bought all high-quality ingredients. He'd also hit the liquor store and got a few slightly extravagant bottles of wine to pair with the meal. But just in case, he'd gotten a case of the beer they'd drank after packing up her apartment.

"You cooked for me?" she asked, eyes big as he put the plates on the table.

"I invited you for dinner. Did you think I was going to give you a bowl of cereal?"

"I thought you'd get takeout, I guess."

He sat across from her and stroked his jaw. "You always underestimate me."

"How was I supposed to know you could cook? How did you

even pull this off? Your kitchen looks like it belongs in a kindergarten classroom."

He laughed. "I've got skills."

"Thank you," she said softly. "For inviting me. For cooking for me. For all of it. It's incredible."

Hearing appreciation for his efforts made it all worth it. He couldn't think of a more intimate date than this. The two of them surrounded by the calm water, the bluesy jazz turned on low, the warm glow of the candle in the glass lantern as the sun sank beyond the horizon.

"We could make it a recurring thing." *Play it cool.* Either they did or they didn't. No big deal. No reason for his stomach to knot waiting for her response.

"For how long?" She pushed a mushroom around the plate with her fork.

"However long you want."

"Or until you leave," she said, eyes glued to her plate.

"I'm not going to leave."

Her gaze slowly lifted. "Why not? Did something happen with your sister?"

"No."

They stared at each other for several seconds.

"You're staying for me," she finally said. Then her tone turned playful and teasing. "You like me."

He grinned, then tipped his head. "Yes, I like you. Finish your dinner so I can show you how much."

32

DARLING, YOU...ARE A MANIAC

DREW WOKE UP ALONE. AGAIN.

She dressed in the navy-blue pajama shorts and matching top she had packed but hadn't put on last night before she fell asleep tangled in Logan, then climbed the stairs leading to the living room.

Logan sagged against the arm of the captain's chair, his feet dangling, his hand clutching an empty double old-fashioned glass.

After taking the glass out of his hand, she sniffed it. Bourbon. Last time she'd spent the night, she'd woken up just before dawn as he'd stumbled into his bedroom, smelling like he'd bathed in the stuff. She'd pretended to be asleep, and he'd snuggled up to her and passed out.

She set the glass on the coffee table, then put her hand on his arm. "Logan."

He jumped, almost falling out of the chair, then tipped his head back, eyes shut tight and groaned. Not exactly the good morning she had been looking forward to.

"Do you always drink yourself to sleep or is this another defect that only occurs when I'm around?"

He scrubbed his face with his hands, then shook his head and blinked, as if in doing so, he could purge his hangover.

He stood, then tried to move around her without answering.

She didn't budge, glaring at him, waiting for his answer.

"Mostly when you're around."

"How flattering."

He shoved his hands into his hair.

She searched his face for an indication of his mood. *Damned poker face.*

Even though they were toe to toe, it felt as though they were worlds apart. A tangle of emotions swamped her. Insecurity being the strongest, circling her throat like a noose. Had she crossed some unspoken boundary? Maybe he'd expected her to be gone come morning.

"I don't have to sleep over if it's a problem."

Logan turned his head toward the open cabin door. Nothing but marsh and horizon in view. His attention swiveled back to her, his expression a mix of boredom and exasperation. "You think I expected you to swim to shore?"

Point made. If he didn't want her to spend the night, he probably wouldn't have held her hostage in the middle of Wassaw Sound.

"Working today?" Without waiting for her answer, he slinked down the steps to the galley.

"I work every day," she said, following him. "Do you have plans?"

"I'm taking Morgan to lunch." He shook coffee grounds right from the bag into his coffee maker's filter, then hit the start button. "It's her birthday."

He reached into an above-head cabinet and pulled out two coffee mugs.

"Did you get her a present?"

"Buying her lunch isn't enough?"

"Not on her birthday. You know girls like presents, right?"

He went into his bedroom and came back out with a small box, its blue color leaving no question where it had been purchased. He tossed it to her.

"Can you teach my brothers how to shop?"

"Morgan is hard to shop for. I got that the last time I was in New York."

She opened the box. It was a wide silver cuff bracelet embellished with anchors linked together by a chain and bordered by coiled ropes. Impressive taste. "When were you in New York?"

"About three months ago. Uncle John likes shopping there. He says the stores on the strip rip you off with their jacked-up prices. I tried to tell him that with airfare and hotel prices, he ends up spending more, but he won't listen. He can't stand to feel like he's been swindled."

Logan poured them each a cup of coffee, then handed her one. His groggy state seemed to clear after he'd taken a sip. His eyes turned stormy as they swept from her head to her toes.

Her nipples scraped against the cotton of her pajama top as they hardened. She sucked in her bottom lip in an effort not to moan.

He stalked to her and set his mug on the table behind her. "Maybe I should give you that bracelet. It goes with the outfit you came strutting up the dock in last night."

"One, I did not strut, and two, I'm not accepting a gift that was intended for your sister." She put the bracelet back in its box and shoved it at him.

"You always strut." He put the box on the table.

"No, I don't."

"Yeah, baby, you do." Before she had a chance to argue back, he kissed her. The buttons on her pajama top popped open as he tugged at the fabric.

His lips left hers and lingered close to her ear. "I like your jammies."

He ran his hands inside the opening and trailed his fingers down the valley between her breasts.

Shivers rushed through her. Her body said, "Bring it." But her mind wasn't on board. It was at the marina, where she'd expected to be headed this morning.

"I have to get back," she whispered.

His body tensed, making her wish she could take back what she'd said. Logan brushed her hair over her shoulder and stared into her eyes. "You never played hooky, did you?"

She shook her head. "Intentionally sabotaging my goals? Not my idea of a good time."

"Sabotaging your—" He stared up at the ceiling for a few moments. "Don't you get burnt out working nonstop?"

"No." Like everyone else, she got tired, but she made a point to take care of herself. She ate right. Didn't mess with drugs. Drank in moderation. Got plenty of sleep.

"What about your creativity?"

"What about it?" Her being a slave to her work shouldn't be news to Logan. It'd seemed like he understood and accepted it, maybe even respected it. Now, she wasn't so sure.

His fingers leisurely stroked the skin above her waistband. "You never get in a slump and need to recharge?"

"My feelings don't dictate whether I create or not. I don't wait for inspiration to strike. I strike."

His caresses came to a halt, and he shook his head, like he was trying to keep her words from embedding into his memory. "You are a maniac."

Fantastic. Just what every girl wants to hear as she's standing nearly naked in front of the guy she's into. Drew narrowed her eyes and raised her arms to push away from him.

He grabbed her wrists and pulled her arms around his neck, then crushed his mouth to hers.

She resisted, trying to wriggle free from his grip.

Logan groaned into her mouth and dug his fingers deeper into her hip. In a slow, deliberate move, he slipped his hand from the back of her head, down her spine, over her ass and under her knee. Simultaneously, he dipped his pelvis at the same time he lifted her leg, rubbing his hard length against her.

The throbbing between her thighs began sharply, taking her breath away. Drew tightened her arms around his neck, which delivered an exquisite shiver as her nipples dragged against the crisp hair on his chest.

His tongue rubbed hers in a rhythm that matched the pulsing of her clit.

Her moan broke the connection between their mouths, but he wasn't fazed. His lips found her throat and planted hot, wet kisses along it.

"Logan…" Oh, hell. Did that pathetic, begging tone belong to her?

Her feet left the ground. She squealed as he lifted her into his arms and headed for the bedroom.

Toes connecting with the soft carpet, she held on tightly to his shoulders as he set her down.

Movements as fluid as mercury, Logan sunk to the mattress edge, the rough texture of his palms against her breasts stirring an intense warmth that spread over her like sunshine.

Drew lowered her face to his, wanting a hot and wet, hungry type of kiss, and that's exactly what she got. He moved down her body and placed a path of wet kisses from her throat to her waistband. She tried to reach for the tie on his pajama bottoms, but he wrapped his fingers around hers and squeezed.

"Patience," he whispered, then ran his tongue across her neck and captured her earlobe between his lips. She couldn't suppress her whimper.

"That's not one of my virtues."

His hot breath tickled her ear. "I know."

Without warning, her top hit the floor, and she landed on her back on top of the bed. Logan covered her body with his. His tongue flicked her nipple, once, twice, before his lips closed around it.

She moaned and ran her hands through his hair, moving restlessly beneath him.

He discarded his bottoms and then slowly inched her shorts down. Being skin to skin felt so good her eyes fluttered shut in ecstasy.

"Look at me," he said in a gravelly voice as he rolled on a condom.

She opened her eyes and stared up at him. He stared back, entering her without any hurry. Each time he withdrew, he came back to her ever so slowly, his warm chest and his hard stomach skimming against her.

The consuming sensations that swept over her left her feeling raw and powerless. Not feelings she'd normally embrace, but with Logan, she didn't mind so much.

His dark gaze held her captive in the dim bedroom.

Her chest clenched, every part of her body aching, but in very different ways. She reveled in Logan's mastery over her body, but the way he unarmed her emotionally…not so much.

She slid her hands up his chest and around his neck, trying to focus only on her physical responses to him.

He turned his head and kissed the inside of her biceps, then pressed his forehead to hers. "I wanna see you lose control," he whispered against her lips.

With those words her orgasm grabbed hold and dragged her into oblivion. She moaned his name.

"Not yet, baby. Not yet." He braced himself above her, both palms flat on the mattress by her head.

She met his gaze, paralyzed by the restrained primal lust there. Waves of ecstasy rippled through her as he continued his slow, controlled movements. Her eyes started to roll back in her head, and she gasped and moaned.

"Oh, fuck." He buried his face in her hair and groaned as the force of his thrusts increased. As the spasming of her walls slowed, so did his movements, until he stopped altogether and sunk onto her, not crushing her, but lending enough of his weight to immobilize her.

When her breathing leveled, he pushed his body off her, kneeling between her thighs. He slid his arms around her, holding on while he flipped over, positioning her to straddle him. His hands rubbed up and down her thighs, creating a friction that rebuilt her subsiding lust. "Stay with me. Fuck work."

She stiffened. It wasn't fair for him to ask that right now. Not when she was feeling all warm and dreamy.

Logan pulled her against his chest and rubbed her back until she softened into him. "Let me show you what playing hooky is all about."

That was like asking a fish to spend a day on land. "Do you want me to have an anxiety attack?"

"No," he whispered. "I'm just curious what will happen if you learn to breathe."

Her face scrunched. "I'm not that uptight."

"Prove it."

Drew sighed so hard her chest vibrated against his. They weren't doing this. When her schedule would allow, she'd spend time with Logan, but she wasn't going to change her plans to do it. Besides, he had plans of his own. "Did you forget it's your sister's birthday?"

He squeezed his eyes shut and put a hand to his forehead. "Damn it, it's going to take a good forty minutes to get back to the marina and get everything secured. Morgan is going to kill me if we're late."

"We? I'm not going."

He bumped his hips upward and gave her ass a playful swat. "The fuck you aren't. Get that sweet ass in the shower."

She rolled off him and crossed her arms. "I'm not crashing your sister's birthday lunch."

33

INSOMNIACS IN GLASS HOUSES

Drew

"I'M NOT GOING TO BE ABLE TO USE CHOPSTICKS if you're wearing that...that..." Logan waved his hand up and down at her outfit. "I like being the only guy who knows what you look like naked. Let's keep it that way."

With one foot already in the passenger side of his car, she froze. "Are you saying my outfit is sleazy?" Did he realize the severity of his insult? If there was anything she knew more about than he did, it was fashion.

The stretchy high-waisted skirt ended below her knee. Admittedly, the black-and-white striped fabric clung to her curves, and the black cropped T-shirt was no less snug. The space between the two garments revealed two inches of bare midriff, but other than that, there was nothing revealing about the ensemble.

"Not sleazy. You could never look sleazy." He put his hand on the roof of his car, crowding her, and ran his hand over her ass. "It's just going to be impossible to quit thinking about what I want to do to you when I get you alone."

Drew placed her foot back on the ground and looked up at him through her lashes. "If you want me to go, this is what I'm wearing. Whatever goes on in your dirty little mind is your problem."

He smirked. "I'm going to make it your problem when we get back here."

She rolled her eyes and folded herself into the car. Sounded like a good problem to have. Playing hooky with Logan was absolutely not happening beyond this one time, but since she'd been persuaded into it, she might as well enjoy it.

So far, she had no complaints.

Taking a shower on the boat should have been awkward. The shower stall was a tight squeeze for the two of them, but she didn't mind being pressed against Logan's naked, soapy, wet body. Getting her hair shampooed by those long, strong fingers of his? Also, not the worst experience. Then there was the way he'd lathered up her breasts while he'd sucked on her earlobe. After a solid minute of that, it'd only taken thirty seconds of his finger teasing her clit for her to come.

Drinking coffee on the deck of the Gypsy, alternating between watching the scenery and the captain, as he drove them back to the marina, might forever be her favorite way to spend a morning. Living on a boat full time was preposterous, but for a weekend getaway, it was pretty sweet.

When they got to the restaurant, Morgan was out front, waiting for them. No question she was Logan's sister. Where his hair was dark, his sister's was blond and framed her face in voluminous sweeping layers, the longest cascading to the center of her back. But the resemblance wasn't in their features, it was the vibe they exuded. Effortless cool.

Drew's skirt might be tight, but Morgan's jeans fit her like a second skin. Black, with zippers at the ankles and across the pockets, they looked like something from a rock star's dressing room. Her shirt wasn't tight at all. The white tank top she had on hung off her slender frame, and was nearly transparent, revealing her black, lacy bralette, and the entire side of her torso. She'd accessorized with gold frame aviator sunglasses, a chunky gold choker, and black platform wedge sneakers. Even with the little boost from her shoes, she was still shorter than Drew.

Morgan's mouth formed a crooked smile as they walked toward her.

"This half-naked person is my sister, Morgan," Logan muttered.

"You can't see my eyes, but I want you to know I'm rolling them at you." Morgan turned her head in Drew's direction and thrust her hand out. "It's nice to meet you, Drew."

"Happy birthday. Thanks for letting me tag along. I didn't want to intrude, but your brother insisted."

"Are you kidding? I've been dying to meet you." She gestured to Logan with her thumb stuck out. "He's only here to pick up the bill."

Logan shoved his hands into his front pockets and bobbed his head. "Love you too, sis."

As soon as they were seated and the server appeared, Morgan ordered an espresso.

"Been up all night?" he asked.

Morgan shot him a dirty look. "Insomniacs who bring an overnight guest to lunch shouldn't throw stones."

"You told me the insomnia was new." And he'd implied it was her fault. Drew glared at him.

He grinned. "It *is.* Morgan has trouble respecting personal space. I can't get a papercut without her knowing about it." He turned back to his sister and raised his chin. "You promised me you'd stay out of trouble."

"It's my birthday, Logan. Cut me some slack."

He shifted on his seat, propping one forearm on his chair back and the other behind Drew, his fingertips skimming the skin at the base of her neck left exposed by her hair being in a bun.

A shiver ran through her, and out of the corner of her eye, she caught the twitch of his lips.

"Please tell me the keys to the *Gypsy* are my birthday present," Morgan said.

"Prove to me that you've given up your little hobby, and I'll hand them over."

"Where will you live if you give her the boat?" Drew asked, not liking the anxiety laced through her voice.

Maybe he still had the penthouse he'd mentioned. In Las Vegas.

Will he keep in touch? Will he even remember me in a few months?

Her brain wouldn't shut off. She couldn't even redirect it.

Logan's voice cut through. "You don't have to worry about me being homeless. Morgan is incapable of meeting the terms of our agreement."

Morgan flashed him a you-know-you-love-me smile and finished it off with an even-if-I-am-a-pain-in-your-ass eyebrow raise.

He ordered for the table and the waiter came back with a bottle of sake and three ceramic shot glasses.

Morgan clapped like a happy toddler. "Let's get drunk."

"Thought you had to work tonight?" Logan filled each glass with the hot liquid.

"I traded shifts with one of the other nurses. I don't have to go in until tomorrow night. Make a toast, Logan." She held up her glass.

He groaned. "Not in front of Drew."

"Why not?" Drew asked.

"Because his toasts are notoriously vulgar. One leads to another and before you know it everyone at the table, including him, is roaring drunk," Morgan said. "That's why he won't do it in front of you."

Logan roaring drunk. She couldn't imagine. So far, she'd never seen him lose control. Except when they were getting hot and heavy, but even then, it had only slipped for a moment before he reined it back in.

"Come on," Morgan whined. "It's my birthday. This only happens once a year. Let's have a good time."

He stayed quiet for a minute, rubbing his thumb around the rim of his glass, then lifted it. "Here's to another year of trying not to openly laugh when I look across the room and see you're mentally making fun of the same person, another year of not paying for therapy because we have each other, of doing absolutely nothing and still having the time of our lives. Here's to a million more memories, ten thousand inside jokes, and not a single secret. Happy birthday to my best friend, my partner in crime, my favorite human."

Morgan's eyes watered a bit and she blinked to clear them before clinking his glass and downing her sake.

No one moved across the country for no other reason than to help their sibling if they didn't care deeply for them, but that speech exposed that Logan didn't simply love his sister. He cherished her.

The waiter delivered two large platters with a colorful assortment of sushi.

Logan ordered another bottle of sake, much to his sister's delight, and excused himself to the men's room.

Morgan's big blue eyes assessed Drew. *Thoroughly.* "The subject of Logan giving me the *Gypsy* bothered you."

Drew set down her chopsticks. "He's never mentioned it. I was surprised, not bothered." He'd told her he was staying. No doubt he could afford to rent a swanky condo but signing a lease was more of a commitment. A commitment that lured him farther away from the life he'd planned. Besides, even though the concept of living on a boat had seemed wild to her at first, it'd grown on her. Living aboard the *Gypsy* was as much as part of Logan's identity as playing poker and his quick wit.

"I've never seen Logan with a woman. I mean, never *ever*. I know he's not a monk or anything. But he'd never introduce me to anyone he didn't plan on keeping around."

Drew didn't hate hearing she was the first woman Logan had been involved with that Morgan had met, especially considering how close they were. Ah, man, where was the emergency brake on this runaway train of romantic entanglement?

"You don't need to reassure me of your brother's intentions."

Remembering her own intention to have a fling with Logan wouldn't hurt, though.

The way he looked at her when he returned made her toes curl and her stomach flutter. His deep blue eyes communicated that in the brief time he'd been gone, he'd replayed memories of the things he'd done to her. And fantasized about the things he wanted to do to her yet.

She swallowed hard.

Logan turned his attention to his sister but brushed his thigh against Drew's. He poured another round from the fresh bottle the waiter brought to the table. "Here's to you, and here's to me. May we never disagree, but if we do, fuck you, and here's to me."

He tossed back his shot, then slammed the glass down. "That was the last one."

Their stories about their uncle entertained Drew through most of lunch. Not only had he taught them how to run a con, but he had elaborate tea parties with Morgan, and coached Logan's little league team.

After their plates had been cleared and more sake ordered, Logan put Morgan's present on the table in front of her.

She opened the box, her eyes sparkling as she slid the cuff onto her wrist. Then she jumped out of her seat and came around to their side of the table, throwing her arms around Logan from the back and giving him a loud smooch on the cheek.

"You know," Drew said, "I haven't heard any of these vulgar toasts Morgan spoke of."

Logan shook his head. "You aren't going to."

"I have brothers. Three of them. I've heard my share of obscenities and dirty jokes."

"She probably knows more swear words than you," Morgan said.

"Playing hooky is more tame than I'd expected." Drew faked a yawn.

Logan let go of an exaggerated sigh, then raised his glass. "Here's to rattlesnakes and condoms; two things I don't fuck with."

Morgan kicked him under the table.

"What?" he asked with innocence so insincere it was comical.

"That's terrible, and hopefully, has no truth to it." Morgan shot Drew an apologetic cringey face.

"Well, I don't fuck with rattlesnakes. That'd be dumb."

Drew pinched her lips together to prevent laughter from spilling out.

By the time they'd finished their meal, none of the three of them were in any shape to be driving. Logan ordered a cab, and they made their way to the marina.

Morgan walked to the *Gypsy* ahead of Drew and Logan. She tripped over a rope, stumbled, and dropped her phone. "Shit."

"You're too drunk to be texting and walking," Logan said.

She picked the phone up, but Logan snatched it from her.

He looked at the screen and his eyebrow shot up, then he swiped down.

Morgan tried to grab the phone back. "Logan…"

A devious look crossed his face. Then he pitched her phone overboard.

"Logan!" Drew smacked his shoulder. "I can't believe you did that."

"She'll thank me tomorrow."

"No, she won't," Morgan slurred. "You're buying me a new phone."

"When I do, I'm going to have his number blocked." He had to lift his sister onto the boat. She was so drunk she could barely stand. Logan brewed a fresh pot of coffee while Drew helped Morgan get situated in one of the chairs on the deck. She sat with her while she smoked a cigarette and then helped convince her to drink some coffee.

"Sorry about her. She usually knows when to quit," Logan said after he'd tucked his sister in on the settee and tugged Drew into the bedroom.

She shrugged. "It's her birthday."

Logan sat on the bed, shoulders pressed against the headboard, knees bent, and motioned for her to sit in front of him. Once she'd gotten comfy, he took a deep breath.

"The reason I came to Savannah is because Morgan was in trouble." He held her eyes captive with his, his voice low and serious. "She met Eric in Vegas. Three days later, follows him back here, convinced she's in love."

Morgan seemed like she had it together. Drew couldn't imagine her uprooting her life to follow a near-stranger across the country.

"I told you about her talents. Well, Eric found out about them and decided she could be useful to him and his boss. She started working at the hospital and they convinced her to lift some prescriptions. It went on for a while. Then Morgan found Eric in bed with another woman.

"She wanted revenge, so she broke into his boss's office and cleaned out his safe. Figured she'd been the one taking all the risks to earn all that cash, so she was going to take it back."

Logan stretched his neck to one side, then the other. He looked desperately in need of some type of tension-relief. "I moved here to help her clean up her mess. I'm still working on that."

Drew hiked her skirt up to her thighs, then crawled up next to him, and rested her head on his shoulder. "Why are you telling me this?"

He rubbed a piece of his bedspread between his fingers. "I'd move heaven and hell if that's what it took to protect Morgan. Most of what I've had to do was in the hell sector."

She swung one of her legs over his lap to straddle him, and touched his cheek, his whiskers tickling her fingers. "I don't care that you color outside the lines. I can see how much Morgan means to you, and I get that you would do anything to protect her, whatever the risks."

He put his hand on the back of her neck and brought her face closer to his, until their foreheads touched. "I'd do the same for you."

34

EAVESDROP ENERGY

Drew

DREW RUBBED HER EYES and stared at the open hatch above the bed, trying to focus on the voices drifting through.

"I have to tell her." Logan's voice was low, an angry whisper, but she could hear every word.

Morgan groaned. "I like her. Why do you want to fuck it up?"

"I don't. But I can't keep this from her."

Logan was keeping something from her?

Her skin went clammy and all the warmth surrounding her from the past twenty-some hours with Logan eviscerated.

"It's a tiny detail," Morgan said, immediately hushed by him.

"She was my mark. I conned her. That is a big fucking detail."

Drew sat up and hugged the sheet to her chest, her breath frozen in her lungs.

The rest of the conversation was drowned out by her heartbeat pounding in her ears. Hot tears streaked down her cheeks. She wiped them away, angry for shedding one tear over Logan Cash.

Wait. How exactly did he con her?

Holding her breath, she listened closely, hoping their conversation hadn't turned to something else.

"—steal the painting."

She gasped. *Shit, that was loud. They're going to know I was eavesdropping.*

Maybe she wanted them to know. She should march right up to the flybridge and let Logan have it. Put him in his place. Kick him in the balls.

But she was paralyzed. Her head dropped into her hands. The room spun. Her body shook.

How could this happen? The first guy she'd ever let in, let touch her, had lied to her. Manipulated her. Stolen the one thing in the world that made her feel connected to her mother.

She had to pull herself together.

Lifting her head, she tucked her hair behind her ears and wiped her cheeks.

I'm naked, in his bed. What am I still doing here?

Drew flipped the sheet away and plucked her dress off the floor. In the bathroom, she splashed cold water on her face. She swiped the toiletries she'd left on the vanity into her tote bag. She gathered up the rest of her things from his bedroom and was about to make a fast getaway when the door opened.

Logan stopped short. "You look like you're going to puke."

"I feel like I might." Her voice shook, but hopefully he'd blame that on her being ill. She breathed deep through her nose. Being in the same stupid beige, claustrophobia-inducing room with him was a hell she'd never imagined. She didn't know if she wanted to cry or yell or beat the crap out of him. Inside, she was a swarming mess of emotions, but outside, she was frozen numb.

He rubbed his palm over his five o'clock shadow. "Lie back down. I'll get you whatever you need. We can get takeout for dinner. Whatever sounds good to you."

"I just want to go home."

"Let me drive you."

She didn't bother to remind him they had left his car at the restaurant, nor did she care that they had planned for her to drive him to get it once they sobered up.

Drew shook her head and tried to squeeze past him. He put his hand up on the door frame, blocking her path with his arm. Bamboo whirled into her personal space. The bastard didn't have to smell so good. She'd never be able to experience that scent again without thinking of him.

"I want to take care of you." He trailed his knuckle down her arm, sending an explosion of tingles in its wake.

His words gnarled away at her rationale. Her icy armor started thawing from the outside in.

Damn him. He was such a good liar. She had to force herself to believe he didn't mean it. *This is what he does. It's what he's good at.*

"If you don't let me past, I'm going to barf all over your obnoxious beige carpet."

His arm dropped to his side.

Drew fled to the living room, snatching her turquoise wedges off the floor without breaking stride. Her eyes stung, but no way was she going to cry in front of him.

As she passed Morgan, who was drinking coffee and smoking a cigarette on the aft deck, she kept her eyes ahead, making a beeline for the parking lot. Drew had foolishly liked her too. Logan had said she was a brilliant thief. That was probably the only thing he'd said that wasn't a lie.

DREW DROPPED HER BAG ON THE KITCHEN COUNTER AND LISTENED. Today had provided plenty of practice for her eavesdropping skills.

The white Volkswagen Beetle was in the driveway again.

Her dad had a girlfriend. She was going to have to face it sooner or later. It might as well be now while her world already felt as if it were ending.

She zeroed in on a royal purple faux snakeskin clutch on the sideboard. That shade of purple was not easy to pull off. Making it resemble scaly skin from a reptile did not help. Hopefully, her dad had better taste in women than his girlfriend did in accessories.

Seeking out a hairbrush, she tiptoed down the hall. Running her tongue over her teeth, she accepted she was in need of a lot more.

In her bathroom, she peeled off her skirt and almost tossed it in the hamper. In the middle of wiping off her eye makeup with a cotton pad, she froze. Oh God, was that…a hickey? No, no, no.

Her eyes closed as the memory of Logan kissing his way down her neck, lingering above the swell of her breast, grabbed hold. *Stupid girl. You stupid, stupid girl.*

After a steamy shower, Drew braided her hair over one shoulder, concealing the mark. In a pair of yoga pants and a SCAD hoodie, she trudged back down the hall, ready to plaster on a phony smile for her dad's company.

When she poked her head into the living room, it was dark and quiet. She frowned, then checked the kitchen, dining room, and sunporch. All vacant. Which meant they could only be…

Upstairs.

Ew.

Laughter—giggling, actually—caught her attention. She whipped around as a blonde in a paisley print maxi dress appeared from the basement stairs. Aubrey followed in the woman's wake.

"Hey," he said. "Where you been?"

"Nowhere special." She gave the woman standing next to her brother a quick perusal. "Hi."

"This is Holly." He looped his arm around her waist. "This is my sister, Drew."

"Is that your Beetle in the driveway?"

Holly nodded. "Is it in the way?"

The tension in her shoulders released. "No. I was just wondering.

It's cute." And its presence had been the entire reason she'd spent that first night with Logan. Okay, maybe not the *entire* reason.

"Oh, thanks."

Drew ran her hand down her braid. "Where's Dad?"

"Atlanta. He and Uncle Rich took some paintings to a gallery."

"Oh."

"I'm going to walk Holly out." He flashed her an odd look. "Don't go anywhere. I want to talk to you."

She moseyed into the living room.

Aubrey had been so, so wrong. Their dad had nothing to do with the theft.

She stood in front of the fireplace and stared up at the blank spot over the mantel. Outrage drowned her hurt.

By the time Aubrey joined her, her mind had churned a crazy plan. She turned to face him. "Let's get the painting back."

His eyebrow darted up. "Come again?"

She hadn't told Aubrey about Logan yet. Lee and Grant had met him, but she hadn't had time with Aubrey. "I started seeing someone," she said, her voice nowhere near steady. "But today, when he thought I was sleeping, I overheard him talking to his sister. He conned me, Aubrey. They stole the painting."

"Are you drunk?"

She shook her head. "No. Why?"

Aubrey dropped into their dad's leather club chair, his forearms across his knees, fingers steepled. "I don't know why you would make something like that up, but it's bizarre. Maybe start at the beginning. How did you meet this guy?"

She told him the story of how she'd crossed paths with Logan in the coffee shop, then asked him to photograph Claire's wedding, leaving out the part about losing her virginity on his boat.

"Hold on a sec." Aubrey pulled his bottom lip between his fingers while he thought for a moment. "You met him *after* the painting was stolen?"

"It doesn't make sense to me either. I don't understand why, but I know what I heard."

He stood and paced the room, hands clasped behind his back. All he needed was an ugly plaid detective's hat and a pipe. "He's circling back to make sure he didn't leave a trail."

"What?"

He paused in front of the window. "Did he ask you any questions about the theft?"

"No, none. I mean, I did tell him a little about Dad not reporting the crime, but I volunteered that information."

Aubrey titled his head slightly, giving her a tight smile. "He let you think you volunteered it, but I bet he was orchestrating the whole thing."

"No." Drew refused to believe that. "I asked him to photograph the wedding. I approached him."

"Which I'm sure was a stroke of luck for him."

She shoved her hands into the pocket of her hoodie and waited for Aubrey to make eye contact. When their gazes connected, she stared at him, waiting a long moment. "He doesn't know I overheard him."

A slow grin spread over his face. "You've already cooked up a plan to exact your revenge, haven't you?"

"I'm going to con the con man."

Logan wasn't going to get away with this. She'd take him down.

"I thought you needed to focus on your collection?" Aubrey cracked his knuckles. "If you're going to do this right, it's gonna take time. And patience, something we both know you don't have much of."

"What I lack in patience, I make up for in determination. I'm going to give Logan Cash a taste of his own medicine, get the painting back, *and* win that freaking contest by a landslide."

35

GRANNY PANTIES

"TELL HIM YOU HAVE A HEADACHE. Tell him you're on your period. Tell him anything, but do *not* sleep with him."

Drew glared at Aubrey in the mirror and set down her eyeliner pencil. "You don't have to tell me that."

"Good," he muttered. "After he goes to sleep, you have to look through the boat."

She spun around and braced herself with her hands on the bathroom vanity, scrunching her face. "That might be a problem. He has trouble sleeping."

Aubrey flicked her forehead. "And you're just now telling me this?"

Rubbing the sting out of her forehead, she scowled at him. "I thought I could just...ask him to go get me a coffee in the morning."

"And if he says no?"

"Why would he say no?"

He threw his head back and groaned. "Whatever, Drew. I don't care how you do things as long as you're careful."

"Good." She smiled and turned around to finish her makeup. "Can you grab the white garment bag out of my closet?"

"*This* is what you're wearing?" he asked, coming back into the bathroom with the bag unzipped.

It was the LBD—little black dress—she'd worn to her dad's exhibition. It was made of Guipure lace with a satin underlay. Short, but not too short, and it had cap sleeves.

"We're going to an upscale place. This is suitable."

"No, this is the kind of dress women wear when—"

"When what, Aubrey?" she asked, snatching the bag from him and carrying it to the bed. She laid it across her duvet and turned.

"When they"—he scratched his chin—"plan on putting out."

"You're an idiot. It's a martini bar. And this," she pointed at the dress, "is a cocktail dress."

"To you, it's a cocktail dress. He's going to read something else into it." Aubrey stacked his hands over the backwards ball cap perched on his head. "I don't like this. There has to be another way. I feel like I'm prostituting my sister."

"Oh, shut up. If Logan thinks my dress means I'm going to sleep with him, then he's going to be disappointed."

"Promise me one thing."

She crossed her arms and glared. "What?"

"That you'll wear granny panties."

DREW SWALLOWED THE LUMP IN HER THROAT as Logan shrugged out of his jacket and draped it over the captain's chair. They'd had the best date in the history of dating—except it was a sham.

But it didn't feel like a sham when he'd come to pick her up looking like every woman's fantasy in a black suit and crisp white shirt. He'd gotten his hair trimmed, manicured his ever-present five o'clock shadow, and he smelled *so* good.

It continued to not feel like a sham while he opened doors and pulled out her chair. The martini bar was a freaking aphrodisiac. Designer cocktails, dim lighting, a jazz band playing on the stage.

By the time the bartender set her first martini in front of her, she was tingling, and Logan hadn't even touched her. At least not with his hands. His eyes, however, had done shameful things to her.

Spending the night and avoiding anything sexual had seemed a lot easier when she wasn't standing in his living room, watching him take out his cufflinks and roll up his sleeves. Her heart pounded in her chest and heat pooled between her legs. Oh, Jesus, she was hopeless.

She had to stay the night. Otherwise, she couldn't snoop through his stuff.

Should have worn the granny panties.

One little crook of his finger and she walked straight into his arms.

He cupped her neck and massaged in a circular motion using his thumb. "What's going on with you? You're never this quiet."

"Nothing." The word came out hoarse.

Logan heaved a sigh. "You're the worst liar I've ever met."

And you're the best one I've met. "I shouldn't have had that second martini. Vodka always makes me lightheaded."

There. That was the truth. Except it usually took a little bit more vodka and a lot less Logan.

"Try again."

She wet her lips, stalling. Her gaze drifted around the room, but he put a finger on her jaw and guided her to look at him.

"Stop overthinking and tell me what's going on in there." He tapped her temple.

That'd be fun. *Hey, it's just that I'm reeling in disbelief that the way you look at me, the intensity behind your kisses, and the chemistry between us, everything we've shared, has been fake. I'm trying to figure out how to let go of feelings so visceral they're embedded in my soul.*

"You're doing it right now," he said, his voice low, and oddly, soothing.

"You can read my mind?"

"Every thought." A shiver rushed through her from the warmth of his breath against her ear. "You better stop thinking about me naked so often."

Fighting her smile and trying to rebuild the ice fortress around her heart that he was melting put a strain on her determination. "Hmm. Maybe you *can* read my mind. I'm going to need further proof, though. What am I thinking right now?"

He pulled back and studied her face. "That we're going too fast. That you're feeling too much. You're worried that you're wrong about us. About what we have." His eyes softened, and warmth simmered in her chest. "But you're not wrong," he whispered and God, she wanted to believe him.

His prediction was freakishly spot on. Damn it.

"Am I close?" he asked.

"No." It sounded like she had swallowed a frog.

"Look, I wasn't expecting this, either." He ran his hands up and down her arms. "But it happened, and I don't wish that it hadn't, even if I have no idea how to navigate it."

Could that be true? Could Logan have not meant for them to get involved?

He had tried to warn her off sleeping with him that first night. But she'd pushed. He'd told her it'd never work between them. But she'd pushed. After he'd helped her pack her apartment, he'd tried to leave. But she'd pushed.

He could have done a better job resisting, though.

Not that she had any business judging his willpower. Her own was frayed to the snapping point. Maybe their chemistry was legit. Maybe his attraction to her had gotten in the way of whatever plan he'd devised.

But did that change anything? Bottom line, he'd had a plan.

Somehow, the idea that having a romantic relationship with her wasn't a part of that plan made it seem less sordid. Wanting his touch felt less shameful.

"I know you like everything mapped out and I'm more of a *go with the flow* type." He pulled her closer, their hips touching. "But maybe that makes us a good fit. We can learn from each other. Balance each other out."

She fiddled with the collar of his shirt. "Or drive each other crazy."

"We already do that." He dragged his hand from the small of her back to her ass and rubbed his palm over it. "What's driving me crazy right now is this dress. For my mental health, I'm going to have to ask you to remove it."

Drew snorted and rolled her eyes. His knack for diffusing the mood when it got heavy fit that balance he suggested they could have. Her usual pattern was to get progressively worked up until she exploded. That hadn't happened since…she'd blown up on him at Claire's.

Even when Logan wasn't around, she had more patience with others. Her stress levels had taken a nosedive and it showed in her interactions.

Would it be wrong to enjoy the perks of being with Logan while she searched for clues about where the painting had gone? What was the harm in having sex with him when they'd already done it before? In the grand scheme of things, did it really matter?

He kissed her jaw, next to her ear, then worked his way toward her mouth one shiver-inducing kiss at a time.

"I need your help with the zipper," she said softly.

Logan brushed his mouth across hers. His fingers wove through her hair as she pressed her lips to kiss, seeking one of those feel-it-in-her-bloodstream kisses he was so good at. He obliged her until she started to move against him restlessly.

He walked around her and pushed her hair over her shoulder, out of the way. The zipper was the only sound as he pulled it down the length of her spine. His palms were hot against her shoulders as he guided the sleeves down her arms. The dress pooled at her feet, leaving her standing there in a black lace bra *and* matching thong.

The air in the room crackled. Logan's hand drifted across the lace covering her hip. "What's this?"

"Underwear?" she asked in a you've-heard-of-it-right? tone.

He nipped at her shoulder as his erection pressed into her ass.

She gasped, then tilted her head, giving him better access.

While he used his tongue and teeth on her neck, his hand flattened against her stomach and descended until his fingers slipped under the lace edge. "Did you wear these for me?"

Her eyes flickered closed. The answer to that question wasn't something she wanted to deliberate on. When she'd taken them from her lingerie drawer, she'd told herself that they'd be more of a hindrance than not wearing any. Turns out she was an easy person to lie to, even when she was lying to herself.

Logan moved his hand up her ribcage and cupped her breast. His warm breath tickled her ear. "Answer me."

She nodded and turned in his arms, going straight for the top button on his shirt, hastily undoing it.

Logan grabbed her hands and gently squeezed her fingers. "In a rush?"

She nodded again and pressed up on her toes to kiss him.

He dropped her hands, and placed his palm flat against her lower back, pulling her tight against him. "I'm not," he whispered before claiming her mouth.

No urgency existed within the movements of his lips or tongue, but he still managed to erase every intelligible thought from her brain. The pace he set teased her sanity. Slow hands and soft kisses. Scorching fingertips against her spine as he unclasped her bra. His thigh rubbing against her, hitting her, the texture of his pants and her thong against her flesh dragging her to a place of pure need.

He walked her backward until her calves hit the edge of something. She tugged her mouth from his to look. A chair. The kind with the seat on an angle, making it perfect for sinking into.

Her core throbbed as Logan pushed his thigh farther between hers.

He wrapped one arm around her and braced himself with the other by placing his hand on the back of the chair. His chest pushed against hers, forcing her to sink until her ass connected with the cushion.

"What are we doing?" she asked breathlessly as he trailed his mouth down her torso.

He knelt between her thighs, pushing them wider. "Everything, Drew. "I'm going to do *everything* to you."

She parted her lips to speak but the words lodged in her throat as he lifted her thigh and kissed a path from her knee to her thong.

His tongue swept over the narrow strip of fabric covering her aching pussy.

Her eyes fluttered closed. He'd never put his mouth there before. She nearly whined out loud when his lips moved to her other knee.

He followed a mirrored path back to her, this time pushing the fabric aside and dipping his tongue between her folds.

Involuntary noises escaped her throat. She put her hand in his hair and arched, her back bending away from the chair.

Logan licked and kissed her wet pussy at a torturously slow place. Not until she lifted her hips, begging without words for more, did he spread her with his fingers and connect his tongue with her clit.

Such exquisite sensations wrapped around her that she cared about nothing else. She wanted this, and she didn't care what type of person that made her.

She could hate herself in the morning.

36

SHAME RISING

LOGAN WAS STILL SLEEPING when she tried to ease over him and out of bed. Just as she braced one knee on his side of the mattress, he grabbed her and tossed her down next to him.

"I thought you were asleep."

"I am," he whispered. He buried his face in her hair, outspread on the pillow. "I love the way your hair smells."

She sighed.

He snored.

He was fast asleep, and she was trapped under the weight of his thigh and torso. *Perfect.*

After twenty minutes of letting shame wash over her for sleeping with a man who had conned her, she fell back asleep.

The next time she woke up his lips were running over the sensitive skin along her collarbone. She gasped and arched her body. His T-shirt and jeans felt significantly inferior to the warm, bare skin she'd been expecting.

"Why are you dressed?" she asked.

He grunted. "Get up. I have a surprise for you."

He disappeared, and Drew blinked until the room came into focus. Her dress hung from the door of Logan's closet, her bra and thong looped around the hook of the hanger. The overnight bag she'd brought with her was on top of his small dresser. Instead of putting on the sexy-but-not-too-sexy pajamas she'd packed, she snagged Logan's Violent Femmes shirt and a pair of his boxers from his dresser, and trudged into the kitchen, frowning when the aroma of freshly brewed coffee hit her nose.

So much for Plan A.

Logan carried a steaming mug to the table and set it in the center, next to a bowl of cut fruit and a plate with a croissant. He'd provided more than breakfast, though. He'd set up a makeshift art studio with pads of various types of papers, charcoals, markers, watercolors, brushes, and color pencils.

"Where did all of this come from?"

He leaned his shoulder against the wall next to the booth. "The art supply store."

Drew shot him a glare, then slid onto the bench and fingered the bristles of a paintbrush. "But why?"

He grabbed his own mug of coffee next to the maker and took a sip. "Because you need to be productive, and I need you here looking all sexy in my shirt. Besides, when you're a famous designer, I want to be able to say I supported your dream."

He was willing to do all this to spend time with her?

She couldn't help smiling. "What are you going to do?"

"Not gonna lie. I'll probably try to distract you." He walked over and planted a kiss on her forehead, then disappeared up the steps and into the living room.

While she sketched, he moved about the boat, doing what, she had no idea. Probably something she knew nothing about, like checking lines and making sure everything was in tip-top shape.

Her pencil glided along the page, creating the S curve of a female form with elongated legs and exaggerated stilettos. With a Filbert-shaped brush, she swept ink over her design, angling the brush to create varying stroke widths. She blew on the paper to help the ink dry and then squeezed blue and yellow watercolors from a tube, onto a piece of palette paper.

A flash caught her attention.

Logan had crouched at the top of the steps and had his lens aimed directly at her.

She scowled. "I just got out of bed."

He slinked down to the galley and snapped another picture. After flashing her a wolfish grin, he brushed her tangled hair over her shoulder and whispered, "Yeah, but it was *my* bed."

Deciding to ignore him and delete the pictures later, she went back to work on her illustration.

He continued to snap shots of her, getting closer. And closer. There was a close-up and then there was macro-photography. Her pores on film. Not gonna happen.

She covered the lens with her hand. "I can't concentrate."

"Sorry." He set the camera on the table. "I'm gonna go have a smoke and call Uncle John."

Before he was out of sight, she said, "I need to check my e-mail. Can I use your computer?"

"It's in the bedroom," he called over his shoulder. "The password is gutshot672."

Could it be that easy? She waited until the boat dipped and bobbed as he got off, then rushed into the bedroom. After grabbing his laptop from the small desk in the room, she sat on the bed and typed in his password.

His files were mostly photographs, and his internet browser history for the past few days was limited to restaurant reviews and his e-mail inbox. Feeling lucky, she tried the same password to log in to his e-mail account.

Bingo.

Bill payment reminders. Penis Enlargement Spam. An order confirmation for an SD memory card.

"Aha," she said to herself as she clicked on an e-mail from John Cash. It was an informal message, basically saying he missed Logan and Morgan.

Drew raked her hand through her knotty hair as she went through the rest of his e-mails. Nothing connecting him to the painting.

The computer *ping*-ed. A notification from his message app icon in the dock. She clicked it.

A message from Morgan.

> Sushi tonight? You can bring Drew.

How nice of her. Drew rolled her eyes and scrolled through their message history. Boring.

He had few other contacts in his message history. Charlie, who Logan congratulated for winning something—a poker game, maybe?

The next one was his Uncle John. Probably another dead end. They probably didn't talk about the kind of stuff she needed over e-mail or text.

As predicted, nothing noteworthy. Except for the last few messages.

> When do I get to meet Drew?

> Going to ask her to come home with me for a weekend.

She put her hand to her temple. He was going to go as far as introducing her to his uncle to keep up this charade?

Drew slammed the computer closed and paced between the kitchen and the bedroom. None of this made sense.

She stared at the table laid out with art supplies. That wasn't the type of thing a guy would think of if he was working her, or even using her for sex.

Her eyes settled on his camera. Her hand shook as she hovered it over it. She might not like what she found if she browsed through his memory card.

Screw it. She snatched up the camera and went to the living room. Out the window, she saw him in the parking lot with his phone to his ear, kicking at pebbles, sending them flying into the water.

Drew sat on the settee and pressed the on/off button on his camera. Might as well go ahead and delete those humiliating bedhead photos. She hit the trashcan icon on the close-up of her. The next one wasn't so bad. Her hair was clearly morning-after hair, but he'd done a pretty good job with the composition of the shot. In the picture, she was chewing on her lip, her hand filling in intricate details on her sketch. Something about the way he'd captured the light shining in through the window of the otherwise dim room, and focused on her hand, rather than her face, made her smile.

My boyfriend is so freaking talented.

No! Not her boyfriend. Drew squeezed her eyes shut and swallowed the shame rising in her throat. When she opened them, she flipped through the rest of the photos quickly. All landscapes.

She tapped her finger against her lip. Where was his camera bag?

She found it on the floor by the captain's chair. Before picking it up, she checked out the window again. He was still on the phone, but she had to hurry. At any minute, he could come walking up the dock.

She set the bag on the chair and rifled through it. Extra memory cards were in the bottom, all organized in a little clear box. Each one had a letter, or a combination of letters, written in black marker. Selecting one at random, she exchanged it for the card in the camera.

Claire and Matt's wedding. C&M. Duh. She ran through the first few dozen photos, stopping on the ones of Claire's gown. She'd been too stubborn to look at the photos when Logan showed them to Claire and Matt.

And her stubbornness was biting her in the ass. The photos Logan took of the gown were a hundred times better than the ones she'd taken on the dress form in her studio.

Without looking at the rest, she inserted another card, this one labeled B. Her forehead wrinkled as she looked at high-resolution photos of people she didn't recognize. They weren't artistic shots. She paused and studied a photo of a man in a suit and a woman in a teensy mini dress outside of some type of office…or a hotel? And his hand was on her ass.

She scanned through more photos of men and women being affectionate, and one of two men entering an adult novelty store. Mixed in were shots of men in what looked like vacant lots, standing next to expensive cars and making some type of exchange.

Just when she'd seen enough to leave a bad taste in her mouth, a picture of her appeared in the stream. She was working at the restaurant, on the upper deck, and it looked like the shot was taken from the walkway below.

Drew almost dropped the camera, but fumbled and caught it. There weren't many pictures of her, but all of them were taken from a distance. Her coming out of her apartment, walking into her studio, and through the coffee shop window.

Seeing photos of herself, unaware that she was being watched, sent a chill down her spine. She glanced out the window. Crap. Logan was halfway up the dock.

She scrambled to switch the SD cards and get the case back into the camera bag.

"What are you doing?"

Her head shot up.

Logan's gaze flicked from her face to the camera in her hand.

She lifted her chin and smirked. "Deleting the pictures you took of me this morning."

He stalked toward her.

Drew slipped around the captain's chair and started for the kitchen, but Logan grabbed her around the waist and hauled her up against him.

"Give it to me."

Holding the camera as far away as her arms allowed, she wiggled in his arms. His hold on her tightened, and he grabbed for the camera but couldn't quite reach.

Drew gasped for air between bursts of laughter. "Promise to stop taking pictures of me and I'll hand it over."

"I'm not promising that." He placed his hand on her stomach, his fingers sliding under the hem of her shirt.

Her breath caught. "Logan." His hand dipped under her pajama shorts and between her thighs. "Logan!"

"Screaming my name will only encourage me." His fingers skimmed her flesh. On the next pass, one finger worked its way between her folds, catching her wetness and dragging it to her clit. "Give it to me," he said again, his voice low and dangerous.

The camera had gotten heavy. "Fine," she said, her voice cracking. "Take the stupid camera."

"I'm not talking about the camera anymore."

37

HELLCAT WITH A HICKEY

THE WALK OF SHAME. Everyone had done it at some point or other. But how many people could say they'd made the walk of shame in front of their brother, while wearing her lover's underwear and favorite shirt less than twenty-four hours after swearing she wasn't going to put out?

Drew squirmed while standing in her dad's kitchen, the hanger holding her black dress dangling from one hand, and her shoes dangling from the other. Thankfully, her lingerie was tucked away in the overnight bag slung over her shoulder.

Aubrey's face was a rare shade of furious and he had a death grip on his freshly made sandwich. Peanut butter and jelly oozed from the edges.

She pointed at him. "Don't judge me."

His gaze softened and he licked the jelly from his hand. "I'm guessing you didn't find anything incriminating?"

"No. I went through his emails, texts, and the memory cards for his camera. He's too smart to leave a trail, Aubrey."

He finished chewing the half of the sandwich he'd shoved in his mouth and gulped down a third of the tall glass of milk on the counter. "You like this guy, despite everything. If you're going to keep seeing him, I think we should revisit my idea to simply ask him how he was involved."

"It'd be a waste of time. He's not going to admit to anything." She draped her dress over a stool and plopped her bag and shoes on the floor.

"How do you know?"

"Because I figured out what happened." She'd been replaying the oblique conversation Logan and Morgan had at the restaurant regarding Morgan's "little hobby" and what she'd overheard when they thought she was sleeping. If his interest in her was legit, then only one explanation made any sense. "His sister stole the painting and Logan wanted to make sure she wasn't a suspect. He'd rather take the fall for her than admit her guilt."

"Then confront *her*. Give her a guilt trip about Logan keeping secrets from you to protect her."

"I've only met her once. I don't know when I'm going to see her again."

"Meet her again. Say you want to get to know her better and invite her to do girl shit."

"Girl shit?"

"Get your nails painted, shop for tampons. Whatever." He smirked. The gross simplification of how women spent their time didn't offend her. Aubrey was far from sexist. He just liked to get a rise out of her.

"You're hilarious, Aubrey." She was about to berate him on the various reasons why asking Morgan to hang out would make Logan suspicious when the sound of the front door opening traveled through the house.

Drew widened her eyes at Aubrey and snatched up her bag, dress, and shoes. It was one thing to let her brother see her in Logan's clothes, but her dad…she was not ready for that.

She rushed down the hall into her room, took the quickest shower of her life, threw on a soft, comfy nightgown and wrapped a lightweight cotton robe around herself.

The smell of pizza caused her stomach to growl as she walked back into the kitchen. She went right for the box.

"Hey," her dad said from the sink. "There's mail for you on the kitchen table. From New York."

She dropped the pizza back into the box and dashed to the table. A letter size white envelope addressed to her waited, leaned up against the fruit bowl.

"I can't open it," she said, wringing her hands. "Someone open it and tell me what it says."

Aubrey launched himself over the back of the sofa, a slice of pizza in his hand. "I'll do it."

"You'll get it all greasy."

"No one else can open it for you," Uncle Rich said from the spot next to where Aubrey had previously been. "That's not how it works."

She looked to her dad who was walking toward her with a beer and a slice of pizza on a plate. He placed them both on the placemat in front of the letter.

"I'm not reading it. If I do that, I'll miss getting to see the look on your face when you read that you're a finalist."

"Or the look when I read that I'm not."

Her dad wrapped his arm around her shoulders. "I doubt that's going to happen, but if it does, you're very talented and I know you'll find another way to achieve your goals."

She took a deep breath, then grabbed the letter.

Aubrey pulled his pen knife from his pocket and handed it to her.

Her hands shook as she ran the blade along the edge of the envelope. She pulled the paper inside free and unfolded it. Inside her chest, her heart beat wildly. This was it. Her eyes scanned the letter. She only needed to see one of two words, either congratulations or unfortunately.

She lifted her gaze from the letter to her dad. "I'm in."

"Yes," he shouted and pulled her in for a hug.

As she received hugs from Aubrey and Uncle Rich, she made a

mental list of all she had to do. Constructing an entire collection for a
runway show was no small undertaking.

"We're having a family dinner to celebrate," her dad said. "And
you're bringing that boyfriend of yours."

"Dad, I don't think Logan—"

"Logan?" Uncle Rich's head snapped in her direction. "Your
boyfriend's name is Logan?"

"Yeah. Why?"

He ran his hand over his shiny scalp and shrugged. "I can't see you
dating a Logan. A Jonathan or a Paul, maybe."

"Um, okay…"

"I want to meet him," her dad said, his tone verging on irritation.

"Me too," Aubrey chimed in.

Drew gave him a look that subtly let him know to shut his big
mouth. "Our relationship isn't at the meet-the-family stage."

"Grant and Lee met him." Aubrey took a swig of his beer, then
smiled.

"Your relationship reached the meet-the-family stage when you
started spending the night with him," her dad said. "So, he better be there."

Her face blazed with the heat of a third-degree burn. "What about
the woman Aubrey's been seeing? They've spent the night together.
Shouldn't he have to bring her?"

"That's over," Aubrey said, avoiding eye contact with her.

"Why? What happened?" she asked.

"She's married. That's what happened."

38

DATE NIGHT DETOUR

LOGAN

LOGAN FELT LIKE A DICK for attending the celebratory dinner with Drew's family, but he couldn't pass up the opportunity to meet Aubrey. Continuing to see Drew while hiding the truth from her ate at him like a vulture gnawing on a carcass.

If he didn't find out anything useful from Aubrey tonight, he'd fess up. His conscience couldn't take it anymore.

He parked on the street outside her studio, but before he got out of his car, Drew emerged from the building and made a beeline for the passenger side. Seeing her delivered a buzz better than a shot of vodka. Regardless of what she wore, or how she did her hair, she was beautiful. But man, her style, and the way she carried herself, put her in a class of her own. In the light green sundress that swished around her thighs, the tan fedora, and big, gold framed sunglasses she'd dolled herself up in today, she looked like royalty.

Logan made long strides to reach her before she reached the car. He caught her around her waist, spun her, and pulled her up against him.

She squealed and grabbed onto his shoulders.

"Slow down. We're not even late." He'd gotten there five minutes earlier than she'd requested. Even though he'd said he would come with her to her dad's house tonight without hesitation, between then and now she'd asked him over and over if he was sure, and then last night when they'd settled on the plan of him picking her up and them riding there together, she'd reminded him of the time they'd agreed upon—for the eighth time.

"I've been going full throttle all day so I could relax and not beat myself up over not working on my collection for the rest of the day. It's going to take more than a minute for me to resume a normal pace."

"Does that mean you're coming home with me after dinner?" A small, private celebration waited for them back at the *Gypsy,* but Logan wanted it to be a surprise. So far, she hadn't committed to coming because she wanted to return to the studio after they had dinner with her family.

"I don't know yet." She wriggled away from him and unlatched the door.

He placed his hand on the top of the door and slowly pushed it shut. With his other hand splayed across her pelvis, he pulled her into him, so the curve of their bodies aligned, and whispered against her ear, "We're not going anywhere until you make up your mind."

"If you're going to pressure me into giving you an answer, you're not going to like it."

Logan smirked. No timidness in her personality. Her pushback always forced him to get creative in swaying her.

He took a step back, reached to open the door, and held it for her. "You look beautiful, by the way."

She cut her eyes at him as she slid into the car. "You should have led with that."

Logan bit his tongue, bobbed his head, and shut her door.

The drive to her dad's house was less than ten minutes. When they pulled into the driveway, he went to get out, but Drew grabbed his arm.

He glanced at where her hand cuffed his forearm, then up at her.

"Are you sure you want to do this?" she asked.

His sigh was so loud the windows almost shook. "I am. I don't think you are, though. Are you afraid they won't like me?"

She stared at the dash, shaking her head. "I *know* they're going to like you. That's the whole problem."

"How is that a problem?"

"I don't want them to get attached, okay?" She flung her door open and started toward the house.

He muttered a few choice words under his breath. She wanted to avoid her family forming an attachment to him because she believed there was chance—probably a big fucking one—that they wouldn't work out. He shouldn't be bothered by that. It was logical to think any new relationship might not work out. She didn't even know about the bullshit they had working against them.

He didn't want her to be logical where he was concerned though. He wanted her to be twisted up inside like he was, to think crazy shoot-the-moon type things about their future.

Logan grabbed the bottle of wine from the backseat and caught up with her where the sidewalk forked, one path leading to the front door, the other to the backyard. "You can't say something like that and run away."

She turned and grabbed the wine bottle from him. "I know. I'm sorry. Can we talk about it later?"

"No. Hell no." Logan shoved his hand into his hair. "Tell me what—"

Drew pressed her mouth to his, derailing his train of thought.

He froze, flummoxed by the unexpected kiss. As soon as her lips left his, his brain resumed functioning, and he asked, "Did you just kiss me to shut me up?"

"Yes." She ran her finger over the foil covering the cork on the wine bottle. "The vision I used to have of my future gets blurrier each day. And what unsettles me is that I don't care. I don't want to fix it. But that's not who I am, Logan. I'm a total control freak. My plans don't have backup plans. My journeys don't have detours.

"Or at least they didn't before I met you. Now, nothing is the way I'd intended it to be. But it's somehow better. Like having to re-do my illustrations. I don't think I'd have made it as a finalist with the originals. Or me having a panic attack about introducing you to my dad, but at the same time, I have no doubt the two of you will click."

"Still not seeing the problem, Drew."

"Winning this contest comes first. I don't know how not to hyperfocus so hard that I forget anything else exists but my art."

Logan crossed his arms. "I know what you're like. I'm not going to let you forget I exist."

"But you will get tired of having to remind me."

He pulled her sunglasses off and got in her face so she couldn't look anywhere other than into his eyes. "I'll be okay."

She opened her mouth to speak, but this time, Logan cut her off with a kiss. The hard, cold glass of the wine bottle sandwiched between them dropped to her side, immediately replaced by warmth and softness.

He cupped the back of her neck and slanted his mouth over hers.

She clutched at the fabric covering his chest and whimpered.

It had only been a few days, but it suddenly felt much longer since he'd had her in his arms, devouring her sexy, pouty lips. The thin fabric of her dress made him ache, too much like having her naked body against his.

Her tongue swept across his lips.

Logan growled. This was some sweet fucking torture. So good but destined to be over too soon. But not just yet. He sucked her bottom lip between his while sliding his hand down her side. He grabbed her hip and squeezed.

A very distinct throat clearing interrupted them as he moved his hand toward her ass.

He reluctantly pulled his mouth from hers.

Beyond them, closer to the house, a man with a mess of wavy light brown hair and eyes the same shade of green as Drew's stood with one hand shoved into the pocket of his jeans. His gaze shifted between Logan and Drew, his lips in a tight line.

This had to be Aubrey.

Logan imagined he'd wear a similar expression if he caught some guy kissing and touching Morgan the way he'd been kissing and touching Drew.

She turned and faced him, arms crossed, her back to Logan. "Creepy much? How long have you been standing there?"

The man held up a lit cigarette that had been down at his side. "I came out to smoke and heard voices. It got quiet, so I walked over to see what was up."

Logan moved from behind Drew and thrust out his hand. "I'm Logan."

"Aubrey." They shook hands, then he took a drag of his cigarette. "Glad you could come. It's about time we met."

Drew looped her arm through his. "We'll see you inside."

"Why rush off? Afraid I'm going to embarrass you?" Aubrey flashed her a crooked smile.

"You're more likely to embarrass yourself, Aubrey."

That only made his smile grow.

"Drew told me you're an archaeologist," Logan said, not budging despite her trying to tug him along toward the door. This was his chance to find out about Aubrey's investigation.

"Not a very good one, apparently, or I wouldn't be here."

"Are you considering changing occupations? Drew said you were doing some detective work."

Aubrey cut his eyes in Drew's direction. It was the type of non-verbal communication he and Morgan shared whenever they questioned the other's motives. The Millers had agreed to keep their mouths shut about the painting. To Aubrey, Logan was an outsider, not someone to share secrets with. To get him to talk, he'd have to change that.

"Nah. I can't wait to get back in the field," Aubrey said. "How about you, Logan? What line of work are you in?"

"He doesn't work." Drew let go of her death grip on his arm and propped her hand on her hip.

He squinted at her. "I recently photographed a wedding."

"Doesn't count. You wouldn't let them pay you."

Logan's gaze dropped. *Busted.* Taking money from her friends didn't sit right with him. Not only had he agreed to the job as a favor to her, but he'd used it as an opportunity to squeeze her for information.

"Oh, you didn't think I knew that?" she asked.

He ignored her and knelt, spotting something sparkly in the crack of the sidewalk. It was so small he had to pinch it to pick it up. He let it drop into his palm and examined it. An earring. He stood and held it out to Drew. "Is this yours?"

She shook her head. "Not my style."

"Didn't think so."

"Maybe Marjorie's," Aubrey said.

Drew's eyes lit up. "Let's go ask her." She grabbed Logan's other wrist and pulled.

In the house, a very pretty, very pregnant woman sat at the table, folding napkins on top of her belly.

"Marjorie, did you lose an earring?" Drew took it from him and held her palm out so the woman could see it.

She shook her head and turned to Logan with a smile. "Hi, Logan. I'm Marjorie, Drew's sister-in-law."

Marjorie went to stand, but he waved her off.

"Don't get up."

"Logan," Grant said, wiping his hands on a dish towel and walking from the kitchen to the dining area. He put his hand out. A brightly colored tattoo of a bleeding heart peeked out from his short sleeve T-shirt. "Good to see you again."

"Where's Dad?" Drew asked.

"I'm right here," her father answered as he appeared from the hallway and pulled her into a hug. He released her and gave Logan a quick once-over. "Nice to finally meet you, Logan. I'm Sam."

He shook his hand. "Yes, sir. I was beginning to think your daughter was ashamed of me."

"I'd like to say she's told me all about you, but I haven't seen her enough lately to drag any information out of her."

"What do you want to know?" He wanted Sam to trust him, as fucked up as that was.

"Let's start with where you're from."

Easy. "Las Vegas, Nevada."

Drew pressed herself into his side. "He was a poker player before he moved to Savannah."

Sam glanced at the Richard Mille watch Uncle John had given Logan for his twenty-first birthday. "I'm going to make an educated guess and say you didn't retire from poker because you went bankrupt."

"I didn't retire. I'm just taking a little break."

"So, you're going back to Vegas?" Lee asked, looking from him to Drew and back.

Marjorie cleared her throat. "Simmer down, Lee. He's not going to drag your sister back there with him by her hair." She threw Logan an eye roll and a smile. "You have the extreme misfortune of being the first guy Drew has brought home to meet her three insanely overprotective brothers."

"And the night has only just begun." Aubrey smirked and elbowed Lee.

"We should play cards after dinner," Grant said.

Shit. No, they shouldn't. Meeting Drew's family hadn't stressed him until now. Her brothers weren't going to cut him a bit of slack.

"I'm in," Sam said.

"Daddy, I don't think you want to play poker against Logan." At least Drew could see what a bad idea it was. He wanted her family to like him, not despise him because he'd beat them at something he clearly had an advantage in.

"Sure, I do."

"Well, I don't." Drew set the bottle of wine on the counter and opened a drawer.

"I'm not playing if you don't," Logan said. Having her in the game meant he could help her win. Which meant he wouldn't win, but it also wouldn't seem like he'd thrown the game to get her dad or brothers to like him.

"Nope. Not doing it." She pulled out a corkscrew and opened the wine.

"Come on, Drew," Grant pressed. "We can all take turns embarrassing you in front of Logan if you don't play."

"Daddy!" She stomped. "Grant is being mean to me."

Sam chuckled. "You're on your own, kiddo."

"Hey, Logan," Lee said. "Did she ever tell you she was David Bowie for Halloween when she was in middle school? We have photographic proof."

"Daddy." Her plea was as soft as a breath, and chilling.

The energy in the room changed.

Sam made a cutthroat sign. "Enough. This night is to celebrate Drew, not humiliate her."

After that, her brothers mostly behaved themselves. Dinner was overwhelmingly southern. Oven-fried chicken, potato salad, okra, macaroni and cheese, biscuits, and corn bread.

During the meal, Aubrey paid attention to little else besides Logan, watching him like a hawk. It felt like more than standard protective brother behavior. Instead of dessert, Aubrey went outside, and Logan followed, ready to get to the bottom of whatever his problem was.

39

YOU PLAY WITH HER FUCKING HAIR

LOGAN

AUBREY'S EYES NARROWED as he stared at Logan and exhaled a cloud of smoke.

"If you have something to say, just say it." He needed to prove to Aubrey he was a straight shooter. No bullshit. If he had a problem with Logan, he wanted him to lay it out. They could sort through their shit and move on. No more seeing him as an outsider.

"Fine. I'll say it." Aubrey hopped up onto the hood of Drew's car and leaned back on his elbows. "You're in love with my sister."

It took him so off guard, he flinched. Too late to hide his reaction. A wave of lightheadedness crashed into him. He leaned back against his own car, not liking how his knees shook. "Come again?"

"You hardly ever take your eyes off her. You play with her fucking hair."

"That means I'm in love with her?"

"You aren't?"

Fuck. He'd backed himself into a corner. Denying it seemed worse than owning it.

By his tone, you'd have thought Aubrey was accusing him of something heinous, like in some way he'd wronged his sister. Seconds ticked by but no words came to him. His thoughts were a clusterfuck.

"Oh, damn. You hadn't realized that yet, huh?" Aubrey smirked and took another drag off his cigarette.

His own cigarette had an inch of ash hanging from the tip. Logan flicked it off. Skirting around admitting to anything, he said, "It's too soon."

Way too fucking soon. That didn't mean he wasn't guilty of it. He didn't want anybody else, and that wasn't going to change. They hadn't known each other long, but things were getting serious. He'd come to a family dinner. What was next? Moving in together? Damn. He didn't hate that idea.

Drew wouldn't commit to anything that major, though. Not right now. Probably not for a long time. If he moved into a place with a full-size bathroom, maybe she'd start spending the night more often. Baby steps.

"I don't think there's a set germination time." Aubrey's you're-an-idiot tone pissed him off.

He didn't want to talk about this. Especially not with one of her brothers. He'd rather not think about it at all. Not until he'd found out who stole the painting and how to get it back.

"Maybe not with other women, but Drew's not an easy person to get close to. She overthinks everything and does her damnedest to keep me at arm's length."

Aubrey tilted his head. "Yet, here you are, the first guy she's ever brought around her family. I'm pretty sure you're the first guy she's ever given the time of day."

And despite that, it wasn't enough for Logan. He wanted more. He wanted those walls she'd built around her burned to the ground. But again, this wasn't what he wanted to talk about. Time to regain control of the conversation. "Are you an archaeologist or a love doctor?"

"Neither. I'm an archaeological anthropologist. I study people who've been dead for hundreds, sometimes thousands of years. Figuring out what their lives were like. What was important to them. Figuring out those same things about living, breathing people is a cakewalk."

He didn't like being told he was easy to read. It was the worst thing someone could say to him. "Your sister *is* important to me. Is that what you want to hear?"

Aubrey slid off the car and stubbed out his cigarette. "Nah. I want to make sure you know that you're never going to be as important to her as her art."

His gut twisted. He understood that winning this competition came first for the foreseeable future, but *never*? He'd been hoping once she'd achieved her goal, she'd be less stressed and more interested in a future with him. But her brother, the person she'd claimed she was closer to than anyone, said otherwise.

"Did she inherit that trait from your dad?" Logan needed to bring things around to the painting. Letting his emotions get all fucked up by whatever Aubrey was trying to convince him of was amateur hour.

He scoffed. "No. She's one-of-a-kind. Got her own, unique brand of fucked-up-ness thanks to the way her life has unfolded."

"How has it unfolded?" Drew hadn't shared much about her past. Maybe if he could drag some of it out of her brother, he could get her to confide in him about it if he handled it delicately.

"Did you notice our mom isn't here?" Aubrey asked, his voice thick with bitterness. "Have you ever heard Drew talk about her?"

He shook his head. And maybe he hadn't thought that was strange because he didn't talk about his own mother, or really even think about her. But it probably wasn't normal.

"She died when Drew was eight. Drew was with her when it happened. They were at the grocery store, picking out apples for a pie. She collapsed, and that was it. She was gone. A brain aneurysm. The smell of apples still makes Drew sick to her stomach." Aubrey clenched his jaw and stared off in the distance.

Logan didn't know what to say, so he didn't say anything. He waited for Aubrey to collect himself enough to say more.

"You'll never hear her mention our mom. We can't even bring her up in front of Drew. Her art is her drug. It's what she uses to self-medicate. She can get lost in it and ignore her pain." Aubrey took two steps closer to Logan, bringing them eye-to-eye. "I've always thought someone would come along and show her how to stop hiding from her feelings, someone who would be so open and honest about themselves, that she'd slowly start to open up to them. Is that going to be you, Logan?"

◈ ◈ ◈ ◈

"FIVE CARD DRAW ALRIGHT, OR ARE YOU A TEXAS HOLD 'EM MAN?" Sam asked Logan as he tore the cellophane off a new deck of cards.

Drew's brothers had badgered her relentlessly until she gave in and agreed to join their poker game. No way in hell did Logan want to play cards with the Millers, but there was no getting out of it. Maybe he should wipe them all out as quickly as possible, so he could take Drew, who still hadn't agreed to come home with him, back to the *Gypsy*.

He put his arm around the back of Drew's chair. "I'm a play 'em any way they're dealt man."

Grant set a poker chip carousel on the table. "I don't know that it's a good idea for you two to sit next to each other."

"Why?" Drew asked, her tone brimming with defensiveness.

Grant smirked and took his seat next to Lee. "I don't want it to be easy for you to conspire. Seems safer to keep you out of whispering distance."

Logan snorted. This wasn't a partner game, but okay. He'd roll with it because sitting across the table from Drew meant he could see her better, which meant it'd be easier to watch for her tells. No need for him to cheat. Helping her win was going to be a cinch.

"*Roi des cons*," Drew muttered.

"What did you say?" Logan asked.

"She said her brother is the king of idiots. In French." Sam smiled wide, like he was as proud of her for insulting Grant as he was for making it as a contest finalist.

"You speak French?" he asked, turning toward her in his seat.

"My mom was a high school French teacher." Her gaze connected with his and held steady.

The room had flatlined. Logan could feel the weight of every single stare on them, but he couldn't take his eyes off Drew to note their expressions. The rawness in those green eyes slayed him. Something soft and fragile and enigmatic about her shone through. And, not for the first time, he realized how badly he wanted more of her. More than she might be able to give.

Aubrey told him she didn't talk about their mom. So, what was this? He didn't know what to do or say. If this was a breakthrough moment, he should probably do *something* to encourage her to talk more about her mom.

"How did she learn French?" *Keep talking. Don't shut down.*

A whisper of a smile flitted across her lips as she turned her attention to the stacks of chips Lee had pushed across the table to her. She rearranged them into smaller stacks as she spoke. "Growing up she was obsessed with the idea of living in Paris, so she started studying the language."

"Did she ever get to live there?" he asked.

"She visited a few times. We took our honeymoon there," Sam said. "But she never got to live there. Drew did, though."

Logan raised an eyebrow. "You never told me that."

She shrugged, still devoting her attention to her chips. "I was in a study abroad program. Just one semester."

He had come to understand Drew. Her ambition, her goals, her triggers, her insecurities, her moods—he'd unraveled the intricacies of her personality. But her backstory remained a mystery. He didn't like that.

Clearly, that's where her pain resided. He couldn't—and didn't want to—rely on her family to fill in the blanks. Aubrey was right. She wasn't going to volunteer that information. If he modeled sharing deeply personal details of his life, would she respond in kind?

"I agree with Grant," Aubrey said. "Drew shouldn't be allowed to sit by Logan."

She shot him a look so dirty it rivaled the one she'd given him when he'd spilled coffee on her illustrations.

Logan leaned closer to her and whispered, "It's fine, babe. Sit across from me and I'll help you stomp your brothers at poker."

Her frown shifted into a grin. She scooted her chair back and stood. "Trade me spots, Aubrey."

Aubrey hesitated for a second, and then as if he'd resigned himself to his little sister's bossiness, swapped places with her.

"It was lovely to meet you, Logan," Marjorie said. "Lee, can you give Grant a ride home? I'm beat."

Lee nodded, then finished doling out the chips.

Grant craned his neck back to kiss his wife. His eyes stayed glued to her until she'd disappeared out the door.

Once everyone had anteed, Sam dealt everyone five cards.

Logan left his face down, studying Drew as she scooped up hers and arranged them.

Her eyebrows pinched together. She didn't have shit.

He lifted his cards enough to see their faces and used his thumb to fan them out. One card short of a flush.

"I'm raising." With a smirk, Lee tossed three chips into the pot. Either he had a lousy poker face, or he was bluffing big time.

"Fold," Grant said and slid his cards toward Sam.

Drew pulled her bottom lip between her teeth. Her gaze lifted to his.

"It's three chips, baby," he said. "It's not gonna break ya."

She rolled her eyes and added her chips.

Logan, Aubrey, and Sam followed suit.

Once everyone had replaced their discards, Lee once again upped the bet. This time another ten chips.

"Nope," Drew said, popping the P. She shoved her cards toward her father.

Logan had a flush, Queen high. He saw Lee's bet and raised him fifteen.

Aubrey groaned and folded.

Sam folded.

Lee narrowed his eyes at Logan and pushed fifteen more chips into the pot. "Call."

Logan revealed his hand.

Lee's jaw tightened. He turned his cards over, revealing three jacks.

"I told you you guys didn't want to play against him," Drew said as he collected his winnings. "Would you listen to me? Of course not."

Sam laughed. "The game's not over yet, sweetie."

And it wasn't. Sam won the next two hands. The next round, Logan won on a bluff, with Grant and Lee both folding after donating half of their remaining chips to the pot.

The game went on, back and forth, with Drew the only one who had yet to win a hand. Sam and Aubrey ran out of chips at the same time.

He knew when she had a hand that wasn't complete trash and set his plan into action. With his chip count, he easily pushed Grant and Lee out.

Drew chewed her lip, checking and rechecking her cards while he waited for her to make a call.

"Scared?" Logan asked.

The look she shot him made him laugh. "Of you? Never."

She went all-in.

Logan feigned uncertainty, fiddling with a stack of his chips. Then he shook his head and folded.

"Oh, come on," Lee muttered. "You gave her that."

He shrugged. Maybe she'd give him something later to say thank you.

40

A CHARMING CONFESSION

DREW STEPPED INTO THE LIVING ROOM of the *Gypsy* and stopped short. An enormous bouquet of black and pink roses—at least three dozen—and two glass flutes and an ice bucket holding a bottle of champagne waited on the coffee table. Next to the vase was a long black box.

Logan squeezed by her and made his way inside. "I wanted to have our own celebration." He rolled the sleeves of his shirt up to his elbows and ran his hands through his hair.

Since they'd left her house, he'd been acting strange. He'd hardly said a word in the car. He was fidgety and that was so unlike him it made her suspicious. Something wasn't right.

"You're nervous."

"Yeah," he said, slipping his hands into his pockets. "I'm nervous."

She tilted her head and studied his face. "I thought you were the master at hiding your emotions."

He leaned against the captain's chair and crossed his arms. "When I'm trying. Why would I try to hide how I'm feeling from you?"

Why wouldn't he? This wasn't real. As much as she wanted to believe otherwise, she knew better.

Dinner with her family had been great. Her dad liked him—not that she'd doubted he would. Even though he'd set her up to completely murder her brothers at poker, they all seemed to like him. Except Aubrey, but he had his reasons. They'd all have their reasons when this was over.

Her gaze dropped to the coffee table. "You didn't have to do all this."

"You don't want to open your present, then?"

She did and she didn't. That box very likely held jewelry. Whatever it was, it'd be exquisite. But if it was a part of his con, she didn't want it.

"It's shiny," he said in a teasing tone.

Her curiosity won out, and she opened the box. It was a white gold bracelet, with three charms dangling from it. A coffee cup, a sewing machine, and a hand of cards—a royal flush.

Logan took the box from her, removed the bracelet, and set the box on the table.

She held out her wrist.

He wrapped it around and joined the clasp. With one finger, he lifted the coffee cup charm. "How we met." His finger moved to the sewing machine. "This one is kind of obvious." The hand of cards sparkled in the light. "And this one is because I want to take you home and introduce you to Uncle John."

"When?" she asked, her voice quiet. This shouldn't be a surprise. She saw the message he'd sent saying he was going to ask her, but she'd never thought about her answer.

Logan took a few steps backward and pulled the champagne from the ice bucket. "I know you're crazy busy right now, and you're only going to get busier as the deadline for the show gets closer. I'm anxious to introduce you to him, but we can do Vegas after the show."

"That's over six months from now." Did he think they'd still be together then? Her temples throbbed. She'd kept herself from imagining a time when this was all over, when Logan was no longer in her life.

He poured champagne into the two glasses and handed her one. "Don't you think you'll be ready for a vacation by then?"

"I don't know."

"You don't have to decide when right now. I just want to hear that you want to."

Drew took a sip of champagne. "Is this what you were nervous about? Asking me to go home with you?"

Logan shook his head.

"Then why?"

"I need to tell you something and I'm worried about how you'll react."

That didn't sound good. She took a deep breath. If he was going to tell her the truth now, she wasn't so sure she was ready to hear it. She wasn't sure she'd ever be ready.

"Aubrey accused me of something tonight," he said and rubbed the back of his neck.

Her heart seized. Aubrey wouldn't—

But what else would he have accused Logan of? Now that she thought about it, Logan's behavior had been off since he'd come inside from having a smoke with Aubrey.

Damn him. Her brother couldn't trust her to do this her way.

"He accused me of being in love with you."

Her heart stopped beating. "What? Why would he say that? That's absurd."

Logan stared at her with an expression that said, "Is it really, though?"

"No. Logan, no. You can't." She shook her head hard enough to send her earrings swaying and hitting her neck.

He glanced at the floor, and then back at her, expressionless. Okay, *now* he decided to hide his emotions. Awesome.

She set—okay, slammed—her champagne on the table. "You're not supposed to say that."

"Are you mad that I just told you I love you? What the fuck,

Drew?" That dark, feral intensity flickered in his eyes. He was clearly trying to rein it in, but it seemed to be slightly beyond his control.

Logan plopped onto the settee and pressed his head back into it.

The room began to spin, but she didn't want to sit, she needed to move. She walked to the captain's chair and grabbed the armrest to steady herself. "I'm not mad. I'm…" Indescribable emotions wrapped around her like a boa constrictor, tightening until she got woozy.

She turned to him.

He'd shut down. Avoiding eye contact with her, he clenched his jaw and glared at the wall.

A feeling she *did* have a word for overrode the others. Guilt. "You mean it, don't you?" she said, almost choking on the words.

"Do I seem like a guy who would say that if I didn't?"

Did he? Maybe she could answer that question if she actually knew him. But he had secrets. Big ones. And yet…her gut said she did know Logan. It believed he'd *never* say that to her if he didn't mean it. Not even to pull off whatever con he was running.

Her legs wobbled. She crouched and hugged her knees. A sob slipped out. She hastily wiped a tear that spilled down her face. "No one has ever said it to me before. Not like this."

"Baby…" He walked over to her and knelt. He swept his thumbs over her cheeks, wiping away fresh tears.

Crying in front of him would have humiliated her a few weeks ago. But it didn't now. And being held by him felt safe, like he'd protect her from anything and everything.

Logan slowly lowered his mouth to hers.

She tasted the salty wetness of her tears on his lips.

His mouth slanting over hers again and again dissolved all the negative feelings. A warm knot emerged in her stomach. She wrapped her arms around him and pressed closer. This felt right, even though she knew it was wrong.

Logan pulled his lips from hers. He held her face in his palms and stared deep into her eyes. "I promise you, I've never meant anything more in my life."

41

OUR FRIEND BOB

LOGAN

SHE NEVER SAID IT BACK.

Logan swung his car door open and lit a smoke. Drew hadn't said she loved him the night before, or this morning when he'd dropped her off. She needed time, and he was going to have to find a way to be okay with that.

He strolled up the dock toward the *Gypsy* but froze when he spotted Professor Richard Anthony—who he'd taken a photography class with—sitting on the back deck.

What the fuck?

He pinched the cigarette between his lips and stepped on board.

"I got a message that you wanted to talk to me." His stare was hard and his shoulders tense.

Logan squinted as he took a drag. After he'd exhaled, he said, "I didn't leave a message for you."

Anthony raised his foot to rest across his knee. "You didn't tell our friend, *Bob*, to pass that message along?"

Holy fucking shit. He'd been antsy as hell waiting for Bob's associate to contact him. Until he had an idea of what his odds were for getting the painting back, he didn't want to tell Drew. Didn't want to get her hopes up for nothing.

He also didn't want to lose her. Knowing there was a good chance that he would if he told her, he'd kept it to himself.

He stabbed his cigarette out in the ashtray and took the other chair. "How'd you know where I live?"

Anthony rolled his eyes. "The same way I knew you worked for Bob. I followed you." He shook his head. "We can talk about that in a minute. First, I want to talk about you dating my goddaughter."

Logan almost fell out of his chair. "Come again?"

"Drew Miller is my goddaughter," he said, enunciating each word with emphasis as if Logan had some type of mental handicap.

His head spun with questions. His favorite professor was not only a blackmailing art thief, but Drew's godfather? That didn't add up. The only thing that made sense was…

"You're not trying to steal the painting from the original thief. You're trying to get it back."

"Good job, Logan." He applauded while rolling his eyes.

"Start at the beginning."

"I'll tell you everything," he said. "And then you're going to stay the hell away from Drew. Got it?"

Logan's throat tightened. "Why?"

"Why?" he shouted. "You don't sleep with the mark."

He threw his head back and squeezed his eyes shut. "It's a little more complicated than that."

"Why'd you go after her in the first place? Sam and his family don't know anything. There are no clues there."

Logan threw his hand up. "I didn't know that! If you wanted my help, why didn't you just come to me? You didn't have to go through Bob."

Anthony released a loud burst of air. "I was trying to help *you*. I negotiated your freedom. No need to thank me."

"Why?"

"Because I liked you." He rubbed his scalp with one large hand. "I used to do what Bob had you doing. Only no one was twisting my arm."

Logan raised an eyebrow.

"I started when I was just a kid. Petty theft. By the time I was twenty, I was stealing cars, taking blackmail photos, hustling anyone I could get an angle on. Not that I had anything to show for it. I spent it all bailing my dad out of jail every other week."

If Logan was going to listen to this, he was gonna need a drink. Didn't matter that it wasn't even ten. He shoved himself to his feet. "You drink bourbon?"

His uninvited guest chuckled. "I do when I have to tell a story like this one."

Logan grabbed a bottle and two glasses. After pouring, he lit another cigarette and sat, resting his glass on his knee.

Anthony threw back half of his bourbon. "I had a little brother. Julian. Smart kid, could have been anything." His voice, filled with emotion, revealed a hint of an accent. Boston, maybe. "Maybe not so smart, 'cause all he ever wanted was to be like me."

He paused, downed the rest of his bourbon, and let out a deep breath. "He came up with this idea that we'd tail other thieves, figure out their next hit, and then we'd let them go through with it. Afterward, we'd snatch the goods from them. They couldn't report us for stealing something they'd already stolen, and if the cops found any evidence at the original crime scene, it would point to them, never to us. The perfect crime."

Logan refilled both of their glasses. "Did it work?"

"Yeah, until we crossed someone we should have known better than to fuck with." He pinched the bridge of his nose. "Julian's girlfriend was pregnant, and she wanted him out. We were going to do one last job. The payoff was big, and of course, so were the risks. Julian ended up with a hole in his brain, and me with one in my chest."

Bile rose in Logan's throat. He washed it down with more bourbon. "That's brutal."

"Sometimes, I still wish I'd bled to death." He shook his head. "I left everything behind—not that there was much for me to leave. Shortly after, I got off a bus in Savannah and a few days after that, I met Sam. To this day, he's the closest thing I have to family."

"So, you thought you'd come out of retirement and get him his painting back."

Anthony shrugged. "It's been a while. I'm rusty. Not to mention I don't have the same kind of contacts in Savannah as I did back in—" He cut himself off. "I don't usually take a personal interest in my students, but you had this talent—raw talent—that I don't often see in first year students, something I can't teach."

Logan lit a cigarette and turned a deaf ear to the flattery. "Can you just get to the part where you felt you had the right to get involved in my personal business?"

"You had a long-range lens in your camera bag. Most college students' cars don't cost as much as a lens like that. Not to mention, you never turned in one photo taken from that kind of range." Anthony raised a suspicious eyebrow at him. "I didn't have to tail you for long before you led me to Bob. I couldn't figure out why you would work for a low-rent crook like him. You didn't need the money."

Logan pushed up from his chair and paced the short distance to the cabin doors. It really got to him that this man he'd seen as a mentor had stalked him, learned intimate details about his life, thought he could be his savior.

He jammed his hand through his hair. "Fine. You thought you'd kill two birds with one stone. What'd Sam think of your plan?"

After a stretch of silence, he spun around.

Anthony took a sip of bourbon, but his face stayed expressionless.

"You didn't tell him you had a double motive." Logan scowled.

"He has no idea who I am, other than some guy Drew brought home for dinner, does he?"

"I told him to keep the police out of it, and I'd handle the rest. After you quit, I figured it was for the best, but then Drew mentioned her boyfriend. I'd hoped it was a coincidence you had the same name."

"And now that you know it's not?" Logan asked.

"Time to clean up the mess. Sam thinks Drew's in love with you."

Logan leaned against the ladder leading up to the flybridge and crossed his arms.

"Is she?" Anthony asked.

"I don't know," he snapped, then ground his teeth together.

Anthony stood and poured himself two more fingers of bourbon. "How could you let this happen?"

"So, I was good enough to blackmail someone for, but not good enough to date your goddaughter?"

"You lied to her." He shook his head, his lips set in a scowl. "I'm not going to stand by while you go on deceiving her."

"You want me to stay away from her?" Logan stepped forward. "What're you gonna do if I don't?"

Anthony stared at his bourbon while swirling it like a mini tornado.

"You need me to disappear because you don't want Sam to find out you put his daughter in the position to be my mark," Logan said. "You're fucking lucky that it was me, and that after I quit, I stuck around, because when you decided to keep dealing with Bob, he sent a real criminal after her, one with absolutely no morals. I protected her and cleaned up your mess, so it looks like I'm the one with the leverage here."

Anthony's chuckle irritated him. His intentions had been good, but the man had used horrible judgment. "What do you want?"

"Nothing. Not right now anyway."

He stood, glaring at Logan. "What are you going to do?"

"Something I should have done a long time ago."

42

PRETENDING? PSSHHH...

DREW TIP-TOED AROUND THE KITCHEN, grabbing a banana and a bottle of water. She'd worked at her studio until after midnight. The stress of the competition had started to weigh down on her like ten Louis Vuitton suitcases filled with cement.

She had to create a collection so undeniably beautiful and innovative that her competitors didn't stand a chance. And she had to do it with limited funds. Hiring help wasn't in her budget. She didn't know how she was going to buy shoes and accessories for the models after she bought all the fabric she needed. Thank God the foundation sponsoring the contest provided models for the runaway show.

Between her worries over the collection and her anxiety over Logan telling her he loved her, she wouldn't be able to sleep, but she headed down the hall to her bedroom anyway.

"Avoiding me?" Aubrey's voice came through the darkness.

She stopped short and turned toward the family room doorway, squinting against the darkness. "Trying to be creepy?"

Her hand grappled for the light switch.

Aubrey laid stretched out on the sofa, feet propped up on the arm, a stack of throw pillows elevating his head. "I fell asleep waiting for you to get home. Lucky for me, your car is in need of a new muffler. Otherwise, you'd have slipped out in the morning, like you did today."

He'd still been in bed when Logan dropped her off earlier today. Her head swimming with confusion, she'd showered and dressed like someone had hit fast forward on her personal remote.

She slinked into the room and dropped onto the blue chair. "Okay, yes, I was avoiding you this morning, but I'm just getting in now because I was working late at the studio."

He swung his legs, landing his feet on the floor. "Why did you go home with him last night? I thought you'd already looked for clues."

With the cold water bottle pressed to her temple, she geared herself up to tell her brother off. "Logan said you accused him of being in love with me. Why'd you do that, Aubrey?"

"Because he clearly is. And I thought I could guilt him into coming clean with you."

"Well, he didn't," she snapped. "And I'm not even sure if Logan did it anymore."

His lips turned downward. "Because…?"

"I know we didn't meet by coincidence. I know he followed me. But…" She released a heavy breath. "He hasn't done anything else suspicious since we've been going out."

He crossed his arms and leaned back. "Since you've been pretending that you're going out, you mean. Right?"

Drew took a sip of her water, then shrugged. "I thought we were both pretending, but now, I don't think he is."

He smacked his hand over his eyes, his mouth twisting as he scrunched up his nose. "I guess I should be the protective brother and tell you that he's bad news and warn you to stay away from him."

She snorted. "You're not going to?"

His hand slid down his face, revealing his eyes. Serious eyes. Even at funerals, his expression was never that somber. He always made silly faces and crossed his eyes to lighten the mood. "He's enamored with you.

There's no way someone can fake that so convincingly."

The rims of her eyes tightened, battling against the stinging tears determined to escape. She'd convinced herself she was a fool. Hoping for something impossible. Having Aubrey affirm it filled her with relief.

She bit her lip to keep from smiling. "What am I going to do?"

Aubrey rubbed his palms together. "Do you love him?"

"I shouldn't, but I do."

Aubrey rolled his eyes, then a smile tugged at his mouth. "Just ask him, okay? That's what I thought you should do from the beginning."

"No," she blurted out.

"Why the hell not? Please tell me you aren't just going to sweep all this under the rug."

She shrugged. "I don't want to hear his excuses. Logan might have done some shady things, but he wasn't being malicious, he was just protecting his sister."

"What about the painting? You're willing to forget about it?"

No, she'd never forget. But she was a realist. There was no chance in hell they'd ever get it back. "I can't believe Logan knows who stole the painting or how to get it back and hasn't told me. He wouldn't do that."

He nodded. "I trust your judgment."

43

LAUNDRY ROOM LEGEND

LOGAN

LOGAN GULPED, FORCING DOWN THE BILE ratcheting up his throat like a roller coaster on its way to the crest. Today—the day he'd spent more time horizontal than vertical, vowing he'd never again drink anything stronger than water—*would* be the day Drew conquered her fear of stepping off the dock onto the *Gypsy*. And in her typical fashion, she didn't do it half-ass. The boat pitched back and forth as she leapt aboard.

Whether the half of a bottle of bourbon he'd drank yesterday or the idea that Drew was probably going to walk out of his life today was more to blame, he didn't know. Didn't care.

He had his hand across his eyes, additional protection against the cheerful fucking sunlight, and splayed his fingers to peek through them.

Drew leaned inside the doorway, her hands braced on each side of the frame. Her lips—painted the exact roulette red as her heart-shaped sunglasses—lifted on one side. "Is that what you're wearing?"

There was no denying he looked like shit. He hadn't showered or shaved. His clothes were yesterday's leftovers, a dark gray T-shirt and black jeans. Not the ideal outfit for a Fourth of July beachside party.

Miss Miller, on the other hand, was her usual put-together self in a breezy white dress with her hair down and wavy. He peeked from behind his hand again to see her shoes. Flip-flops? That was new. And blue.

Patriotic. He wouldn't have expected any less of her color coordination skills.

He closed his fingers and uncrossed his ankles, then recrossed them in the opposite order on the arm of the sofa. "Is that what *you're* wearing?"

"It is until you take it off of me," she said, her sultry voice stroking his lust to life.

His hand dropped to his stomach and his head rolled to the side.

She knelt next to him and placed her hand on his chest, her sunglasses on top her head.

"You don't feel good?" She'd never sounded so concerned. Maybe he ought to take advantage and let her give him some TLC. Just one more day of being able to touch her. To breathe in the orange blossom scent on her skin. To be someone she didn't want to punch in the face.

He stared into her eyes. He'd given himself more than his fair share of those days. Time was up. If he could get his words right, and if she held onto her temper while he pled his case, maybe she'd still end up in his arms tonight.

"I'm a little hungover, but it's not so much that. When I said I love—"

Her fingers flew to his lips. "Wait. If you're going to take it back, fine. But don't say anything else until you hear what I was too afraid to say the other night." She took a deep breath. "I love you."

He nipped at her fingers with his teeth.

She yelped and pulled her hand to her chest.

Everything had to be a fucking ordeal with her. He couldn't gain her guilt at the coffee shop because instead of spilling coffee on himself, she'd impaled his foot with her stiletto, resulting in him ruining her illustrations. Then she'd enticed him to kiss her. It got worse, though. She'd let him—no, seduced him—without telling him she was a virgin. Somehow, because the universe must hate him, they'd ended up here, with her telling him she loved him right before he got ready to confess his dirty deed. She couldn't have just told him when he'd wanted to hear it. Too easy.

Her lips puckered. "Why are you being such a bear?" She stood and smoothed her skirt. Her voice filled with pout when she spoke next. "It's my favorite day out of the year. Barbecue and watermelon and corn on the cob and parades and fireworks. And this year was going to be the best because well…" She threw arms up.

He propped himself up on his elbows and forced a less grouchy tone. "Because what?"

She paced to the open doorway and leaned against the frame, her hands behind her. Her shoulders rounded into a shrug. "Because I thought I'd be spending it with you."

"Baby." His voice splintered like firewood split by a maul. "I didn't know it was that important to you."

Her finger hooked inside the center of her shades and pulled them down from the top of her head, obscuring her eyes. "Maybe you just didn't know how important *you* are to me."

LOGAN CARRIED A COOLER FILLED WITH BEER, champagne, and bottles of water to the picnic area in Matt and Claire's yard. Red, white, and blue balloons bobbed in the breeze, colliding, and making a *bop-bop-bop* sound. A large assortment of patriotic embellishments that Matt had bitched Claire had spent a fortune on decorated three long tables set up with food. Classic rock boomed from speakers on the deck and kids darted between adults standing around with icy beverages in hand.

Matt slapped Logan on the shoulder. "I heard you met the fam."

"Does Claire have brothers?"

"Only child." He flashed his teeth and then tipped his beer bottle to his lips.

"Lucky bastard."

"My brothers like you." Drew appeared next to him and propped a hand on her hip.

Logan stared at her, kind of liking the few extra inches he had over her without her heels. "Even Lee?"

She covered her grin by taking a swig of the beer Matt had handed her.

Claire had pulled out all the stops for the twins' birthday party, which meant Logan and Matt got roped into all sorts of menial tasks. After they had enough water balloons to fill a twenty-gallon tub, they were designated team captains for the water balloon war.

"Alright, soldiers." Logan squatted in the middle of a group of preschool and kindergarten-aged kids. "This may seem like an unusual approach, but see that woman over there?" He pointed to Drew, who was lost in conversation with Matt's mother. "When the whistle is blown, instead of charging the enemy, we are going to run in the opposite direction and open fire on her. The enemy will be confused. We will use that weakness. As soon as you throw your balloon at Miss Drew, run back here, reload, and charge the enemy. Any questions?"

"Are we going to get in trouble?" a little kid with freckles covering his face asked.

"No, I won't let you get in trouble. Anything else?"

Autumn inched closer to Logan's side. "Is Aunt Drew your girlfriend?"

"Yes. That's why I have permission to use her as a diversion," he told the white lie with a straight face. He stood and gave the ready signal to Matt by whistling.

Eight bloodthirsty tots charged, unloading an arsenal of water balloons on Drew. The first balloon hit her foot, but the rest pelted her stomach and chest. The children's accuracy impressed him.

She shrieked and whipped her head left to right, murder in her eyes.

He shot her a *bring it* smile.

Before she got halfway, Matt rounded his troops and sent them in her direction. Half of the second round of balloons missed their target, but enough made contact to thoroughly soak her.

She stood, dripping wet and seething mad. Her white cotton dress clung to her body, exposing the red bikini underneath.

Logan's cock twitched.

A whistle of appreciation snapped him out of his stupor.

Colin, Matt's brother stared at her, his expression lustful.

Logan glanced around for a towel to wrap around her but found none. He grabbed her hand and dragged her toward the house.

"Where are you taking me, you asshole?"

"To get some dry clothes."

"I didn't bring a change of clothes."

He ushered her up the porch steps. "You can borrow something from Claire."

"She's two sizes smaller than I am."

"You can put your dress in the dryer, then."

He shoved her into the small laundry room and hiked her dress up over her hips.

She pushed it down. "Logan! I'm not going to run around in my bikini while my dress dries."

"You're right about that." He worked the dress up again, being quick about getting it over her head before she stopped him. "I'll keep you company while you wait."

He tossed the wet dress into the dryer and turned it on. When he turned back to her, he scraped his gaze down her body. A sheen of moisture and goosebumps covered her skin. The top covered most of her breasts but the ties on the bottoms begged to be undone. He reached past her and pulled the laundry room door shut.

"People have been coming into the house to use the bathroom all day," she said. "We can't fool around in here. Someone will catch us."

He captured her hands, held them above her head, and pushed her against the closed door. "Then you're going to have to try to be quiet." He tickled her neck with his tongue.

She whimpered.

His swim trunks became even tighter.

"Really, Logan—"

"Shhh." He sealed his mouth to hers.

Letting go of her hands, he yanked the ties of her bikini bottom, then shed his T-shirt. He lifted her and set her on top of the dryer, then plucked the flimsy top from her body.

Her tits were so full and round, he couldn't stop a loud growl from escaping as he cupped them in his hand.

Her hand flew to his mouth.

He laughed beneath her palm. Then his amusement dissipated. "Shit."

"What?" Her eyes searched his, worry growing in them.

"No condom."

"Oh. Yeah." Her cheeks pinked. "I'm on the pill."

His eyebrow shot up. "Since when?" And did that mean she was going to let him inside her without anything between them? The idea made him harder.

"Not long after you spent the night at my apartment." Her cheeks went from pink to red. "I didn't know how to ask—to make sure—"

"I'm clean."

She grasped his hips and pulled him closer, wrapping her legs around him. "Okay, then."

With his hands on her hips, he tugged her to the very edge of the dryer and pushed down his swim trunks. He crushed his mouth against hers, muffling her moan as he eased inside.

Her body curved into his, breaking their mouths apart. Hard nipples scraped his chest.

He dipped his head to take one into his mouth. Her heels dug into the backs of his thighs and her fingers squeezed his shoulders.

Logan tightened his grip on her hips and increased his pace. He didn't have the luxury of drawing this out. As exhilarating as the threat of being caught was, he didn't want anyone to walk in on them. Because if someone did, she'd want to stop, and holy fuck, he didn't think he could.

He switched his attention to her other breast, rubbing his thumb across her nipple while his mouth sought the soft spot behind her ear that made her squirm. She whimpered and his hand flew to her mouth. Beneath his chest, hers vibrated.

They were a pair. There'd never be anyone that'd make him happier—or crazier—than she did. Losing her scared him, but he loved her enough that he couldn't keep doing this to her. She had to know everything.

Tomorrow.

She wanted today. And damn it, she'd have today.

Friction grew between their joined bodies and her insides spasmed. Her walls squeezing him sent him into oblivion. He closed his eyes and slammed into her.

His thrusts stopped and then picked back up in a shallow rhythm, his forehead on her shoulder.

"We're never using condoms again," she whispered.

He lifted his head and watched her face as he withdrew. Her mouth opened but no sound came out. He loved the look on her face when he did that. Like he'd taken something she needed to be whole.

The sound of silverware rattling jerked him back to reality.

Drew's eyes widened and she scooted off the dryer, scrambling to get back into her bikini. He sighed and pulled on his clothes, fully clothed before she was able to get her bottoms on. He had to help her tie the strings on her bikini top and pull her dress over her head, her hands fumbled so bad.

"I love you," he whispered before pulling the door open.

44

FUCKERY ON THE FOURTH

LOGAN

LOGAN AND DREW CLEANED UP IN THE BATHROOM, then walked into the kitchen.

Claire stood at the counter, sticking candles into the birthday cake, a rectangle decorated with strawberries and blueberries to give it the appearance of an American flag. "Have fun desecrating my laundry room?" she asked without looking up.

Drew turned a fiery shade of red.

Logan coughed to cover his laughter. "Do you want me to take the cake out for you?"

"Yes, thank you for offering." Claire beamed at him.

He lifted the cake from the table and carried it outside.

The women trailed in his wake, whispering. The next hour was spent singing *Happy Birthday*, eating cake, and watching the twins open their presents.

Once the birthday rituals had all been carried out, Matt invited Logan to pitch horseshoes against his brother and father. As much as he liked Matt, he wouldn't mind hitting his brother in the face with a horseshoe. The way he looked at Drew really irked him.

After a few rounds of horseshoes, Logan didn't hate him so much. Like their father, Colin was a dedicated serviceman. It was hard to hate someone who volunteered to serve their country. He was also a good sport when he lost, making jokes about his father not holding up his end of the partnership.

Logan couldn't blame him for being attracted to Drew. If she had been Colin's girlfriend, he would have done more than just look. He would have tried his damnedest to steal her.

When they'd had their fill of the sport, the sun had already set. He was about to go to the beach where a crowd had gathered, waiting for the fireworks show, when he spotted Drew coming from the porch with a stack of quilts and towels in her arms. He tried to take the stack from her, but she resisted.

"Claire is in the kitchen. She's got stuff for s'mores and ice cream and popsicles, go help her bring them down to the beach." She was bossing him around, but he didn't mind. It turned him on a little.

He found Claire in the kitchen, like she'd said he would.

She was loading a basket with chocolate bars, marshmallows, and graham crackers. "Hey, Logan," she said as he opened the screen door.

"Hey," he said. "I'm at your service. What do you need me to carry?"

"There's boxes of popsicles and a big bag full of ice cream cups in the freezer. You can take those down and pass them out to the kids."

He walked over to the freezer and gripped the handle.

"Things have gotten pretty serious between you two," she said without looking up from the basket. "Drew was having a rough time for a while there, with her father's painting being stolen and then her apartment getting broken into, plus the stress of the competition. I don't know if she could have handled it all without you. She's never been this happy."

"I don't know if I should be flattered or think that's sad."

She turned and braced her hands behind her on the table. "I met Drew the year after her mom died. All these years later, she's only talked to me about it once, but I can tell she feels a void in her life where her mom should be. It's like everything in her life that should make her happy is bittersweet because her mom's not here."

He turned his head and stared out the window in the direction of the beach. All he could see was the glow of the bonfire and a few silhouetted figures moving around it. Maybe that's all he really saw of Drew. A silhouette. He knew the outline of who she was, but he didn't know much about what went on inside.

She'd been a little girl, all alone in a grocery store, with her mom dying. He couldn't even—

And she didn't talk about it. Not to her best friend. Not to her family.

As if reading his mind, Claire said, "It's hard for her to talk about it. I don't think she has a lot of memories of her mom besides that one." A far-off, sad smile appeared on her face. "She does have a very vivid memory of her mom reading to her in the garden. That's why she took it so hard when the painting was stolen. It was like losing her mom all over again."

"The painting was of her mother?" He swayed, dizziness swamping him.

Claire nodded. "Of the two of them. They're in her garden, reading a book on a blanket. It's really a very beautiful painting. Drew says she remembers everything about that day. The way her mother's voice sounded when she read her the story, the smell of the garden, how it felt to be in her arms."

His heart shriveled into a hard, decrepit heap. What he thought had been a harmless secret was a terrible tragedy for Drew.

Claire backed out of the screen door, the basket of s'mores ingredients in her arms. "C'mon. The fireworks are starting."

Logan snagged the popsicles and ice cream, then followed.

He set down the icy treats and children swarmed the picnic table.

He spotted Drew standing beside the bonfire, her auburn hair illuminated by the flames. With her skin a variety of gold highlights and curvy shadows, he wanted to put his hands on her. Kiss her under the colors exploding in the sky. Jellyfish had more spine than him.

He inhaled, exhaled, and marched forward. His arm circled her waist and tugged her away from the fire. "We need to talk."

"What?" Her bare feet dug into the sand, resisting him, but her hands locked onto his biceps, attempting to keep him close. "The fireworks just started."

"It can't wait." If he didn't do this now, he would lose his nerve.

Her lips parted and her gaze opened into his. She nodded and let him lead her away from the party, halfway between the beach and the house.

"You're scaring me, Logan."

"I know, baby." He rubbed his forehead.

"Well?"

"We didn't meet by coincidence."

Her arms locked across her chest. "I know."

He shook his head. "Drew, listen to what I'm telling you. I came to the coffee shop looking for you. I knew who you were."

Her bored expression stayed in place. "I *know*."

He stepped back. "What do you mean?"

"I overheard you talking to Morgan."

"What did you hear?" he asked through clenched teeth.

She blew out a breath. "You were involved in the stealing of the painting."

What the flying fuck?

"No," he dragged out the word. She thought he was involved? And she didn't say a word? "I had nothing to do with it."

"Right. Whatever." She crossed her arms in front of her chest.

"Drew, how could you think that I—if you thought that, why the hell are you with me?"

She looked at her hands and picked at her nail polish.

His spine stiffened. His hands reached for her, wanting to shake her, but he lowered them to his sides. "Answer me."

"Aubrey and I wanted to find out how you were involved. We thought maybe we could get the painting back if—"

"You tried to hustle me?" Logan couldn't believe it. He wanted to break something. He settled on kicking at the ground.

"I didn't try," she said, voice filled with fury. "I did hustle you."

"So, none of it was real? You stooped to having sex with me to pull the wool over my eyes?"

"You did the same thing to me!" Drew's eyes narrowed and her lips pinched together.

"It's not the same. Not at all." Logan had made the mistake of sleeping with Drew, but he'd quit the next day. He'd tried like hell to do the right thing and stay away from her. "When?"

"When what?"

"When did you decide that you would fuck me if it meant finding out where the painting was?"

Drew shoved him, but he didn't budge. "That's not what happened."

"I didn't try to sleep with you after the wedding. You came on to me, remember?" Logan pointed his thumb at his chest. "The next morning, I quit the assignment. I was going to leave you alone after that. But it didn't work."

Drew's face fell. She shook her head, taking a step back. "I don't want to talk about this anymore."

"I love you, Drew." Logan reached for her, but she jerked back. "I want to get this straightened out. It's been hanging over my head for weeks."

"Oh, it's about easing your conscience?" She blinked rapidly and took a deep breath. "You don't love me, Logan. If you did, you wouldn't be doing this right now. When I'm having one of the best days of my life."

"I do love you," he shouted. "And you love me. We'll work this out."

Of all the sappy shit he'd never thought he'd say. Jesus Christ. What the hell had happened to him? He wasn't *this* guy. He'd never felt so vulnerable in all his life.

And he fucking hated it.

She shook her head. "No. This was wrong from the beginning. We don't belong together."

"Bullshit."

Drew kept her gaze to the ground. "I want you to leave."

A flurry of fireworks burst in the sky, signaling the finale.

Logan raged inside too much to speak. He ground his teeth, his mind jumping from one fucked up thought to the next. She'd manipulated him. Aubrey had been in on it. What kind of brother encourages his sister to sleep with a man to get intel?

He tried to go over everything from the time he'd helped her move from her apartment to now, but it was one giant clusterfuck in his mind. Maybe he *should* leave. He could never think straight around her.

He looked into her eyes one last time, incensed and miserable. Then he left her behind, not knowing if the damage between them could be repaired.

45

GYPSY GET-TOGETHER

Drew

DREW PULLED DOWN THE VISOR in Aubrey's Bronco and blotted at her swollen, watering eyes. Her jaw trembled as she tried to ward off another crying jag.

"Take your time." Aubrey cranked down his window and lit up a cig. "Sure you don't want to come back in a day or two? Take some time to digest things and figure out what you want?"

She fanned her face with her hand and blew out a breath that puffed up her cheeks. Until they'd driven through the gate to Logan's marina, she'd really thought she could do this. Whatever information Logan had about the painting's theft, was information they needed. And he *owed* her.

If she focused on being pissed-off, everything would be peachy. But her heart—wobbling inside her chest like a piece of china about to fall and shatter—kept getting in the way of her mad.

Breaking up with Logan was the right thing to do. She had spent too much time trying to justify her feelings for him. No matter how she spun it, they'd built a relationship on lies.

She flipped the visor back into place and grasped the door handle. "Let's get this over with. I have work to do today."

Her pulse dialed up and her lip quivered as she walked the dock. Even though Aubrey was by her side, she wanted to bail. Seeing Logan, well, she wasn't sure she could handle it.

When he stepped onto the back deck with a cigarette dangling from his lips, his hands poised to light it, she was more than sure she couldn't. She grabbed onto Aubrey's arm and dug her fingers in.

Logan's head turned, the lit cigarette tumbling from his lips as their eyes made contact. He muttered an obscenity and reached to retrieve it.

Drew and Aubrey came to a stop in front of his slip.

He tossed the still-lit and perfectly good cigarette overboard. His hair was a rumpled mess, which fit well with his wrinkled white T-shirt.

She adjusted her big sunglasses and hoped the lenses were dark enough to hide her tears.

He stared for a few seconds, the corners of his mouth tight.

Aubrey snapped his fingers in front of Logan's line of sight. "She's not here to make up with you or fight with you. We need to talk. Invite us in?"

His eyes shifted to the right, through the open door, into the cabin. When he looked back at them, his mouth opened, then shut.

He had company? Drew clamped her molars together. "You already found another innocent girl to con and take to bed? Wow. You work fast."

He rolled his eyes. "No. And I didn't trick you into getting into my bed. I think it was the other way around."

"Oh, right." She huffed a phony laugh. "This is all *my* fault."

His expression melted into a guilty one. "No, baby—"

"Drew!" Aubrey glared at her. "Do you want me to handle this, or do you want me to leave so you two can hash this out?"

"Handle it," she said in a low voice.

At the same time Logan said, "Yeah, leave."

A tall figure emerged from the cabin.

"Uncle Rich?" she and Aubrey blurted out at the same time. That's who Logan's company was? What the F?

She whipped her head in Aubrey's direction.

He stared at her with wide eyes.

"I think taking this inside is a good idea," her godfather said, not quite meeting her gaze.

Logan held his hand out to her.

Out of habit, she almost slipped her hand into his, but Aubrey stepped onto the boat ahead of her, turned his back to Logan, blocking Drew's view of him, and looked up at her. "Need help?"

"Nope." She planted one wedge sandal on the gunwale and swung the other leg over, stepping onto the boat in one stride. All three men stood out of her way while she walked inside the cabin, then one-by-one followed. She boosted herself into the captain's chair and crossed one leg over the other, straightening her yellow sundress to make sure she wasn't revealing too much leg or cleavage. She'd really wanted to mope around in jeans and her softest, comfiest T-shirt, but she didn't want Logan to know how badly their breakup had devastated her. No matter how badly she was hurting, forgiving him, forgetting all of this, and fixing what had been broken, wasn't possible.

He was the last to come through the door, sliding it shut after him. Aubrey sat on the settee, hanging his hat on his bent knee, his body leaned forward, like he wouldn't be sitting still for long.

Uncle Rich took up the other end, his long legs out before him, arms stretched across the back cushion. Comfortable for a guy who didn't even know her boy—Logan. How much time had he spent here?

She refused to so much as flick her gaze in Logan's direction. As long as she avoided eye contact, she should be able to keep her shit together. Somewhat.

Aubrey bounced his leg. "I've got about ten different scenarios in which you're both involved with the painting running through my head, and I don't like a single damn one of them, so someone better clear this up quick."

Her godfather sighed from deep in his chest. "Logan was my student. We weren't working together, though. Neither of us stole the painting or were in any way involved."

"Bullshit." The words came sputtering out of her mouth. She pinched her lips together to keep anymore from escaping.

Logan exhaled through his nose—like an irritated dragon. He was peeved with her? *Really.*

"It's true, Drew." Uncle Rich held her gaze and gave a slight nod. "Before I met your dad, I was a thief. I stole from other thieves. So, I told Sam not to go to the cops. I thought I had a better shot at stealing the painting back."

She blinked at him, willing herself to absorb the information, but it wouldn't sink in. It was like her brain had been shrink wrapped. She looked at Aubrey.

His gaze was down, focused on his hands, clasped together over his knees. "And you recruited Logan to help you?"

"Not exactly," Logan said under his breath.

Unable to help it, she cut her eyes in his direction.

He was slouched in the chair just inside the door, his head tilted back, resting against the wall.

Her stomach wound itself up, like a bobbin wrapping with thread. She was beginning to get the feeling that Uncle Rich hadn't given Logan a choice in any of this.

Don't feel sorry for him. Don't feel sorry for him. Don't feel anything *for him.*

"I did need Logan's help," Uncle Rich said. "And I thought he needed mine. I came up with a way to help get him out of the tight spot he was in, and have him get some answers for me, only he had no idea it was me blackmailing his boss to get him to do the job."

"What the fuck," Aubrey muttered under his breath and shot him a tight-faced glare. "Why did you need him to ask Drew about the robbery?

Why couldn't you just ask her yourself?"

"He didn't send me to talk to her." Logan straightened in his chair and looked Aubrey in the eye. "My assignment was to find suspects. I figured someone had to do recon and they probably posed as a repairman or housekeeper. Turns out, Drew was the person who let them all in the house, signed their checks, whatever. She knows more than she thinks she does."

"Hellooooo." Drew waved her hand through the air. "*She's* sitting right here."

His gaze shifted to her. "I never found out what you knew. I quit the morning after…the wedding."

"You want a medal for that or something? Maybe we should knight you," Drew snapped.

Uncle Rich cleared his throat, just as he did when trying to regain command over one of his classes. She could kick herself for not considering he'd have taught Logan, but then again, it was impossible for underclassmen to get into one of his classes. Drew had to have a few strings pulled to get into one as an elective while earning her Master's. Of course, Logan Cash had found a way around that. Probably a counterfeit transcript.

"We all want the same thing, right?" he asked. "To see the painting back where it belongs."

"That's why we're here." Aubrey stood and walked to Drew's side. "Tell us whatever you know."

"That isn't much," Logan said. He propped his elbow on the arm of the chair and rubbed the stubble along his jaw with his thumb. "Together, we might be able to pull this off. If Drew will cooperate—"

"We're not working with you," she blurted out, then looked to Aubrey for backup.

He gave her a weak smile. "I get why you wouldn't be thrilled about the idea, but Logan and Uncle Rich have more experience in this kind of thing."

She gave him her best you're-a-dirty-traitor scowl, then turned her gaze to Uncle Rich. "What about Dad?"

"He's got enough on his plate right now."

"What Professor Anthony means is, he doesn't want your dad to find out he's responsible for getting you mixed up with riffraff like me."

Uncle Rich leaned forward. "Sam likes you, Logan. Did it ever occur to you that maybe I'm trying to keep you from screwing that up?"

"It doesn't matter if my dad likes him or not." Drew slid out of her chair. "Because I don't."

"And if you change your mind?" Uncle Rich stared up at her, eyebrow raised. "Do you really want Sam to have anything to hold against Logan?"

"I'm not going to change my mind."

Logan stood, opened the door, and disappeared.

Aubrey jabbed his finger in her side.

She swiveled and got in his face. "Don't. I'm not the bad guy."

"After what we just heard, I'm starting to think he might not be, either."

Uncle Rich stood and took a few steps closer, which was all it took to put him in her personal space inside the small boat cabin. "You have every right to be mad, but if Logan thinks you might be able to narrow down suspects, and you want to help, you're going to have to talk to him."

"Fine. But for the record, I think this is a waste of time." She plopped onto the settee and crossed her arms while Aubrey went to smoke and lay out her stipulations for working with Logan. No apologizing. No talking about anything besides the painting. No touching. No exceptions.

Uncle Rich skimmed his fingers around the captain's wheel and covered the throttle with his palm. "Pretty nice boat."

"Mmmhmm. Not really a proper place to live though."

His eyes cut to her. "You don't approve?"

She ran the pad of her middle finger over the smooth edge of her thumb nail. Say things were different and she and Logan stayed together a few months. If he asked her to move in, supposing she wanted to, they'd have to find an apartment. It wasn't just lack of space for her clothes and shoes. The shower was a ridiculous hassle. The fridge was a midget. It wasn't like the place was decorate-able. Don't even get her started on all the beige. "It's fine for him. I mean, he'll probably be living in some swanky condo in Las Vegas in no time."

Uncle Rich shrugged. "Unless you want him to stay in Savannah."

Drew picked up the deck of cards on the coffee table and flipped it over in her hands. This was never supposed to be like that. One or both of them changing their lives to maintain their relationship. She had no intention of making any sacrifices. Whatever decisions she made about her future were hers to make alone.

But Logan had up and moved to Savannah for his sister. If she moved back to New York or some other metropolis, he'd come with her. Her tattered heart knew that much.

"You ready?" Logan asked from the doorway, his voice brushing down her spine like a calloused hand.

She set his deck of cards on the table and tucked her hands under her thighs. "Ready to get it over with."

Uncle Rich shot her a look before leaving. He'd been friends with her dad since before she was born, and never shied away from telling her to suck it up or to keep her temper in check. This time he didn't need to say it, that look communicated it clearly.

He perched on the edge of the coffee table, his knee next to hers, and hung his head, his hands running through his hair. After a deep inhalation through his nose, he reached for a black folder on the end of the table. He set it on his lap and opened it, flipping through a few pages of handwritten notes.

She had never seen his handwriting, which maybe wasn't that

surprising in this digital age. Curious, she glanced over, not actually reading the context but trying to get an impression of his penmanship. The lines were crisp, and all slanted a touch. Far from chicken scratch.

She tried to get a better look at the page of notes while he studied a photocopied document. Her thigh brushed his. With a small gasp, she pressed her knees together.

He lifted his head, slowly. Hooded eyes landed on her.

The irritation and clouded hurt that had been there earlier was gone. The color of his irises darkened.

Her body flushed from that one look. She tried to swallow subtly.

His gaze slid to her chest, where the exposed skin above her neckline pulsed with heat. She didn't have to look to know her skin was splotchy, and her nipples were hard, and her pounding heart was obvious.

Logan raised his chin a notch, meeting her eyes. If Aubrey and Uncle Rich hadn't been just outside, she was certain his hands would be on her. Regardless of her stipulations.

He cleared his throat and focused back on the documents in his lap. "Do you remember the cable guy?"

She shrugged. "He kind of made an impression."

His head snapped up and his eyebrows merged.

"He hit on me." Drew stood and walked around the coffee table. She couldn't bear another second of being so close to him. She stopped in front of the open doorway that led to the galley and Logan's bedroom. "He was chatty the whole time and before he left, he gave me his card and wrote his personal number on it. He said I could call him at any time if I had problems with my service—or anything else."

He clenched his jaw and shook his head. "You were with him the entire time he was in the house?"

"Yes."

"Was the TV he was working on in the same room as the painting?"

"No."

"Did he have a chance to see the painting?"

"No."

"Okay." He snagged a pen off the table and crossed out something on the paper, then turned it over. "The cleaning lady. Your dad has someone come in every other week?"

"Yes, and it's always the same woman."

"Do you ever see her, or just send in the check?"

"I send in the check. I do all my dad's bills." Her dad wasn't an idiot, or bad with money, or even forgetful. It was her way of taking care of him.

She wasn't a great cook, and she couldn't always be there to do the grocery shopping and prepare meals anyway. Trying to keep a clean house with three boys had been a lost cause, thus he'd hired the cleaning lady. They used to have someone once a week, for an entire day. Now that Grant and Lee lived on their own and Aubrey only lived at home sporadically, every other week for two hours was sufficient.

As a single dad, he had shouldered all the responsibilities and done it well, but she wanted to lighten his load, even if just a little. So, she made sure all the bills got paid on time.

Logan scratched the side of his nose while he stared at the paper on his lap. "I did a little digging. The cleaning lady has worked for the company for over three years, so I want to look at the other suspects first."

"What suspects?"

He flipped another page. "The landscaper?"

"Matt's mom." She crossed her arms. "Don't go there. Besides, she doesn't come inside."

"Right. Can you think of anyone else, repairman or anyone like that, who came to the house in the past six months?"

She leaned against the captain's chair and tried to walk herself through the past six months. "An energy conservation guy did an audit on the house."

"Did you set that up? Or did they offer you a free consultation?"

Her lips parted, then pinched together. *Uh-oh.* "He was going door-to-door."

"Did you see him go to any of your neighbor's doors?"

She shook her head. "But I wasn't paying attention. I didn't have any reason to be suspicious."

"What did he do while he was in the house?"

"Checked the windows and light fixtures and stuff like that."

He muttered something under his breath. "Was he in the room with the painting?"

She winced and nodded. "Oh, God. I let a thief into my house, didn't I? I made it easy for him."

"We don't know that yet. But if this guy was posing as an energy-whatever-consultant, it's still not your fault in anyway."

"How are we going to find out?"

"Did he give you any paperwork?"

She nodded. "Yeah. He did an estimate on his tablet of what it would cost to get everything up to snuff and what it would save us annually. He e-mailed it to me, and then I got a hard copy in the mail a few days later. Dad wanted to talk to him and schedule to have his company do the installation, but we never got around to following up."

"Get me the paperwork. I'll find out if the company is legit and if this guy really works for them."

Uncle Rich stuck his head through the door. "You narrow it down?"

Logan nodded. "Gotta check some stuff. I'll let you know what I find."

"Give me a call. I'm heading out." He winked at Drew. "See ya, kitten."

Once he was out of the way, Aubrey came inside the cabin. "You gonna fill me in?"

"Hang on," Logan said and stood, tossing the folder on the settee.

He leaned halfway out the door. He waited a few and then turned back to Drew and Aubrey. "I'm not ready to rule out Anthony as a suspect."

"What?" Drew wanted to punch him in the face. Who the hell did Logan Cash think he was? After everything he'd done, now he had the balls to accuse her godfather of stealing the painting. "He didn't do it!"

"He's right, Drew." Aubrey sat with his hands on his knees. "I don't believe he did it, either, but we need to be sure."

She crossed her arms and shook her head. "His word isn't enough?"

"I want to do a sweep of his house." Logan said it as though it was an everyday occurrence, like doing the dishes or taking out the trash. "If I don't find anything, we'll move on."

"You're going to break into his house?"

His eyes said, "Duh."

"No need." Aubrey stood and pulled his keys from his pocket. "I have the key. I fed and walked his dog when he and Dad went to Atlanta the other weekend."

46

UNTIL YOU CAME ALONG

LOGAN

LOGAN FLIPPED HIS GREEN POKER CHIP over each of his knuckles and then back again. And again. And again. And again.

"Can you quit that?" Drew snapped.

They sat in his car, being lookouts while Aubrey searched Anthony's house. It really wouldn't matter if he came home, since Aubrey had an excuse for being there, but if they could avoid it, it would be better.

He reached for his pack of cigarettes.

"Isn't it a little cliché for you to be carrying around a poker chip?"

He rolled his window down and lit up. "Probably."

"Is it your good luck charm or something?"

"Not exactly, but I did have it in my wallet the night you got a flat tire, so I guess it has brought me some luck." She wasn't going to like hearing that, but he wanted to remind her how good it had been between them that night.

"Did you forget the rules?"

He snorted. "You broke them first. You asked if it was my good luck charm. That doesn't exactly have anything to do with the painting."

She stayed quiet for a while. Then huffed. "What's the deal? It's just a twenty-five-dollar chip, right?"

Releasing the tension from his shoulders, he sank into the leather seat. "Uncle John gave it to me before my first high-stakes game. I guess he could tell I was pretty worked up about going against such big players. He said it didn't matter if I was playing against those guys for five million, just that I was playing. And if I lost my buy-in, then I'd still have this chip," Logan laughed, "and I'd start all over again, and when I saved up another 50K, I'd get into another big tournament."

"What happened?"

He took a few more drags from his cigarette and then threw it out. "I still have the chip, don't I?"

"You won five million dollars?" Her jaw dropped. "That's just… *crazy*."

"Any crazier than beating out hundreds of other fashion designers in a contest? My odds at winning that tournament were a lot better than yours."

"Yeah, but even if I win the final round, I'm not going to walk away with a million-and-a-half dollars."

"You're going to get a lot more recognition than I did, though. You'll end up making way more than that in the long run."

"What's up with all the faith in me?"

His eyes met hers in the shadow-filled car. "You're not just talented, but you're driven. Which are only a few of the reasons why I love you."

She shook her head slowly, mouthing "no" a second before his hands cupped her face and his lips landed on hers. She didn't put up a fight, but she didn't kiss back either. Something wet slipped between their lips.

He pulled back and swiped his thumb over her cheek, brushing away her tear track.

"It was always my intention to tell you. It was the 'when' that I struggled with. But I couldn't go on keeping it from you once I found out the painting was of you and your mother," he said, his voice as heavy as his heart. "If I'd waited even a few more hours, I'd have found another reason to put it off."

She pushed his hands from her face. "Do you feel better now? Is your conscience appeased?"

"No." He shook his head. "Not telling you was eating away at my sanity. And now that I have told you, you hate me. Either way, I lose."

"I don't hate you," she murmured.

"You don't?"

Her sigh filled the car. "No. That doesn't mean I like you enough to work things out."

"Don't have to like somebody to love them."

"Oh, shut up, Logan." She twisted her body and stared out the window. "You know, there were only two rules, and you broke them both."

"All I've done since I met you is break rules."

She snorted. "Because you were a regular rule-follower before."

"I might not always drive the speed limit, and I can't say I've never tapped into another person's Wi-Fi, but I do have a code and I've always stuck to it."

"Until I came along." Her eyes darted to him.

He turned his head and smirked. "Until you came along."

Drew rubbed her lips together.

Damn. He wanted her bad. Since she'd come walking down his dock yesterday, he had ached for that connection. Something between them had been damaged, maybe lost altogether, but the sexual pull between them was alive and well.

Maybe they could just fuck it out.

Logan reached for her, cupped her neck, and merged their lips. A pissed-off whimper vibrated from her throat. He nipped at her bottom lip. She leaned into him, bracing herself with her palms on his thighs. Her fingernails dug into his muscle, their sharpness dulled by the denim.

Her head angled to the side and her mouth opened. He groaned, then stroked her tongue with his.

The distinct sound of knuckles rapping on glass killed the moment. He pulled his mouth from hers and turned his head and looked up at Aubrey's fire-ant red face.

Logan ran his thumb across the corner of his mouth as he hit the button to roll the window down.

"If you were going to molest my sister instead of keep a look out, you could have stayed the fuck home." His voice was quiet. The I'm-so-mad-I can-barely-talk kind of quiet.

"You're right. Sorry, man."

Aubrey looked past him. "Get in the Bronco. You can ride with me back to the marina."

Drew nodded and reached for the door handle.

Before she stepped out of the car, Logan said, "Told ya."

She whipped her head back toward him. "Told me what?"

"Whenever you're around, I can't do my job right. I was supposed to be watching your brother's back."

Her big green eyes shrunk into dark slits. "Don't kiss me again."

DREW LEAPT UP FROM HER PERCH ON THE GUNWALE and stuck her finger in Logan's face. "I told you."

It felt so good to say it. Especially after Logan's I-told-you-so earlier.

He leaned forward in his deck chair, his forearms on his thighs. "Nothing?"

"Nada," Aubrey said. "He didn't do it. Unless he anticipated us checking him out and set up all that shit."

According to her brother, Uncle Rich's home office was full of research he had done, trying to find the painting. Aubrey had snapped photos with his phone. Profiles on professors at the college, copies of the notes Logan had taken, a file on Logan's old boss, and a list of random, unlikely suspects and their possible motives.

"Shit." Logan ran his palms down the sides of his face. He hadn't bothered with his usual manscaping. His five o'clock shadow was more of a forty-eight-hour shadow, and the crisp line normally present along his jaw was filled in with whiskers.

The tidy bad boy image he had always presented appealed to her. But this…scruffy, rumpled, antihero-thing he had going on. It did things to her.

Things that had her so hot, the trickle of sweat that dripped down spine, cooled by the breeze, turned to vapor. Things that made her forget relationships shouldn't be based on sex alone. Things that made her want to tell her brother she didn't need a ride home.

"The guy from that energy conservation company was legit," he said.

Aubrey plunked into the chair he had offered to her four times already. He pulled a cigarette from his pack with his lips and struck his lighter. After exhaling, he said, "We're missing something. There's gotta be someone we overlooked."

Logan rubbed his index finger against his bottom lip, his eyes locked on her. "We need to dig deeper. But not tonight."

Her lady parts went on high alert. *Stop looking at me like that.*

"I think we should ask the neighbors. Too many people live on our street for nobody to have seen anything," Aubrey said.

She tore her gaze from Logan, feeling like she'd broke the surface after a dive and could finally take a breath. "If they saw something suspicious, they would have said something by now or called the cops."

Believing they would get the painting back was foolish. The only progress happening was Logan getting back under her skin. She needed to get away from him. For good.

She squared her shoulders. "I can't waste any more time on this. I'm behind on all my deadlines. I'm going to have to work day-and-night to get my collection done as it is."

"Okay," Aubrey said soothingly. "You're right. You need to focus on your collection. We can handle this."

She stomped her heel before realizing how childish that was. "You aren't going to get the painting back. Stop kidding yourself!"

"I'm not ready to give up yet."

"Neither am I," Logan said.

"I'm not going to take you back if you find the painting." The words tumbled from her mouth. They had been in the back of her throat since she had agreed to work with him.

47

LET LITTLE SISTER HELP

LOGAN

LOGAN SORTED THROUGH the files laid out on his coffee table, trying to find the one with the list of cleaning ladies the Miller's had used over the past six months, when Morgan came through the cabin door, wide-leg white linen pants swishing around her ankles.

"What's wrong with Drew? I just passed her on the dock."

"Nothing," Logan said, retrieving the file and handing it to Aubrey.

"She was crying."

Aubrey blew a breath through his nose and sunk into his seat. His hand squeezed his forehead. "Maybe she's right and we should let this go."

Morgan propped a hand on her hip and looked from Aubrey to him. Her diamond stud earrings—a score from a job she'd done in Vegas—sparkled in the summer moonlight. "Let what go?"

"Don't worry about it."

Her forehead bunched. She walked to the coffee table and peered at the scattered papers and files. "What's all this?"

"Morgan." Logan couldn't help his grouchy tone. He had enough to worry about. "It's not a good time, okay?"

"No, not okay." She scooped up the sheet with his notes about the cable guy. "You're looking for the painting?"

He closed his eyes and inhaled. Waited for what he knew was coming.

"Without me?"

He opened his eyes.

Aubrey looked uncomfortable as hell. But he was trapped. Unless he wanted to squeeze by Morgan to get to the door.

"You're in Aubrey's way."

She folded her arms across her chest. "Why haven't you asked me for help?"

"Because I have bigger things to worry about than babysitting you."

"Babysitting me?" Her face fell. "Can you please stop holding that one mistake against me?"

"It was a pretty big fucking mistake."

"That doesn't mean I'm not the best person to help you with this."

"I wouldn't have this problem in the first place if it weren't for you."

Aubrey took a step in Morgan's direction. "I'm just going to…" He gave Logan a quick wave and waited for Morgan to move out of his way, then disappeared.

"I don't know why you're suddenly so bitter toward me," she said, her voice soft, avoiding eye contact. "I never asked you to come to my rescue, and I told you not to get involved in this. But if you don't want me around, then I don't want to be around."

She made her way off the boat. All alone, Logan stomped to the galley and grabbed a bottle. The irony of it all was that if Morgan hadn't screwed up and he hadn't come to Savannah, he never would have met Drew.

48

DREW 2.0

DREW STOOD IN FRONT OF HER DESIGN WALL and pinched the edge of her favorite sketch between her fingers. A gray silk dupioni dress with a tuxedo-shirt-inspired bodice. She had been saving the design for last, to keep herself psyched up while making the other muslin samples in her collection.

She tugged on the paper, sending the pushpins flying, and crumpled it in her palm.

The instant she'd stepped inside her studio this morning, everything had felt wrong. The seven completed muslin samples she had been satisfied with, now seemed like junk. This collection wasn't going to win any contest. Not that she had the time—or the money—to start over.

She tossed the balled-up paper in the bin with the others and covered her eyes with her hand. *Don't cry. You don't have time to cry.*

After a vain attempt at meditative breathing, she walked to her drafting table, and spotted Aubrey in the doorway.

He grinned at her, touched his palms together and gave her a slight bow. "Namaste."

She really didn't feel like being laughed at. With a glare, she said, "I just decided to scrap all the work I've done up until now, so I really don't have time for your bullshit."

He pressed his hand over his heart. "Me? Bullshit? Never."

She sat on the stool and crossed her arms. "What do you want?"

"To make sure you're okay."

"I'm fine."

"Now who's bullshitting?"

She turned to stare out the window. She was far from fine. But dwelling on it wouldn't help. What was done was done. She and Logan were over. "What do you want me to do? Sulk around in my pajamas, eating ice cream by the tubful, crying my eyes out?"

"If it helps." He picked up a tracing wheel, spinning its sharp spokes around and around and around. "*Or* you could talk to Logan."

"Get out."

"Drew, you've got to stop doing this. You repress all your pain, and it kills me to watch you do it."

"You want me to openly express my pain so you can watch?"

He grabbed hold of her shoulders and gave a squeeze. "Of course not, but I don't want to see you carrying it around, dying on the inside. You need to deal with it."

"I'm not good at talking about my feelings, okay? Just let me be."

"No," Aubrey said. "I won't. When you were with Logan, you were different. You, but better. Drew 2.0. You talked about Mom. If Logan can bring that out in you, I'll do everything I can to convince you to work things out with him."

Since she was eight years old, she had held everything inside, because she couldn't talk with her mom about it. All the confusion of adolescence she'd dealt with on her own. Talking with her dad or her brothers wouldn't have been the same.

After her mom had died, her dad had taken her shopping for a new leotard, shoes, and tights in preparation for her next season of ballet lessons. Before the first class of the year, she'd looked into the mirror at her lopsided bun and that had been the end. One look at her hair and everyone would know she was the girl who no longer had a mom.

She was still that girl. The girl who didn't have a mom to talk to about heartbreak. It wasn't fair. She wanted to tell her mom about Logan. In the beginning, she'd wanted to tell her how he'd stood up to her in the coffee shop. How she danced with a dozen different guys at Claire's wedding, but Logan was the only one who made her palms sweat. How he'd set up a mini art studio on his boat because he wanted her around.

And now she wanted to tell her mom how bad it hurt that it was over. To ask her how to fix things. What to say to him. If it was even okay to love him so intensely when their relationship was built on lies.

49

FORGIVENESS, FINALLY

LOGAN

LOGAN LET THE HEAVY DOOR SLAM and took a long, deep breath of night air—muggy and swampy air, but still better than what was floating around on the inside of the strip club he'd spent the past two hours in.

He lit a cigarette as he walked to his car, pissed he hadn't gotten anything more than a stripper named Glitz's phone number. Over the past week he had been in all caliber of nightclubs. Members only. LGBTQ+. Places where the drinks were served out of crystal and strings of diamonds encircled women like lights on Christmas trees. Places where people bragged about how much they had blown on art they didn't even understand. Places where people bragged about crimes they had gotten away with.

People told Logan things. His ears bled with the useless information. Of all the unimaginable things strangers had confessed to him after he'd wormed his way into their circle, buttered them up, made them feel like he knew them as well as their own mother, none of it had a damn thing to do with art theft.

Tomorrow, he'd meet up with Professor Anthony and Aubrey to tell them *again* that he hadn't gotten any closer to finding answers. Neither of them had gotten anywhere either. Things weren't looking good.

As his car sped onto the bridge over the Savannah River, he

wondered how Drew would react if he showed up at her house and told her he needed her. That he couldn't stand to spend another night without her.

Staying away, giving her space—it wasn't his style. He wasn't a fade into the background kind of guy. He was the kind of guy that got in her face and remind her what they'd had.

No, things weren't perfect. Were they ever? Didn't someone inevitably always fuck shit up?

Before he approached Drew, he needed to make amends with another person.

A simple sorry wouldn't do. But his brain was so tangled with this mess he couldn't think of a gesture to prove to Morgan how sorry he was.

He was too old to be mean to his sister because he was having a shitty day and she'd happened to walk in when it got ten times shittier.

Logan parked in front of her apartment and removed the keys to the *Gypsy* from his keyring. He knocked and listened to the sound of her feet beating down the stairs.

She opened the door of the duplex and frowned.

He reached for her hand and placed the key in her palm. "I love you, and I'm sorry. Make sure you get your boater's license."

For a few seconds, she stared at the key in her palm. Then she looked up at him and threw her arms around his neck. "I love you too. And I forgive you. Also, I'm sorry for all the grief I've caused. I know you'd rather be in Vegas."

He kissed her temple then held her at arm's length while he said, "I need your help."

She propped a hand on her hip. "Finally."

50

THE HELPFUL ANTIHERO

HIDDEN BEHIND THE CURTAIN OF HER HAIR, Drew opened her eyes and listened, praying that the knocking had been a dream. She wet the corners of her mouth, trying to rid them of the gross paste that had formed.

Rubber soles drummed against the wooden floorboards, coming closer to her drafting table, where she'd fallen asleep. She whipped her hair off her face and straightened, saying another prayer that it was her father or one of her brothers.

"I didn't mean to wake you."

Shit. Shit. Shit.

Drew faced Logan. He looked exactly like she remembered—amazing. The universe seriously hated her.

"How did you get in here?" she asked, crossing her arms.

"Aubrey. He called me, worried because you didn't come home last night."

"And he thought I was with you?" She rolled her eyes.

"No. He's worried you're pushing yourself harder than necessary, so you don't have to deal with your feelings about me."

So, he'd brought Logan here to confront her? What the fuck? Aubrey needed to stay out of her business.

Logan held out one of the two paper coffee cups in his hand.

Drew pushed herself off her stool and walked to him. "The last time you tried to apologize to me with coffee, you ruined my illustrations."

"Who said I was going to apologize?"

She wasn't going to take the bait. If she did, the next thing you know they'd be having hot, hot sex. Drew took the coffee from him and walked to the full-length mirror. And almost screamed. Her hair was a chia pet on steroids. Her makeup was chimney-sweep-chic. Her clothes were rumpled, and when she looked at the clock, she added the fact that they were from yesterday. Last she remembered, it was three in the morning. It was now close to ten.

"I'm going to be late for work." She rushed around, grabbing things. Her phone. Keys. A box of granola bars—empty.

"Stop." Logan blocked her path, preventing her from grabbing her purse. "When was the last time you slept in an actual bed?"

Three days ago? "I don't need your concern, Logan. I'm a big girl. Been taking care of myself for a while now."

He glanced around the room.

Her studio was normally very tidy. But right now, there were bolts of fabric haphazardly leaned up against the wall. Beads and sequins spilled on the floor. Color pencils and crumbled papers strewn over her worktable.

"Let me help you," he said.

She snorted and pushed past him. "I seriously doubt you could even sew a button."

"That's not the type of help I'm offering. Quit your job. Hire a few assistants, or seamstresses. Whatever employees you feel necessary. I'll pay for all of it."

"I don't need employees." Ridiculous. So ridiculous. "And I'm not taking your money."

"Drew, think of what you could accomplish if you could focus on this, and only this, if you didn't have to do *everything*. Throw some of the menial tasks to someone else."

"I can't."

"Is it against the contest rules?"

She shook her head. The other two contestants probably had people helping them. But that wasn't her style. The only way she could control the quality of the work was if she did it all herself.

"Don't risk the competition because you're too proud to accept my money. If you want, consider it a loan."

"Are you trying to buy back my love?"

Logan ran his tongue over his teeth. He looked like he wanted to chew her out for even suggesting it. "No. Trust me, I learned a while ago that manipulating you is impossible. I want you to win, and I'm willing to do whatever I can to help make that happen."

"I can do it on my own."

"Yeah, I know you can. That's not the point."

"You didn't come here to offer me money. And I doubt you came simply to deliver coffee. What do you want?"

He slipped his hand around her neck and looked deep into her eyes. "You. You're all I want."

Her studio suddenly felt very small. Heat flushed through her system. She was such a sucker for those eyes of his. So intense. She thought about Logan, and a moment exactly like this countless times a day.

Her eyes welled up. She pulled away, turning her head. *Get it together.*

She'd thought back over every detail of every minute she'd spent with him. He'd been acting, at least in the beginning. Which meant her reactions to him were influenced by dishonesty. She couldn't trust her feelings for him. She refused to be a fool.

"I need time," she said, her voice quiet and shaky. "My collection comes first."

She turned in time to see him hang his head. Her chest ached with a crushing force. It wasn't true. Her heart struggled to decide which was more important—Logan or her career. But she needed it to be true. Her career had to come first. She would have no self-respect if she lost the competition because she made her love life top priority.

Logan said she was all he wanted, but that wasn't true. If he gave up his poker career, he'd be miserable. How long before he left Savannah behind? Then she'd be left with nothing. No career. No Logan. No self-respect.

51

BEATRICE BENENATI

WITH TWO CARRY-OUT SHRIMP BASKETS, two lemonades, and an ass-load of determination to find a new direction for her collection, Drew let herself into the studio and called out for her father.

"Just me," a voice hollered from the back.

She navigated through her dad's maze of canvases.

A petite blonde in a black romper had one foot on the top step of an eight-foot ladder, the other braced against the wall, both hands tinkering with one of the security cameras Drew's dad had installed after the break-in at the house.

"Morgan?" She set the carry-out on her dad's worktable. "What the hell are you doing?"

She glanced over her shoulder. "Hi. The number of blind spots in the security system here was making me itchy. Your dad said it was okay for me to make adjustments."

Her body flushed as her pulse accelerated. "You met my dad?"

"Logan told you I was helping him and Aubrey, right?"

Her throat tightened. "Logan and I don't speak. Aubrey didn't mention it."

Morgan backed down the ladder, stopping four rungs from the bottom, then sprung off. "How are you?"

It was after nine, and she'd been on her feet waitressing all day, fueled only by a cup of coffee and a B.L.T. "Peachy."

"Logan was protecting me. He didn't know—"

"Stop." She held up a hand. "I don't want to hear it."

Morgan inhaled loudly, then slowly released it. "I have something for you." She snatched a black canvas bag off a stool by the table and pulled out a thick white envelope and handed it to Drew.

A flip of the flap revealed a wad of cash. She raised an eyebrow.

"The person who broke into your apartment was my ex. When I found out, I stopped by his place and browsed his precious sneaker collection. Do you know my friend that has a vintage clothing boutique off the strip said since they were all in the original boxes, he'd give me twice the amount Eric stole from you? He even paid to have them shipped," Morgan said in what-a-nice-guy energy.

Drew counted the bills. "Isn't he going to be pissed?"

"God, I hope so."

"No, I mean, isn't he going to retaliate?"

Morgan rolled her eyes. "First, he'd never believe I'd do that to him. He's under some delusion that I'm still in love with him."

"Maybe because you do things like text him when you're drunk?" Not that she was one to judge. Earlier in the week, she'd had a few too many while telling Claire what had happened between her and Logan. She'd gotten the bright idea to call him to give her a ride home since she was in no shape to drive, but Claire had talked her out of it.

"That was one moment of weakness after seeing how in love my brother is with you. Eric never loved me. I couldn't see the difference then, but I can now."

"What finally opened your eyes?"

"You and Logan breaking up."

Drew squinted, trying to make sense of the nonsense Morgan spewed. "I'm not following."

"Logan would do anything to erase the hurt he caused you. He'd move hell and earth to win you back. Eric never even said sorry."

"He's never going to find the painting, and even if he did, I still wouldn't forgive him."

"He's not trying to find the painting to earn forgiveness. It's important to him that you and your family get it back."

Drew didn't care. And she didn't want to keep talking about it. "By the way, where is my dad?"

"He went home."

"And he left you here? Alone?" Did her dad not see a problem leaving a known thief alone in his workspace? Perhaps no one had told him. It would be typical for Logan to omit information to protect Morgan.

"You think I'd rob him?"

"That's what you do, right? That's how you got this money." She held up the envelope.

"Eric stole from you first. I was evening the score."

"But this is twice the amount he stole."

"Consider it interest. And retribution for being a cheating asshole."

"He cheated on you, not me. You take the other half."

Morgan shook her head and held up her hands. "I don't want it. No amount of money could make me feel better about what he did to me. Trust me, I've already tried that route."

Wanting to eat her dinner and get to work, Drew popped open the Styrofoam container containing fried shrimp she'd gotten to go from the restaurant. She pushed the extra take-out box a few inches in Morgan's direction. "I got extra, thinking my dad would be here, but it's yours, if you're hungry."

"Aubrey and Logan went to get pizza, but thanks."

"Logan's coming here?" Damn it. All she wanted was to eat and get in an hour or two of work. Fat chance of that happening with Logan in the same vicinity. If hell froze over and he didn't come upstairs and attempt to hash things out again, knowing he was here would drive her crazy.

Morgan tilted her head toward the opposite side of the building. "I want to show you something."

Drew followed, coming to stand next to her by a large table her dad used for organizing his tubes of oil paints and his brushes. But those items were missing. Papers and folders covered the surface. Each folder had a photo clipped to it.

Morgan climbed on a stool, then onto the table and sat cross-legged in the middle.

"What are these?" Drew asked, even though she had firmly told Aubrey she didn't have the time, patience, or desire to be involved in the investigation.

"Files from the college on the students your dad invited to your house last February."

Her hand stopped mid-reach for the lemonade cup. "How did you get their files?"

Morgan twisted her hair up and stuck a pencil through it to secure it. "I'm resourceful."

She shook her head and took long pull from the straw. Once a year, her dad invited interested students to the house to see his work. This last year, he hadn't brought them to the house because he'd relocated his workspace to the studio. "You think one of my dad's students did this? And they started planning it eighteen months ago?"

"It's possible. Logan spent a few hours with your dad, asking him questions about every aspect of his life, and it came up that he's had his students over before. Your dad was skeptical, but he understands we have to rule them out."

"He spent a few hours with my dad? Does he know about Logan's involvement?" Drew hadn't told him that they had broken up. Pretending she hadn't seen him because she'd been busy working hadn't been hard to pull off.

Morgan chewed her bottom lip. "Logan told him everything. At first, I think he wanted to kill him for hurting you, but once I explained he'd gotten close to you to protect me, he chilled out a little. Then he and Aubrey had a talk in private, and after that he calmed down enough to let Logan interrogate him for leads."

Her stomach tightened, and although she'd been starving a minute ago, her appetite disappeared. A little tiny sliver of yearning to work things out had kept her from exposing the truth about Logan to her dad.

Drew picked up a folder with a photo of a girl clipped to the outside. She looked familiar. Beatrice Benenati. Didn't ring any bells. Hometown of Omaha, Nebraska. Got her bachelor's at RISD. It didn't mention her graduating with her master's from SCAD. What would draw someone from Omaha to Rhode Island and then to Savannah? Talk about a drifter.

"I've seen this girl somewhere," she said.

Morgan's head snapped up. "Let me see that."

Drew handed over the paper.

"You went to SCAD, yeah? Maybe you had a class with her?"

She shook her head, trying to place where she knew her from. "She only took a few courses here, and they weren't any I enrolled in."

Morgan pulled the photo free and held it in front of Drew's face. "Coffee shop?"

She shook her head again. "No. I don't think so. I need to eat." Even though she didn't feel like eating anymore, she had to, or she wouldn't be fit to get any work done.

After grabbing both take-out trays and her lemonade, she came back to the table. "Are you sure you don't want some?"

"It smells delicious, but we ordered an extra-large pizza."

"Oh, trust me, Aubrey can eat an entire extra-large pizza by himself."

Morgan laughed and hopped down from the table, pulling a stool across from Drew. She was kinda-sorta—okay, *absolutely*—adorable. Her fingers were crossed that Aubrey wouldn't become involved with her. Maybe she needed a better strategy than hope, though. If they started dating, that would be awkward.

Too bad that last girl he'd been seeing had turned out to be a homewrecker. Wrecker of her own home anyway. Hold on a—

"I know!" Drew said around a mouth full of shrimp and breading and cocktail sauce. Once she had swallowed and taken a swig of her drink, she snatched the photo of Beatrice and waved it in the air. "Aubrey dated her. Well, maybe you wouldn't exactly call it *dating*."

"Did she come to the house?"

Drew nodded.

"When?"

"Two weeks ago? And before that too. The same night—the first night—I stayed with Logan. She spent the night with Aubrey." She looked at the photo again. "Her hair was different, though. And her name wasn't Beatrice. I can't remember what it was, but it wasn't Beatrice."

The door to the studio opened and Aubrey came through with a huge pizza box balanced on one palm. When he noticed them staring at him, unsmiling, his own smile disappeared. "What?"

Logan followed him, but Drew wouldn't meet his gaze.

She held the photo for Aubrey to see. "Remember her?"

He came closer, slid the pizza onto the table and took the photo from her. "Yeah. Holly. Why do you have her picture?"

"Because she was one of the students your dad had to your house to view his work last year. And back then, she went by Beatrice," Morgan said.

He scratched his chin. "Well, I don't get the name change thing. Other than maybe she just hated her name. Beatrice is kind of—" He scrunched his nose. "But we didn't meet until after the painting was stolen."

"Maybe she needed to come back for some reason. Like she left something by accident that could have been incriminating." Morgan paced the area. "Or maybe she was going to run another scam on you. Find out how to get in here or take something else from the house. Did you talk to her about the painting being stolen?"

Aubrey tossed the photo on the table and took a slice from the pizza box. "No. We didn't talk much."

Drew rolled her eyes. "She's married. Aubrey found out because he had to fish her ring out of the bathroom drain."

Morgan stopped pacing and folded her arms in front of her chest, a lock of hair falling free from her makeshift bun. She blew it off her forehead. "Was she there the whole time? While you were taking apart the pipes or whatever?"

Aubrey froze, pizza to his lips. "No."

"It wasn't me," Drew said under her breath.

Morgan, Aubrey, and Logan looked at her.

She shrugged, then focused on Aubrey. "You and Logan kept harping on it having to have been someone I let into the house. I knew my instincts would have told me if someone was there under false pretenses."

"Of course, you would," Morgan said. "Women have fantastic instincts. But put some cleavage and a short skirt in a man's path and the only instincts he knows are basic."

Aubrey blushed and dropped his half-eaten slice of pizza back into the box. "I had no reason to suspect she had ulterior motives."

"We need to talk to Sam. See what he remembers about her," Logan said.

Her heart clenched. She hadn't made up her mind about Logan, but if she kept spending time with him, her decision wouldn't be made with a clear head.

"I have my own work to do." And plenty of it. It was already late, and she planned to work until she couldn't keep her eyes open. She'd lost so much lately, there was no way she was going to let this dream slip through her fingers.

52

JULIAN BENENATI

DREW PIVOTED in her crouching position to grab her pins and found a pair of blue eyes staring at her. She jerked back, landing on her ass. "Morgan!"

Morgan, squatting with her arms resting on her knees, smiled. "I wasn't trying to sneak up on you. I found out Beatrice Benenati is the curator for an art gallery in Omaha. She's clean as a whistle, but her dad, Julian Benenati? Not so much. Theft of all sorts."

On her knees, Drew pinned the gown to be hemmed. "That's fishy, but how can you be sure it was her?"

Morgan held out an open palm. Resting in the center was an opal earring. It was the one Logan had found the night he'd had dinner with her family.

"I think when Beatrice noticed she lost it, she decided to go back for it. That's why she hooked up with Aubrey, and I don't think it's any coincidence that both times your dad wasn't home. He'd have recognized her."

"She purposely dropped her ring down the drain to distract him so she could look for this?"

Morgan laughed. "She's not even married, Drew."

She took the earring, twirling it between her fingers. It didn't look expensive. It must have been extremely special for her to risk returning to the scene of the crime. "What now?"

With her usual grace, Morgan straightened and hoisted herself onto the worktable, tucking one leg under her chin. "She's in Omaha. As far as we can tell, she doesn't have any property here, or any intentions of returning. That means the painting is in Omaha too. At least we hope. Logan has a plan."

A tinge of hope swelled in Drew's heart, but she tamped it down. She didn't want to go through the disappointment of Logan's plan failing.

53

DOMINIC BENENATI

LOGAN

LOGAN ZOOMED IN WITH HIS LENS, making sure he saw what he thought he'd seen, then shook his head. He lifted his camera back up in time to snap a few shots before the bastard got into an SUV and disappeared. Then he dug his cell from his pocket, found the name he wanted in his contacts, and held it to his ear.

"Yo, Aubrey. How soon can you get to Omaha?"

The line was silent for a minute, then Aubrey said, "How soon do I need to be there?"

"Richard Anthony just came out of your girlfriend's gallery with another man who could be his twin, but I'm guessing he's the brother he told me had his brains blown out."

"Holly—I mean, Beatrice—was working with Uncle Rich?"

Logan grabbed the file off the passenger seat of his rental car and opened it. He rattled off the profile Morgan had put together. "Beatrice Antoinette Benenati. Age twenty-five. Daughter of Julian Antonio Benenati. Julian had some trouble with the law when he was younger, but he traded his life of crime to work in construction. His brother, Dominic Benenati, disappeared twenty-five years ago and has never resurfaced."

"You think Uncle Rich is Dominic?" Aubrey asked.

"It'd be a pretty big fucking coincidence if Beatrice's father just happened to look exactly like Anthony." He hadn't had enough time to mull it over, but somehow Anthony was involved. Pretty fucking convenient that he had unfettered access to the Miller home *and* Sam trusted him enough that he'd allowed Anthony to talk him out of reporting the theft.

"She's his niece?"

"I'd say. Good thing he's not actually your uncle, or you'd have fucked your cousin."

"Shut up," Aubrey muttered.

"I'm gonna make a play to get the painting back, but I need you here."

"CONGRATULATIONS ON YOUR WIN LAST NIGHT, MR. CASH."

Logan tipped his head to the bartender and slid his favorite dead president across the bar. The guy probably wouldn't have made that much in tips in the hour if the Diamond Lounge wasn't closed at Logan's request. At least not at noon. Especially not in Nebraska.

He took a sip of his Drambuie and followed it with a swig of coffee. The Omaha Hi-Lo tournament hadn't been part of his plans, but when he'd checked into the casino's hotel and saw the poster advertising it, he figured what the hell. He'd had a few hours to kill before Aubrey's plane got in, so might as well.

"Your guest has arrived, Mr. Cash," the casino host announced after opening the doors to the VIP lounge.

Logan adjusted his cufflinks, stood, and buttoned his suit jacket.

A woman in a classy black dress walked through the doors, three bellhops pushing carts carrying crates the size of a Smart Car trailing her. A short black bob and bangs framed her round face. He couldn't fault Aubrey for being lured in by her. Her level of glamour didn't even begin to touch Drew's, though. Logan missed her so much his chest ached. The image of her beautiful face had been burned into his brain, and when he closed his eyes, she was all he saw.

Beatrice was prettier when she smiled, which she did as she met him in the middle of the room, hand extended.

He shook her hand. "Thank you for coming, Mrs. Benenati."

"Thank you for inviting me, Mr. Cash. It's Miss Benenati, but please, call me Bea."

"Only if you'll call me Logan."

"Deal."

"Hopefully, one of many." He motioned to the bar.

She set a thick leather portfolio and her purse on the top.

Logan stood next to her, close enough to make it seem like he was interested in her, but with enough distance that he could stomach getting through this charade. Every ounce of his mind, body, and soul belonged to another woman. "Let me buy you a drink."

"I better not. I haven't had lunch yet."

"Then I'll buy you lunch *and* a drink." He shifted his gaze to the bartender. "A menu."

"Oh, that's very nice of you, but—"

"You boxed up all these paintings and drove them across the Missouri River. The least I can do is feed you."

"Actually, it was my staff that packed and transported them."

"Alright, then." He turned to the bartender again. "Would you send a filet mignon and crab cake to Ms. Benenati's driver." Logan looked at her. "Is there more than one?"

She shook her head.

"Okay, then. Send that out to him, and then I'd like to have—" He turned his hip into the bar, leaning closer to her. "How many employees at your gallery?"

"Five."

"Five of the same to-go before she leaves. Put it all on my tab."

"Yes, sir. And for you, ma'am?"

"A crab cake and a house salad, vinaigrette dressing," Beatrice said.

"Mr. Cash?" the bartender asked.

"I'll have the scallops."

"Right away."

She shook her head and smiled up at Logan. "That's very generous of you."

He shrugged and reached for his coffee.

"I'm sure you're anxious to see the paintings I selected for you."

"I was, but I've got to admit, I'm pretty damn content looking at the work of art right in front of me."

It was a corny line, but lucky for him, she ate it up. She blushed and bit her lip. "Let's get started."

He helped her open the three crates, then surveyed the canvases leaned up against the wall. He pressed two fingers into his chin, his other hand cupping his bent elbow, and stared at the first painting.

It was a blue monochrome abstract. Not the least bit his taste. "Love it."

"It's a favorite of mine."

He moved down a few steps, stopping in front of the next painting. It was something he might consider hanging on his wall—if he owned any. Somewhere between Pop Art and Art Deco. A girl with a ponytail and white sunglasses, sipping coffee on a cafe patio while reading a newspaper.

He'd had no intention of buying any of the paintings. Until now. This one reminded him of someone he knew. As he moved through the rest of the line, nothing else jumped out at him, but he said, "I'll take them all."

"I haven't given you prices."

He grinned. "I'll give you cash for that one right now." He pointed at the painting of the cafe girl. "I'll have it sent to my room. Pack the rest and have them sent to my address. You can give me an invoice, including the shipping costs, tonight."

"Tonight?" she asked, toying with the pendant on her necklace.

"Assuming you'll have dinner with me."

"Oh. I suppose I could do that."

If she believed he was spending a wad on these six paintings, and she was smart, then yeah, she'd better.

"Our lunch is here."

As she poured dressing over her salad, he asked, "I assume you're a collector?"

She nodded. "I'm also actually a painter myself."

"No shit?"

Beatrice laughed. "Don't be too impressed. My work isn't fit to hang on a wall."

"I'd like to be the judge of that." He smiled at her, even though he could give a flying fuck about her talent, or lack there of.

"I learned a lot in college, but you can't teach talent."

"You're being too critical of yourself. I bet you're a brilliant painter."

"Let me prove you wrong. Instead of you buying me dinner tonight, come to my place. I'll cook and you can laugh at my pathetic attempt at being an artist."

And there it was. The opening Logan needed. "Deal."

54

HEY, SUGAR

LOGAN

BEATRICE BENENATI MUST BE ONE HELL OF A GRIFTER. A curator working for a tiny gallery in downtown Omaha couldn't afford digs like this.

From the outside, it didn't look like much. An older brownstone on the corner of a downtown street. But inside was another story. An antique chandelier in the entryway, art on every wall, period furniture in exceptional condition, and a kitchen that spared no convenience.

She had skills. Logan wondered what scam she planned to run on him as she led him down the hall, sashaying her ass in a tight red dress.

He wanted to play the gull just to find out what her scheme was, but there wasn't time. He needed to wrap this shit up. He had a lot to take care of before New York.

"I brought you a gift," he said, standing across the kitchen island from her as she poured red wine. He pulled the small velvet box from his pocket and set it on the counter.

"That's really nice of you, but entirely unnecessary."

"It's not much." Logan flipped the top of the box open and held it closer to her.

He caught the flare of her nostrils even though she got a handle on it quick. "One earring?"

"I'm pretty damn confident you have its mate."

Beatrice looked at him like she thought he was whacked. "I don't understand."

"It's simple. You're going to hand over the Sam Miller painting you filched and then you'll have a matching set of earrings. Get me?"

Her mouth opened, a gasp slipped out, then she shut it. With her wine in hand, nose up, she said, "You can keep the stupid earring."

"You spread your legs for Aubrey more than once trying to find this thing. Don't act like it means nothing to you."

"It's cute you think I would trade you the painting for a worthless earring."

Logan snapped the lid on the box shut and tucked it back into his breast pocket, then slid his hand into his pants pocket and covertly called Aubrey. Ten seconds later, there was a knock at the front door.

"Gonna get that?"

She glared at him, set down her glass, and strode to the entry.

Logan watched from the hall as she opened the door to Aubrey's wicked smile. "Hey, sugar."

Logan snickered. If Aubrey ever got into running cons, he'd make a damn good roper. The guy had charm out the wazoo, even when faced with a woman who had done him dirty.

Beatrice looked over her shoulder at him.

"Don't be rude. Invite him in, *sugar*."

Her face fell and she stepped to the side, head hung, and allowed Aubrey in.

Logan led Aubrey and Beatrice into the living room, where he made himself at home at the baby grand.

"You know, Bea, I was raised by a con artist too. Likewise for my sister. My uncle would flip his fucking lid if he found out she prostituted herself as part of a con." He had read Logan the riot act for sleeping with his mark. But Beatrice didn't need to know that.

Her face turned red. "I did what I had to do."

Beatrice had spent an entire weekend in bed with Aubrey in Destin. She had gone above and beyond to make him malleable enough to get what she wanted.

He snorted. "Whatever you need to tell yourself, doll. Why didn't you get Anthony to find the earring for you? He spends plenty of time at the Miller home."

"I'm not telling you anything."

He ran his hand across the piano keys, filling the room with sound. "I didn't expect you to. All I want you to do is hand the painting over."

"Not happening."

He shot a look at Aubrey. "Ready to go? I can't wait to see the look on her father's face when he hears his daughter sold her pussy for a worthless earring."

"What makes you think he's going to believe you?"

On cue, Aubrey stretched and draped his arms across the back of her sofa. "Because how else would I know that you have a birthmark on your hip, or a tattoo of a feather under your left tit." He smirked. "Or that you give *phenomenal* head."

Logan could have given the dude applause for delivering that so well.

"Go to hell." She drained the rest of her wine. "Dominic couldn't convince me to give the painting back, and neither can you."

Dominic, aka Richard Anthony, tried to convince her to return the painting. Interesting.

"Why do you want it?" Aubrey asked.

She laughed. "I don't."

"Then why'd you take it?" He couldn't understand why she'd gone back for the earring herself, instead of getting her uncle to find it, but now it made sense. Anthony wasn't in on it. But at what point did he figure out Beatrice was the thief?

"Dominic left my father to die. All these years, he thought his brother was dead and never bothered to make sure that his niece was cared for." She pinched her lips together. "My dad always wondered what happened to him. So, I found him. And you know what else I found? He had a new brother, a niece he treated like a fucking princess, and nephews he joked around with and took to baseball games. One big happy family."

Jealous bitch. He checked to see how Aubrey was taking all this.

All he saw was pity. Not pity that her uncle had abandoned her and her father. No, it was the pity someone would give to a person in a padded room.

"You took my dad's painting to get back at your uncle?" Aubrey's fingers curled, like he wanted to strangle her.

"No," Logan said, finally getting the whole picture. "She wanted to hurt Sam for taking her father's place and Drew for taking hers. The way she got back at Anthony was *telling* him she took it, knowing he would never turn her in. He couldn't betray his brother by ratting Beatrice out, so he needed someone else to figure it out and get it back without involving the police. That's why he got me involved."

Beatrice uncrossed her legs, then crossed them in the other direction.

Squirm a little more, sugar. She didn't like that he had pinpointed her motive. She didn't like hearing that her uncle believed Logan was more clever than her. And she hated that he was right.

"We're not going to go to the police," Aubrey said, his voice calm and rational. "That's not what Uncle Rich wanted and regardless of this fucked up situation you put him in, he's always looked out for me. That being said, you're giving the painting back. Don't care if you don't want to. You are. Or I tell your daddy and your momma what we did, and I'm not gonna be a gentleman about it."

She scrunched up her face until there was nothing attractive about it. "Fuck you."

"Ya already did. It ain't happenin' again. Now, where is the painting?"

Maybe Logan ought to start taking notes from Aubrey. He had yet to raise his voice, or even sound the least bit angry, totally in control of the situation. And it looked like Beatrice was about to cave.

"Give me the earring first."

"You aren't in a position to negotiate," Logan said.

Like a bratty kid, she slapped the arms of her chair and got up, stomping to the kitchen.

Logan motioned for Aubrey to follow and caught up with her. He grabbed her arm before she opened a door in the back corner of her kitchen. "We're coming with you, so if you're thinking about pulling anything, get it out of your head."

Beatrice kept her eyes downward and opened the door.

He followed her closely down a flight of stairs, keeping alert. He didn't trust this chick.

The ground floor was being used for storage, frames stacked against the walls and drop-covered furniture and a fireproof safe big enough to hold a motorcycle. She unlocked it and pulled out a long mailing tube. She took the cap off the end and pulled out a rolled piece of canvas.

"You cut it off the stretchers?" Aubrey asked, his voice losing a bit of that tranquil facade.

"Trust me, I didn't want to."

"I *don't* trust you."

She unwound the canvas and held it up for them to see.

Logan ran his hand through his hair and stared.

A woman and a girl. Same shade of green eyes, same nose, the full mouth. The only difference between them their hair color. Drew's mother had long, dirty-blond hair. Drew's auburn hair color came from Sam.

Beatrice rolled the canvas and slid it back in the tube. "The earring."

Logan took the box from his pocket and held it out. "They say opals are bad luck. Guess that was true for you."

She snatched it out of his hand and flipped it open to make sure it was there.

"You might want to think about having those posts replaced with screw-ons." Logan had only bought one pair of earrings in his life. For Morgan. A pair of sapphires for her sixteenth birthday. The salesman told him you could tell an expensive pair of earrings from cheap ones by whether they had regular or screw-on posts.

"Oh, and one more piece of advice, stay away from the Millers or I will make your life a living hell."

ONCE LOGAN BOARDED THE FLIGHT FROM OMAHA TO SAVANNAH,

he closed his eyes and tried to make up for lost sleep.

Unfortunately, Aubrey was feeling chatty.

"I wanna get the canvas reframed before Dad or Drew sees it."

"Uh-huh." Logan shifted in his seat, tilting his head back.

"I can't wait for you to tell her. She's pretending she's resigned herself to it being gone for good, but I can tell she's been holding onto hope. Now y'all can work out your shit, and she can stop stressing about everything else and focus on the contest."

"You tell her."

Getting the painting back did not equal Drew forgiving him and them going back to the way things were. Even if it did, he wouldn't want that. Every time he'd seen her lately, she was a frazzled mess. She kept blaming it all on the pressure to win the contest, but he saw through that excuse.

Logan had every intention of giving her the time she needed. He already had an idea how he'd distract himself while he waited.

"You don't want to be the one to give it to her?"

"No." The painting would be home where it belonged soon. Logan didn't care who got credit.

"Are you giving up? My sister isn't worth fighting for?"

"I'm not giving up. She's gotta deal with her shit, and I gotta give her the time and space to do that. Even if it fucking sucks."

"What are you going to do in the meantime?" Aubrey asked.

"I left Vegas in a hurry. I gotta put my penthouse on the market and look for something in Savannah." Living on solid ground again was going to take some getting used to. Morgan was chomping at the bit to move her stuff to the *Gypsy*.

Maybe he'd look for something on Tybee Island. He'd seen a few For Sale signs in Matt and Claire's neighborhood.

"Does Drew know you're staying in Savannah for good?"

"No. Don't tell her, either. She needs to focus on the competition. Not worry about what I'm doing."

Aubrey stacked his hands behind his head. "She's gonna worry about what you're doing no matter what."

Logan hoped that was true.

55

LOGAN'S TELL

DREW WAS SCHEDULED TO FLY TO NEW YORK with eleven pieces of luggage. She wasn't sure what she was doing, walking down the dock to the *Gypsy*.

Logan had found her dad's painting. Even though Aubrey was the one to bring it home, he'd made it clear that he was only a sidekick in Logan's scheme to get it back. She'd spent the rest of that day and night with her phone in hand, contemplating calling him. The memory of telling him he couldn't earn her forgiveness by finding the painting kept her from doing so.

She hadn't been lying. It wasn't his efforts to find and return the painting that made her want to talk to him, to see him, to tell him she still loved him. She loved Logan because of who he was, and who she was when she was with him.

Her hands shook, making it difficult to hold onto the envelope. But she couldn't get on that plane tomorrow morning without doing this.

Drew didn't know if it would ever not bother her that their relationship had started out as a big deception.

Until the coordinator from the contest asked her how many tickets she would need for family and friends, she hadn't been sure what she wanted. But the idea of not having him there made her eyes prick and her nose burn.

How did she even begin to tell him everything she felt?

Drew had herself so worked up over seeing Logan she was thrown off guard to find Morgan sitting on the deck. And she had company.

The man sitting with her was spectacular. Not a hair out of place—hair the same color and thickness as Logan's. His suit had without a doubt been made custom. Shoes shined. Nails clean and neatly trimmed.

It wasn't just his appearance. He had a presence. Confident, but not too confident. Cultured, but an everyman's man. Charming, but sincere.

Morgan's forehead wrinkled. "Hey, Drew. What are you doing here?"

"I came to talk to Logan."

"He doesn't live here anymore. He gave me the boat," she said. "He's in Vegas. I can give him a call."

"No, please don't."

Her heart felt like it had sunk all the way to the bottom of the river. She shouldn't be surprised. Logan had never intended to stay in Savannah. He wasn't a settle down type of guy. But he'd promised to wait. So much for that.

"This is Uncle John." Morgan motioned to the man who had rose from his seat.

"Come aboard," he said, extending his hand to assist her. "I've heard a lot about you."

Drew took his hand and stepped onto the boat.

"This works out great." Morgan slipped on a pair of white clogs hiding under her chair. Leave it to Morgan to look glamourous in scrubs. "I got called into the hospital. Now you can keep Uncle John company and I won't feel like a horrible host."

"Oh, um," Drew looked from John to Morgan, "I'm sure he doesn't want me hanging around."

"I absolutely do."

Morgan pulled Drew in for a hug. "It's good to see you."

"I almost forgot—" She opened her purse and pulled out an envelope. "I'll understand if you can't make it, but the show is three days from now. You can bring a guest. There's a ticket for Logan in there too."

Morgan took the tickets and pulled her in for another hug. "I'll be there. I can't wait."

Drew forced a smile. She was happy Morgan would come, but she'd been hoping to deliver the tickets to someone else. Someone she wanted with her the night of the show more than anything.

"How are you?" John asked once Morgan had walked up the dock.

"Great," she politely lied. What was she supposed to say? I'm miserable because your nephew gave up on me?

"You are a very bad liar," he said with a huge smile. "Have a seat."

Her next smile was genuine. "I guess my poker face could use some work."

"In the time you spent together, Logan could have turned you into a fine poker player."

A laugh burst from her lips. The thought of her being any more than a mediocre player was absurd. "I'm hopeless when it comes to hiding my emotions. Logan has already pointed out my very transparent tells. *Several* times."

"Everyone has at least one tell. The trick is to keep your opponents from noticing it. Even Logan has a tell."

"He said that you're the only one who knows what it is." She was suddenly very curious to discover what gave Logan away when he bluffed or lied.

"Logan was always honest when he was a little boy. Except for when it came to protecting Morgan. This one time, she was only three, and she put damn near an entire can of fish food in my aquarium. Logan told me he did it. I knew he was lying. He had been feeding the fish for years and knew to take just a pinch." He shook his head. "Aside from the smoking, I don't think Logan has any secrets from me and if he's lied to me, I'm not as perceptive as I give myself credit for. The only time I've seen his tell is when we're playing cards."

Drew gasped. "You know he smokes?"

"Of course. Morgan too. Drives me crazy and costs a fortune in whitening treatments. They love thinking they're so clever pulling one over on me all these years, so I let them." He leaned back in his chair and propped one foot on his knee. "There's not much my kids do that I don't know about."

"I'd love to know what Logan's tell is."

John shifted his head from side to side, his eyes narrowed and shifting back and forth. "If I tell you, will you use it for good or evil?"

"Evil, of course."

His soft laughter warmed her insides. "You'll keep him on his toes. He needs that."

She pulled her hair over one shoulder. Broadcasting the pity party going on in her head would be inappropriate. Logan had gone back to his life, which he had every right to do. And sure, long-distance relationships worked for some people, but neither of them would be satisfied with one. Rather than tell his uncle that there was no future for them, she said, "His tell?"

"It's more of what you don't see than what you do. That's why his opponents don't stand a chance against him. Logan's eyes…"

"His eye color darkens when his emotions intensify."

He nodded. "Exactly. When he's bluffing—or lying—he turns off his emotions, and if you pay careful attention, you'll see that intensity missing from his eyes."

A new weight found its way into her chest. One of the reasons she hadn't been able to stay away from Logan was because of that intensity. It was always there. It had never not been there. Did that mean—

She stared at her hands. "Things got so screwed up between us."

"You'll straighten it out." He sounded so sure, as though he could see into the future.

A tear fell into Drew's lap. If she started ugly crying in front of Logan's uncle, she'd never get over the embarrassment. She wiped at her face.

A handkerchief appeared before her. She glanced at John, who held it out, and he nodded. "It's okay. I've seen women cry before. It didn't kill me then, and it won't kill me now."

Drew let out a little laugh and accepted the handkerchief. She blotted her face. "He's already given up on us."

"He has?"

She sniffed and nodded. "He told me he'd give me time. I guess he got tired of waiting."

"You don't really believe that?"

She sobered, and a tiny bit of her sorrow lifted. "Is there a reason I shouldn't?"

"Logan's in Las Vegas finalizing the sale of his penthouse. He'll be back in a few days. I'm going to stay for a few weeks and help him look for an apartment." He shook his head. "That boy has ridiculously high standards. But I guess you're living proof of that."

Her face heated, but her embarrassment was overruled by the euphoria growing inside her. He was buying a house in Savannah. He hadn't given up.

"I want Logan there the night of my show." More than anyone else.

"I don't think I'll have to twist his arm to get him there."

"Thank you. I'm sorry, but I really need to be going."

John ignored her extended hand and pulled her into a hug. It should have been uncomfortable hugging a near stranger, but it wasn't. Almost as though he had never been a stranger at all.

56

WELCOME TO NEW YORK

Drew

ALL THE MODELS WERE LINED UP, ready to show the audience Drew's vision, her life's sole purpose for the past several months. The judges had already made their decision during the dress rehearsal, but they wouldn't announce it until all three contestants had shown their collections to the public.

The other collections were incredible. Her original designs would never have been able to compete. But with her new designs, she felt she had a chance.

Minutes before the show was scheduled to begin, a stage crew member brought Drew a small black box. "Someone sent this backstage for you. They said it was important you get it before the show starts."

"Thank you. Did you see who delivered it?"

"One of the ushers brought it to me."

The box was tied with a green satin ribbon and when she pulled it free and removed the lid, there was a short note inside.

No matter what happens tonight, you're an incredible designer. If you don't win, consider this a down payment on my investment in your collection.

Underneath the card was a green poker chip. The chip was worn, the white markings barely visible any longer.

Drew took a deep breath, dabbed at the corner of her eyes, and took the microphone from the sound man. She walked out on stage, the green chip concealed in the palm of her hand. The spotlight made it impossible to see into the audience, but she knew her family was there.

After introducing herself and her collection, she curtsied and slipped backstage.

She closely scrutinized each garment before it hit the runway. When the last model returned backstage, she took a deep breath. None of the models had tripped, each garment was flawless, there were no wardrobe malfunctions. The models passed by her in sequence, taking their final walk down the runway. As the last model reached the curtain, she grabbed hold of Drew's hand and led her onto the stage. Applause sounded through the tent. Following the progression of models down the runway, she spotted her dad and brothers. She waved to the audience and blew a kiss to her family, and then waited with the other contestants for the winner to be announced.

White noise flooded her senses. This was *it*.

All her hard work, her stubborn determination, her obsessive attention to detail, it had led her to this moment. Her heart pounded. Her knees locked. Her mind raced in a million directions, bouncing from one outcome to another.

"The winner of this year's Emerging American Designer contest is—"

Her name coming from the contest spokesperson's mouth barely registered. When the other contestants took turns hugging her and giving their congratulations, it finally hit her.

She'd won.

She'd done it.

She'd won!

Backstage reporters and designers alike wanted a word with Drew Miller, the designer. It was all a little much. She took meditative breaths between introductions, politely answered each question, and graciously accepted their compliments.

"Drew, you are amazing!" Morgan thrust a bouquet of pink gerbera daisies into her arms and hugged her, almost crushing the blooms. "I cannot believe how talented you are."

She laughed. "Thank you."

John appeared and squeezed his way in, giving her a pride-filled hug. "Never had a doubt you'd win."

She tried not to be obvious about looking for the third member of their gang. He wasn't with them, though. She wasn't sure if he had been in the audience. Maybe he had sent the poker chip with his sister and uncle.

Drew stayed in one place for the longest time, her own little one-person receiving line. She must have shaken hundreds of hands and exchanged air kisses half as much.

Aubrey brought her a second glass of champagne and disappeared just as fast. He and Lee were running around, talking to models. She'd have to drag them out of here at the end of the night. Personally, she was anxious to get back to her hotel. Her feet hurt, her stomach was empty, and she was sick of standing here by herself talking to strangers.

"How is it possible to look so dejected when your dream just came true?"

Drew whipped her head to the right. Logan. Her smile was so wide it hurt. She leaned up on her toes, her cheek next to his, and pressed the poker chip into his palm. "Not being with the person you want to celebrate with kind of sucks all the fun out of it."

When she lowered herself, his lip curled a notch on one side, but his eyes narrowed to razor-thin slits. "Why don't I ever get the reaction I expect from you?"

Her smile dimmed. "You didn't think I'd be happy to see you?"

"Not really, no."

"I invited you."

He held his hand out, revealing the poker chip. "This wasn't on loan."

"I can't keep it. It's special to you."

"Not as special as the last thing I lost."

Being with Logan again was like trying to walk through the spinning tunnel in a funhouse. Every time she took a few steady steps, she lost her balance. She was all discombobulated and dizzy.

She cast her gaze down. Those potent eyes were too much for her right now. "How long are you in New York?"

"Two more days."

She'd be in the city for another week. She didn't want to wait until she got back home to see him again.

She opened her mouth to ask if he'd escort her back to her hotel, but one of the judges—a toothpick of a man with a skunk-stripe through his jet-black hair—approached.

He reached for her hand and shook it enthusiastically. "Most designers your age don't have half your talent. Can't wait to see where your career goes."

Logan gave a small wave and mouthed, "Bye."

Before he walked away, she grabbed his forearm. "This is my friend, Logan. Logan, this is Will Snyder. He was one of the judges and he's the head of merchandising at Macy's."

She didn't let go of his arm while he used the other to shake Will's hand. Her crazy was showing, but she didn't care.

Four introductions later, she whispered, "Thank you."

Logan took the monotony out of the conversations. Mentioning that he was from Las Vegas or that he was a poker player garnered interest, and therefore took some of the spotlight off herself.

The event coordinator approached her. "The editor of Elle

magazine wants to see you."

Elle magazine! "Hold on a sec." She turned back to Logan.

He winked at her, then turned and walked away. No goodbye. No plans to meet up again. No indication that he even cared if he never saw her again.

57

DONE WAITING

Drew

FOR TWO DAYS, DREW WAITED. But Logan didn't call. He didn't track her down.

Everything she'd worked herself to death for had been realized, yet there was an emptiness in her heart.

The night of the show, she'd been open about her feelings for him. She hadn't spelled it out that she wanted to get back together, but she hadn't thought he'd need an explicit proposal. Maybe his visit to Las Vegas had changed his mind about making Savannah his permanent residence.

He'd said he'd be in New York for two days. It had been two days.

Drew wasn't an idiot. If he'd wanted to see her, he would have.

After signing the contract with Macy's, she returned to the hotel. The front desk manager met her in the lobby and presented her with a long, slender silver box with a green ribbon around it. She removed the card and opened the box first. There were a dozen black and pink roses mingling with baby's breath.

She opened the card. It wasn't from a floral shop. It was a business card for North Cove Marina. She flipped it over. The message was short:

I'm done waiting.

C5

She recognized Logan's handwriting. What did C5 mean? The address of the marina on the business card was Manhattan. She asked the desk manager if he knew where it was. He explained it was located on the Hudson River, only a few blocks away. He offered to call her a cab.

She declined. Drew needed the fresh evening air to clear her mind.

Before entering out into the icy streets, she tightened the belt on her ivory wrap coat, pulled on her long black gloves, and positioned her beret on top of her loose curls.

During the walk, her heart beat wildly. Snow flurries surrounded her, catching on her eyelashes and in her hair. She tugged the collar of her coat up to her ears.

By the time she reached the ramp to the docks, her head was pounding with unanswered questions. She couldn't make out where the marina office was located in the dark. An older couple sat on the back deck of their boat, so she decided to ask them. Before she had a chance to open her mouth, she noticed a letter and a number had been assigned to their slip. B9. She walked along the pier, looking for C5. It was on the outer dock, farthest from the street. The yachts docked along the outside of the marina were monstrous. The getaways of millionaires. She was getting closer, C3 and then C4. When she saw the boat docked in C5, her jaw dropped.

It had four visible levels, with another level, maybe two, below deck. It was modern, yet softened by curved lines and honey colored teak. The name on the stern read: *The Splurge*.

The city painted under the name was Savannah, GA.

Logan had said one day he would splurge and buy something expensive.

That was a gross understatement.

She had to climb a narrow flight of stairs to reach the deck. The door to the cabin was open an inch. She glanced inside. The interior was as impressive as the exterior. The furnishings were chic. The colors were perfect. Navy and white and terra-cotta. A splash of yellow with throw pillows and a vase on a side table.

"Hello?" She waded into the living room.

Logan appeared from down a hall, wearing jeans and a black crew neck sweater. "Hey."

Her mouth opened but nothing came out. Inside, her stomach spiraled with nerves.

"What do you think?" He motioned around the room.

"It's beautiful."

"Good, because it's yours."

She shook her head. "What? No. Mine?"

"Well, it's *ours*. I looked at twenty different apartments and none of them felt right. Then I saw this and…it did."

Her chest was so tight. All she'd wanted was to see him, to try to work things out.

He could have rented an apartment and gave her a key like a normal person, but no. He'd bought a flippin' luxury yacht. "Logan, you've lost your mind. This is too…extravagant."

He struck a finger into the air. "That reminds me, I did get you a *little* something else." His hand lowered and disappeared into the coin pocket of his jeans. It emerged with his thumb and his index finger pressed together, holding a ring.

She took a deep breath, which she was sure sounded like wheezing. Now would be a good time to not hyperventilate.

The ring *was* smaller than the yacht, but by ring standards it was a whopper. A three stone, emerald cut diamond ring.

"Is that—"

"An engagement ring?" The corner of his mouth lifted. "Yeah."

"Are you insane?" she said, her legs boneless. "I need to sit."

She was about to wilt onto a buttery leather chair when he stopped her.

"Wait."

Her mouth went dry. "You shouldn't be doing this, Logan."

He frowned. "The other night, it seemed like you were ready."

"To get back together," she said, her freak out ratcheting up. Not to get *married*.

"Your vibe is telling me you're going to say no, but I'm a gambling man, so…" He took her hand in his and got one on knee. "I've never needed someone in my life as much as I need you. I can't change the past, but I promise to be a better man from here on out. I know I can make you happy."

She wiped at her watering eyes.

"Marry me, baby?"

While she was trying to unlock her tongue, he released a long, drawn-out breath.

"Are you sure that's what you want? To be stuck with me?"

"Being stuck with you, as you put it—very eloquent, by the way—is exactly what I want to do *forever*." His eyes were dark and fierce and beautiful.

Hello vertigo. The Logan-no-gravity effect. She squeezed her eyes shut.

When she opened them, she knew his heart was beating just as fast as hers because she could see his pulse in his neck. "Yes."

He glanced at the ring, then back at her, like he didn't know what to do now. Second thoughts?

"We don't have to get married," she said in little more than a whisper.

"You already said yes. It's too late to back out now." He stood and pulled her over to the sofa, then tugged her onto his lap, slipped off her glove, and slid the ring on her finger.

"I'm not taking anything back. I was giving you an out. You looked panicked."

He ran his thumb across her bottom lip. "I didn't expect you to say yes that easily. I had a plan to get you to accept, and a backup plan for if that didn't work. And as a last resort, I was going to beg. I don't know what to do with all that now."

She traced his collar with her fingers. "Save it. I'm sure it'll come in handy in the future."

"That's a solid prediction. There's a lot of things I plan on talking you into doing with me." He untied the belt on her coat.

She draped her arms around his neck. "We're really going to live on this boat?"

It was a thousand times bigger than the *Gypsy*. But normal people lived in houses. She tried to picture her and Logan doing normal people things in a normal house. It didn't work.

"It's a *yacht*." He smoothed her hair over her shoulder. "But no, not if you don't want to."

"I want to."

His face lit. "Yeah?"

"Yeah."

He slid her coat off her shoulders. "Wanna move in tonight?"

"I'll have to get my things from the hotel."

"That can wait. This can't." He leaned in and captured her lips in a kiss.

EPILOGUE

Morgan

Morgan pulled her uncle's Ferrari into the valet lane outside the hotel entrance of the Venetian. Her heart pulsed wildly. She was about to allow someone—who probably wasn't even old enough to buy beer—to unknowingly drive off with a very delicate package in the trunk.

She took a deep breath. It would be okay. She didn't have time to self-park. Not when she had to make a complete wardrobe change. While waiting for the line to move, she put the car in park and pulled off the shag wig and wig cap she'd been wearing for the past three hours. To try to revive some volume in her natural hair, she fluffed it with her fingers, but it was no use. Having flat hair at her brother's engagement party was the price she'd pay for pulling off the Bellagio job.

Between the duffle bag on the passenger seat and the garment bag hanging in the backseat, she had everything she needed to make her transformation from tourist to supportive and stunningly stylish sister. After kicking off her canvas sneakers, she tugged the "What happens in Vegas, stays in Vegas" sweatshirt over her head and shoved it into the duffel. The dark tint of the windows kept bystanders from catching a glimpse of her in her bra as she rid herself of her tank top.

The dress she'd chosen for the engagement party hadn't seen the light of day—or rather, the neon glow of a Las Vegas evening—in four years. It'd been waiting for her in the back of her closet at Uncle John's condo, right where she'd left it after she'd worn it to the World Series of Poker Main Event. That'd been a memorable night for Logan, but with any luck, he wouldn't remember what she'd worn. Not that her brother would care that she'd worn the dress twice, she just didn't want him tipped off that instead of shopping for a new dress, she'd been busy planning a heist.

Twisting in her seat, she freed the black sequin number from the garment bag. Before she could pull it over her head, the valet line moved, and she put the car in drive and inched forward.

A light rap on the window caught her attention. She hit the automatic window button and smiled up at the baby-faced valet attendant as his jaw dropped. Getting to see a woman in a demi-bra might be the best tip this kid got all weekend.

She lowered her lashes and chewed her bottom lip. "I'm not quite ready."

He sputtered before finally managing to say, "Take your time. I'll come back."

She winked at him, then rolled up the window. Once she'd pulled the dress over her head, she unhooked her bra and discarded it. The severe scoop of the back of the dress made going bra-less necessary, but lucky for Morgan, she wore bras to conceal hard nipples more than she did for support. With her arms in the long sleeves and the dress tugged over her hips, she shimmied her jeans down her legs and worked them over her ankles.

Her phone buzzed from the passenger seat as she retouched her lipstick. She silenced it and shoved it into her clutch, then wiggled her feet into her slingback stilettos. The last step was to put in her sapphire earrings.

A mere second after her foot hit the ground outside the car, the valet reappeared. "Ma'am."

"Could you?" She turned her back to him and gestured to the

sparkly cord hanging limply from one side of her dress. "There's a tiny hook on the other side where it attaches."

"S-sure," he stammered. He fumbled a few times, then finally succeeded.

"Thanks," she said. "I owe ya, one."

The kid's eyes widened, and a goofy smile appeared.

"Take care of her." Morgan gestured to the car and sauntered off to the entrance.

In the lobby, she forced herself to walk at a normal pace, even though she was dying to make a mad dash for it. Her phone vibrated in her purse for the fifth time since she'd left the Bellagio. She didn't have to look to know it was Logan. It tugged a little smile out of her knowing that even through all the hell he had gone through because of her, he didn't want to celebrate tonight without her there.

She stabbed at the elevator key a few extra times, as if that would make the car arrive any faster. After the passengers exited, she jiggled her leg, wishing she'd taken the escalator or the stairs. Standing idly made her antsy.

On the second floor, she beelined toward the restaurant where Uncle John had rented a private room. Only the best for Logan, the golden boy.

Morgan took a deep breath and released it before entering the restaurant. Logan deserved this. His engagement to Drew was wonderful news, and she couldn't be happier for them. It was her own life that had her feeling blue.

The hostess escorted her to the private room and Morgan crossed her fingers, hoping she could slip in unnoticed. No such luck. All eyes landed on her when the door opened, and she strolled in. She gave a shrug and a mischievous grin, hoping everyone would think, "Classic Morgan, but you gotta love her," and not "What a hot mess."

Logan stood at the far end of the room with Drew and Uncle John.

He raised an eyebrow at her, then crooked his finger.

Morgan ignored him and walked to the bar. "A shot of Sambuca and the blondest beer you have in a bottle."

The bartender nodded, pulled a long neck bottle from some hidden cooler beneath the make-shift bar, then set it on a napkin in front of her.

She lifted the beer and examined the label. It was her favorite. "I didn't know any bars in Vegas stocked this."

"I'm not sure about other places, but we don't. The client requested it special for tonight."

For her. *Thanks, Uncle John.*

Her fingers had just closed around the shot of Sambuca the bartender poured when Logan appeared beside her.

"What did you do?" he asked, his voice verging on irritated.

She tossed back the shot, then smiled at him. "What are you talking about?"

He shoved his hands into his pockets and huffed. "You only drink Sambuca when you're celebrating, and you're twenty minutes late. So, sis, what the fuck did you get into before you came here?"

Her brother knew her far too well. "I'm *celebrating* your engagement, you big dummy." Not a lie. She wouldn't lie to Logan, but if she told him the full truth, he'd not only be disappointed in her, it would ruin his mood, and she didn't want that tonight of all nights.

His jaw ticked. "Why were you late?"

"You look beautiful," Uncle John said, joining them and pulling her into a hug.

She kissed him on the cheek. "That's a lie, but a sweet one, so I'll take it."

"You're late." He raised his eyebrow to let her know they'd be circling back around to talk about why she hadn't arrived on time, but she wasn't worried. Morgan might be the screw-up of the Cash family, but she was also the baby. She'd been the apple of Uncle John's eye since the minute he held her as a rosy-faced angel wrapped in a fuzzy pink blanket—his exact words whenever he wanted to remind her that he loved her unconditionally. Tomorrow, she'd tell him everything—right before she asked him for help with the last little bit of her plan.

Morgan turned to Drew, who had also joined them by the bar, and smiled brightly. "Your dress is stunning. Thank you for accepting my brother's proposal, by the way. I didn't know you did charity work."

Logan shook his head, then downed the glass of champagne.

Drew snorted and pulled her into a hug. "It's good to see you. You look lovely."

"Now that we're all here, let me make my toast, so we can get on with the night and feed our guests before they get too drunk," Uncle John said.

Throughout the party, Morgan couldn't stop watching her uncle. He looked happier than she'd seen him in as long as she could remember, and it stung. She wanted to see him happy. It just sucked that she was the reason he'd been through so much grief for so long.

"Getting drunk at your brother's engagement party and making a fool of yourself is not going to make you feel better. Quite the opposite," Lucy said, scooting closer to her on the bench in the semi-circular booth.

Facts. Morgan tossed her head back and let out a long, deep sigh. "I know."

"You'll have your turn one day." Lucy was the closest thing to a mother that Morgan had. She'd been Uncle John's bestie since before Morgan was born. There were times she appreciated Lucy's wisdom, and then there were times like now, when she wished she'd zip it.

"My turn at an engagement party?" Morgan cringed. "Hard pass."

"There's plenty of men out there that would treat you like gold, if you'd give them the chance."

"Can we not, Luce? I'd rather talk about anything else right now." Everyone knew Morgan's taste in men was subpar. She had a knack for picking the scummiest of losers.

"Okay. Fine. Let's talk about why you were late, and why your hair looks like that."

She passed her hand over the back of her head and down the hair draped over her shoulder. "I forgot to pack my heat tools."

Lucy sighed heavily. "Fine. I'll cut to the chase. Did you talk Brody out of demolishing the Mermaid?"

"Talk him out of it?" Now, why would she do that?

Two days ago, when Morgan had arrived in Las Vegas, Lucy had spilled some very interesting information regarding one of her clients. Lucy had a reputation for being the best money launderer on the West Coast. In the past, she'd never talked to Morgan about any details of what she did for her clients, or what they did that put them in need of her services.

At first, Morgan couldn't understand why a construction worker would need money laundering services. Brody Lewis was going to demolish the Mermaid but turns out, the man wasn't a construction worker. No wrecking balls for this job. He'd been contracted to level the Mermaid by blowing it the fuck up.

Even though the building hadn't been inhabited in years, it was prime real estate. The problem was, it'd take a ton of mold remediation to get it to where it could be viable for residences or a business. It was also considered a historical building and couldn't simply be torn down.

All of Morgan's early memories took place in the penthouse of that casino. Sure, it wasn't inhabitable anymore, but she couldn't stomach the idea of it being destroyed so some shiny, hoity casino could go up in its place.

"Morgan," Lucy said, a heavy warning in her tone. "What did you do?"

"I made sure that lunatic won't be destroying the Mermaid. Isn't that why you told me what his plan was, so I could stop him?"

Lucy *never* breached her clients' confidentiality. She said it was unethical, which was hilarious considering every one of her clients was a criminal. But she'd told Morgan about Brody's plan to demolish the Mermaid. The only reason she'd do that was if she wanted her to interfere.

Lucy lifted her glass of red wine and gulped the rest of it down. "Is this the part where you tell me he's tied up in the trunk of your car?"

A laugh burst from her, and she slapped her hand across her mouth. The file she'd snagged from Lucy's desk didn't reveal much about Brody Lewis, other than he was in his early thirties, had some offshore accounts, and a military background. Didn't matter. Odd were, he was bigger than she was, because most people were. "I'm not exactly cut out for kidnapping."

"If you didn't talk him out of it, how are you sure that he's not going to go through with it?"

She lifted a shoulder, and flashed Lucy the smile she'd been using on her for years any time she got caught doing something mischievous. "I imagine it'll be pretty hard to blow up the Mermaid without explosives."

The way Lucy's eyes nearly popped out of her head made it nearly impossible for her not to burst into laughter. Fortunately, at that moment, Uncle John *clinked* a fork against his glass and launched into a toast.

continued in BANG, book two of the
Troublemakers and Heartbreakers series

Support an Indie Author

If you enjoyed this book, please review it and tell your friends about it. By doing so, you'll be helping me spread the word about the book, which means I can spend less time marketing and more time writing.

—

Learn about my upcoming books, ARC opportunities, bonus content, and interact with me. Join my invite-only reader group, the Troublemaker Society.

https://www.facebook.com/groups/mctroublemakers

or sign up for my mailing list:

https://www.authormarycain.com/newsletter

—

Subscribe to my Ream Stories

What is Ream Stories? It's a bookish OF. Oh, did that get your attention? Well, I'm not lying. That's exactly what it is. Subscribe to become a superfan, and in return for your support, you'll get exclusive content like bonus scenes, early access to my books as I write them, and you might even get to video chat with me—I promise you, I will be fully clothed!

https://reamstories.com/marycain

—

Follow Me

Yo, you got that stalker energy? If you roll with me on any of my socials, I'll hit you back with that follow, no questions asked. We're fam now, so let's keep it real and keep it tight.

https://www.facebook.com/marycainauthor

https://www.instagram.com/author_marycain

https://www.tiktok.com/@author_marycain

https://www.threads.net/@author_marycain

—

Printed in the USA
CPSIA information can be obtained
at www.ICGtesting.com
LVHW021556110724
784897LV00001B/16